THE MAMMOTH BOOK OF
EGYPTIAN
WHODUNNITS

THE MAMMOTH BOOK OF
EGYPTIAN
WHODUNNITS

Edited by Mike Ashley

Introduction by Elizabeth Peters

CARROLL & GRAF PUBLISHERS
New York

Carroll & Graf Publishers
An imprint of Avalon Publishing Group, Inc.
161 William Street
16th Floor
NY 10038–2607
www.carrollandgraf.com

First Carroll & Graf edition 2002

Reprinted 2002

First published in the UK by Robinson,
an imprint of Constable & Robinson Ltd, 2002

ISBN 0–7867–1065–9

Printed and bound in the EU

CONTENTS

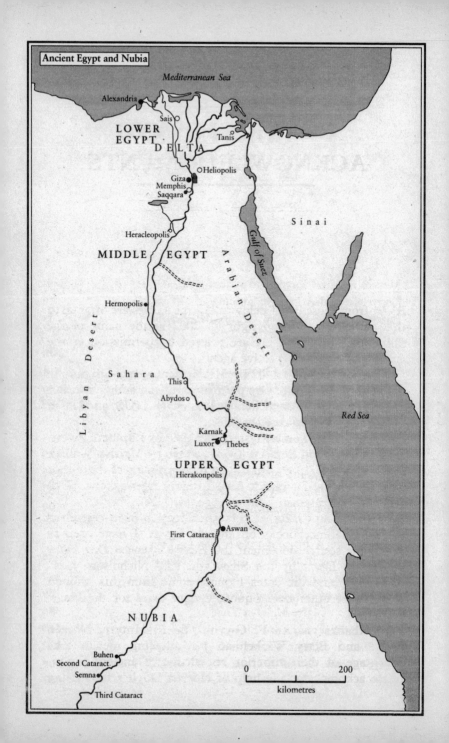

Ancient Egypt and Nubia

Mediterranean Sea

Alexandria

Sais

Tanis

LOWER
EGYPT

DELTA

Heliopolis

Giza
Memphis
Saqqara

Heracleopolis

MIDDLE   EGYPT

Hermopolis

Libyan Desert

Sahara

Arabian Desert

Sinai

Gulf of Suez

Red Sea

This

Abydos

Karnak

Luxor   Thebes

UPPER   EGYPT

Hierakonpolis

First Cataract   Aswan

NUBIA

Buhen

Second Cataract

Semna

Third Cataract

0   200

kilometres

COPYRIGHT AND ACKNOWLEDGMENTS

In the compilation of this anthology I have consulted several reference books on ancient Egypt. I have used as my prime source document the *British Museum Dictionary of Ancient Egypt* by Ian Shaw and Paul Nicholson (London, 1995) and the dates I quote come from this, though I am aware other books quote variant dates for the kings' reigns.

My thanks also to F. Gwynplaine MacIntyre, Noreen Doyle and Betty Winkelman for allowing me to take advantage of their superior knowledge of ancient Egypt. I also acknowledge the help of Noreen Doyle's fascinating website about ancient Egypt in fiction, which can be found at:

< http://members.aol.com/wenamun/Egyptfiction.html >

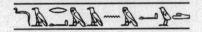

FOREWORD:
THE SANDS OF CRIME

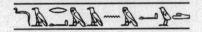

Mike Ashley

Of all the ancient civilizations none seems to hold more fascination for us than that of Egypt. So much was recorded at the time about their everyday life that the people seem just like any one of us, with the same problems and worries. And yet there remain such mysteries as the Pyramids, the Sphinx, the Exodus and the Plagues of Egypt and, of course, the Curse of the Pharaohs, that we continue to look upon them with awe and fascination.

And then there is the sheer immensity of time! The predynastic period dates from over 7,500 years ago. The earliest known kings ruled about 5,000 years ago and the first pyramids were built over 4,500 years ago. The Egyptian civilizations rose and fell and rose and fell again and again, yet there was a continuity stretching for some three thousand years, three times longer than England has existed and fifteen times longer than there has been a United States of America.

The Egyptian civilization had laws and rules like ours, rules that were just as easily broken and had to be enforced. The worst crime of all was that of tomb-robbing, which was deemed even more serious than murder. Theft was not an especially common crime – there were apparently few muggers or highwaymen. Tax evasion or non-payment of a debt was far more common, so some things have stayed the same. At the time of the New Kingdom the law was enforced by a group of

mercenary soldiers known as the Medjay, but there had been a
police force for centuries before, charged with guarding the
mines and quarries and cemeteries.

This anthology takes us through the ages, and features
whodunnits from the dawn of civilization, at the time of the
first pyramids, through all the well-known rulers down to the
time of Cleopatra. It also includes a few stories set during the
early days of Egyptology from the Napoleonic period to the
years just before the First World War, all of which draw upon
the magic and mystery of ancient Egypt.

All of the major writers of Egyptian mysteries have con-
tributed new material, from Elizabeth Peters to Lynda
Robinson, and from Lauren Haney to Anton Gill and Michael
Pearce.

The fascination with the magic of Egypt isn't a recent
phenomenon. It goes back at least as far as the ancient Greeks,
whose historian Herodotus (who appears in one of the stories in
this book) described the mysteries of Egypt in his travels and, in
so doing, also described one of the world's oldest mystery
stories. The modern interest began in Napoleonic times with
the growth of archaeology and the emergence of the science of
Egyptology. The rediscovery of ancient Egypt began to fuel
fiction, such as the work of Théophile Gautier in France, and
mummy's and Egyptian curses soon became a staple of horror
fiction and macabre mysteries. The fascination in fiction really
took off with the success of H. Rider Haggard's books which
evoked a mystique of lost times and other days.

Although I have encountered a few early short stories set in
ancient Egypt involving a crime or a mystery, I don't know of a
genuine 'whodunnit' set wholly in ancient Egypt earlier than
Agatha Christie's *Death Comes as the End*, published in 1944.
The story is set in around 2000 BC, though in fact reads every
bit as cozy as a traditional country-house murder. Christie was
married to the archeologist Max Mallowan and joined him on
several archeological digs in the Middle East. Several of her
stories are set in Egypt or involve an Egyptian theme, most
notably "The Adventure of the Egyptian Tomb" (1924) and
the novel *Death on the Nile* (1937).

Despite setting a novel entirely in ancient Egypt, Christie's work did not in itself set a trend for such works. In fact it was not until the current fascination for historical mysteries, in the wake of the Cadfael books by Ellis Peters, that several authors began series set in the Land of the Nile. These include Lynda Robinson's novels set at the time of Tutankhamun and featuring the pharaoh's inquiry agent, Lord Meren; Lauren Haney's series featuring Lieutenant Bak of the Medjay Police during the reign of Queen Hatshepsut and Paul Doherty's novels featuring Egypt's principal judge, Amerotke, in the reign of Tuthmosis. All of these characters feature in new stories in this anthology.

All of the authors have endeavoured to make the stories fit into the known historical period. This occasionally means using special words and terms but, have no fear, they are all explained in each story.

The word you will encounter most is *ma'at*. *Ma'at* (with a capital M) was the goddess of truth and justice and represented harmony in the universe. She was the goddess in whose name the king ruled. If *ma'at* (small "m") means order then the opposite, chaos, was represented by *isfet*, which also represents sin or violence. Then, as now, society was the constant tussle between *ma'at* and *isfet*.

Egypt was divided into a number of provinces. In later years these were called *nomes*, though that is a Greek word and the original Egyptian was *sepat*. There were 42 provinces, each governed by a *nomarch*. For a couple of hundred years (from the sixth to the twelfth dynasties) the nomarchs became hereditary rulers, but were eventually stripped of their power (see Keith Taylor's story).

The ultimate rule of law was vested in the king, but it was delegated to a vizier, the equivalent of a modern day prime minister. Cases could be heard by a vizier but for all practical purposes each town had its own magistrate, the *kenbet*. The royal palace, which was the basis of all administration, was called the *per-aa* (or "great house") and in later years the Greeks corrupted that word into *pharaoh*, the name we all associate with the king. The proper Egyptian word for king was *suten*.

The ancient Egyptians never called their country Egypt, of course. Their name for their land was *Kemet*, which means "black land", because of the silt from the Nile which spread over the land during the annual inundation. The northern part of Egypt, around the Nile delta, is called Lower Egypt. This is where most of early kings ruled and where the main pyramid complexes were built, at Saqqara, Giza and Memphis. The southern part of Egypt is called Upper Egypt. This was the main home of the pharaohs in the Middle Kingdom and is the site of Thebes (also called Luxor) and the Valley of the Kings. If you continue further south along the Nile, you reach the first cataract at Aswan, which was the old boundary of Upper Egypt. Beyond that was Nubia, or the Land of Kush, also known as Wawat, roughly equal to modern Sudan.

And that's about all you need to know. Now it's my pleasure to hand over to Elizabeth Peters to declare this anthology open.

Mike Ashley

INTRODUCTION

Elizabeth Peters

I spent the earliest years of my life in a small town in Illinois – and when I say "small", I mean fewer than 2000 people. It was an idyllic sort of existence, I suppose, except for a few minor disadvantages like a nationwide Depression and the fact that my home town had no library. For a compulsive reader this was a tragedy more painful than the Depression. Luckily for me both my parents were readers. From my mother and a wonderful great-aunt I acquired most of the childhood classics and some classic mysteries. My father's tastes were more eclectic. By the time I was ten I had read (though I won't claim to have understood) Mark Twain, Shakespeare, Edgar Rice Burroughs, H. Rider Haggard, Sax Rohmer, *Dracula* and a variety of pulp magazines, to mention only a few. I don't doubt that the sensational novels and magazines influenced not only my reading habits but my later plots. There was quite a lot in them about lost civilizations, ancient curses, and animated mummies.

Ancient Egypt has always been an inspiration to writers of sensational fiction. There is probably no other ancient culture so evocative and so seemingly mysterious. Bizarre animal-headed gods, monolithic temples, tombs filled with treasure . . . it's great stuff, even if you know that the historic facts do not substantiate that view of Egyptian culture.

My love affair with the real Egypt began when that same wonderful great-aunt took me to the Oriental Institute Museum at the University of Chicago, in which city we lived at the time. Everyone should have a great-aunt like that; she considered it her duty to pound culture into the unwilling heads of her younger kin. After that experience I was no longer unwilling. It's impossible to explain an obsession. That is what Egypt was for me, from then on. A goodly number of young people feel the fascination; it usually follows the dinosaur craze. Most of them grow out of it. I never did.

After graduating from high school I went to the University of Chicago – not because it had a world-famous department of Egyptology, but because it was close to home and I had received a scholarship. Practicality was the watchword. I was supposed to be preparing myself to teach – a nice, sensible career for a woman. I took two education courses before I stopped kidding myself and headed for the Oriental Institute. I studied hieroglyphs and other forms of the language, and got my doctorate when I was twenty-three.

Much good it did me. (Or so I believed for many years.) Positions in Egyptology were few and far between and, in the post-World War II backlash against working women, females weren't encouraged to enter that or any other job market. I recall overhearing one of my professors say to another, "At least we don't have to worry about finding a job for her. She'll get married." I did. And they didn't.

During the next few years I did manage to get to Egypt several times, and each visit strengthened my initial fascination. I had given up the idea of a career in the field. Instead I had begun writing mystery stories, because I enjoyed them and I hoped to earn a little money. They were terrible. My first book to be published was not a thriller but *Temples, Tombs and Hieroglyphs, A Popular History of Egyptology*. It was followed by *Red Land, Black Land, Daily Life in Ancient Egypt*. Finally that degree had "paid off" – in a way I never expected. Perhaps I should have taken this as an omen, but I kept on writing mysteries and finally got one of them published. It was a "Gothic romance", as they were erroneously called in those days, under the name of Barbara Michaels. The first book I wrote under the Peters pseudonym proved I hadn't got Egypt out of my system. It was a contemporary thriller, *The Jackal's Head*, without any of the appurtenances of supernatural fiction; but there was a lost tomb and a golden treasure and considerable skullduggery.

It has taken me over a quarter of a century to realize that I love to write, and that that career is the one I should have pursued from the beginning; but my obsession with Egypt has not faded and I doubt it ever will. I go "out", as we say in the trade, at least every other year, and I use my training and my experience in what is probably my most popular mystery series, written under the Peters name: the saga of Victorian archaeologist Amelia Peabody, who has been terrorizing 19th-century England and Egypt through fourteen volumes (so far). The effects of my childhood reading linger; Amelia has encountered walking mummies and found lost tombs and lost civilizations. The books are fantasies in that sense, but they are soundly grounded in fact and they give me the best of two possible worlds. I collect Egyptological fiction, and attend every film featuring archaeologists, good and the bad. Some of the books are very bad indeed – not because of the wildness of the author's invention but the ineptitude of plotting and style. The wilder the better, say I. One can never have too many mummies.

SET IN STONE

Deirdre Counihan

One of the great geniuses of the ancient world was Imhotep. He was the vizier of the Third Dynasty king, Djoser, and the architect responsible for the construction of Djoser's tomb, known as the Step Pyramid. That pyramid complex, at Saqqara, was constructed around 2650 BC and was the first known stone building in the world. The following story takes place in Imhotep's old age but refers back to an incident in his youth. Most of the characters named actually existed, including Peseshet who, like Imhotep, was a physician. She became the "overseer" or director of female doctors.

Deirdre Counihan comes from a literary family. Her grandfather was the prolific writer W. Douglas Newton. Her father, Daniel Counihan, was a writer, painter, journalist and broadcaster and her mother, Joan, is an historian. With her sister, Liz (who is also a writer – see my anthology Mammoth Book of Seriously Comic Fantasy*) they produce a small literary magazine,* Scheherazade. *Previously a teacher, Deirdre is a specialist in art and art history, particularly archaeological art, and runs an artist's Open House.*

M id-morning of the second day after their arrival, they found Udimu dead.

His nursemaid had missed him at first light, but finally found him when the ape Huni ran screaming out of the garden latrine. Small white feet and little legs down to the knees protruded from the sandbox; the rest of him was crammed incongruously inside. Horrified, the two gardeners looked at each other and then, taking one small leg each, hauled him out.

They laid him on the mud floor, the favourite son, to await Lord Kanofer, his father. His pathetic lock of childhood hair swung to one side as his head lolled backwards. They saw that his throat had been slit from ear to ear, but a length of fine linen had been rammed into his mouth, so hard that some of it protruded through the jagged cut. His pointed child's face was bloated by his agony, his lips forming a rigid circle of horror, drawn back from the pearly milk teeth. His eyes were closed. His chubby infant fingers gripped into the fists of his final agony.

"Ah, no! This cannot be – he is just a baby!" The desperate nursemaid wrung her hands in horror. "Who would do such a thing?"

"Udimu? Have you found him?" His three older sisters came hurrying up, gathering round the door of the latrine, peering in and then falling back in disbelief. Peseshet, the eldest, broke through the others and knelt down beside the pathetic body. She dabbed at the jagged end of the cut with the edge of her kilt.

"Poor beautiful, baby – you that are always so pale." Tenderly, she eased open the tiny clenched fist. "Ah see!" Her voice broke. "Here is a bit of his sleepy-shawl – he would never go to bed without it – they must have wrenched it from him!"

"He is dead?" The baby's other sisters, Intakes and Meresank, had now been allowed through the throng of horrified servants. "This is insane."

"Someone has cut his throat, poor little *ka*."

"This must be the razor that did it!" Intakes stood poised, not daring to bend down and touch it, but pointing to something that lay further into the darkened hut. "I think it may be Father's."

"Oh, don't be crazy." Meresank was sobbing uncontrollably. "It could be anyone's! Hasn't anybody been sent to fetch Father and our brother Imhotep and the doctor? We shouldn't be touching anything till they get here."

"Insanity on insanity," wept Peseshet. "There is the razor, but where is all the blood?"

Someone had recaptured the pet ape Huni, and he stood whimpering, tied to a palm by the walkway. And maybe he was the only one of them that knew that this was not the first murder in the family he had witnessed – if he understood what murder was.

It was fresh mid-morning – still too early for polite visiting – but the young Royal Physician Iry was received with all the deference due to one permitted to touch the body of God. As impeccable servitors ushered him through the vast, faded opulence of Imhotep's family mansion, Iry found himself, yet again, astonished that someone with the taste and austerity of this venerable lord should continue to live there.

There was no one in the two kingdoms of Egypt whom Iry revered more than this increasingly frail old man. While the inspiration of Imhotep's thought reigned proverbial on every lip, and all stood in awe before the breathtaking splendour of the sacred edifices that it had been his to mastermind, Iry, uniquely, understood that while his own powers as a physician were a remarkable gift from the gods, they paled into insignificance when compared to those of this discreetly dying gentleman.

Iry was ushered through the great studio – scale models, the fruits of Lord Imhotep's life of labour for the royal family and the gods, lay everywhere bathed in the amber mote-flecked silence. A sudden beam of golden light from the garden came flooding over the masterpiece, Great Djoser's pyramid tomb, stepped in stone and pointing to heaven.

Iry drew a breath of awe – today, over on the far banks of the river, its vast completion stood surrounded by the pyramids of those lesser deities, Djoser's descendants, all set in stone for eternity. This workshop of vacillations attested to the patience and forbearance with which Imhotep the wise, over the years, had conducted them on their path towards immortality.

The light glanced across the statue of Thoth, benign in baboon form, naturally presiding over any such place of endeavour. "O Thoth, grant me wisdom like Imhotep," begged Iry. "Steer me lest I offend or hurt him!" For that great old gentleman – showing no professional or family jealousy – had once steered Iry towards the exalted position of service that he held today, always reminding him that service must be pivotal to everything he did.

Now, in the course of that service, Iry was obliged to perform a most distasteful task. Something His Sacred Majesty had been reading in the royal archives had intrigued him – something on which Lord Imhotep could likely shed some light!

"He will fall for your honey-tongue, Iry!" the fascinated Pharaoh had decided. "Everyone knows he respects your integrity!"

Doctor Iry shuddered. Nothing was less likely in this case. If Lord Imhotep had considered something better left unrecorded for all these years, he had good reason – better reason than serving as salacious entertainment for a bevy of inquisitive young princesses, which was probably the real driving motive behind the royal interest. Righting uncovered wrongs, somehow, did not ring true from King Huni.

All too soon the young doctor found himself sitting nervously by the cool tranquillity of Imhotep's lily-covered pond. Things were not going well. At any moment, Iry sensed, his lordship's legendary restraint could be in jeopardy.

"So, his majesty has finally taken to a quest for knowledge!" Imhotep sat, taut and fastidious in his cushioned chair. "But what wonder of Earth or stars succeeds in prompting him? A disgusting family murder, best forgotten – thoroughly investigated years ago! Why, I was scarcely a boy at the time!"

"But . . ."

"Contrary to popular belief, I do not know everything," hissed the old man; then, suddenly, he smiled. "You know, Iry, they even say I leapt from the womb issuing instructions to the midwife! Such nonsense. Why does the king imagine I might have any important observations concerning such ancient darkness?"

But Iry's imagination was awash with crimson – the blood of a two-year-old with a slit throat. "Obviously his majesty has read what exists about the case," Iry gulped. "He knows who the culprit was said to be – but it was not a simple death – he feels there cannot be so simple an answer. I was astonished to be told the murdered child was one of your brothers . . ."

"My only brother; Udimu was my half-brother. My father had two wives."

"Truly, I did not appreciate that! Royalty – you constantly confuse me!"

"Ah, Iry – how deftly you flatter, these days – but we were only fringe royalty. Like you, our duty lay in serving those at its core."

"And were you happy? I had always found your family such an inspiration. Could such horror have been foreseen?"

"Foreseen? Yes, we were, originally, a very happy family, my elder sisters Peseshet, Intakes, Meresank and I. We were the children of peace after all those years of civil strife. Our dashing father, Kanofer, had risen through it all by his talents. Our dear mother, Princess Redyzet, was a half-sister to the Great Queen Nemaathap."

"Indeed, it is the records of her inquisitors that have captured Pharaoh's imagination!"

"Then I need hardly remind you that this beautiful and wise lady enshrined the royal blood-line. Originally she was married to the king, their father, and was mother of our favourite young uncle/cousin, Crown Prince Djoser.

"But the old king, my grandfather, suddenly died. To everyone's surprise – but presumably hoping to avoid the sort of anarchy that having a child-king can bring – Queen Nemaathap chose to marry her only half-brother, Senakhte, thus making him the new Pharaoh.

"To be able to do this, my half uncle Senakhte quite ruthlessly divorced his seemingly barren wife Lady Heterphernebti – who was a particular friend of Mother's. My sympathetic parents rushed to provide a loving home for her and her disturbingly light-fingered pet ape (whose name, if I recall aright, was Huni), and so all our troubles began."

"Heterphernebti – not a name that I recall from the transcripts. And as for the ape . . . !"

"But crucial – his majesty may not be wrong, possibly much lies unrecorded – probably better so. Well, my two younger sisters took to our ex-aunt at once, but the eldest, Peseshet, and I could never really trust her. Within the family, Heterphernebti and Senakhte held a clouded reputation, hints of intrigue around the throne – but now she was stranded high, dry and very bitter. You would think that a rich commoner would have expected no less.

"But the royal barns groaned with produce to preserve the land from famine and the royal nursery was filling with half-sisters for our beloved Prince Djoser, so the gods clearly endorsed Senakhte's stark decision (anyway, that was what Peseshet and I were amused to conjecture).

"Innocent days! Father, now Royal Supervisor of Works, would take me out with him at each fecund brown Inundation to inspect construction – and I learnt the months and years of careful preparation needed for any plan to reach fruition.

"At harvest time when this labour ceased, we always sailed down to our Southern estates, where my father had been born."

"Where your brother was done to death?"

"Indeed. Then one year brought another newcomer to my parents' household – her name was Miut – kitten. She had a remarkable story."

"That name is mentioned!"

Imhotep paused and Iry fancied a slight smile creased his mouth.

"This stranger, Miut, strode into my father's fields, claiming to be the wife of one of our tenants, Bedjames – met while undertaking a distant voyage for Pharaoh, but now gone missing. To my adolescent eyes – I was just into my eleventh year – the most striking thing about her was that, unlike the rest of the field workers who were sensibly naked, this young woman kept herself covered. A superb shawl was wrapped clingingly around her most curving parts – 'stolen, no doubt,' Mother laughingly observed – yet Mother and her perpetual guest, Heterphernebti, acquired shawls of equal quality at the soonest opportunity!"

"Quite so, my lord, but . . ."

"But keep to the point, eh, Iry? Lady Heterphernebti expressed great sympathy for this abandoned wife and so Miut joined our household while we investigated whose responsibility she was. She became a favourite with everyone.

"But dear, beautiful Mother's health was starting to give us concern. Poor Peseshet was studying to be a female doctor and was desolate at proving unable to help her. Lady Heterphernebti, assisted by Miut (who had wonderful ways with headaches), was all solicitude. It was Heterphernebti's hand that mother held, not my father's, not mine, in her final moments. I have never, ever, recovered from the desolation of that thought."

Imhotep paused, and Iry noticed his eyes had moistened.

"And so to Udimu. The swiftness with which Father and Heterphernebti chose to marry after Mother's death and the arrival, scarcely eight months later, of my little brother, was a shock for everyone. Heterphernebti had been considered barren, old, yet here she was producing a child, and a child phenomenon at that."

"I see the complexity of it! Tell me more about Udimu."

"Many of the exaggerated tales that have been put about concerning my birth and earliest years have probably originated in real stories of my pale new brother. He was born with teeth, he could talk well before he could crawl – and he was crawling early too. He was like a young adult even before he was three. 'This is a full-term baby!' Peseshet insisted at the birth, daring to voice what none of the other women wanted to consider – that Udimu had been conceived well before his parents' marriage or Mother's death.

"So the notion that my sister Peseshet hated Udimu started the moment he was born – everyone knew she remained irreconcilable to the circumstances of Mother's passing. However, I can affirm that with the rest of us, Intakes, Meresank and I, she was fascinated by, and rather proud of our new brother.

"Heterphernebti found the joint roles of Lord Kanofer's consort and happy new mother draining. Though Father ensured that she was pampered and cosseted, she preferred only Miut in attendance to soothe her head. The other maid-servants were needed to monitor poor Huni, the pet ape, who could not decide if Udimu was meant to be some new toy to be dismembered or some titbit to be eaten!"

"But was Udimu such a truly remarkable child, my lord?" Iry tried to steer the old man back to the point. "Pharaoh particularly wanted to understand this – the death was so thorough, so brutal – three different ways! You were such a brilliant family, did he so outshine you all?"

"Absolutely! A complete enigma – from his earliest words, we never heard him make a grammatical error, yet he was baby enough to require a neatly hemmed section of his mother's expensive shawl to comfort him to sleep.

"He loved to be told stories; he didn't mind if they were truth or fiction, but he understood the difference, which astounded me because one of our favourite family diversions was convincing poor Intakes of complete nonsense. She used to look so like Mother when she opened her eyes wide in wonder, it was almost like having her back, laughing amongst us. Everyone joined in the task of keeping Udimu captivated – and stayed to be captivated as well.

"Miut's tales were the ones that held the biggest audi-ence. Prince Djoser, and sometimes other friends and re-latives, would sit enraptured here under the stars as she described her epic journey and the astonishing things that she claimed she had witnessed – perhaps, strangest of all, in her own land, a well that could turn any object into stone. You could give a leaf eternal life, she said, or preserve a flower forever.

"Prince Djoser was deeply taken by that notion of eternal stone, but Udimu became obsessed. He would build tiny stone casings for the spent flowers that dropped here on the garden pathways, in hopes to keep them fresh forever. He wanted to tell stories too. One evening, when most of the family were gathered here by the pool, he said to us:

"'Last night I had a dream that I was a little bird, but Imhotep was a big bird, and I flew under the shadow of his wing. At the edges of the earth, we were met by a vast, golden ship, hauled on golden ropes by a crowd of golden men. Imhotep and I perched on the ship and it took us deep into darkness until we stopped at a huge gate. I peeped out from under Imhotep's wing and saw that the gateway was made of writhing bodies, and that the gatepost was turning in the socket of a lady's eye. Everyone got off, and we went into a vast hall alive with flames. In the middle were some huge golden scales and a big black dog and the most lovely golden feather.'"

"Incredible!"

"Yes – we were all shaken – could someone his age know about 'The Boat Of A Million Years' and the judgment hall of heaven? Whose heart was about to be weighed against the Feather of Truth on the scales of Anubis? Was Udimu a seer on top of everything else?"

"Yes . . . his majesty was wondering . . ."

"But Udimu had not quite finished. 'I thought I would try to fly down and pick up the pretty feather, only Nurse woke me up. But that lady who was lying with the gatepost through her eye – she looked like Intakes.' The effect of this on poor Intakes was terrible – she fled in tears, followed by the other girls. Father and Heterphernebti were ashen-faced. Miut sat very still, hunched in her shawl – she recognized a dream of power when she heard it."

"Only the immediate family were there?"

"On that particular occasion – but Father tried to discourage Udimu from story-telling after that. Poor baby, he was just approaching his third summer, when we set off up-river for the most tragic harvest of our lives.

"Mid-morning of the second day after our arrival, they found Udimu dead. His nursemaid missed him at first light, but they only finally found him when the ape Huni ran screaming out of the garden latrine."

Imhotep drifted into silence and Iry wondered whether he had fallen asleep. The two sat quietly for some while, Iry listening to the laboured breathing of this most remarkable man. Then

Imhotep raised his hand and a servant brought water and dates. He invited Iry to partake and then continued.

"In the fields the harvest ceased. My father stood on the terrace, white-lipped. He could not bear to go back into the house, he could not bear to go deeper into the garden and look again on what he had seen. This was the terrible death of a child, his child, and in the territory of his jurisdiction.

"We had a doctor with us, of course. The poor man had known us all since birth and now had to speculate on who might have done this. After a careful examination, he allowed Udimu's tiny body to be taken back to his sobbing nurses and tight-lipped sisters to be washed and wrapped in linen ready for burial.

"Heterphernebti would not look on him. Perhaps she thought that if she didn't, the horror would go away. She sat in her room, alternately whimpering and wailing, and refused to see even the indispensable Miut. Father made no attempt to comfort her at all.

"By evening the last layer of linen, soaked in resin, was wrapped round our darling and he was placed in the clothes chest of cedar that was my pride and joy — but I wasn't going to stint my poor brother in his final moments. A proper coffin would be made for him as soon as we returned to civilization. Tenderly, my sisters and I placed Udimu's comforter, found crumpled on his bedroom floor, beside him for his longest sleep.

"Then happened one of the strangest things. By that evening, my father had Peseshet quietly separated from my other grieving sisters and locked in a storage room. We were all crying and repacking our belongings, Father being able to commandeer transport at short notice. I was dumbstruck when he sent for me and said that my sister Peseshet was the culprit and that he was sending her home under guard ahead of everyone else. I was to travel with her to maintain the proper propriety.

"'Whatever can have given anyone such an appalling idea?' I had blurted out before I had stopped for thought. 'Did the doctor tell you something that the rest of us didn't see? Why,

Peseshet wouldn't harm a fly – more likely she would splint the leg of one that someone else had swatted!'

"But he was adamant; this was not the dashing father of my childhood but the solemn hypocrite who had married Heterphernebti with Mother still fresh in her grave."

Imhotep sucked for a moment on a date, gradually removing the stone and looking at it as if it were something dredged from his memory. He placed it on a plate and stared at it for a while before continuing.

"That silent boat journey homewards was the most miserable experience of my life. Peseshet was completely bewildered and the guards, longtime family retainers, did not know how to treat her. 'Why does Father imagine that I did this awful thing?' she repeatedly asked.

"'Father told me that you had found out that he was going to share Mother's Legacy for us with Udimu – and, with your training, you, uniquely among us, have the knowledge of how to kill.'

"'Since when have I cared about riches – enough to murder? And in that way – his throat was slit from ear to ear, for heaven's sake – where did I get the razor? Why, I've never touched one in my life! What woman would kill with such a thing?'

"'You muffled him in his sleepy-shawl and swept him out into the garden so that you could kill him silently. The doctor says Udimu was throttled – there were finger-marks on his throat. You had stolen Father's razor but wrapped it in the bandage so as not to cause more defilement by touching it – but chiefly to make people imagine that the killer must be a man.'

"'Incredible – so it was Father's razor!'

"'Yes – but it was one of your bandages!'

"'There is no shortage of them about!' She smiled at me, almost to break my heart. 'How is your poor leg now?' I had hurt my leg on the voyage out – how typical of her to be thinking of me at such a time. 'It seems I can trust no one,' she said. 'How could anyone concoct such a terrible scenario? This must be one of Heterphernebti's imaginings. Once we are back, Imhotep, I beg you to go to Prince Djoser. I would feel safe to tell him.' Naturally, I had never intended doing anything else.

"Outside on the deck the poor ape Huni, sent back on the same craft and securely tethered to a rail, whimpered all through the night – but they would not let Peseshet comfort him."

Iry's mind sifted these facts against those recorded in the archives. So far Imhotep had added much flesh to the ancient bones, but not revealed anything new. Even though Imhotep was remembering back some sixty years, Iry believed he knew far more than history had told, but he knew his old mentor had to tell the story in his own time. For all that Iry wished he would come to the point, he harnessed his impatience and sat back, trying to look relaxed and hoping this would encourage Imhotep to reveal more.

The old man looked at him briefly before his eyes once again receded into the distant past. Iry had known him all of his life, and yet this was but a fraction of Imhotep's many long years and he wondered just what mysteries there were to reveal.

"Typically, our prince was there to meet us," Imhotep resumed, "the tragic news having been sent ahead. We all knew the story must come out, but horrifyingly, in the short time our journey had taken, it was already assumed that my sister was guilty and that my poor father's problem, apart from burying Udimu, was to find a tasteful way of disposing of her.

"Our ship arrived in darkness and, as we left, they were shoving poor Huni, screeching, into a cage. Peseshet, her wrists bound, was taken, heavily veiled and in a carrying chair, torchlit, through the sleeping town. I still remember following, limping beside my Prince – the blessed relief of talking to one, who after all, knew all about trusting nobody and watching one's back! Me, a young lad of just thirteen summers, and Djoser, my hero, being scarcely twenty.

"We went over and over the details of the murder, trying to fathom out a perpetrator for that frightful death. 'Udimu couldn't have known the latrine,' I remember explaining to him. 'He hadn't been shown the garden yet. But he needed little sleep and sometimes wandered at night.' His nurses, exhausted from supervising him on the boat, unfortunately, had relaxed once back on dry land.

"I'd heard no report of a break-in at the villa and had to assume the guilt of someone from within – if Pharaoh now has visions of dark magic being involved, I fear nobody saw any trace at the time.

"I had tried to establish where everyone had been. Heterphernebti and Father, I knew, seldom slept together in those days. She had been in her rooms attended by her maids, while Father had spent much of the night poring over details of the harvest in his office. Intakes and Meresank and I had also been sleeping in our rooms, exhausted servants in attendance. So, too, had Peseshet – but somehow in her case this had become negative evidence as to whether she had been in her bed or not!

"Prince Djoser was outraged. The Prince always loved children and so was appalled at the details of Udimu's death when I described them. We racked our brains in the darkness all the way back to this house, but to no avail."

Again, Iry had to blink away that terrible crimson vision of the baby, head yanked back by his child-lock, eyes rolled up in fear.

"They took poor Peseshet to a secluded room that they had readied for her over there in the south wing. Prince Djoser would take no nonsense from my father's steward when he tried to discourage him from coming in with us.

"'Whoever can you have offended, Peseshet, to incur this sort of treatment?' said our cousin. 'How could anyone imagine you capable of such an atrocity? Whoever killed poor Udimu certainly meant to do it, didn't they – but why?'

"'Peseshet,' I said to my sister, trying to encourage her. 'You told me there was something particular you wanted to say to the prince, something that you could trust only to him?' She looked so beautiful at that moment – could she trust me enough to tell me too?

"'Something to show, not something to say.' She had hidden it in a tiny screw of papyrus and slid it into the hem of her kilt. She dropped it into his outstretched palm.

'It's part of what Udimu was clutching.' It was a bit of tied-off fringe.

"'It's from Udimu's sleepy-shawl,' I said. 'We all know that. They must have ripped it out of his hand when they grabbed him.'

"'No!' she said. 'Look again. We assumed as much, but when it came to folding Udimu's shawl to put . . .' – her eyes filled with tears at the memory – '. . . to put beside him, I noticed that it was perfect – there wasn't a bit missing from the fringe at all. It doesn't come from Heterphernebti's shawl. Look at the colours in it, Imhotep – tell me whose shawl it really came from!'

"The dye was most distinctive, fabulously expensive, which was why it had been suggested that it was stolen. It was Miut's shawl, carried from her distant land.

"'This requires most serious consideration from a higher authority.' Prince Djoser said. He rewrapped the scrap of thread and took it with him.

"The next day Prince Djoser and I came to the peace of this garden. Just over there, by that clump of iris at the edge of the pond, I almost tripped on one of Udimu's tiny towers, built like a stairway around all four sides. The gardeners had left it, I suppose, out of respect that it could have been fashioned by a two-year-old, and I must admit that I broke down and wept at the sight of it.

"'Oh, this is terrible,' I said. 'For how many years are we going to be stumbling into his eternal little piles of stone?'

"Djoser laughed in sympathy. 'Eternal stones – now there is a thought. If we ever make a royal tomb together, Imhotep, it will be of eternal stone!' and I limped beside him up to the desolate house.

"The rest of the family arrived two days later; Udimu was laid to rest with due solemnity in the family grave. Everyone managed great dignity, just as they had after Mother's untimely death.

"Lady Heterphernebti, though, was privately giving cause for concern. She refused to eat any food that she had not prepared herself – nor would she have her devoted Miut anywhere near her.

"My father, who had the Pharaoh's authority for the territory in which the dreadful crime had been committed, let it be known that it was now a matter for the past. To his shame, it was all a tragic domestic incident. No–one was allowed to see Peseshet. I lived in terror that she might be 'disappeared'.

"I did not know what to do. Should I share my knowledge with my other sisters? Peseshet had feared trusting anyone. They were bewildered. They could not believe that Peseshet could do something so terrible, but equally they didn't believe that Father would do anything so unjust. It must be some court secret that he could not tell us.

"But for the Prince and myself, it seemed the other way about. If Miut was involved, why was my father protecting her at the expense of his own daughter?

"At last the prince came quietly to me and said, 'When I told my mother about what has been done to Peseshet, she cried. Miut may go missing very shortly.'

"I found it difficult to imagine Queen Nemaathap allowing herself to be moved to tears. But then there was little that that great lady did not understand about being a sacrifice for the good of her family."

Imhotep paused again. Iry had some sense of what was to come and knew the next part of the story would be painful for Imhotep to recall. Iry bowed his head, hoping to appear as a pupil not inquisitor. With a voice broken by emotion, Imhotep continued.

"When my father discovered that Miut had been taken by agents of the Great Wife, he hanged himself from a beam. Everyone was numb with astonishment – and poor Intakes and Meresank devastated by this new grief." Again he paused but Iry said nothing. Imhotep coughed to clear the emotion from his throat and continued in more defiant tone. "But Father had known his time was up – he was just a poor upstart who had made himself too many enemies. Under interrogation much emerged. Miut had been a uniquely skilled poisoner and Father had found out. It transpired that this was not such a surprising thing for him to light upon, because he was a consummate poisoner himself. His swift rise to riches in his youth had been based as much on these skills as on any of those immense talents for which he was later justly revered.

"Miut's services had been used on countless occasions – starting with the removal of my beloved mother when Heterphernebti found, to her astonishment, that she was expecting my father's child. Mother would never have been reconciled to his betrayal of her with her best friend. She would have insisted on a messy divorce and taken all her riches and probably his good name with her."

Imhotep smacked his hand down on the armrest of his chair as if that were an end to it and stared at Iry intently. Iry found himself almost cowed by the steady gaze and had to look away towards the garden. He spoke, his voice sounding distant, but with enough conviction to remind Imhotep of his purpose.

"But Udimu was not poisoned, my Lord. The files record the death of your father and the fate of Miut, but say no more. One is left to draw conclusions that your father was directly involved in the death of his own son."

Imhotep struggled to lean forwards and locked Iry fiercely in his gaze.

"We could not bury Father with Mother and poor little Udimu. He was a great man but now he is forgotten. His name was erased everywhere in his tomb and you will find no mention of any relative or companion, or any provision for mortuary priests to remember him. Kanofer is entirely alone. I did that to him and he deserved it for what he did to Mother and Peseshet and Udimu. They loved him and he betrayed them.

"Toddling out into the darkness of the garden, what did little Udimu find? Father and Miut at a tender moment? More likely, he overheard something it was vital he did not repeat and so had to be silenced. He may have been only two but he understood all that he heard even if he did not always appreciate its significance. He would certainly have told others of plots and schemes. Silence and secrecy are the essence of the poisoner's art. Father, realizing that hardly anyone would ever know the exact details of Udimu's murder, must have ruthlessly decided on finding a quick scapegoat in Peseshet. Why would Miut, who was so very useful to him in his craft, ever be implicated at all?

"Heterphernebti got her just deserts. She must have known something of my father's secret business all along. Her fear of Miut once her mind started to go after her baby's death was enough to convince me. Mighty Pharaoh, not wishing his previous wife to know any hardship, took her into his keeping. I do not know when or how she died, or where she rests. I do not care.

"Miut met the fate of any poisoner who has lost her friends. She was rather more loyal to my father than he was entitled to expect. I later discovered that she had not revealed all that she might have done to the interrogators of the Great Queen.

"Peseshet survived to be set free, as I am sure I need hardly tell his majesty, who shares her blood. She would have been destined for removal when the time was right, but her servants were vigilant. She was happy to be a minor queen for love of a prince with so many charming sisters – her name forever kept alive by the disciplines of medicine that she founded.

"So there you have it, Iry, all very shocking – but a tidy ending. What more could his majesty require to know?"

Now was the moment that doctor Iry had been dreading. He cleared his throat. "My Lord. Forgive me if I think on this." He got up, a trifle stiff from sitting for so long on the hard stone, and walked around the pool, where Udimu's potent story had been told and where Imhotep had stumbled on the tiny tower of stone. He looked at the venerable gentleman sitting among the irises and noticed the slight trembling of the long-fingered old hand against the whiteness of the fine linen kilt.

"Thank you, Mighty Thoth," breathed Iry. Fine, white linen. Imhotep had stumbled. Imhotep had limped. Imhotep had found it hard to face Peseshet's concerned eyes on board the transport home. The bandage mattered. Could it be that Imhotep was involved some way in his baby brother's death? Again, Iry seemed to see the world flood crimson as he turned to face his childhood mentor.

"Dear master, you must know what you have just said – that Miut had not revealed all she might. How could that be, if you did not know much more than you have told me? If, indeed, you were not in some way implicated yourself?"

Lord Imhotep laughed. Iry watched the tension drain from the frail shoulders. "Whatever your private thoughts of Pharaoh, Iry, he chose you well. He is the Morning and the Evening Star and maybe he understands better than I do, that now I approach my end, as we both know I do, I need to search my soul for the truth of things. Ask me then, what more troubles you?"

"Firstly, why was that poor infant killed not once, but three times – the death for one of power? That fascinated his majesty and horrified me. What was the significance of Udimu's dreams? Did your father truly leave his razor at the scene of the crime, an intelligent man like him? And what of the linen bandage – are you somehow concerned in that – were you jealous of him, surely not?"

The old man smiled sadly, looking back, Iry felt, across all the years to his family gathered in this garden. "What Miut never revealed was hidden in the dream, but she did not truly understand that herself. Yes, I am sure that Udimu saw the Boat Of A Million Years and was about to watch the weighing Osiris. I no longer mourn my little brother. He will come again, he was of the kind that does – a great magician. It was I who flew out from under the shelter of his wing and, yes, I was jealous of his abilities. As I draw near to the weighing of my heart, I hope I did right – but fear that I did not.

"That night, like Udimu, I could not sleep. On board ship I had hurt my ankle and we'd bound it with a strip of linen. In the heat of the night, I got up to bathe it with cold water. I entered the hallway and Udimu suddenly came scuttling out into the moonlight and toddled off into the garden. Naturally, I followed, but instantly sensed that we were not alone. A garden is a place for secret meetings, but Udimu failed to understand. There were voices coming from out there. Like Udimu, I heard what they said, but unlike him, I recognized its implication. To my horror, Udimu came running out to the two of them, all laughter. Miut was on to him swiftly and, without remorse, throttled him with the ruthlessness of any cook. Father stood dumbstruck.

" 'What is the matter?' Miut said callously. 'He would have spoken. Did you want that?' Savagely, Father wrested the limp child from her grip, breathing deep gasps of horror as Miut continued relentlessly: 'You don't think he was your child, do you? Lady Heterphernebti thought she was barren, she comforted herself with many men.'

"I could not see Father's face to judge his reaction, but from then on he moved as if in a dream. They bundled Udimu in Miut's shawl and carried him deeper into the garden, finally ramming him down the latrine – a piece of unspeakably pointless violence. Perhaps it was Father's anger at what he had just heard.

"I hid in the bushes until they were done, creeping into the latrine hut once they had gone back into the house. I pulled him out and tried to revive him. Remember, Iry, how young I was, how little I knew of death or how a dead body will react when moved. I even thought that he choked once or twice. I was filled with rage and fear at what I had heard and what they had done.

"When I saw what the sand had made of his poor little eyes, I closed them. His baby's mouth, pulled back in the rictus of death, terrified me. I unwound the bandage from my ankle and placed it as a pad between his lips to hide the horror of his tongue and I left him sitting upright, decorous.

"I had no idea what to do or who to turn to. As I ran from the latrine in a panic of grief and terror, something slithered and fell in the darkness behind me. It must have been the poor baby slumping over because I had failed to prop him up correctly – but I did not turn back. I knew that if the tiny soul was still living, the pad that I had placed in his mouth would probably stifle him – but I ran on. I have lived with that burden ever since.

"When they found Udimu's body the next morning, that razor slash was as complete a mystery to me as it was to Father. He must have been sick with shock when he saw that someone else might have discovered his wickedness – but I gather that he and Miut decided that it was the random work of Huni, who had stolen the razor. They were probably right in this. I swear to you, I left my bandage as a neat pad – not rammed right down Udimu's throat. The ape must have done that. But for a long time afterwards I lived with the belief that Udimu could still have been alive and that had I acted responsibly I might have saved him, instead of leaving him to become a victim as Huni's plaything. That is why, at the time and to my eternal shame, I said nothing to anyone, not even to Prince Djoser and why – " and with this Imhotep's shoulders stiffened, facing up to his guilt " – why, for a while, I let Peseshet appear to take the blame."

"But surely the ape would have been covered in blood?" Iry interjected. "Was there not blood everywhere?"

"No, Iry, there was scarcely any blood at all, not even on the bandage peeping from the wound and this puzzled everyone greatly at the time. Later, of course, I understood." Venerable Imhotep held his former pupil deep in his gaze. "Now tell me, Doctor Iry, why would that be?"

In Iry's mind the crimson became white, fine white linen, reverently placed. "No blood flowing, even through a gaping neck wound with the poor child upside down – why, he must have been dead long before the wound was made!"

"But of course," Imhotep sighed. "We can see that now – I did not know then." Again he looked deep into Iry's eyes. "It does not absolve me. Maybe the gods decided that it was only right that such a great magician as Udimu should know a triple death. Father and Miut never appeared to suspect anything of me."

Iry listened aghast – great Imhotep complicit in his small and brilliant brother's death and silently allowing his sister's accusation! However, he was on Pharaoh's business, whether he liked it or not – he licked his lips and continued. "So what was it that you had heard that night which neither you, nor the dead, have ever revealed until now? What was so terrible?"

"It was something personally terrible for me, worse for my beloved sisters. I should have understood the meaning of what was told me by Udimu, when he sat here and described his dream of judgment, but neither he nor I understood that at the time. He thought that he saw our poor sister Intakes writhing under the gate of the judgement hall, and she fled in tears. But the person he had seen was the Princess Redyzet, our dearest mother, whom Intakes very closely resembled, and who was dead before he came into the world. She, it seems, had been as bad as, if not worse than, my father.

"My parents owed their rise to riches and success to judicious poisonings. I am convinced that their chief clients must have been my mother's half-brother, the sinister Prince Senakhte, and his wife Heterphernebti. With Mother's death, Father lost his chief technician.

"Later, when some particularly challenging commission arose, my stepmother had revealed that her maidservant Miut had poisoning skills as yet unknown in Egypt. Father would have understood the implication of what that meant. This must have been when he stopped sleeping with Heterphernebti. But he still made use of Miut. I think he was even sleeping with Miut, fascinated by her – another peasant made good.

"But ironically, what I and my brother (for that he will always be for me) overheard had been plans to murder the great Pharaoh Senakhte himself, for a suitable fee. However popular his regime, and exalted his godhead, he remained a person who made enemies.

"That was my terrible dilemma. Who should I tell and how? I knew that Peseshet was innocent, but I wasn't entirely sure that I was myself. I wanted to save her, but I had not yet thought out how I could. As it was, as always, it was she and Prince Djoser who saved us all.

"I do not know who planned Senakhte's death – if there is no information about this in the records of the Great Wife Nemathaap's inquisitors, that could be interesting in itself. What I do know is that I preserved the good name of my mother, the incomparable Princess Redyzet, and saved my poor sisters from even more pain.

"But there it is; she whom I had thought was most good,

most beautiful, turned out to be only an illusion. That is how one becomes a man. But I avenged my loss – and all my life I have tried to repay what I gained. That is all one can do. So let them weigh my heart. I, who have the reputation for understanding everything, have learned that I understand nothing at all. But thank his majesty, Iry – for his kindness of thinking of me at so auspicious a time."

"And so Udimu's triple death was coincidence?" gasped Iry. "His majesty had notions of mighty magic at work. He wanted Udimu's story set in stone for him to find when he came again."

"And he will let me fashion it? Who is to doubt Great Huni's wisdom?" Lord Imhotep's smile was eager and sincere. "It was not coincidence – who but the god of wisdom takes the form of an ape?"

SERPENT AT THE FEAST

Claire Griffen

We move on a hundred years to the time of the great pyramid builders and the reign of king Khafre (called Chephren by the Greeks). His name is associated with the second pyramid at Giza, only slightly smaller than that of his father, Khufu (or Cheops). Khafre's image is also said to have been the original face of the Sphinx.

Claire Griffen is an Australian who has been both an actress and a dramatist. She has written several mystery and fantasy stories.

On a barge made of cedar from Byblos, Baki, Chief Physician to Pharaoh, lay under a canopy on a couch with jackal-headed armrests and watched the river slide past to the deep sweep of the oars. His destination was the summer palace of Metjen-hotep, Chief Architect to Pharaoh and designer of his tomb at Giza. Metjen's *ka* had stretched out the hand of generosity to his friends, fellow imakhu, those permitted to kiss the feet of Pharaoh and not merely the dust before him.

Baki had been glad to escape Pharaoh's city of Memphis. On certain days a humid wind blew from Giza the stench of the Mortuary Temple and the latrines of the countless builders, craftsmen, overseers and labourers.

Yet he wished Metjen's summer palace was in the Ta-meh, the Ostrich feather-nome for instance, where a fork of the Nile flowed into the sea and cool breezes wafted across the marsh-lands.

This was a long journey he was undertaking, one made by Pharaoh only every second year when he inspected his king-doms and the reports of his nomarchs. Baki would have to spend some nights moored to the riverbank, listening to the croaking of the Nile frogs.

To Ken-hotep, Metjen's adopted son, the palace was ideally situated across the river from the city of Abydos, where he could indulge his carnal urges in the houses of pleasure, and between the Nile where he could hunt hippopotami and wild-fowl. Beyond was the desert where he hunted lion and leopard and sought the legendary monsters of *sag* and sphinx. And down river was Aswan where Metjen could check on progress at the granite quarries, although this was a somewhat perilous foray since it brought him close to the warlike Nubians, who harried the quarry workers.

To one who rarely left Memphis, the river held a fascinating vista. A crocodile sacred to Sepket glided past, its snout barely above water. Storks, nesting along the bank, preened their new-sprung feathers ready for flight. Fowlers knotted webs and spread them for the unwary water-fowl, fishermen in frail boats speared the water in hope of prey, launderers washed garments in the same water where oxen drank and children played among the reeds.

In the fields it was the Time of Shemu – harvest, and the mertu, the lowliest in rank, were harvesting the barley and emmer to be threshed by oxen and carried by donkeys to the Granary House. Baki reflected what a hot summer it had been. Like all who dwelt in the Land of Kem, he was anxious about the Time of Ahket when the Nile would flood its banks and deposit on the fields a fertile black silt. In the time of Pharaoh Djoser, the Land of Kem had experienced seven years of drought and famine. The Two Kingdoms relied on the annual flooding of the Nile for its prosperity.

When the barge rowed into the Serpent-nome, the Red Land where the desert stretched to the Red Sea, Baki grew tired of the unchanging scene and played *Hounds and Jackals* with his sandal-bearer Paser. He listened to the songs of his harper, who beseeched him to follow his heart and forget the past, an exhortation the physician viewed somewhat cynically.

When the pillars of Metjen's palace appeared he was glad to alight and stretch his legs. Downriver a skirmish was taking place, a group of youths trying to snare a hippopotamus with ropes. The animal bellowed its fury as one more daring or more foolhardy than the rest climbed upon its back. Baki recognized him as Ken-hotep, the Chief Architect's son, his face alive with the joy of the struggle, his half-naked body gleaming with oil and sweat.

As he walked barefoot up the slope, with his sandal-bearer following, Baki glimpsed a woman borne in a gilded chair watching Ken-hotep. The physician stepped behind a palm tree to observe her. It was Iras, the wife of Metjen-hotep, and she was watching the primitive struggle with shining eyes and moist lips.

Another man stood on the bank above her, also observing her. When he saw Baki he approached him and stretched out his uplifted palm in deference. "Lord Baki, Chief Physician to Pharaoh, we all know your fame."

Baki could not have said why he disliked this young man's greeting. Was he embarrassed at being caught spying on his friend's wife or was the youth too subservient? He pretended not to remember his name.

"Horiheb, Chief Scribe to Lord Metjen-hotep, Chief Architect to Pharaoh, High Priest of Ptah." The youth flushed slightly, recognizing the insult. "My lord Metjen awaits your coming in his pleasure garden."

The small garden was shaded by trees of olive, sycamore, fig and date palms, adorned with lily, iris and acanthus and cooled by pools of ornamental fish and water-lilies. Metjen lay on a couch under a fringed canopy, but rose as he entered. With him were two servants, one with a fly-whisk, the other with a fan of ostrich feathers. He greeted Baki enthusiastically.

"Baki, Physician to Pharaoh. May you live and flourish forever! How do you stay so lean? Your ribs stick out like bleached bones on the Sinai Desert, while I resemble nothing so much as the hippopotamus Ken-hotep is out hunting."

"And has snared. I saw him just now." Baki returned the greeting. "It is our natures to be what we are, fat or thin, ugly or beautiful. Speaking of beauty, how is the Lady Iras, your wife?" He refrained from mentioning the glimpse he had had of her.

Metjen sighed. "Ah, if only Ken-hotep was the son of my loins, but it has never been granted me from my wives or concubines to have a child. When I adopted Ken-hotep, I chose him for his beauty and his spirit. I should have chosen a plainer, more studious youth. His wildness flourishes rather than declines with the coming of manhood. He is bored with the study of architecture, he grows surly if he has to accompany me to the site of Pharaoh's tomb. He lives only to hunt in his papyrus boat on the river or to cast his spear in the desert at lions and leopards, or feast and get drunk and lie with the hand-maidens. He is yet to take a wife."

"He has the spirit of a child even if he has the form of a man. Be patient."

"I will heed your advice, you who saved the sight of my left eye, with the concoction you poured in my ear and by making me sit in my chair night and day with charms of rotten fish and herbs tied to my person." Metjen-hotep pretended to grumble.

From the experience of long years, Baki believed it was the prolonged sitting that had drained the blindness from Metjen's eye. But he had known that the architect would not be satisfied without medicine, so he had ground together a mixture of honey, red ochre and pig's eye and twice chanted a spell while he poured it in Metjen's ear. In his gratitude, the architect had brought Baki to the attention of Pharaoh and his present exalted state.

"If you continue to visit the quarry, your god Ptah may decide to teach you a lesson and not even my skill can save your sight."

"Yes, I'm aware the granite grit blinds most of the workers."

"Small wonder they have to be conscripted. Between the grit and sand, the blistering sun, the whips of the overseers and the Nubians over the border it's a wretched existence." Baki halted abruptly. He had often wondered where Metjen had found his young wife. There was a touch of the Nubian in her features and her colouring, nothing definitive, almost an illusion.

The architect shrugged off the warning. "As for the Lady Iras, her beauty blooms forever." He looked at the sun. "Soon she will go to her chamber and spend hours enhancing that beauty."

Baki could imagine that preparation, without closing his eyes. Iras, dusky-skinned, gazelle-eyed, narrow-waisted, narrow-loined, bathing in a pool where the blue lotus floated after purifying her body with senna and fruit, lying on a stone slab while her handmaidens shaved her skin with copper razors and anointed her with perfumed oils. Her robe would be sprinkled with myrrh and frankincense, her hair braided and coiled, her eyelids coloured with blue from copper sulphate, and encircled with kohl of crushed lead, her lips reddened with ochre, her nails and the soles of her feet painted with henna. Her robe would be white linen tied under one breast and swathed in folds to make her figure both angular and seductive, her jewellery copper and turquoise from the mines of Sinai. All this she would observe in her hand-held bronze mirror and smile.

Metjen studied Baki. "The journey from Memphis is a long one; no doubt you prepared your attire and cosmetics on board your barge. Allow my servants to freshen your clothes with perfumed water and your breath with honey pills. I too must prepare myself for my guests."

Baki wore a loin-cloth and ceremonial skirt. Paser had dusted his feet and inserted them into papyrus sandals. His clean-shaven chest was bare beneath the elaborate jewelled collar bestowed on him by a grateful harbour master for bringing his wife through a difficult childbirth. His body, while not as cadaverous as had been described by Metjen, did not boast the leopard-like sinewy grace of Ken-hotep. It was his eyes, green as the Nile, that gave him a hungering, almost wistful look that some mistook for naiveté.

He followed Metjen to his chamber and submitted to the administrations of his servants with a rueful smile. It was the horror of all nobles that they might not smell fragrant during a feast, which was why their plates were strewn with flowers and their heads adorned with incense cones to gradually melt onto their shoulders during the long summer night.

Metjen sighed again as his servants settled his wig over a shaven head anointed with a preparation of gazelle dung. He surveyed his reflection in his mirror mournfully. The cosmetics that enhanced the beauty of others only served to make more obvious his slightly grotesque features. Under his priestly leopard-skin, he wore a garment that covered his body and upper arms, but did nothing to conceal his paunch. While Baki was being tended, his host picked up a flute and began to play.

The physician had heard him play many times before, for recreation or to soothe his troubled spirit. "Like a mertu in the fields who tootles to inspire his fellow workers and remind them that Osiris was once cut into pieces by his wicked brother Seth yet restored by Isis, his sister and wife," Metjen said whimsically.

"You should take care, my friend, you'll be luring all the serpents in the nome to your chamber," warned Baki flippantly.

"Or be thought a hired musician at your own feast." A dry voice came from the doorway.

A shadow crossed Metjen's face. "I did not hear you announced, Horiheb." He glanced mischievously at Baki. "My chief scribe disapproves of my playing."

"It does not befit my lord Metjen-hotep's high degree." Horiheb extended his raised palm in praise of Pharaoh's Architect. He was a slightly built youth with sallow skin and an unsmiling mouth.

Metjen snorted softly, but laid down his flute. Baki wondered at his tolerance of the young man's criticism, until he remembered a rumour he'd heard that Horiheb was the architect's son by some dancing girl. If that were so why hadn't he acknowledged him or even adopted him in place of Ken-hotep?

"Is there anything my lord requires of me before or during the feast?"

"Only your presence."

Horiheb bowed and withdrew.

"Your flute has already lured one serpent to your chamber," murmured Baki.

He was surprised that the architect would invite his chief scribe, a man of inferior rank, to his table; it only added dried grass to the fire of rumour.

Metjen ignored his jest. "Shall we go down to the feast hall? I should be on hand to greet the Chief Judge, Lord of the Treasury and the Granary, Ramose and his wife the Lady Meret. With so many duties, one wonders Ramose can tear himself away from Memphis."

Baki glanced about the hall with its limestone pillars painted with symbols of lotus and papyrus and images of the god Ptah. Jars of wine, light and dark, waiting to be mixed, stood against the walls. Each guest was presented with a white lotus flower to hold in the hand and an incense cone by the Chief Anointer.

Iras, attended by two handmaidens, was already waiting. Curled about her arm was a small monkey. Her eyes flashed when she recognized her husband. "You are late, Metjen."

"My beloved." He touched his nose to each of her cheeks, then eyed the monkey dubiously. "My beloved, should you bring your pet to the feast? It may create a disturbance leaping from table to table."

Iras shrugged her shoulders under the heavy turquoise and copper collar. "It was a gift from your son."

From Ken-hotep emanated not only the perfume of oils, but an aura of challenge and high mettle. He wore a loin-cloth and lapped skirt of sheerest linen, arm rings and collar studded with lapis lazuli. In defiance of custom he did not shave his head, but wore it in small, tight, oiled braids. He was staring at Iras; although she disdained his glance, she smiled as if her mouth had a secret she had hidden from her eyes.

Baki, surveying the guests, felt the Pharaoh must be bereft of most of his friends, since he counted many Imakhu there, ministers in charge of trade in the Lands of Punt and Cush, or in charge of Pharaoh's army. Some had summer palaces at Abydos, others would return to Memphis in the morning; it was not wise to be too long from Pharaoh's sight lest his favour should fall on another.

A tall, angular man with cheeks so sunken they made dark triangles on his face in the torchlight acknowledged Baki. This was the *Tjati*, spoken of by Metjen, long-time friend to them both.

Baki greeted him with mock deference. "Ramose, Chief Judge in Memphis, Lord of the Treasury, Lord of the Granary and so on."

"How is the living god you serve? Will you be able to preserve his life indefinitely?" murmured Ramose.

"At least until his tomb has been cased with the white limestone of Tura and the red granite of Aswan and the capstone set in place."

"I understand sculptors are busy carving an outcrop of rocks into a giant sphinx, its human head bearing the features of our beloved Pharaoh."

They both hid a smile. Khafre was the first Pharaoh to assume absolute power and to call himself "the great god, the son of Re". In imitation of the gods he had taken as consort his sister Khame-re-nebti.

"No man is a god to his physician," muttered Baki.

Ramose raised his brows, but said no more. Jealous ears were everywhere and to speak against Pharaoh was high treason and carried horrendous penalties.

A gong summoned guests to the tables. Men and women sat apart from each other. Serving girls, naked but for the leather pouches that concealed their private parts, brought exotic dishes to the tables. Onyx, basted in balsam honey, antelope and goose flavoured with herbs and spices, lumps of fat served with cumin, radish oil and juniper berries. Metjen served his guests no fish for to him as a priest it was traditionally unclean, but he denied them nothing else. Beer was flavoured with figs, mint and honey. Duck from the Nile was served with celery, parsley and leek. Brown beans, wild sedge roots in olive oil and lotus seeds were set out in bowls. Girls danced to the music of lutes, zither and sistrum.

True to Metjen's prediction, the little monkey made a nuisance of itself, chattering, screaming, leaping along the tables, snatching food off plates and clawing at wigs. Horiheb rose from his place at the end of Metjen's table and beckoned one of the guards. The monkey eluded capture, creating more havoc among the guests and screaming defiance, but was eventually seized and carried away by the guard, not before it had sunk its teeth into Horiheb's hand.

"You must let me look at that," offered Baki. "A monkey's bite has been known to hold a latent poison."

From her place among the women Iras glared at Horiheb, her expression more poisonous than any monkey bite.

As the feast progressed she frequently summoned the wine steward, laughed and talked loudly and even hummed while a male harper urged the guests in song to enjoy the pleasures of the hour and have no regard for the morrow. The Lady Meret was shocked. Not only were they guests of Metjen-hotep but of the gods and should behave with decorum.

As the last course was being served, dates, grapes, honey cakes and jujubes accompanied by palm juice, the dancing girls again performed their slow, stately dance. To everyone's embarrassment, Iras rose and joined them, her body twisting sinuously, seductively. The buzz of conversation abruptly shut off and all eyes turned to Metjen. He smiled indulgently, but clapped his hands. The music dwindled away, the dancers fled, leaving Iras alone. The Lady Meret tried to persuade her to rejoin the other women, but Iras stalked out of the hall.

"Your wife compromises your dignity, my lord Metjen-hotep," murmured Ramose.

"What should I do? Have her beaten? She is young. Sadly, the cure for that will come all too soon."

Ken-hotep rose and left the hall. No one marked his going; with so much wine and beer flowing the latrines were in constant use. No one but Horiheb, who presently followed him. Why this aroused Baki's curiosity he could not say, but he too excused himself from the table.

Out on the terrace, the night winds were sultry and the Nile sparkled darkly in the distance. Peering over Horiheb's shoulder as the scribe hovered in the doorway, Baki saw the pale glimmer of a woman's dress, the glitter of jewels on dusky skin, suddenly concealed by a tall shape. As his eyes became accustomed to the night he saw Ken-hotep and Iras pressing their bodies fervently together, nuzzling each other's cheeks and throats and whispering words of passion.

"I think we should leave," advised Baki. "This is not our concern."

Horiheb started at the sound of his voice, but said, "It is my lord Metjen-hotep's concern. They have spat on his honour."

Iras, looking over her lover's shoulder, saw them in the doorway and hastily pushed Ken-hotep away. Horiheb strode back to the hall, Baki following.

"I beg you will say nothing to Metjen."

"You must have witnessed Ken-hotep wrestling the hippopotamus. You must have also seen the lady Iras as I did. When I saw her eyes I knew she had spat on Metjen's couch."

"If you must run to him with your tittle-tattle, wait until he is alone."

"No, he should learn of her betrayal before all his friends."

By this time they had reached the feast hall. Seeing the expressions on their faces, Metjen rose abruptly. Again, the chatter among the guests broke off.

"My lord Metjen-hotep, Chief Architect of Pharaoh, High Priest of Ptah." Horiheb extended his upraised palm. "Allow your scribe to speak."

Metjen frowned in irritation. "What is it, Horiheb?"

"As Lord Baki, Physician to Pharaoh, is my witness, just now I saw your wife and your so-called son in lewd embrace. They spit upon your name and on your house in the presence of your friends . . ."

"You lie, Horiheb." The woman's imperious voice cut across his. "My lord and husband, I speak the truth. I went out onto the terrace to cool my brow. Ken-hotep came upon me and tried to lie with me by force. I fought him off . . .''

Baki, glancing instinctively at Ken-hotep, saw him recoil in shock.

"Is this true, my son?" demanded Metjen tremulously.

"Should I refute the lady's virtue?" Ken-hotep's gaze scorched his erstwhile lover's face, his naked chest rose and fell in panting breaths, the melted incense gleamed on his shoulders. "Should I say her tongue is forked like a serpent's fang, one fork dripping honey, the other poison?"

"Is it true?" Metjen rapped out.

"Think what you will," muttered the youth.

Metjen glared from one to the other, at their smeared cosmetics, at the rent in his wife's robe. His face darkened.

"Go from this house, Ken-hotep. You are no longer my son. If your shadow falls across my threshold again, my servants will beat you away with rods. Hand-maidens, walk behind him as he leaves, brush away his footsteps with your whisks, so there will be no trace left of him in the house of Metjen-hotep." He turned to Horiheb. "Come to my chamber tonight, bring your implements. I wish to change my choice of inheritance."

Again, the scribe extended his palm. "All men can see how righteous you are."

As he backed away Baki murmured in his ear. "Don't gloat. He will not love you for this deed."

In compassion and deference, the guests continued their feasting and drinking but in a more subdued manner. Iras disappeared and reappeared with a fresh robe and her cosmetics restored. Her behaviour was faultlessly decorous for the rest of the evening.

When Metjen was retiring he drew Baki to one side. "What did *you* see? Who was the seducer: Ken-hotep or Iras? Or both?"

"I would not hurt you for all the wealth of Kem," Baki said reluctantly.

Metjen nodded as if satisfied by the reply. "I will need to play my flute long hours to ease my soul."

In the chamber allotted to him, Baki divested himself of his finery and washed away his cosmetics. He tossed restlessly on his couch. Metjen was not a man to make enemies, but what if news of this scandal should reach Pharaoh's ear? He could lose his exalted position. No man could bear such humiliation. He would serve himself well if he put away his errant wife.

He was drifting into sleep when his door burst open. Iras appeared beside him, her hair hanging down her back, her face distraught.

"Come quickly, my lord physician. My husband loses blood."

Baki threw on his clothes, seized his box of medicines and followed her.

"I went to his room to humble myself before him, to beg him to take me to his bed in token of forgiveness. 'I found him lying on the floor, face down, blood spreading from beneath his body. I pray to Isis he still lives. Use all your skills, physician."

When Baki turned the body over he saw at once that Metjen had embarked on his journey to the Afterlife. He was still fully dressed in wig and leopard-skin, his cosmetics intact. His limbs were convulsed, his eyes protruding. Imbedded in his breast was a dagger with a gold hilt in the design of a *sag*, half-hawk, half-lion. He glanced from the peculiar contortion of the limbs to the stain of blood on the antelope skin on the floor.

"Whose dagger is this?" he asked, although he felt he already knew the answer.

"Has my lord Metjen-hotep's soul fled?" whispered Iras.

He nodded. "Have your handmaiden fetch Lord Ramose."

Servants drawn to the hall outside were already wailing and tearing their robes.

"Go to your chamber, my lady Iras," Baki requested. "We will bring you the results of our investigation."

She stole a glance at the body before she left the chamber, but did not meet his eyes. Her lips, devoid of ochre, had an ashen, almost bluish tinge.

When Ramose, stern and stately, even in just his loin-cloth and without his wig, entered, Baki was scanning the floor. The

Tjati took in the situation with a glance. "That dagger belongs to Ken-hotep. It was a gift from his father because the youth was always hunting the *sag* in the desert, but in vain."

He walked out onto the terrace and looked over the wall. "A man as young and agile as Ken-hotep could climb this wall, commit the deed and then escape the same way."

"Leaving behind a dagger that would incriminate him?" Baki made a wry mouth.

"Perhaps the knife caught in Metjen's breast-bone, or he could have heard someone coming."

"Like the lady Iras. Why not avenge himself on her?"

"It's possible that that embarrassing scene was concocted between them to delude us all, while all the time the lady Iras was conspiring with Ken-hotep to murder Metjen for his wealth."

"She hated Ken-hotep. It was on her lips and in her eyes while she watched him wrestling the hippopotamus and hoped he'd die."

"You are always cynical about women." Ramose came back into the chamber. "What are you seeking?"

"Metjen's flute. He always played it before he went to his couch. I can't find it."

"Is it under his body?"

"I've already looked. He's not wearing his sandals."

"He may have kicked them off for comfort."

"Or . . ." He drew up Metjen's robe. "Look there. A tiny nick above his ankle, a slight trickle of blood. His sandals were removed in case they were stained and drew attention to the wound."

"What does that signify when the dagger in his breast killed him?"

"If the nick had been on his arm, nothing. It could have been a defence wound. But on his ankle, that signifies something else. It explains why Metjen did not see the serpent that killed him."

"But the dagger . . . ?"

"Was placed there by someone who wanted to disguise that he had been bitten by a serpent and to incriminate Ken-hotep.

See, the dagger comes out quite easily and the wound bleeds little."

"It was opportune for someone that the serpent chose to invade Metjen's chamber this very night."

"Not so opportune. Not by chance. If it hasn't been removed, I think you will find its basket below the terrace wall."

"And the serpent?"

"Has curled up in a corner somewhere."

Baki was amused at the nervous glance the dignified Tjati cast about the room.

"Don't be alarmed. A flute player will draw it out presently."

"Are you saying the serpent was deliberately loosed on Metjen?"

"And lured by his playing,"

"By whom? Ken-hotep?"

"Ken-hotep had already left the hall when Metjen announced his intention of changing his will. We have both heard, my lord Judge, of husbands adopting their young wives as daughters to ensure they will safely inherit. I think we should talk with Scribe Horiheb, who claims to be Metjen's son."

"A foolish piece of tittle-tattle. Metjen tolerated it because it amused his pride that other men might think he was able to procreate."

"I thought as much. Metjen came to me many times for a cure for his infertility."

A second, wholly unexpected shock awaited them in the scribe's room. Horiheb too lay sprawled on his sleeping mat with a dagger thrust through him.

"You cannot tell me this is not Ken-hotep's revenge," said the Chief Judge, grimly. "Or will you search his body for a serpent's bite?"

Baki was silent for a several minutes, utterly disconcerted by this new turn of events. "Is this also a dagger belonging to Ken-hotep?"

"I don't know," replied Ramose reluctantly.

"I shall examine his body, more precisely his finger. See the black smudge. He wrote to Metjen's dictation last night. Where is the roll of papyrus, where the changed will of Metjen-hotep, Chief Architect to Pharaoh, High Priest of Ptah? Search the room, my lord Ramose. I trust you will not stumble across the serpent."

Ramose dealt him a sour look, but complied. The physician continued to examine the body, noting traces of vomit on the pillow beside the mouth. The scribe's lips, usually flesh-coloured and barely discernible on his face, were blue.

The Tjati suddenly summoned him in an altered tone. Lying in a corner was the monkey, dead, a dark fluid issuing from its mouth.

"That explains the vomit on Horiheb's pillow and the colour of his lips. I thought it might have been occasioned by the knife thrust, but I was mistaken. I would refrain from partaking of the dates in that dish beside Horiheb's sleeping mat."

"We must return to Metjen's chamber and see if we can discover the scroll."

"I fear it will have already been stolen."

Again, he was mistaken. Beside Metjen's body knelt one of the two servants who always attended him. He was rocking himself with grief and smearing his face with ashes.

"Where is your friend?" Baki asked him, gently.

"He has gone across the river to Abydos with a letter for Lord Ken-hotep."

"From whom?"

"From Lord Metjen-hotep, dictated before he died. When Ken-hotep quarrelled with his father he always sought out a certain house of pleasure in Abydos to burn away his rage. My friend was sent to seek him in this house with the letter."

"Do you know what the letter held?"

"No, but I can guess. My lord would have offered Ken-hotep reconciliation and begged him to return." He gave a wan smile. "This has happened before."

Baki and Ramose exchanged glances. Of one accord they went to the chamber of the lady Iras. With her hand-maidens she was on her knees, wailing and strewing her hair and garments with ashes.

"Lay aside your grief, my lady," said Ramose, quietly. "We know it is false."

Her eyes flew open. "Have you arrested Ken-hotep?"

"Ken-hotep did not kill your husband," intervened Baki. "Your other lover Horiheb instigated his death."

"Horiheb!" She shrank from him.

"After he had written the letter to Ken-hotep for Metjen, offering reconciliation instead of the change of will removing his son's name and leaving you, his wife-daughter, all his wealth, which you had promised to share with Horiheb. It had been planned long before, Horiheb had the serpent to hand, the humiliation scene was played out before Metjen's friends, Ken-hotep banished. How galling it must have been to Horiheb when Metjen dictated the letter begging him to return. When Metjen began playing his flute, his scribe vindictively released the serpent. You were waiting in Horiheb's room, eager to hear of the change of will. Why did you bring your monkey? To jest with him about the game you'd played at the feast to make everyone think you hated him. When he told you what he'd done you were furious. He had prematurely engineered a murder that no one would have suspected yet Ken-hotep's name had not been removed from the will.

"You didn't just bring your monkey to his room. You had long plotted to remove Horiheb from your path. Your own weapon was to hand. You brought the poisoned dates and wine to his chamber. Did you feed him death with your own fingertips between your caresses? Push dates into his mouth with your tongue? Is that why your lips are blue. When he was dead you put the dagger in his breast. It was a mistake to leave the monkey in the room.

"You realized Metjen suspected you, so you did nothing to prevent his death. It was clever of you to disguise the serpent-bite with a nick of the blade, clever too to plunge into his breast the dagger you had stolen from Ken-hotep. Not so clever to remove the flute, since its absence drew attention to the possibility that we were being deluded as to the real cause of Metjen's death. You should have left well enough alone – no one would have suspected it was not an accident – but you wanted to incriminate Ken-hotep of both murders and be Metjen's sole heir."

Iras had sprung to her feet, panting, her eyes darting from side to side, like those of a trapped wildcat.

"You will be taken to Memphis bound with cords and tried before me," pronounced Ramose. "If you do not confess you will be beaten with rods. When you do confess, such was Pharaoh Khafre's love for his Chief Architect, his wrath against you will be mighty. You will be entombed alive with Metjen-hotep and there enjoy your portion of his treasure."

Later, Ramose joined Baki on the terrace where he stood gazing at the flamingo-coloured clouds on the horizon that heralded the sun-god's boat. He handed the Tjati the dagger he had picked up from the floor in Metjen's chamber.

"The *sag*, half-hawk, half-lion. The Sphinx, man, lion and eagle in one. Will Ken-hotep ever find them? Do they really exist?"

"Do you doubt the gods, Baki?"

The physician shook his head with a whimsical smile. "Only love, my friend, only love."

THE SORROW OF
SENUSERT THE MIGHTY

Keith Taylor

After the reign of Khafre the Old Kingdom civilization of Egypt sank into decline and for several hundred years (known as the First Intermediate Period) the local provincial nomarchs established themselves as hereditary kings. It was a period of social and civil uncertainty. It suddenly came back into order during the Twelfth Dynasty kings at the start of what is called the Middle Kingdom. This dynasty had several important rulers, but none so powerful as Senusert III. His name is spelled several ways and he's also known as Sesostris III, a near legendary king, who re-established a central power in Egypt and reorganized its social and administrative structure. He also undertook immense building works, including reopening and expanding a canal to bypass the first cataract at Aswan and so open a navigable link between Upper Egypt and Nubia. Senusert reigned from about 1874-55 BC, so although we have moved on about seven centuries from the last story (as big a gap as from today back to the time of Robert the Bruce), it is still vastly distant in time.

Keith Taylor is perhaps best known for his Celtic fantasy series featuring Felimid which began with Bard *(1981), but he has recently been exploring ancient Egypt for a new series of historical fantasies.*

I

. . . and he becometh a brother unto the decay which
cometh upon him . . .

– Papyrus of Nu

An extreme contretemps is needed to panic a woman who has
been chief cook – and therefore poison taster – to a Kushite
king. Tamaket had not trembled at the prospect of cooking for
Egypt's royalty. The King of Egypt would not fling her to
crocodiles if displeased. Tamaket had felt almost tranquil as
she put the kitchen staff to work.

Until she discovered poison in the dinner wine.

Rakheb discovered it, really. And that was the end of him.
Among other duties, he had to fill the wine-bowls from a great
river-cooled jar. When he thought that he was not observed,
he swigged the wine.

Tamaket noticed. With a dozen kitchen workers and fifty
dishes from roast goose to melons to supervise, she saw. In the
Egyptian governor's house at Semna it was no serious crime.
At the Kushite court it would have meant death.

This time, death struck quickly. Rakheb groaned with
stomach pains in a few moments, then fell down convulsing.
A shower of pots crashed down with him as he clutched at the
rack which contained them. They bounced and rolled through
the kitchen.

Tamaket moved to his side swiftly. She could do that, when
she wished, even though her shape was almost a sphere. She
carried her weight adroitly.

"Salt water!" she snapped. "*Now*, O you staring asses!"

She forced it down his throat herself. In a racking heave he
brought it straight up. Not nearly enough of the mortal wine
accompanied it. With a final spasm of legs and head he
perished.

Tamaket rose, shaking. This was an attempt on the life of
Egypt's godking, and she was apt to be suspected. She had no
time to feel horror at Rakheb's vile end. No time at all. She had
come into peril; her wits must now avert it.

She tasted the wine, then rinsed her mouth in a hurry. A faint undertaste, thick and murky, told her the nature of the bane: juice of a certain fungus combined with other ingredients, complex and lengthy to brew. It agreed with Rakheb's symptoms.

She considered hiding the truth, and dismissed that idea as impossible. Rakheb had died before a dozen witnesses. If the wine had been poisoned, so might other dishes be. Nothing, nothing would go upstairs that Tamaket did not know was safe, which meant a delay she must explain, as there had been a death she must explain.

Maybe to Governor Antef only. A clement man, he enjoyed the king's favour to a high degree, for they had been friends from boyhood. Let him decide how much to say.

Bringing the shaken kitchen staff under control with a blistering lecture, she mounted the outside stair. Her heart hammered with more than the effort of climbing. These people were the tyrants of the earth as far as Kush was concerned, habitually coming upstream with fleets and armies when each new reign began, while Kush made as steady a custom of rebelling. Now someone had tried to assassinate Egypt's lord – in a household which she administered.

The archers stationed around the roof's edge knew her, and gave her ingress. Tamaket had arranged the roof garden herself. Small sycamore trees planted in pots gave shade; flowers in coloured brick troughs, perfume. She usually felt proud of it whenever she looked upon it. Now she wondered if she would be strangled here.

"My lord Governor!" Tamaket wailed. "Mighty Khakaure, Living Horus! Great Royal Wife, Mistress of the Two Lands! Your slave implores mercy!"

She pleaded in faultless Egyptian which had been good even before she entered the Governor's service. Haughty, frowning faces turned towards her, seeing a young Kushite woman huge as a hippopotamus, breathing hard and badly worried. Governor Antef alone replied.

"Tamaket. What delays the food?"

"Hand of the King! I have tested the food constantly as it

was prepared. Some – " She hesitated artfully, in a way that betrayed the artifice. "Some appears tainted. Meanwhile I am sending up roast goose slices, bread and fruit of which I am certain. I beg the Great Ones' indulgence."

Antef realized, as he was meant to, that something was amiss. Making an excuse to the King and the Royal Wife, he came near Tamaket. Tall and wide, younger than thirty yet, hard-muscled as a quarryman, he looked down at her.

"What's this talk? You have never let tainted foodstuffs get as far as the kitchen benches while I have known you – or lost your head like this, either! You are hiding something."

Tamaket's glance moved to the royal couple. She said for Antef's ears only, "Poison in the wine. I ensure there is none in the viands also. A cook is dead."

It was masterfully done. No one else apprehended it. Hugely taken aback (he was not a devious man), Antef stared at the woman he had made his major-domo, flat against precedent. In about three heartbeats he decided against secrecy.

"Say it now," he commanded, "and to all. Clearly."

"O Hand of the King – "

"Forget the honorifics and speak! No Kushite subterfuge with me!"

Tamaket bowed low to them all, with effort. "Your pardon, Great Ones. It's a hideous thing, but I have found what I am sure is poison. In the wine. The wine which came in the royal ship," she added hastily. "I am proving all the food for safety's sake."

"Our wine?" Dahi echoed. "Not possible, woman! You imply that it was poisoned before we left, before the jars were sealed at the palace?"

"Your foot is upon my neck. But I supervised while the seals were broken, and with one jar the wax was newer, with crumbs of older, darker wax in it, as though it had been replaced. This I set apart, but one of my lesser cooks drank from it and suddenly died. I know it was bane."

"You do?"

The words came from the king. His formal royal name, Khakaure, taken when he assumed the Double Crown of

Khem, was always used to address him in public. Only his intimates still used his personal name, Senusert. Surely nothing personal or intimate informed his manner to Tamaket. He looked upon her sternly, the god incarnate of Egypt.

"You know much about poisons, in that case," he said.

"I do, mighty Khakaure. All that there is to know! At Kermah I was the king's chief cook, and taster of his viands. I had to learn to know and guard against poison, though it were given never so craftily, or have a short life."

"And *she* prepared our meal?" Dahi said, with an astounded look at Antef.

"Who better, Great One? Particularly in these parts. I'm told the savage she served never had so much as a bellyache. Yet Tamaket prefers to serve me. Had she outlived the King of Kush she would have been buried alive in his tomb with his other servants."

"It is very true, O brother and sister of the gods," Tamaket affirmed.

"And what sort of alleged food did you cook in Kermah?"

"Egypt's cuisine is much in favour there, Great Royal Wife. I learned from Egyptians. I believe the meal will not offend even your divine mouth."

Dahi considered the rotund figure before her. The Kushite woman was young, her face pretty within her orb of crisp dark hair, and fresh-skinned as a child's despite her bulk. The round dark eyes looked guileless. Dahi did not believe it for an instant. Kushite cunning was a byword in Egypt, and not without reason; under cruel tyrant kings, the crafty survived longest.

"Tell me," Dahi demanded, "how did you come to serve our valued Lord Antef?"

"I was sent to him as a gift by the king."

"Because of the love he bears Egypt's governor?"

"I wasn't told why," Tamaket answered, wholly aware of the irony. And the suspicion. She continued deferentially, "However, I did beg the Lord Antef as a favour – and a precaution – to bring my entire family to Semna also. Or someday an ill-disposed person might threaten them, to make me a traitor."

She dropped her gaze before the sudden fire in Dahi's. Had she sounded too simple, or too impudent? No. She believed she had said it with enough spirit, but not too much, and the Royal Wife must have been thinking it anyhow.

Dahi laughed aloud. Not cruelly, to Tamaket's relief.

"Provided the meal is good," she said, "I think, my lord, that our friend should bring this woman back to Egypt with him – and even her kin, for safety."

"Let it be so," the king decreed, "if the warning about the wine proves true. Woman, you say a man died after drinking it?"

"Truly, O Living Horus."

"Have the wine-jar brought here now, and a kid to test it. I take no Kushite's word."

Yet he discovered that in this case he could have done so. The kid died as the man had done. The remainder of the meal proved both superb and safe. Tamaket duly left with the royal ships when their prows turned downstream again. Her brothers and children went also, as ordained by Dahi.

II

May your heart be cheerful, my lord, for we have arrived at the country of Egypt. My sailors have driven home the mooring-stakes, the vessel is attached to the shore safely, the offerings to the gods have been made. We have lost none of our sailors although we went to the furthest parts of Wawat, and we have returned in peace.

– The Shipwrecked Sailor

"Magnificent," Senusert enthused, with a final glance back at the great dam spanning the Nile. Five hundred paces long and almost two hundred thick, faced with stone, it had been endowed with massive stone sluice-gates at either end for those years when the Nile rose excessively high.

"Yea, magnificent," he repeated warmly. "I never doubted

you would perform the task, but you have surpassed yourself, Antef. This is your greatest work yet."

Antef smiled with pleasure. He had been appointed Governor of Semna and sent upstream chiefly for the purpose of building the dam, anyhow. He was an engineer above all; some said the greatest since Imhotep. With the dam complete, his work had been done, and a new governor had replaced him.

Montumes, the Keeper of State Records, coughed primly. "The *king's* greatest work. What he commands done, he has done himself."

This bit of sycophancy drew no response at all from Senusert. The Royal Wife vented a small snort and said audibly, "Jealous old crocodile."

Tamaket rather agreed, except that to her Montumes looked less like a crocodile than a hoopoe with draggled feathers. His wig had been poorly curled, while the pleats and folds of his linen robe might have been crisper. For that matter, saving the royal family themselves, all the king's entourage bore little resemblance to the comely, dignified images of folk in their prime that Tamaket had seen on the walls of temples and tombs. They displayed the usual incidence of flab, meagre calves, paunches, boils and eroded teeth, while one army officer possessed a spectacular wall-eye. Tamaket had begun putting names to these physical characteristics, and later she would add ambitions, fears, prejudices, rivalries – all the things she must know to survive in Egypt.

The royal family looked uncommonly handsome, though, she had to admit. Senusert made a splendid figure of a man, tall, athletic and straight-featured, and the Royal Wife also needed no artist's flattery. She stretched her lioness body on the gold-worked couch beneath the deck awning, easy and assured, while two servants stirred the air above her with long-handled fans. *It's as well*, Tamaket thought, *the king is young and mighty*.

Amenemhat was comely too, a slender boy of twelve who seemed to hero-worship his father. And perhaps Antef as well. The latter, Senusert's friend from boyhood, stood even taller and wider than the king, with a rough-hewn, amiable face wide across the cheekbones and short from brow to chin. She had discovered him to be a kindly master, and hoped he would continue to protect her.

Because she was in dire trouble. Someone had tried to poison the godking of Egypt, the Living Horus. Well – presumably the king. Now she had boarded the king's own ship for the return to Egypt, with her children and brothers in one of the others, separate from her. Clearly, she was suspected.

It was greatly to her advantage to catch the guilty, then. A long road. She did not even know with certainty whom they had meant to kill. Comprehensive testing had shown that of all the wine-jars brought from Egypt in the royal ship, one, and one only, had been rendered lethal. One out of dozens. Tamaket had chosen it herself and personally seen it carried to the kitchen. (Her idiots of porters might have dropped it otherwise.) The poison must have been added to the jar in Egypt, either before it was loaded in the ship's hold or during the voyage – but not in Semna. *And none but Tamaket could be sure of that*.

The longer she cogitated, the less likely it seemed to her that Senusert had been meant for the victim, unless the assassin was crazy, for so much could go amiss. A cook or scullion might drink of the fatal wine before it so much as reached the royal taster, as had in truth happened; poor Rakheb. In fact the king's taster began to look like the most likely intended victim. She vowed to find out who his enemies and rivals were.

If death *hadn't* been meant for the taster, then Tamaket had to conclude that the murderer was not very clever. One who tried to destroy a king by such slipshod methods in Kush would be lucky if the killing dose reached his dog! Why, Tamaket had known poison to be added to one half of a fig only, by a hollow needle so fine it left no mark, so that a murderer might bite from the fruit and hand the rest to his victim, smiling – and that was considered elementary cunning past the Second Cataract.

You worm-wit! *Throwing the blame for your baby plots on one who survived two years of the Kermah court is going to be less simple than you suppose*!

The three royal vessels proceeded down through the cataract, fifty miles of river studded with islets and boulders. This being low water season, they bulked black and dry everywhere. Because of them, the region had its common nickname – the Belly of Stones.

There were villages, of course, with fields and groves but few irrigation canals. They passed a number of stations, wavering in sun-shimmer, where crushed gold ore fetched across the desert by donkey trains was further crushed, and then washed for its shining content. Kings of foreign nations enviously said that gold was as common as dust in Egypt.

At Antef's suggestion, she cooked for the royal party at several stopping places. She was closely watched, of course, and each dish tasted at most stages of the cooking. She extended herself to give them superb meals. Oryx roasted over charcoal; spiced pigeons and cress; duck flavoured with garlic and wine; fresh delicate lettuce from the river-side gardens; chick-peas fried with chopped onion and spices; triangular *shat*-cakes made with date flour and honey; all irrigated by wine and black beer.

No one fell ill. Tamaket, alert and anxious, was more concerned than any of them to prevent it. The poisoner might be aboard this ship with her; in fact, she suspected he was. Outwardly she took great care to seem cheerful and relaxed. She and the king's taster, Ipi, a handsome slave with an ironic sense of humour which he greatly needed, found common ground in discussing the vicissitudes of a taster's position.

For days the royal vessels bypassed the series of huge forts Egypt had built along the Belly of Stones; Mirgissa with its two-mile slipway by which it could be provisioned at any time of the year, Kor, and Buhen with its rock-cut ditch and massive double ramparts of brick.

The garrison commander at Buhen was a war-comrade of Senusert's from his first – and so far only – expedition into the south. There would be others, of course, as surely as the cranes would migrate. It was why Antef had been sent to build the dam. Now the river had backed up into a long narrow lake and the Nile was navigable far above Semna. The fortress commander looked forward to it, and said so in Tamamket's presence.

He suggested a lion hunt. Senusert came back jubilant, having killed his prey with a single arrow – not the first such feat he had performed. His reputation as a hunter and archer was more than the usual kingly braggadocio.

The young prince, Amenemhat, seemed less of an athlete, though active and healthy enough. It had disappointed him to be left behind during the lion hunt, and after it he increased the diligence of his archery practice, not that he had skimped it before. A conscientious lad. For a boy of twelve, he did not become distracted easily, except when the huge figure of Antef walked by. Tamaket knew hero-worship when she saw it.

The king, it was evident, also thought highly of Antef. One bit of conversation she overheard at Buhen fortress was especially revealing. The pair had discussed the skill of Kushite archers, and Antef had endorsed their famous reputation.

"None knows better than you!" The king had spoken with vehemence. "As Khonsu expels demons, my heart turned cold when I heard you had been laid low by a savage's arrow. I would have come. But I could not. And from Memphis to Semna is so far that I knew you would either recover or join the blessed before I could arrive."

"The doctor you sent south with me saved my life, Senusert."

"He's worth a thousand," Senusert agreed. "I would not have sent you into danger without him. Still, I'd far rather he had never been needed."

"He was needed often enough when the desert patrols came in, and for worse injuries," Antef said bluntly. "Mine was nothing much in itself – but the dog must have steeped his arrowhead in filth."

"Nothing much!" Dahi repeated derisively. "A hand's width over and a hand's length down, Lord Antef, and the king had needed a new engineer. It pleases us both to have you returning to Egypt. It surely pleases Amenemhat."

The prince nodded, tongue-tied. But his heart could be seen in his eyes.

They came to the First Cataract, the southern gate of Egypt, after a few heavy portages. This had always been the first great obstacle to pass on any voyage to Kush. It could be navigated with ease now. Senusert had ordered it cleared and dredged before his first expedition south. One passage, spear-straight, ten paces wide and more than eighty long, had been cut through the sun-darkened granite in a deep-water channel.

Tamaket had learned how to approach those of the king's entourage for instruction. Montumes, Keeper of State Records, the one who looked like a hoopoe, never gossiped with his inferiors and viewed Kushites as barely human savages. Nevertheless, if one asked him humbly and flattered his high concept of his own wisdom, he would grow informative.

"O wise Montumes, who did this work for the king?"

Montumes lifted his round little head with its ill-shaped wig and responded.

"The same who raised the Semna dam. He whom you serve, woman. In the seventh year of mighty Khakaure's reign he accomplished it, by the king's command."

Tamaket widened her glossy eyes. "Truly, he must be a great builder. I saw him plan and raise the dam, but I did not know what else he had done. And he is not thirty yet."

"He was making canals and irrigation layouts at twenty, a noted surveyor. The king appointed him Supervisor of Quarries soon afterwards."

Tamaket could have reeled off all Antef's titles, past and present. Besides King's Friend and Child of the Royal Nursery, they included Master of Irrigation and Canals, Chief Builder of the Two Lands, and – replacing his earlier position as Supervisor of Quarries – Master of the Mines and Quarries. She knew Antef had led a couple of expeditions into Sinai after copper and turquoise, an enterprise less than safe considering the nature of the nomads.

She did not tell Montumes she knew all this. Parading one's knowledge before the little man was no way to gain his cooperation. Tamaket needed friends. Above all she needed her master Antef. Frowning, she asked herself if someone might have been trying to poison *him*, and might try again. A troubling thought.

III

Increase your subjects with new people,
See, your city is full of new growth.
— Instruction of Merikare

Each subsequent day of the voyage downstream brought new matters for awe. Tamaket had never seen the Two Lands before. Oh, Kermah, with its great palace and temple and thousands of folk, had been a respectable city even by Egypt's standards, but not beside Thebes. Looking upon its huge stone wharves, its mansions, the colossal Temple of Amun and avenue of ram-headed sphinxes, Tamaket felt a pang of despair for Kush. How could it resist this?

Well, she could not stop it. Her fate and her family's lay in Egypt now. Her two brothers, brave and loyal but scarcely brilliant, needed her nearly as much as her children. Other Nubians and Kushites had settled in Egypt down the ages – as forced labour, artisans, prisoners of war, honoured hostages, bowmen in the army, and the famed Medjai desert police. Some had risen high.

Antef, she noticed, though cheerful most of the time, appeared downcast in Thebes. She wondered why. She chose the captain of his household spears to ask, feeding the man a magnificent meal to sweeten him.

"The Lord Antef doesn't seem to enjoy his food since we arrived here," she remarked. "Or much of anything else."

That was all it took. "You don't know," the spearman said. "The Lord Antef lost his wife in Thebes. He married young, they had two children, and then she died in a boating accident. The children followed. An outbreak of sickness."

"Ah," Tamaket breathed. "Sad. I knew he had been married, but not that she died in Thebes."

"He's shut-mouthed on the subject, for it pains him yet. Nor should you chatter of it."

"I surely will not, brave captain. Thanks." Tamaket sighed deeply. "My husband died young also. He displeased the King of Kush and was buried in an anthill."

"I've heard that. Here even the king may not violate *ma'at* on a whim. No, not though he is a god. Your husband was a good man?"

"I always found him so. At least our children still live. The twins were born after his death. There were those who wished to slay them at birth. Twins are held unlucky in Kush."

This appeared to be more knowledge than the spearman wished for, but Tamaket was his master's major-domo; he displayed polite interest.

"They could not be more alive, so you would have none of that plan, clearly. *You* must be glad to be out of Kush!"

Tamaket shrugged her ample shoulders. "It was my home, but now my life is here. Yes, I am glad, and also to be serving the Lord Antef. He's been kind. More than kind."

"And to others. It's his way."

But had plotters wished to kill him nevertheless? Or, perhaps, him and all the other important servants of the king they could poison at one sitting? Or just the king and his chief wife? If Senusert were to die and Dahi survive him, the new ruler of Egypt would have to marry her for valid kingship. Tamaket did not like his chances unless Dahi found him attractive! To impose on that one against her will would be a mighty feat.

She observed that Senusert and Dahi had both been much freer, more like natural human beings, beyond the cataracts. Each mile they travelled into Egypt, their royal roles seemed to settle more heavily upon them, and their manner became more remote and high, in accordance with their divine status. Senusert had a dull time in Thebes, rising daily at dawn to read endless reports, records and petitions. Montumes gave him brisk, methodical aid in those duties.

They embarked again. The next important stopping place

proved to be Abdu, burial place of Osiris and pilgrimage shrine for all Egypt. Here, as everywhere, the king must examine the administration of temples, their huge estates, the probity and competence of his officials, and perhaps most ominously doubtful of all, the loyalty of nobles.

Tamaket knew something of that situation, too. Egypt's present king ruled over a land which had descended into chaos, the most feared of all conditions to Egypt's people. Only during this dynasty had the precious principles of *ma'at* been restored. The king embodied these. The nobles, particularly the great nomarchs, had enjoyed autocratic feudal power in the bad times and felt other than comfortable without it.

A motive for poison, and an obvious one.

Tamaket discussed it with her brothers. This far into Egypt, the rulers no longer troubled to keep them apart. Besides, Antef considered them honest; they were archers of his own bow company, nearly as good as the king himself, and like him tall and leanly muscular. Conversing with their sister they resembled a couple of upright sticks beside a ball.

"The nobles are having their wings clipped and their talons cut," she said. "They may not raise war-hosts unless the Living Horus gives the word. They have been forbidden to build, as they used to, tombs and mortuary temples fine as a king's. Khakaure's father took a number of nomarch's sons into the Residence and had them raised with the princes, to be as their foster-brothers. Our lord Antef was one of these."

"We know that, sister," Oruno told her. "We have served him too! His father rules the Heron Nome two day's journey away. The king means to stop there to awe the man."

"Rumour says he's among the most fiercely jealous of his power and rights," Zebei added. "Or was when young."

"All of which may affect us. Listen, my brothers. I will not be with Lord Antef when he visits his father. You and the king will. Observe for me; see how his sire welcomes him! How his family regards him. Tell me how they welcome the king. Certainly they'll be humble before him, but look for what lies beneath."

They would do their best, she knew. They would bring her

their observations without holding back. The king's taster would observe more sharply, and be closely present throughout the banquet, as her brothers would not. However, Ipi had no reason to open his mouth to her, as yet. She must cultivate him and place him under obligation.

"Well?" she said when her brothers returned. "Tell me of Lord Antef's father, this hereditary Nomarch of the Heron? What sort of man do you think him, and how did he greet his son?"

Zebei grimaced. "From what we saw? Cold as deep water, my sister. His welcome to his son was like his welcome to the king. Formal and stony."

"We didn't go within," Oruno added, "but we saw the Lord Antef come out with a sombre look, and he is brooding yet, if you notice."

"Indeed I notice," Tamaket said. "Did the nomarch's servants say anything that can explain it?"

Her brothers shook their heads in unison.

"Not in our hearing," Oruno told her. "They are as closemouthed as Kermah palace guards. All that household. Their discipline must require it."

This was interesting. Seemingly, Antef had a hard man for a father. Formal and stony? When Antef had been long absent from Egypt, a success at difficult tasks, and once almost died from an arrow! Belike he was furious at Antef's being close as a brother to the king, and yearned for the power his forebears had held in the time of chaos.

Nor was he the only one. Gossip, flying like cranes, said there were at least twenty in Middle Egypt. And more elsewhere. Tamaket saw the number of folk who might be guilty multiplying before her eyes.

IV

I swear by my life that when I gained mastery over men it was very pleasing to my heart.

— *The Destruction of Mankind*

"A lioness, a man-eater!" Zebei repeated, his voice excited. "Egyptians call her the Drunkard. She appeared here while Khakaure was in the south. Eight deaths she has caused, sister – eight."

"Eight," Tamaket said sardonically. "How many would she slay sober? You talk as though this is cheerful news."

"It is," Oruno told her. "The king goes to hunt her! He wishes Lord Antef to be there, and Lord Antef is taking *us*."

Well, it made sense that Senusert would do so. The king had a duty to protect his people. Besides, he revelled in lion-hunting.

"Why is she called the Drunkard?"

"She's lame, and runs like one."

Zebei gave that answer. He had always been the more down-to-earth and succinct of the pair. Oruno snorted, and added his own version, that of a man with a flair for storytelling which made him welcome at any camp fire.

"Bah! She's called the Drunkard after the lion-goddess Sekhmet, dull one, that Ra sent to punish a disobedient folk. She slaughtered and tore and would stay for nothing, even when Ra commanded her, fearing mankind would be utterly destroyed. To halt her the other gods had to make a vast flood of red-coloured beer. She took it for blood and drank it all. When she slept, stupefied, the race of men was saved."

Zebei chuckled. "So? Well, and now I know. A pleasant story, brother, but we will not stop *this* lioness with beer! It'll take spearmen, bowmen and a thousand beaters."

"The king will bring them. Sister, the Drunkard may be a demon! Cunning past belief, as the people tell. Why has she appeared here, alone, as one might say out of nowhere? Lions are uncommon so near Memphis and the capital."

Tamaket's heart chilled at the word *demon*. They were real to her, real as stars after sunset, real as food, the dark powers that hunger and lust and gibber in the night. Yes. A man-eating lioness of exceptional craft might be one.

But probably not.

"The desert wastes are close enough," she said. "Maybe this – Drunkard – drifted in from yonder. Maybe the Waters of Shedet. The lake silted up long ago and the fields around it are going back to waste."

"Wherever she came from," Zebei said confidently, "she will soon go to the abodes of the west."

Stringing his tough longbow with a movement that looked easy, he fired three arrows swiftly at a copper target one hundred paces off. They crowded each other in the centre. Oruno cocked an eyebrow, sent four to join them just as swiftly, spaced just as closely, and smirked at his brother.

They left with Antef on the lion hunt a few days later. Tamaket remained, if not in charge of the estate – its steward managed that – at least of the great house, its servants, and all that belonged thereto. The place had betrayed the lack of a woman's touch. Antef absolutely ought to marry again, Tamaket thought. As should she, no doubt. It would be madness to do that before she dispelled the cloud of suspicion hanging over her, though.

Tamaket worked hard while her brothers were gone. Then they returned, and her screams of anguish rang over the immense estate. Zebei came on a bier, ripped and dead, Oruno on a bloody litter, one arm in rags, face grey and wet. She abandoned her duties and tended him only. Antef, who was unhurt, not only allowed it but spent much time with Oruno himself. Her brothers had saved his life, it appeared.

"Sister, she *is* a demon, that lioness!" Oruno raved. "A demon! Two of the beaters died driving her before we ever saw her! The others stayed resolute, else she had escaped."

Tamaket wished fiercely that the Drunkard had. So they had successfully killed her. What of it?

The beaters had moved forwards bravely, it seemed, swinging their torches and great wooden rattles. They advanced at a run in a long crescent three deep. Three groups of hunters waited. Senusert led one, Antef the second, and the king's half-brother Rhamsin, an army commander, the third. Each leader, and two picked men with him, carried bows. The rest had spears and oblong shields.

"We did as planned," Oruno croaked. "We zigzagged, to catch her in a crossfire. It should have worked! But it all went wrong, sister, all! Rhamsin had a clear shot at her flank while she charged the king – and then she turned and charged Rhamsin. She sprang over the men with shields and came down on him. Tore away the top of his head. Then she turned on the others, and sister, *she picked out the bowmen!* Slew them both, then a spearman, and rushed the king's group again afterwards.

"The king shot twice. Hit her once. Behind the neck . . . Lord Antef ran from the midst of us into the open, arrow on string, to draw her attention from the king.

"He did. She charged him next." Oruno's unmaimed hand closed on his sister's. "It wasn't because he shouted or stood alone in the open, but because he held a bow. I swear it! She knew!" He half rose, gasping. "We went to his aid. The king may not trust us, but *he* does. He knows we are true men."

Tamaket did not have to ask what had happened next. The evidence lay here in front of her – and silent in the house of the embalmers, where Zebei's body had gone by now. The doctors shook their heads gravely over Oruno's mangled arm and, when the first touches of gangrene appeared, they tried to save him by amputation. Antef held him down with all his granite strength while it was done, and Tamaket cauterized the stump herself, fast and deftly.

It proved too late. Oruno died two days later.

The brothers were embalmed and buried by Egyptian practice. These rites took seventy days. Long before they ended, Tamaket knew all that had happened on that dreadful lion-hunt, the secret of the Drunkard's preternatural cunning, and the very reason she had become a man-eater. It defied belief. At first.

"Someone split her forepaw lengthwise, when she was a cub, with care, most deliberately," Antef said harshly. "Lame for life, she could not take her true prey. Nor is that all. We found, when she was dead, that her neck was chafed under the fur by frequent use of a choke-chain. She had been a captive for long."

"My great lord!" Tamaket's grief had dulled the sharp edges of her mind temporarily, but this was not difficult to grasp, merely hard to accept. "Did someone cripple that lioness? To make her a man-eater?"

"They must have done more." Antef's broad face was rigid with disgust. "She knew how to avoid hunters, how to pick archers from a group and destroy them. Surely she was *trained* for years in secret, then brought to this region by men who knew the king would act himself. This was another plot to murder him, begun years ago and set in motion if the poison at Semna should fail."

With slow mounting fury of her own, Tamaket said, "*This attempt on the king took my brothers' lives!*"

"Truly. They were brave men. I would not be standing here but for them. It's why I tell you this." Antef added with what seemed real sorrow, "I regret taking Zebei and Oruno on the hunt, now. I might still have come away alive without them."

"No, lord! They would have been hurt in their honour – held that you did not trust them!"

"There is no man who can say they were not trustworthy now. I'll build a fine tomb for them. Offerings shall be made and prayers said while a man of my line survives."

"It's . . . a precious sign of your goodness and regard, lord," Tamaket answered after a moment. "Yet the offering murdered men need most is the blood of their slayers."

"They shall have it."

Oh, yes, Tamaket thought. *I will live to see them seated on tall stakes with their eyes torn out.*

V

His Majesty found me a common builder . . . And His Majesty conferred upon me the offices of King's Architect and Builder, then Royal Architect and Builder under the King's Supervision. And His Majesty conferred upon me the office of Sole Companion, King's Architect and Builder in the Two Houses.

– *Tomb Inscription of Nekhebu*

The Royal Wife had said those same things, and even more violent ones, when the king told her the significance of his fatal lion hunt. Raging back and forth in a broad chamber of the palace, with none but Senusert and Antef for witnesses, she spat corrosive curses and smashed various objects almost as though she had been an ordinary village wife.

"This is vile past belief!" she said at last. "And bizarre, as much as monstrous! How does one train a man-eater at all? How be sure – unless by magic – that it will ever come within reach of His Majesty? What sort of plotters are these?"

"I've begun to see," Antef answered. "Cowards who work at a distance, as from behind two or three curtains. Then if one attempt fails, they are safe, unknown, and can try again from a distance. They attempted such a murder with the poisoned wine, and now with the lioness."

"Who?" Senusert demanded. "I wish you, Antef my friend, to find out! Investigate this matter. Act with my authority. Report only to me – not even to the Vizier."

"*I*, Senusert?" Antef was hugely taken aback. "If you wanted a marsh drained, or the largest obelisk ever quarried brought to Ithej-Tawy, I'd be your man, surely. But am I the one for this task?"

"It's true, my lord," Dahi murmured. "Only liars have ever called our friend subtle."

Senusert dismissed that. "Quarry the truth as you would an obelisk," he ordered, "no matter how hard the stone, or where the chips fly, or whose skin the dust inflames. My Majesty knows that you are direct, not devious. That may be no bad thing. Tell me how you would set about it."

That formal "My Majesty", here in private where Senusert had never employed it before, told Antef that here was a command he might not evade. He said slowly:

"Training a lion is surely no task for any man but a proficient master. The Drunkard was skillfully trained. We have been shown that too well. I'd have thought there was no place in Egypt where lions were kept but the king's own zoo. Therefore I'd begin by asking the keepers there what men, to their knowledge, have the skill. There will be those who know, those who saw and heard. They can be found."

"Let it be done."

Antef thought of his father, and fear touched him. *Great creating Ptah, let him not be involved*!

That thought had occurred to his shrewd major-domo already. Suppose Antef's father should be one of the plotters? Antef was a man of strong, simple loyalties. To stand in the open shooting at a crafty man-eater to draw her away from his friend – that he would do, and think only that this was his friend and foster-brother, not that it was the godking of Egypt. Antef choosing to expose his father, perhaps his entire family, as assassins – that she could not see so clearly.

She had intended to help him find the wretches who had done this evil. She still wished it. However . . . if the trail led to his father, Antef might not be able to face the consequences, and she wanted them destroyed no matter who they were. Better to pursue these hyenas in circumspect fashion, using all the craft she had learned in the life-or-death (more frequently death) atmosphere of Kermah. She needed someone to act for her, someone who would be glad to conceal her part in the affair, and also someone who would be useful. It took no more than two hours' thinking to convince her she knew just the man.

Antef's mansion and estate lay on the outskirts of Ithej-Tawy, the new capital established by Senusert's dynasty south of Memphis. It made the palace easily accessible nearby. Tamaket had smoothly bribed her way to an audience with the Keeper of State Records before her brothers' obsequies were finished.

"You honour me, worthy Montumes," she said.

"Yes, that I do," the birdlike little man answered testily. "What is it?"

Despite the generosity of her gifts, he had no wish to spend much time on her, she perceived. He must reckon everything about her uncouth; her race, accent, size, coloured robe, and the gashes of mourning on her cheeks and upper arms. The sight of them did remind him of recent events, though. He made an effort at compassion, no matter how insincere.

"I'm sorry for your brothers' death," he told her. "Their bravery is much spoken of."

"Yes. I thank you. Have you heard, O Keeper of the Records, that the lioness was *trained* as a man-eater by evil ones who sought the godking's life?"

"I had heard." Despite the guarded words and supercilious tone, he stiffened with interest. "I did not believe it."

"Yet you may. The King and the great Royal Wife believe it. The mighty Khakaure has appointed Lord Antef to find these monsters."

"Antef?" Montumes could not have expressed more eloquently in a long speech that he thought all Antef's talents lay in digging canals.

"He acts with the power of the King in this matter. Yet it's in my mind that he may need assistance from the wise."

Montumes agreed, and she shared her thoughts with him further.

"Nothing so terrible and strange could be done wholly in secret! Those who can train lions are few. Men and women must have disappeared to feed her demon's appetite; at one time she was perhaps carried on a ship to this region. There will be other traces, lost in the records of Egypt, and no man knows those as you know them, O Montumes. I am certain that with your assistance my master can fulfill the king's command."

Montumes's eyes widened in total agreement, and flashed with the hope of gaining credit. He manifestly felt sure Antef had no chance of finding the culprits without him. Before he replied, Tamaket knew she had hooked him like a fish; it had not even taken any finesse. He would help.

Antef proved more competent at investigation than Montumes thought. He had always been methodical and thorough, while his determination was a byword. Inquiries among the keepers at the royal menagerie, where he had said he would begin, proved worthwhile. The oldest man there had served a Syrian prince, long ago, a cruel lord who used trained man-eating leopards to destroy his enemies.

"I was young then," the man mumbled out of his toothless

face. "Never should have left Egypt! I'd not have believed, lord, how you can pervert a big cat if you wish. They can be made so they will touch no prey but live men and women – won't even recognize dead meat as food, if you can credit that! The Drunkard never touched a poisoned bait, did she, or came to a still carcass?"

"No, that is true. She was never known to! How's that done? And what men in Egypt did you ever know who could do it?"

The animal keeper said grimly, "It's done by giving them nothing to eat but live men and women, tied wholly helpless at first, then hocked and crippled, more active as time passes and the cat grows confident, lord. I'd hope there is no man in Egypt who could do it."

"It seems there is."

The old man could think of fewer than half a dozen men he had known with that kind of skill. He gave their names. Antef enjoined him to silence, and went inexorably looking for the men in question. Yes. They were that. Most dreadfully in question.

He also sought traces of strange disappearances. Egypt was an ordered land where almost nothing happened without being recorded by scribes, least of all the bizarre or criminal. Montumes had most of it at his thin fingertips. What he could not recall offhand when asked, he knew where to find in the archives. Harvest figures, the number of priests, servants and artisans in this temple or that, soldiers' movements, caravans across the desert, Nile flood details year by year, legal proceedings – he could provide it.

Odd disappearances had indeed taken place. They had occurred among the pilgrims going to Abdu, over the years of the Drunkard's life. Before then, they had been less frequent or regular.

"Not kidnapped from their homes, then, but in a strange place, nameless among crowds of other strangers," Montumes said.

Antef's big hands closed into fists. "And Abdu, the place of pilgrimage, is above Middle Egypt."

Middle Egypt, where the nomarchs remained most power-

ful, least subdued, and least contented. The two wholly dis-
similar men looked at each other with the same thought in
their heads.

Antef chose his agents while the Nile rose, which it did
poorly that year, and sent them out after the water receded. To
conceal them among the army of scribes who surveyed the
fields and marked the boundaries anew was a simple matter.
Montumes arranged it almost in his sleep, and men under
Antef's orders travelled the desert roads with the Medjai,
camped at obscure oases as well as the greater ones, spoke
with Libyan tribesmen. The reports came back, and in them
now and then there was mention of a lame man-eating lioness.
Usually the mention comprised mere rumour, but sometimes
it amounted to more. They pointed to the same place when put
together; the Boar Nome in Middle Egypt.

"Ushikab, the Nomarch of the Boar," the king said reflec-
tively, reading the summary. "He's a known malcontent, and a
neighbour of your father's, my comrade."

"A close friend too, as you know." Antef looked unhappy.
"He has five sons. One of them married my sister. It comes to
me that it's time I visited them."

"You need not," the king said, "if you do not wish it."

"I began this, O Living Horus, and I'll complete it. Pleasant
or not."

"If your brother-in-law is innocent, he will not suffer," the
king promised. "Indeed, if there's merely doubt, he shall have
the benefit of it, though his whole family should stand
attainted and guilty."

Tamaket remained behind. There was an outbreak of smallpox in Memphis which caused the Vizier to quarantine the
palace, and she took the same measures in Antef's house. Hers,
though, were more stringent; she had seen the same sickness rage
like wildfire in Kush. She accepted no supplies, not even cloth or
leather, except from far upstream, until the danger had passed.

Her vigilance proved wiser than even she had guessed.
Someone tried to smuggle infected matter into Antef's house
so that he would come home to perish. The men trusted with
the task had both had smallpox before, and survived; their

pockmarks were the first thing that made Tamaket suspect them. Just one pitted face might have aroused no misgivings, but both together moved Tamaket to have them taken into close guard and their cart segregated.

They proved to be from the Boar Nome. Although not supposed to know the significance of that, Tamaket was informed. She had taken care to be. The men defied her and refused to say anything – a silly error, when dealing with a Kushite who had brothers to avenge and children to protect. Within a day they had told her all she desired to know.

Their orders had come from a former retainer of the Boar Nomarch's with a grudge against Antef. Tamaket had agents of her own by this time. They discovered the man hiding in Memphis. Again, she passed the knowledge on to Antef through Montumes, letting the Keeper of State Records have the credit. She let him have the men she had questioned, too, or what was left of them.

Antef seized the nomarch's one-time retainer in Memphis. Shown what had happened to his hirelings and promised mercy if he spoke, he betrayed all he knew as fast as he could gabble. His knowledge included the name and whereabouts of the Drunkard's trainer. Before the Nile had receded, that man too had been captured, alive, in the ancient town of Buto.

He was certainly the one. The Drunkard had left her inscription on him by mauling him – when she was only half grown, which doubtless was how he had survived. Nevertheless, the marks of her cleft forepaw were distinctive.

Tried and condemned, he talked volubly in exchange for a clean ending, which the King promised. Thus they gained hard proof at last. Antef travelled south again, and stood in a narrow desert ravine, blocked at the ends and walled at the top, where the Drunkard had been raised. Bones of her victims had been buried in the sand nearby. Several, by the pitiful possessions buried with them, had been pilgrims who vanished from Abdu. The nasty tale appeared complete.

The ravine lay just outside the Boar Nome, and the trainer's testimony implicated its ruler past any man's power to effectively deny.

"And three at least of his sons," Antef said, in the bleakest tone Senusert had yet heard from his mouth. "I believe the last is innocent, for he's both too honest and too indolent to scheme like this, but it's a matter I had rather the Vizier investigated. It's my sister's husband; I am partial."

"He will never be a nomarch." Senusert smiled grimly. "The traitors shall die, I shall deprive their family of the Boar Nome, and you shall be lord there instead, my brother. Let other nomarchs who would plot or rebel see this, and learn their mistake."

His will was done. Ushikab, Nomarch of the Boar, died as a traitor and his elder sons with him. They went to their doom mouthing accusations against Antef's family, which was only to be expected, all agreed, from malice against the man who had exposed them. Antef became Nomarch of the Boar, and Senusert gave him a new title to accompany the province – Chief of the Praised Ones, when his honours had been extensive already, so that many were jealous.

Senusert, Antef and Montumes all knew that certain loose ends had been tucked out of sight and ignored, yet they believed them to be minor, and that the hideous conspiracy was ended.

Tamaket knew better. She saw no failings in the king's good sense, or his justice, either. He had punished only those against whom there was strong evidence. In Kush, the traitor's entire family would have perished with him as a matter of course, like most of his friends and associates. She much preferred Egyptian justice, in spite of the prejudice against Kushites.

But she knew it was not the end.

VI

Be merry all your life;
Toil no more than is required
nor cut short the time allotted for pleasure.
                    – Instruction of Ptah-hotep

Senusert removed the sacred Double Crown with relief, having just worn it through a long morning of listening to petitioners. The false plaited beard of kingship followed. He rubbed the point of his lean angular chin, for the ceremonial beard always itched it.

"I've a task for you, my brother," he said, "which you should like better than the last. It will keep you away from your nome. Appoint a good steward if you haven't done so yet. I desire you to restore the Waters of Shedet."

"Men say it cannot be done," Dahi remarked, with a flash of malachite-painted eyes. "They say the lake is moribund by the will of the gods." She smiled. "Like the mighty king, I'll believe it when you tell us so, Lord Antef, for I have doubts that the others know what they are talking about."

Antef smiled wryly. "I do wonder where their eyes were. I've surveyed the lake and the country around. The trouble lies with the river that feeds it – one of the Nile's offshoots, of course. Once I follow its course from the lake upwards I should know what measures are needed."

"Amenemhat thought you would say that. He wishes very greatly to go with you. Is that pleasing?"

"I'll have joy of his company."

Dahi knew that was no polite formula. Antef felt a good deal of affection for the prince. She was willing to entrust the boy to her lord's friend, even on a journey of some danger.

He returned dark from wind and sun, cocky, bursting with stories. There had been a sandstorm – small – and an attack by some scruffy Libyan bandits. Antef had called them weak beer compared with the Kushites.

"He says he does not know how the story began that the Waters of Shedet are past restoring! There's a gorge, a passage, that has become choked with sand. That's the worst part. Once we clear it the lake will be restored after a few high inundations, he says. Then, with new irrigation channels, all the fields and gardens will be rich as before."

"One wonders," Dahi said with purring amusement, "if there is anything Antef cannot do."

Senusert kissed her. There was passion in the way his hands closed on her waist, even after years and children.

"There was a time when he did not give a banquet or entertain in a way to remember," he observed, "and now even that has changed. A Kushite woman was a strange choice for his major-domo, and all of us looked askance, but now she's the fashion."

"Every hostess in the city would like to win her from Antef for her own household." Dahi shook her shapely head. "I should use my royal power to steal her myself, save that our worthy Antef needs her more. But he should not need her. A wife would be better for him. Will you command him to marry again, Senusert?"

Senusert's lean, energetic face clouded. "Truth. He's been alone too long. I've spoken to him about it and urged just what you recommend, my Isis. But because he is as my brother, I will not command him."

"Tamaket is not enough," she repeated. "Certainly I would never miss a meal she prepared, so long as my tasters were present, but I trust no Kushite. Thieves at the least!"

"Few servants don't thieve," Senusert pointed out, and kissed her again. "Let them, provided they are worth it and keep it within measure."

Antef often came home to his mansion, even with the king's new project begun. The Waters of Shedet lay close to the capital, Ithej-Tawy, as distances in Egypt went. Senusert and Dahi honoured him with frequent visits. Tamaket found herself preparing many a banquet for the royal entourage.

Her temper grew short and her demands perfectionistic at such times. She remembered Semna and the death of Rakheb. She knew that Senusert and Dahi did, also. *If poison appears at one of these meals*, she thought, *I would not give a mildewed wheat grain for my life*.

Once, standing before the Royal Wife to receive a compliment, she had a very bad moment. Dahi was saying amiably that she never feasted better at the palace, and biting with gusto into a steaming quail flavoured with delicate traces of aniseed. Then her expression changed. Clenching her teeth, she bent forwards. The cone of perfumed ointment on her head wobbled. Tamaket, nearest to her, said deferentially, "Your pardon, O Wife of the Living Horus," and steadied her, looking intently into her face. "Are you ill?"

"Of course I am ill," Dahi said harshly. "Ah! I know what this is. I have had these inner pains since I last gave birth . . . they come and go. Forgive me, my lord, I would retire. Send my physician to me, woman."

"At once, Great One."

A common woman's ailment, and her physician confirmed it. The gods be thanked for that! Tamaket sweated to think what might have happened if Dahi's pains had been caused by suspect food. By morning she seemed much improved. Tamaket witnessed two more such attacks over the months that followed, and heard of others, since her master was now something of a courtier – by force of circumstances, not by nature. It always tickled her humour when he appeared at court. Seeing him in ornate formal garments, among soft priests, sleek placemen and over-precise scribes like Montumes, was downright funny.

His father and brothers came downstream to visit him. They seemed willing to treat him as a kinsman again, though the father especially had no warmth. Still, after the fearful blasphemy of murder attempts against the godking had struck so close to his house, he must reckon it wisest to seem more friendly. Tamaket did not suppose the king – or Antef, either – was at all deceived.

Time flowed by as surely as the Nile. The months became a year, then three. After that one meagre inundation, the river rose high two years in a row, and with the obstructed gorge successfully cleared, the Waters of Shedet rose also. So did Antef's reputation.

Tamaket enjoyed success herself. As the Royal Wife remarked, she had become a fashion, almost a craze, in Ithej-Tawy. Her circle of powerful well-wishers increased, and with them the number of spies she now possessed in many places, high and low.

She took to saying, "Oh, my master, may I assist at the feast

Lady Nefer is giving? Her steward has been dropping hints for a week." Then it would be, "The Temple of Hathor wishes me to help organize the moon ceremony, noble one, and the king will attend. May I do so?"

Antef was patient with his servants, even indulgent, but he saw Tamaket had gone to excess.

"You do not serve the whole of Lower Egypt, but me," he warned her. "One last time. Then it must cease."

In the event, *one last time* proved more appropriate words than either of them had imagined.

VII

Those who are in the sky are made wolves, and those who are among the sovereign princes are become hyenas. Behold, I gather together the charm from every place where it is, and from every man with whom it is, swifter than hunting dogs and quicker than light.

– *Papyrus of Ani*

Antef, as the King's Friend, sat on a gold-inlaid chair beside Senusert. Lesser guests used mats and cushions among a forest of dark-red pillars. They made a great throng. Priests, scribes and officials mingled with a group of dignitaries from Crete with their curled dark hair and narrow-waisted kilts, bright with colour in contrast to the milky linen of Egypt. There were no envoys from Kush.

"It's time," Senusert said quietly to Antef. "When the river stops rising, and before it recedes, the fleet will depart."

"Good," Antef replied. "I've heard about the Kushite attacks against Semna. Two major ones in a season."

"They will regret it. The dam you built has opened a door. Now we are going through it. To the ends of the land of Yam."

"Don't speak of it, my lord," Dahi said. "I'll be sorry to see you and our brother, the Lord Antef, go! Conquer these wretches, since you must, and then come home quickly."

Antef did not hear what Senusert replied. Something affectionate, no doubt, but he found himself thinking of what was to come, and thinking of it darkly. He had been with Senusert on one expedition through Nubia. He began drinking deeply in an effort to be merry. This attracted no undue notice; it was a rare banquet at which wine passed around slowly. Dahi did not spare her cups, either, but then she had a good head for liquor.

She raised yet another to her lips. The cone of scented ointment atop her wig had melted to a stub by now, running down over her cheeks and shoulder so that her flesh glistened. She smoothed the remnant back, then drank half the cup's contents in one gleeful draught.

"Fortune attend your campaign, and all that you do, beloved," she said, passing it to Senusert.

The king took it.

His poison-taster, Ipi, plucked the goblet from Senusert's grasp as he had been poised and waiting to do.

"No, mighty Khakaure; this holds poison."

Senusert sat motionless in a haze of perfume and wine and light, calling on his savoir-faire. On campaign or on a throne, one acquired it. His face never changed, and his gaze travelled around to see who else was aware. Nobody, it appeared, except Antef. Then Montumes sidled in beside the taster, busy and knowing.

"He tells the truth, O king."

Montumes dipped a finger in the royal cup and withdrew it with something adhering. Staring, the king saw what seemed to be a fragment of eggshell. He found no especial significance in that.

Montumes could not wait to enlighten him. "A dove's egg, mighty king, blown, filled with death and resealed, ready to crush into your festive wine."

Dahi snatched the cup in anger. "Oh such nonsense! Are you wit-stricken, Montumes? I have just drunk, and I am well. Look!"

In one impatient gesture she drained the rest and tossed the cup aside. People were staring, though it had not been the case before. The attention Senusert had wished to avoid was thoroughly upon them now.

"How did you ever conceive this ridiculous idea?"

Montumes picked up the fallen cup. "Ah. Ah. Great Ones, perhaps I was wrong."

"*Wrong*?" Senusert snapped. "You must explain some way further than that."

"Yes, O Living Horus."

Antef, watching, knew by now that something was deeply amiss, as he saw Dahi's eyes change and Montumes's smirk. He never had cared for the man. Nor did Senusert, in that moment. The contretemps was growing worse.

It might be carried off with discretion yet. Rising with a yawn, the king declared that he and Dahi were retiring, with the ease of one whose word was law, and wished the company goodnight. He returned with Dahi to their private rooms. Montumes shortly followed, needing no command. *You must explain some way further than that*, Senusert had said.

He welcomed the Keeper of State Records with a curt nod, and ordered his guardsmen at the door to admit nobody else.

"There are witnesses I may have to call, O king," Montumes ventured. "That young poison-taster – "

"I will wish to see him in time. Not yet."

Dahi said wearily, "All this talk of poison is folly. I am alive, my great lord, and not even in discomfort, though I drank the cup to the lees before you. Montumes' reasons for doing this I do not know, but I remember he was with us at Semna when that wine-jar proved to be deadly."

Senusert made no reply. Very clearly he was thinking. Frowning, he gazed at the Keeper of State Records, who continued to look at Dahi.

"There is something on your gown, just above the knee – Great One," he said with poorly concealed spite.

Dahi, royal and divine, did not look down like a disconcerted servant. She shrugged in disgust. Montumes caught the king's glance, and pointed to the Royal Wife's gown, whereupon Dahi did lower her gaze, and and bring down her hand in an impatient brushing motion.

Senusert caught her hand before it could touch the linen. What he removed from his wife's gown was a fragment of eggshell, adhering by some dark fluid it had contained, that was certainly neither white nor yolk.

"That isn't proof," Senusert said grimly. "If indeed a dove's egg charged with poison was crushed into our wine, a bit may easily have fallen on the Royal Wife's gown by no action of hers. You have accused her of the vilest crime one may conceive. You must prove it past doubt. You will wail in regret that ever you were born unless you do."

"Indeed and truly!" Dahi concurred. "Where did I hide it, for one thing, you dog? In my navel, perhaps?"

"In your perfume cone, Great One," Montumes answered, "and it is a horror to me to declare it. Your fingers could find the egg readily, once the cone melted to a remnant. Not I alone, but Ipi the taster, saw it happen."

"The taster? Your accomplice in this?" Dahi looked incredulous. To Senusert she said, "Am I to listen further?"

"I scarcely think so." Senusert turned on his Keeper of State Records in anger. "This babble of poison fails on the most important point! Dahi and I were to share the cup you assure me was deadly. First she drank half, and then the rest, while I drank none. She is unharmed. Nothing can surmount that."

Dahi nodded, lips shut hard and eyes fiery. Her look promised ruin to the record-keeper for this.

"Alas, O Living Horus!" Montumes answered. "What your wisdom perceives, the Royal Wife foresaw. She is inured to this poison. Since bearing her last child, she has taken slowly increasing doses, until she can swallow unharmed what would kill a company of soldiers. It is why she gave her child to a wet-nurse this time. She never did before."

"Liar!" Dahi spat.

"That is why she was ill with recurring belly pains," Montumes said inexorably. "Poison, not infection. Her physician was part of this impious scheme. I have had him watched day and night. He supplied the poison, measured the doses, and made lying pronouncements about the results being due to infection! If questioned, I think he will speak."

Dahi's face changed then, so terribly that the king felt a chill rising to his heart, as if he had indeed drunk the lethal cup and its working had begun. He knew Montumes. Scarcely the most daring of men, he would not accuse Dahi unless he was sure of her guilt – and sure, too, that he could substantiate it. The Nile would flow backwards first.

Senusert felt dazed. The air seemed to blacken and curdle around him. Taking it into his lungs became an effort. His face had changed also, and the change was not good to see.

As from a vast distance he heard Montumes say in a low tone, "I am grieved, O Living Horus, grieved – but there is more. I have scarcely begun."

VIII

> The sky pours water, the stars darken;
> The Bows rush about, the bones of the Earth-god
> tremble.
>
> – *Hymn to Wenis*

Senusert entered the empty, darkened banquet hall. Smells of food, wine, perfume and many warm bodies had grown stale in the past few hours. Mixed into the thick miasma were whiffs of vomit, also. Feasts began better than they ended.

The servants who cleaned up the mess had gone. One man had not. One man remained, a cup in his hands, drained to the lees, as he turned and turned it slowly in his fingers.

A brazier standing near cast a dim red glow on the seated man's arm and profile. He never moved as Senusert approached; even his hands ceased turning the empty cup.

The king wasted no time. "How could you do it?"

"What?" The big man shook his head. "I'm drunk."

"You may have emptied an entire wine-jar without help, but I know you are sober," Senusert told him. "I asked how you could do it! Montumes knew everything, Antef. And so do I, now. Explain to me – that's a command. When did you become a traitor?"

"Me?" After a moment Antef said disbelievingly, "*Montumes* says that? Of me? And you credit him? I'd say you must be joking, but this is not your kind of joke."

"It's no laughing matter, and I take oath to that on my father's tomb."

Antef said bluntly, "Then you're the one drunken. Eye of Ra! I'm the one who caught the traitors for you!"

"Dahi confirms him." After a pause, Senusert said in a voice like death, "I discovered tonight that there is nothing she does not know about treason. I credit *her*. You cannot shield her, or your father, Antef. And, by the Double Crown, if you prevaricate one heartbeat longer, I use this dagger."

Antef heard the raw grief in his king's voice, and the certainty. His own came back thick with pain.

"I discovered the traitors. They were guilty, not innocent. I delivered them to you. Senusert, I see you're not joking. *But what makes you believe this*?"

"You know well! You discovered that your own sire was one of them – of the leaders! You did not tell me that."

"No," Antef agreed, his voice flat. "I did not. I warned him that I'd denounce him at any hint of a further threat to you. I left full written testimony sealed and safe lest he should try to silence me first – for he loves me little and I do not doubt he'd be capable of it – and let him know it was written. You will find it with my will in the vaults of the Temple of Sobek. I couldn't hand over my father to disgrace and vile death, Senusert, no matter how black a traitor."

"And so you became one yourself," the king said bitterly. "Antef, you fool! Did you think you could outwit a man like your father, or hold him on a leash by such a simple threat? Dahi informs me – the bitch – that he was glad to have the other traitors caught, and be rid of them, they having proved so inept. I am sure he was. Madmen must have conceived the idea of training a man-eater in the hope that she would destroy me. The night of the lion hunt you were still true, were you not? When did you turn against me?"

Antef said wearily, "Does it matter?"

Senusert had been hoping that it might still turn out to be untrue.

"Not now. No matter when it began, I wonder how you could feast with me, hunt with me, take the honours I heaped on you, all the while intending my death. When did you learn that Dahi shared in the plot?"

He spoke Dahi's name like a man taking his death-wound.

"She was not. Until she became enamoured of me. Then – it happened one step at a time."

Senusert swore vilely. "When I called you a fool it was less than the truth! Dahi brought that poisoned wine to Semna three years ago and longer! She and your father – you don't know it *yet*? They began this treason together."

"No," Antef said harshly. "I became enamoured of Dahi, Senusert. When she loved me also – there was no way to possess her but to murder you. Thus I joined forces with my snake of a father and became a snake myself. My suggestion was that I should kill you in the confusion of battle when we campaigned in Nubia again."

"Your *suggestion*," the king said, sickened. "But Dahi wanted something more certain, didn't she? She has sharper fangs than your sire, knows less about honour – and until tonight I would have killed the man who uttered such things in my hearing. If I have to know it, by all the gods, so do you! Dahi desires power. With me as king, she did not rule. Married to you, with your father as Vizier, she could rule in all but name, for you can be managed, and would be content with building. *She* lured *you*, you dolt, and you do not know it! She loves you not. She loves no man."

He saw Antef's eyes blaze and the great muscles harden. Senusert's own grip tightened on his poniard's hilt. The blade was broad, hard and sharply pointed, and if Antef lunged at him, Senusert was more than ready to drive it through his heart.

"Sit still," he said in the king's voice.

"Not," Antef growled, "if you say that again."

Senusert could almost have pitied him, then, except that his own heart had turned to seared sand and boulders with death resident therein. He wanted to inflict pain so vile that his own pain would vanish. He wanted to drive Antef to attack him so that he could strike with the dagger.

He made his face a mask.

"She rejected your plan to kill me in the tumult of battle. Not certain enough. She was probably afraid that you might remember you had been my friend, and honest, and not be able to murder one who trusted you. It's no failing of hers. She handed me that cup with a loving smile. Does that not tell you all you need to know?"

He knew the message had not come to him yet, either. Soon, he told himself, it is going to strike me, and I shall realize what this means, wholly. My friend, my brother, the one who never failed me, has turned traitor . . . would have murdered me, and she I love, who sat a royal throne beside me, bore my children . . .

"What will you do?" Antef asked.

"Keep this secret," the king answered. "For now. I cannot decide at once, but to my son you are a hero, an example of courage and honour. He should not know the truth too young. With regard to his mother, perhaps he should never know it."

He considered, while Antef waited in silence.

"Keep your great name," Senusert said at last. "Come with me as planned on our expedition to the land of Yam. However, you are not to return alive. My Majesty commands it. Have you heard me?"

"Yes."

Bending forwards, his eyes black in the brazier-glow, Senusert pronounced doom. "Your body shall be lost. You shall have no tomb. Your name shall vanish, and so also shall I deal with your father."

"It is just," Antef said resignedly. "But Dahi is the Royal Wife. You cannot deal so with her."

"She is my children's mother, and that is a great misfortune. She shall bear me no others. Having her buried with me is a thought I cannot stomach, but some way can be found to arrange it otherwise." He added after a moment, "Plausibly."

Antef nodded heavily. "There seems no more to say."

"No."

They spoke so quietly that none watching – and there was always someone watching the king – could have heard the exchange. Tamaket, in the night shadows of the hall, did not catch a word for all her sharp hearing, but she saw both men's faces in the brazier-glow, and it told her enough.

The Keeper of State Records could have the credit and welcome, if he thought that credit would accrue, if he fancied the king would ever like the source of such hideous news. Tamaket knew better. She also knew every poison in three lands, and had recognized the symptoms of the one to which Dahi was inuring herself over a year, no matter what lies her physician told. Dahi had overlooked that. Knowing it, Tamaket had soon surmised that the Royal Wife would hand her husband the bane herself, and choose to do it at some feast where Tamaket was present to be blamed. It had only been necessary, then, to warn Montumes and Ipi, and let them expose the guilty.

"But how did you know?" Montumes had asked her, bewildered. "Guessing that Lord Antef's father was one of the plotters, that I can understand. What brought you to suspect the Great Royal Wife?"

"Oh. I wondered from the start, in Semna," Tamaket had answered. "Someone, it was plain, would find me a useful fool to blame for murder by poison, and that worried me. It has worried me ever since. It was reasonable for the Royal Wife to suspect me, and she does not care for Kushites, nor is she notably kind to subordinates – yet she spoke in favour of bringing me to Egypt. I had to wonder why."

Very softly, she departed.

As Senusert had promised, Antef's body vanished, he had no tomb, and his name perished, with no inscriptions to record it. Senusert entered the annals as a great king, and was worshipped as a god in Kush for long after, but his son succeeded him while still a stripling. There are those who say grief does not shorten life, that this is nonsense, but Senusert was a strong vital man whom his servants had thought would live long.

Also, those sculptors who carved him in granite later, though they could not have known its cause, showed him with haunted eyes and a look of bleak anguish to make the most frivolous halt and wonder.

THE EXECRATION

Noreen Doyle

This story is set during the reign of Amenemhat IV, the grandson of Senusert, from the previous story, and one of the last kings of the Twelfth Dynasty. He reigned from about 1808-1799 BC and, as the story opening tells us, the events happen in year seven of his reign, so we are clearly in the year BC 1801. By now the great power of the Twelfth Dynasty kings is in decline, and the governors are once again exerting their control. The character Senbi, who features in this story, is doubtless descended from the Senbi who lived nearly two hundred years earlier and was one of the powerful provincial nomarchs whose authority was curtailed by the kings of the new dynasty. The resentment of the nomarchs festered for many generations.

*Noreen Doyle is an Egyptologist specializing in nautical archaeology. Although she hails from Maine she is currently undertaking postgraduate work at the University of Liverpool. She has written several historical fantasies set in ancient Egypt since her first story, "The Chapter of Bringing a Boat into Heaven" (*Realms of Fantasy, 1995*).*

The "lector" priest was an important official amongst the priesthood who recited the incantations and words of the gods, keeping track of the rituals and religious ceremonies down through the generations. An execration is a ritual outburst of hatred expressed as a statement of loathing against specific enemies, as the following story makes abundantly clear.

*T*omorrow, this captain tells me, we will be in Thebes, at the Great Prison. The vizier of the south himself will want to see me.

The vizier! My lord, who sent me south to Djer-Setiu, on the order of the king. He will want to see me, but will he believe what I now have to say? I am bound and trussed like a liar and a rebel.

There is a letter that I did not send him, now in possession of others, as is everything else that was mine:

Year 7, first month of the third season, day 21. It is the lector-priest and keeper of secrets Emsaf who says: "By the order of His Person, the king, I, your humble servant, arrived at the island fortress of Djer-Setiu. The commandant, Senbi, has gone away for a time because Nubians are making trouble in the east near the gold mine, but before his departure he assigned everything necessary that you, my lord, did not dispatch with me. I, your humble servant, write that you may be informed that the execration was performed perfectly."

"Did I lie?" I ask this captain.

Nakht – he is the captain – seems reluctant to speak, and returns to yelling at his rowers.

He's afraid, you see, because I killed a man in full view of everybody. He does not yet know what that means for his children, if he has them, or for his wife, or for his mother and father or for the king. Or for himself. Or for the Rightful Order of the world. Neither, in fact, do I.

Perhaps that is the result of my abomination. Perhaps this is why Senbi stood by the riverbank until Nakht's boat was out of sight. Perhaps this is why I killed this man.

But perhaps not, and it happened like this:

In the hour past noon, Kush came, and Libya, and Asia. In the shape of one man, a Nubian, a wretch, all the hostile foreign lands approached the burial place, all wickedness bundled into one flesh and blood and bone, and Egypt watched. Spearmen and scribes and overseers arrayed themselves on this western shore of the river. They knelt aboard boats moored at the bank. Nubian villagers laid down their chores and neglected their herds to stand in the shade of date-palms and rock, curious and frightened by our display of Egypt's might. On a hilly island in the midst of the river, soldiers and Medjays, the strong men of Egypt, stood atop the massive, sunlit heights of the fortress that divided the island along its length. Everyone's eyes fixed upon the wretch as soldiers led him up from the river, to this sandy burial place.

A low chant rose from among the Egyptians and Medjays, the name of this fortress: "*Djer-Setiu, Djer-Setiu:* Destroying-the-Nubians, Destroying-the-Nubians."

The king had ordered that a lector-priest be sent with mutilated limestone figures from Thebes: "Make a very great execration at Djer-Setiu. Melt the wax figurines, break the red pots, put the enemy upside-down in the burial place." And he had sent to the vizier of the south, my lord, the names of Egypt's enemies, along with the names of their children and their servants and all their people. As the king smote them on the battlefield, so would they be stricken here in the burial place.

This Nubian, stripped naked, his head covered only with new-grown bristle, a battle scar on his chest, came to *me*.

I washed my hands in a white calcite bowl, shaking the water from my fingers to hide their trembling.

Into one pit I cast red pots that I broke, and mud figurines of men and cattle and papyrus rafts, and into a second pit I toppled the limestone figures inscribed with the names of those who would harm Egypt and do injury to Rightful Order. Thus did I, Emsaf, lector-priest and keeper of secrets, begin the execration, a spell known since the beginning of the world.

Two soldiers who had fasted and shaved and slept alone for seven days set the wretch – designated from the labour prison by Commandant Senbi – upon the ground. His arms were tied behind his back at the elbows and wrists, and now they bound his legs so that he knelt.

I approached the wretch. He embodied chaos, wickedness, all that would destroy Rightful Order. It was the likes of him who would strip beads from the wrists of high-born ladies and drape them over slave women, give coffins to those who could not afford a tomb, put oars into the hands of nobles, transgress against the god, overthrow the king.

Now, I have in the past wrung the necks of many ducks and even smashed turtles against the wall, but never before had I done this to a Nubian.

He looked at me – turning his head about to see behind him – and, with his mouth open, said nothing, for his tongue had been cut out. He looked at me and for a moment, for just a moment, I thought that he might be not a wretch but a *person* after all.

I did as the king ordered, in full view of everybody. I drew fast across his neck a sharp copper knife, the knife by which Isis and Horus struck Set, the god of chaos. I did this again and again and he bled and he bled and he bled, like the river in flood, as if it would never stop.

And I wondered, as his bowels relaxed and added their contents to the flow, if I were to extend my hand, my other hand, might I control this efflux, slow it, stop it? What mattered, however, was only that I had started it, and I contented myself with this. Contented? I was numbed as if by wine – no, I was filled up – with something –

He was emptied, at last, from throat and anus. He died.

As if he were a small and peculiar ox, I cut away his head and the soldiers cast his body aside.

In due course I placed his skull upside-down in a bowl and I buried it in the last pit, jawless, surrounded by wax figurines that I burned. I cast sand into the pits, which were then filled up with more sand. The spoken word, the written word, every act of the rite, everything was perfect.

"Djer-Setiu!" the men cried, more loudly now, while I washed my bloodied hand and the knife in the white bowl, then lit a brazier of incense. As the purified soldiers swept away our footprints and his fluids, and buried the corpse in so shallow a grave that even a Medjay would not place his dead in it, I retired to the island, where a room of the commandant's house had been reserved for my use.

It is no mean hovel, this house within the fortress walls, and

I was at home there as I might be in Thebes. The ceilings are high and plastered white, held aloft in the hall by columns hewn from wood. The commandant's own wife, a Nubian woman, oversaw the servants who provided me with dates and other good food and saw that I was undisturbed in the small and bright room beside Senbi's own bedchamber.

There I composed my report to tell the vizier that it had been a good execration. I told him of everything but my shaking limbs and my swollen heart.

The enemies of Egypt would tremble and be afraid, I wrote, for they had been overthrown and cast out in the name of the king. Rightful Order would be maintained. With the fate delivered to that one wretch, the enemy, the rebel, whoever, wherever, he was, was overthrown and upturned.

But soon I was to learn that so too, perhaps, was the entire world.

That was five days later when Senbi, commandant of Djer-Setiu, returned from his campaign, triumphant. He had defended the gold mine from rebel villagers and roaming tribes, and ferried their cattle and women and children to the island. The Nubian villagers who lived along both sides of the river put down their water jugs and fishing nets as he disembarked on the island with the wealth of those who, perhaps, had lately been their neighbours. They stared and said nothing, but we, Egyptians and Medjays, called out Senbi's praises.

Senbi made a great procession into the fort from the east bank of the island, with fanbearers and spearmen and crack Medjay archers: up from the river, past the settling basins where gold was collected from ore and the labour prison where the miners were kept, through the cool shadows of the long gateway entrance. There is, within Djer-Setiu, an open court bordered by the fortress walls and Senbi's house and, along the southern side, unyielding knolls of stone that the masons had left in place. Against this little backdrop of desert trapped within the fortress, overseers arranged the cattle and dogs and paraded them before Senbi, who sat beneath ostrich-feather fans with a fly-whisk held to his breast. The captives crawled before him on their bellies. Scribes accounted everything before him.

Senbi then retired to his pillared hall, where he called an audience. He sat on a lion's-foot chair on a raised dais, beneath the attendance of two servants who with slow beats of their fans moved the hot, incensed air – it was exceptional perfume, I marvelled: *antyu* from Punt, which Nubian traders sometimes brought up from the south, much prized in the temples and palace. Senbi was honoured indeed, to have such stuff. Samentju, chief scribe of Djer-Setiu, sat on the floor before him. And he summoned, first, Emsaf the lector-priest and keeper of secrets.

He asked of the execration, and I told him. Those assembled murmured in concurrence as I said that it had gone exceedingly well. When I was finished Senbi asked: "Did you take the tongueless one?"

"I did, my lord, as your instructions directed. Each man in the labour prison stuck out his tongue, and he who did not because he could not, him I took. Samentju may vouch for that."

Samentju's pen slipped across the papyrus. He licked away the unwanted ink and the tip of his tongue turned black. He murmured, "It was so, my lord, it was so."

"It is an excellent thing, then," Senbi pronounced, brushing flies away from his face with his whisk. "A troublemaker among troublemakers that one was, a rebel among rebels."

"He is now turned upside-down in the burial place, my lord. Rebels and foreigners are overthrown with him, in the name of the king."

"In the name of the king," Senbi replied, "many things are done. We stand in his stead here, we commandants at the very borders of Egypt. We are his eyes and his ears and his strong arms. Foreigners are cast down in defeat, gold is dug up from the earth, men fight and bleed and die in his name, for Rightful Order, while the king lies far away downstream."

"Even as ablutions are performed, sacrifices are made, prayers are spoken by priests standing in the king's stead in every temple," I added, "while he is absent."

"*Effectiveness*. That is the function of a priest, no less than the function of a commandant! You know this as well as I do, lector-priest Emsaf. I'm pleased. When you return to Thebes the Nubian herds will go with you, and gold for the vizier. I assume, of course, that you will return to Thebes?"

"I will," I replied.

"A shame." Senbi leaned forward, inviting me onto his dais. "Here we have no priest, no temple, no one who knows –"

Before Senbi could finish, before I could mount the dais, soldiers entered the hall, in the company of several sailors still drenched from their labours. Senbi stood, unhappy at this intrusion.

"For the commandant!" the chief of the sailors called. "Nakht, captain of the ship *Montu-Rejoices-in-Thebes*, seeks an audience."

And Senbi bade forwards the captain, who came with his sailors, who dragged forwards a lean, dark man wearing a leather kilt and his hair cropped short in the Nubian fashion.

"On our way from Iqen we found this man along the river, my lord, nearly drowned," Nakht said. "So we brought him aboard and in doing so found that he had gold upon him, and *beqa*-weights." Nakht presented Senbi with two tiny but weighted sacks and a handful of little square stones inscribed with the diadem-sign. These had only one purpose, to measure gold ingots and dust. There was, though I did not see it, gold dust in the pouches. "We did not know what he might be doing with such things. He cannot trade in this region; he is a Nubian and has no commission. Unless –" Nakht looked at the Medjay archers among Senbi's contingent and seemed unconvinced of what he was about to say. For generations the Nubian-born forefathers of these Medjays had served Egypt's kings loyally. "Unless, my lord, he is one of your soldiers?"

"No, he is not one of my soldiers."

Through all of Nakht's speech, Senbi had taken his eyes from the Nubian only once. When Nakht said *beqa*-weights, I remember very clearly that his eyes went from the Nubian to me for the briefest of moments.

"Where did you find this man?"

Nakht described the spot, a lonely stretch of rocky shore at the bend in the river between Djer-Setiu and the fortress of Iqen.

"You did not moor in the west?" Senbi said. Now he looked at Nakht.

"In the west! No, no," Nakht replied, thinking Senbi made some jest, because *to moor* and *to go to the west* both mean *to die*. "Wet as a fish he was, but quite alive. On the east bank, as it happens."

"Tell me your name." Senbi directed this to the Nubian, who made no reply. Then he said this again, or so I suppose, in the Nubian jabber. Still the man did not answer. "Open your mouth."

The Nubian opened his mouth and Senbi leaned close, and one of the soldiers grabbed the Nubian's jaw and made sure it was open very wide, so very wide that even from where I was standing I could see the mutilation in the moist darkness of this man's mouth.

"Emsaf," Senbi said, his eyes transfixed upon the mouth of the Nubian, that gullet which had no tongue, "tell me again who it is that lies upside-down in the burial place."

"It was the tongueless one," I said. "The tongueless one chosen from among the men in the labour prison."

"That cannot be, for I myself cut the tongue out of that Nubian, and by god, this is he. Emsaf, whom did you kill?"

A heavy stillness fell over Djer-Setiu in that moment. Everyone, not least myself, seemed afraid to move from our places. The world spun like a potter's wheel.

What did this mean? O the terribleness of it for him who had been sacrificed, it was a dreadful fate he had met here and worse in the netherworld. His *ba*-soul, his *ka*-soul, were utterly destroyed – he was *defeated* forever. But for the rest of the earth and for those who still lived upon it, what did it mean? Such an act might be a violation of Rightful Order, an utter abomination. And I had committed it.

Senbi stilled the whirling of the earth by putting both feet firmly upon it, standing, and ordering some men to this and other men to that. Everyone did precisely what he said, grateful to be relieved of the burden of decision. He posted extra archers on the walls and sent out patrols to the four cardinal points. Nakht and the sailors he ordered to the river, to see that none, Nubian or otherwise, passed this way by boat or raft. As for me, he ordered that I stand beside him, leaving me fearful of his intention.

Every man, Egyptian and Nubian alike, in the labour prison was tied with rope and brought before Senbi and me, and Samentju tallied them. Every one stuck out his long, pink tongue between bright white teeth or black rotted gums, every single one of them. The one who had been sacrificed, he could not have done so. *He* had no tongue. It was not there before I slit his throat, nor after. I told Senbi this. He said nothing.

After Senbi had inspected the prisoners, most of whom were runaway labourers now assigned to the gold mine, he himself went to the emptied prison to see that there were no more that the guards had forgotten – or perhaps hidden. Senbi was always concerned about rebels, and I understood, not only because this was the storehouse of grain and supplies for every other fort in Nubia but because there was gold in this land over which the king had given Senbi charge.

"You must know them, rebels," he said, looking about the largest vaulted cell in the prison. It was nearly as large as Senbi's hall, stinking of urine and faeces and buzzing with countless flies.

"And you must write their names upon red pots, cast them down and break them," I said, as we inspected other rooms which stank no less.

"But first you must know them."

He had Samentju and the other scribes make an accounting of all three hundred soldiers within the fortress and every man in the Nubian villages on both shores of the river. Together, Samentju and I checked and rechecked this with an earlier census and with the memories of the scribes. All were accounted for in the prison, barracks, and villages, none were missing.

Seven times Samentju and I examined these figures over

twice as many days. "Have we accounted for Captain Nakht's men?" asked Samentju with some hope in his voice. But we had. Finally, his voice rising from despair to the kind of hope to which only desperate men can aspire, Samentju said, "Does it matter who he was, Emsaf? How many people in the world are wretches? He was bound to have been one of them, and the fewer, the better. The execration will be no different for it."

"That man, whoever he was, did not cut out his own tongue and place himself among your prisoners, Samentju. This means it mattered to someone," I replied. "Which perhaps means that he was not a wretch at all."

"*Was* not," Samentju said, unhappily.

Was not. Whatever he had been, he was nothing now, nothing at all. Who had he been, this one whose *ba*-soul, *ka*-soul, shadow, *effectiveness*, and name I had caused to suffer and to perish utterly. And I had done so under the authority of the king. The execration –

– execution – murder –

– what would become of it? The ritual, it was spoiled. What would come of its power? What abomination had I wrought upon the Rightful Order of this world?

These nights I did not sleep well. Thought of disturbing the pits to look upon the dried remains of his mutilated face haunted me. But I could not violate the burial place. The rite had been done in the name of the king and the god; there was too much Power there. Still, I wondered if the sun would rise in the east, if it would rise at all. I did convince myself that such a worry was foolishness over the course of the next three days, during which Samentju and I tallied and retallied every man, every cow and bull, all the small cattle, all the dogs, each Nubian, within Djer-Setiu and in the Nubian villages. We received reports from Senbi's messengers, who brought word from the fortresses of Iqen and Buhen to the north and the fortress Dair-Seti and the rest to the south. And every day the sun rose, in the east, as was its custom.

Now, I have seen a lector-priest drunk and heard him slur the holy words he was reading, and I have suspected a pure-priest of having slept with a woman or eaten fish when he ought not to have. The world did not end, Rightful Order persisted. But they, and others like them throughout Egypt, had otherwise performed their daily tasks in good order, and that is what matters: if I had slain one who was not an enemy, I had failed in my *unique* task, even if every word of the spell had been uttered perfectly. And the words were uttered perfectly, as anyone who heard them knows and will attest. What is done overpowers what is said: are spoken lies more powerful than silent truths? If a man claims to have given bread to the hungry, clothing to the naked, and a boat to the boatless when in fact he has not, these lies will not serve him in the netherworld.

I did not know if I had lied: I did not know if I had slain a wretch or a *person*.

So even as the sun rose each morning – as it will no doubt do so tomorrow, too, when we have reached the Great Prison – I worried over what chaos would result from my error.

My error! My abomination.

Each morning, as the sun rose, Senbi summoned Samentju and me to a private audience. "What did you find yesterday? Are infants laid on high ground? Does he who had no bread now have a granary?" Such would tell us that chaos had overtaken Rightful Order, and there was little sign of these things, either in Nubia or Egypt, for which I gave thanks. As days passed, however, this began to concern Senbi: I supposed he, a soldier, was waiting for the onslaught of an enemy he knows to be lurking somewhere in the hills, the wait more dreaded than the attack.

Each day, too, he would ask, "What will you do today?" We told him of our next census and accounting; everything that we had done yesterday we would do again today.

When we came to him on the fifteenth day of our labours and he asked, "What will you do today?" I said: "Today, my lord, we must have words with Captain Nakht's half-drowned Nubian."

"Words! Emsaf, I personally cut out his tongue and threw it into the sand."

"He has control of his ears and his hands, my lord."

Senbi's lips turned into a frown. "We can only hope that he likewise has control of his heart. Go then, you and Samentju, and afterwards tell me what you learn."

We went to him with pens – old ones, chewed down and of no use to a conscientious scribe – and ink and bits of stone and broken pots. He had been sequestered in an emptied room in the storehouse beside the labour prison. Samentju entered first; stripped naked, the Nubian watched him calmly until I followed. Then he began to struggle at his bonds, making a breathy noise like a dog. He shook his head, staring wild-eyed at Samentju, pleading with tears, stealing only the briefest of glances my way, as though sight of me were a burning ember thrust into his eyes.

"You've killed someone – someone that should have been *him*," Samentju explained to me. "No wonder he's afraid. Hai, there, Pa-Nehesy," he said to the Nubian, and that was all Samentju or anyone else ever called him: Pa-Nehesy, the Nubian. "That's done with. It's over. Unless the king demands another execration."

This settled him; I wonder how much he understood. Samentju, like Senbi, had learned a little Nubian jabber; a number of the Nubians who lived near Djer-Setiu had some command of Egyptian, and I thought this one might as well, if he recognized the value of the *beqa*-weights lately in his possession. I wondered where they had come from, too. Not from Djer-Setiu; we had accounted for all that had been apportioned to the fortress and indeed found a few weights, and even a little gold, that had never been entered into the accounts, a carelessness for which Samentju severely beat one of the other scribes.

Would we have to beat the truth out of Pa-Nehesy? I wondered. My fingers trembled at this prospect.

"Does he speak Egyptian?" I asked.

"Not any more," Samentju replied. "No doubt he still understands a bit of it."

"Why did Senbi cut out his tongue?"

"He was a rebel."

"So Senbi would want him dead –"

"Of course!"

"– but who would want him alive? What was his tribe?"

"He is from the village on the east bank, and he knows the hill-country and its gold better than any other," Samentju answered. To Pa-Nehesy he said, "The village?" and the Nubian agreed with a nod. "His tribe could not have got him out; they know better than to try. And besides, they have no boats of their own."

"Someone did get him out, boatless or otherwise. Who was it?" I demanded of Pa-Nehesy. "Who got you out?"

He looked at me as if he did not understand, so I repeated myself more slowly. He then looked at Samentju, his expression one of puzzlement.

"Should you translate for him?" I asked.

Samentju paused. "I suppose I should," he replied to me, and did so, haltingly in the Nubian jabber, which he evidently did not speak so well as Senbi. I laid out the bits of broken pottery and an old brush, and crushed and dampened ink for him on another potsherd.

Samentju unbound one of his wrists. Pa-Nehesy shook his arm violently and I jumped back, but he did no more than shake it for a time and then took the pen in hand.

"Can you write?" I asked Pa-Nehesy, who shook his head but proceeded to make a figure on the ostracon. If he could not write, he nonetheless had a little crude skill, and produced the outline of a man. This figure had a staff in one hand and his back was bent.

"An old man?"

"Look, he's lying. There are no old men here," said Samentju. "The frontier is no place for the aged."

"There are none truly old," I said, "but I have seen a few almost-old, with bent backs and with broad bellies. Who are they?"

Samentju thought for a moment, then spoke their names: Hetepi, Ameny –

Ameny. Yes, said Pa-Nehesy's gestures and the look upon his face, it was Ameny. One of the stone-slingers.

Samentju frowned. "Ameny?"

It was Ameny.

So we had one of the soldiers bind up Pa-Nehesy's free hand and went to question Ameny.

Ameny was not an old man, but his belly hung low and hid a little bit of his linen kilt and his hair was thinning. He was vigorous, with a dark, handsome face, and I did not think he would stand still in a fight. Senbi presided over his questioning, which took place in the open yard with men watching from their stations.

"You have put men into the labour prison." Senbi made no question of this statement, and Ameny did not deny it. "How many of the men that you have put into the labour prison are there still?"

"All of them," Ameny replied.

"There is not one who now lies in the burial place?"

Ameny looked at me, then at Samentju.

"I know of none of them who now lies in the burial place, but I do not know every action of these men, lord, nor if one of them might have died by the god's will since yesterday."

"You did not put a tongueless man into the labour prison?"

"I myself have never put a tongueless man into the labour prison nor removed one, nor has any man I have put into the labour prison lost his tongue. At least," he said, again looking at me, "not of which I am aware."

"Did you know the man whom the lector-priest put in the burial place?"

"I could not see from my position on the wall. From there–" he gestured with his head to the soldiers overlooking us from the heights "–all of the prisoners look much alike."

Something was not right here; his answers were too clever. Senbi must have thought so, too, because he gestured that I come forward and take up his part.

"Let the lector-priest try to get the truth out of you. Try to keep your secret from the keeper of secrets!"

"I have spoken with people about you," I told him. "Your wife is a Nubian from the village on the west bank."

"From east or west, so is my lord Senbi's. So would yours be, if you don't already have a wife waiting at home in Thebes or wherever you're from. Or perhaps even if you do."

My wife did wait for me – in the hills, and she would wait for me in our house of eternity until my last day. But I had no such patience to wait for Ameny. There were lies stuffed within these fat truths he told.

"But that is only," Ameny went on, "if you *live* long enough here in Djer-Setiu."

"Enough!" Senbi roared. "Ameny, I will not have you demeaning the lector-priest on whom I would rely, the keeper of secrets who knows the gods and their ways. I do not think you realize your position. Pa-Nehesy has painted you as the man who freed him, so we can assume only that you are likewise the man who put the other tongueless in his place. This will be reported to the vizier."

"Perhaps," I said, thinking to turn Ameny's cleverness against him, "we should ask your wife if she knows Pa-Nehesy."

"My wife?"

"His wife?" Samentju broke in. The expression on his face revealed that he himself had not thought of such a thing. A murmur rippled among the other soldiers.

"His wife," Senbi said flatly. The idea seemed new to him, too, but his surprise was more guarded. "So be it. Samentju, fetch her. Emsaf –" and he gestured again to Ameny.

So I took to questioning Ameny again, and asked him what his duties were, if they had not involved the tongueless. He guarded the wall and accompanied shipments of grain to Buhen and the other fortresses; he had nothing to do with the prisoners except to watch over their passage from the labour prison to the boat that took them to the eastern shore.

"And even then I was atop the wall. If the tongueless was ever among the other prisoners then," Ameny said, "I would not know. They were *all* rendered as tongueless by the overseers' lashes."

I said, "I believe, my lord, that this will require the twisting of hands and of feet."

Ameny blinked and rocked back on his heels but said nothing as the guards laid him down on the ground. At Senbi's order they turned the wooden shackles that bound his hands and his feet, slowly, that Ameny might have time to contemplate his position.

Senbi stood over him for a time as Ameny writhed there, staining the hard-packed dirt with his sweat. Senbi knelt beside his head and said, "You know what will happen if you do not tell the truth."

"I know, my lord, I do!"

They were turned again, a little bit. And again.

"I am innocent of this!" Ameny begged. "I swear, I swear," and after some hours both Senbi and I had had enough. Indeed, Ameny seemed likely enough innocent of this.

By this time Samentju had returned with Ameny's Nubian wife and babe. He gaped to see Ameny on the floor, looking more surprised than the woman. To Senbi Samentju said with hesitation, "I did not think it would come to this."

"Ameny has not spoken," Senbi said. "Except to protest his innocence."

"Perhaps," I said, "it will prompt Ameny's wife to speak."

Her name was Tyetyeb now, but it was not the name she had been born with; Ameny had given her a good Egyptian name. She was young and had given Ameny a son, their only child, not long before. The birth had been hard on her, I could see. Her eyes were sunken and shadowed, her hands shook, and she leaned on Samentju for support; I wondered indeed if he had carried her here. No, no, she could not possibly have freed Pa-Nehesy, not herself. She could scarcely manage the skinny, listless newborn in her arms.

"Do you have brothers here, either in the labour prison or the villages, male relatives of any sort?" I asked.

"I have no brothers anywhere." Her Egyptian was heavily accented but well-ordered. "My father is dead and I have neither uncles nor brothers."

"Do you know Pa-Nehesy the tongueless whom Captain Nakht brought?"

"I do not know. I have been ill in my house with my son and have not seen him."

I believed this but said, "You might yet know something."

"She knows nothing!" Ameny said. Senbi slapped him with his fly-whisk, drawing blood from Ameny's lips.

"You know what will happen if you do not tell the truth," Senbi said to Ameny in measured tones.

Ameny's tongue licked at the seeping blood. "Yes, I do, yes, my lord. My lord, my lord, my lord," he said, and I wondered if he was beseeching Senbi or a god. The note of his desperation and the condition of his woman touched me then and I ended my inquiry. Senbi ordered Ameny released with neither ceremony nor haste.

Samentju said to me, "Pa-Nehesy was mistaken."

"Evidently. I wonder whom he is protecting."

Ameny sat listlessly on the floor for several minutes, as if uncertain that his ankles would ever hold his weight again. He stood at last, stumbling to the wall beside his wife. They left together in the company of a soldier, neither of them well, neither able to help each other, walking like two old persons.

"Do you have doubts, my lord?" I whispered to Senbi.

"No," Senbi replied, looking at the soldiers on the walls, who, having seen everything that had befallen their fellow, now turned away. "I have doubts no longer."

A hot wind blew from the west that night. I lay in my camp-bed with one foot upon the floor, listening as the sand beat against the walls of Senbi's house. I ordered servants to place wet linen over the high windows, and these billowed like sails as the storm bellowed like bulls. I cursed the wind, and blessed the thick walls of Senbi's house.

"Such is Egypt."

I stumbled from the bed, falling to one knee, then both, by no design. Senbi stood in the lamplight, wrapped in a cloak laden with dust. He had been out tonight.

"Stand, Emsaf. I wish to sit."

"Would you care for wine?" I asked as I placed a stool

beside him. Anyone who had been out on such a night would be parched. And desperate – or mad. What was he about?

Senbi took the seat, then the cup that I offered, filled with wine I had brought from Thebes. "This is Egypt's predicament." He gestured around the room. "Orderly, neat, pleasant. Stout walls, good wine, good company."

"The commandant is gracious."

"While outside–" he pointed to the window where the linen was holding its own "–howls all the rest of the world. Hordes beat upon our threshold, upon our windows, upon our walls, upon our roofs. They would sweep the king from the Residence, Emsaf, and would wear Egypt away."

"Egypt is too great for that."

"Do you have a drinking reed?"

"Why, yes, my lord. Would you care for a jug?"

"I have no plans to get drunk tonight! No, I want to show you a trick. It is a good trick. A magician taught me this."

I felt my eyes grow wide beyond my will but, saying nothing, presented Senbi with a drinking reed.

He took, too, from an open chest beside my bed, the calcite bowl that had been given to my father by the king's father. I used it daily in my ablutions. It was old and fine, very white and very beautiful.

"This is like Egypt: fine, complete, beautiful. Pure."

He shook out his cloak, then swept the fallen sand into a mound. "This is the rest of the world, from Asia to Kush, from Punt to Libya. Fragmented, little, irritating." And he emptied the sand into the bowl.

"At the time, did you feel nothing amiss?" Senbi asked, placing one end of the straw against the bottom of the bowl. Idly he began to turn the straw between the palms of his hand.

"What's that?"

"When you killed him, cut off his head with the copper knife of the god."

I remembered what I had felt, and measured my words. "What should one feel? I have burned wax figurines, wrung the necks of ducks –"

"But not killed a man?"

"He was a wretch, my lord," I said with more hope than conviction. "He was not a *person*, not like you and I."

"Now, *I* know what it's like to kill a man. In the name of the king, like you. Many times over. I have brought a rain of arrows upon their fields, stampeded spearmen among their miserable huts. I have poisoned their wells. By the score, Emsaf, I have killed. So very many times have I stood in the same position that you did! We both stand in the place of the king. I understand what you felt."

"There was –"

"What?" He leaned forwards, pausing in the work of his hands, and it was as though a shadow had entered the room, a night upon the night. In that moment something I cannot understand bound us together.

I did not answer at once. I searched for a word, unsure if I should speak it when it came. Senbi resumed his work and did not repeat his question; the echo of it alone prompted my reply.

I knelt before him. "A power."

"Like a god?"

"Like a god – no –" Senbi looked disappointed, perhaps; I do not know. "It was like the king moved within me. His *effectiveness*."

"His *effectiveness*. Yes, that's what it's like, Emsaf. To move in the name of the king is to move *as* the king, in the moment."

"Should I have felt that?"

Senbi shrugged. "Who is to say what we should or should not feel? Did you like it?"

"Like it? I –"

"You did. I can see it in your face, it's so plain."

"*Should I?*"

"Like it?" Senbi laughed, now wagging the worn-down straw at me, and the darkness that had grown close around us seemed to disburse as if a new lamp had been lit. "Emsaf, such power is one of those fleeting things. For such power, such *effectiveness*, to remain in our hands, the whole world would have to be topsy-turvy!

"Do you know what this is?" He offered me the drinking reed, what remained of it, and I shook my head, answerless.

"This is the rebel."

Senbi stood, throwing his cloak across his back. "I thank you for your hospitality, Emsaf. Theban wine is almost as good as the beer my wife brews from the fruit of the date-palm trees of this place." He laughed quietly. "Good night, Emsaf. May you not have to go abroad tonight."

Alone now, I reached for my calcite bowl. The trick of Senbi's magician, I thought, was one of revealing my own gullibility. I would have to find a good stoneworker to polish away the damage. Senbi had scratched it with the reed, no doubt.

But no. As I picked it up a shower of dust fell from the bottom, pale yellow dust and a tiny white disk. There was a hole now, the size of a drinking straw, straight through the stone.

So I left no man unconsidered, nor woman: I wondered if some village wife hated her husband enough to make him drunk, cut out his tongue, and bribe another soldier to place him in the labour prison. A Nubian husband – or an Egyptian one? "After all," I said to Samentju as we sat on the floor of Senbi's pillared hall, "we do not know that the tongueless was a Nubian. His skin was dark." I grasped Samentju's wrist, which was lighter than the skin of my hand, which was not like that of the Nubian. "What does that prove?"

"It proves that he was from the south. Unless he was from the north." Samentju raised his bottom up to sit on the edge of Senbi's dais. "I think you should give up your search, Emsaf. What do *you* think?"

"I think that the world is made up of lies and ignorance. The liar will not speak the truth and the ignorant cannot," I said. "Perhaps that is the result." *Of my abomination.* "There is no more truth in the world. It cannot be twisted out of men like water from a rag. But I will not give up."

"Ignorance?" Samentju said, leaping up. "Ah!"

"What's this, now?" I said. It had been days since I had seen him look so eager.

He laid a hand on my shoulder. "I am going to speak to Pa-Nehesy again."

"Aren't there enough lies in the world, Samentju?"

"There are lies enough indeed," Samentju said, "but one who is ignorant can be taught. Meanwhile, do you wish to question someone? I will have him brought to the courtyard and send for the shackles if you do."

I named two men, scribes. "They might know about the gold weights with which he was found. So," I said, dropping my voice, "might you."

"Indeed, indeed, I have considered that," Samentju said. "I will not be angry with you if it comes to my turn, Emsaf. But I will ask that you turn only my ankles." Smiling, he lifted his left foot and let the papyrus sandal dangle from his toes. "I would happily spend my days seated at Senbi's feet, unable to walk, if it came to that, but a scribe's hands – you know."

And I knew, and hoped it would not come to that indeed.

I had finished with one of the scribes – minding his hands, too, in the event of his innocence, which seemed probable – when Senbi summoned me back into his hall.

Samentju was with him, holding a potsherd, which he presented to me. It held a drawing executed with a bad pen. There was a bold stroke of a crescent; a slanting line balanced at one tip of the crescent, and other little lines fell from it like rain. It was, recognizably, a boat with rudder and oarsmen.

"Pa-Nehesy – he did not know Ameny, any more than Ameny knew him. He merely agreed with a name he had heard before," Samentju said. "What we took for an old man with a staff was a man bent over an oar. It was, it is, Nakht."

"Nakht?" I exclaimed. "And his entire crew?"

"It would have to be," said Senbi, "would it not?"

"Yes, but –" I stopped, trying to puzzle this out. "An entire crew of rebels?"

Senbi shrugged. "Does the idea surprise you?"

"It is only difficult to imagine a gang of sailors at the borders of Egypt having any such need for an elaborate plan. Conspiracy on such a scale is a thing for the court."

"One might think so, but it need not be so."

"If they wanted someone dead, they could have drowned him themselves. And why would Nakht bring back the only evidence that would convict him – the only evidence, in fact, that there had been a crime at all?"

"Why indeed. I make no claim to understand it," Senbi said. "You, perhaps, possessor of secrets, a priest who has been to Thebes and Memphis and to the borders of Egypt, might have more insight."

"Perhaps," I said. "I will investigate Nakht and his crew. You will see that they do not leave Djer-Setiu, my lord?"

He promised this. I went out to tell the other scribe, who had been awaiting the shackles while standing in a puddle of his own urine, that he was dismissed.

I did not summon Nakht or any of his sailors. I had grown tired of listening to wagging tongues, tired of hearing the creak of bones and sinew. I went back to accounting, this time not taking stock of men, nor even gold and *beqa*-weights, but of days. All the dispatches Nakht had aboard his boat I gathered in a basket, and I confiscated, too, his logbook. I spent the evening and next morning reading everything.

When Senbi saw me that next day, Samentju sat with a fresh, white papyrus stretched across his lap and a new pen in his hand.

Senbi said, "Let's take care of this quickly, then. A report of your findings will be delivered straightaway to the vizier, Emsaf."

"A report on an innocent man?"

"Innocent?" Senbi said. "What do you mean?"

"Nakht cannot have freed Pa-Nehesy."

"Ah, then, one of –"

"Nor any of his crew."

Senbi stood. "How is it that you will prove this?"

"The dispatches, my lord. Nakht was moored at Iqen before you left on campaign and did not leave until after the execration. Neither he nor his crew could have been here at Djer-Setiu to free Pa-Nehesy and put the other tongueless one in his place."

Senbi sunk back into his chair, staring blindly at the floor. The situation was wearing on him at last, I thought. This was not the sort of battle he was accustomed to fighting, and he was accustomed to losing no battle at all.

"My lord," I said, "I will find the rebel responsible for this."

His head jerked up, and he stared at me, searching my face, perhaps for lies. But I did not lie. My face, I am sure, made this evident. "Do what you must, Emsaf, and I will do what I must."

In a small ferry-boat I paddled myself to the western shore at dawn the next day, having first performed my ablution – in the river, for my bowl no longer held water – and prayed to god for the strength and the right to do what I was about to do. Perhaps I ought to have gone at dusk, when my destination might have been less obvious in the dying light, but I wanted the great god Re as my witness. Venturing to a burial place is not a thing an honest man does at night, and I was, and remain, an honest man.

That someone had wanted the tongueless dead was one of the very few other things of which I was certain. Did someone want his body, too, some piece of it other than his tongue? Magic could be worked with such things, as Nubian magicians are well aware.

Sherds of broken pots – red – poked through the sand where I had thrown them. Figures of limestone, melted figurines of wax. Teeth intact, and the base of a skull. In a grave shallower than a pan, a length of rope, ribs and drying flesh. The Power of the ritual still hung about the place; I could feel it in my limbs and in my heart, this magic that I myself had worked in the name of the king. Everything but the smallest pieces, susceptible to the wind, lay where it had been thrown.

The pits had not been violated, nothing had been stolen.

I puzzled this, that no Nubian magician had yet stolen his bones, and as I did my eyes were drawn to the scar on the torso. It had opened now, pressed by a few stones, and from it protruded something long and dark, neither bone nor flesh.

My hand reached out to touch it, and my fingers closed about a thin shaft and did not release as my arm pulled back from the corpse.

It was the stone tip of an arrow affixed to an arrow shaft made of reed, long ago buried beneath his flesh, likely an accustomed discomfort. An Egyptian arrow.

Or, an unbidden voice seemed to whisper into my ear, a Nubian arrow?

I threw myself upon my stomach and crawled to the execration pit in which lay his skull. Why had I thought such a thing? In what chest would a Nubian arrow be but an Egyptian one? How could one tell arrows apart? They were the same.

And the wretch whose throat I had slit was a – what was he? Nubian? Egyptian? A wretch? A *person*? Who was he? He had been stripped of everything but his body and his heart and this arrow when I killed him. Stripped of his clothes, of his insignia, of his hair, of his tongue, of his name. Of everything that might have told one sort of man from another.

"O but what was your name?" I whispered across the broken teeth that protruded from the sand.

This was the very body someone had desired, and here was the very place they had desired it to be. Whoever had cut out his tongue might have as easily – no, more easily – killed him outright. Murder was not what they had wished: it was the god's magic, the king's *effectiveness*, they wished to harness. Through my abomination they sought to turn the world topsy-turvy and lay Egypt open to chaos, to overthrow the king. What had Senbi said? For such power to remain in our hands . . .

At that very moment I knew why no one man would speak against the guilty. I knew what would have happened if Ameny, if anyone, had spoken the truth. Senbi had reminded them. They knew. They all knew. As, now, did I.

It was a lie. Everything that they had said, everything that they had done. Help was hindrance. Truth was falsehood.

Chaos had overtaken Rightful Order.

In the name of the king, with my bare hands I tried to

remove the skull from the burial place, to restore Rightful Order, to undo my abomination.

In the name of the king, *this* is what I was doing when they found me. No matter what Ameny says, my story is the truth. In the name of the king.

"He sought to undo the king's execration," is what Ameny said to Senbi. "We found him at the pits, which were much disturbed."

My arms were bound, my feet were bound. I was on my knees before Senbi, naked, Ameny's hand upon my neck, so that all I could see was the chamber floor and my legs and my manhood, and all I could think of was that soon it would be sand beneath my legs, and that I would turn my head to see my copper knife – my? – the god's –

"Only *his* footprints lay about the place, my lord. He had no accomplice."

"You are certain?" Senbi said heavily. I heard the swish of his fly-whisk.

"I am, my lord, as certain as the morning light that comes over the eastern hills like gold."

Senbi grabbed my jaw. Would he tear it off? And my tongue?

"I had thought," he said in a close whisper, holding my jaw tight, speaking across my teeth, "that you might be trustworthy, Emsaf. You understand what you and I truly are, *effectiveness*. You also understand the Rightful Order of the world, with the king in his place – and you and I in ours. But you also understand that it could be otherwise. And it could have been otherwise, Emsaf. You know that. You felt that. You *did* that."

He poked his finger into my mouth, and his fingernails felt like little stone blades along my tongue. My tongue – by which I spoke the words of the gods, as important to a lector-priest as his hands – "Emsaf, you might have stood upon my dais. What king would not welcome beside him a priest who knows the gods and their secrets? And though you are indeed a fine keeper of secrets, for this one you dug too deep, too deep, and then when you found it –"

He ripped his fingers free of my mouth and the taste of salt gushed along my tongue. There was a bit of blood beneath his nails, but that was all; otherwise his hand was clean and my tongue remained in my mouth.

"Samentju will prepare documentation and accompany him downstream," Senbi said to Ameny. "Let the vizier of the south deal with this rebel."

And so I departed Djer-Setiu, trussed to the cabin of Nakht's boat, facing the stern. Samentju lay comfortably on my camp-bed within the vaulted cabin, drinking my Theban wine and writing *his* letter to the vizier. Nakht's crew rowed in silence but for the creak of the looms in their grommets and the lap of their blades across the water.

When I raised my head I saw that everyone in Djer-Setiu had come down to the river to watch my departure, Senbi himself among them.

And they remained there for as long as I could see them, motionless along the stony shore of the island like a stand of so many reeds.

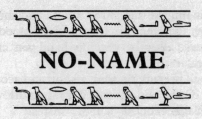

NO-NAME

R. H. Stewart

350 years flash past and we are now in the time of the New Kingdom and at the start of the reign of the eighteenth dynasty king, Tuthmosis (or Thutmose) III. After Amenemhat IV, Egypt entered a second period of decline but recovered under the powerful eighteenth dynasty kings who established the New Kingdom in around 1550 BC. Tuthmosis III reigned from 1479-25 BC initially jointly with his step-mother (and aunt) Hatshepsut. This period, running for the next four hundred years, is the true Golden Age of Egypt. The most famous of Egyptian pharaohs ruled at this time, including Akhenaten, Tutankhamun and Rameses II, all of whom feature over the next few stories.

M en-amun, aged twenty, in his second year as a lector priest, was returning to duty in the great Temple complexes of Amun-Ra.

Slim and personable in pristine white linen, he was shaven-headed; purified by triple washing; waxed and tweaked clean of every last body hair which could be located. He possessed distinct ambitions to set beside his wits and his elegant scribal skills, though possibly a critical superior might have thought – when pushed – that Men-amun's intelligence was likely to outrun his actual courage.

He was not late, but he felt it unseemly to appear laggard. Thus he moved quickly, head down, among the afternoon crowds circulating the outer, public Temple courts. He walked aloof along the shadowed side, avoiding contact with any who might attempt to touch him for the offering of prayers, written Letters to the Dead, or petitions to Higher Authority. And once he had thankfully left the heat and general clamour behind, he took a short-cut which otherwise he might never have considered. Turning aside from the vast columned halls ahead, he sought instead a long, narrow corridor of polished stone unpierced by door or window and therefore dark, except for the dust-hazed indirect blear of day at either distant end.

Traversing this passage was like journeying through a tomb shaft towards Judgment, he thought – toying lightly with the idea of apprehension. All external sound was lost. It smelled of nothing here but the cold, unyielding nature of stone. His awareness reduced itself to the enhancement of his own breathing and the slurred punctuation of his rush sandals on the ground.

The shock he sustained two thirds of the way along was absolute – when the floor in front of him quite simply erupted.

A flagstone lifted before his disbelieving gaze, tilted and crashed over backwards.

From the square black pit thus revealed arose the head and shoulders of a man. The face was frantic – slashed and weeping blood – and he was shouting.

Men-amun skittered to a standstill, transfixed.

"Seek help!" this lacerated visage yelled up at him. "Now! Run! Fetch the First Prophet in person – anyone – but by all that's good: go! Tell them it's real trouble! Say I've got him jammed in, but the frenzy's terrible and he's killed again!"

Men-amun croaked back, sheer fright having gone with his voice.

"Are you daft or what?" the man bellowed. "Hear me, muttonhead! Run!" He ducked down, vanishing as quickly as he'd come.

Men-amun shut his useless, gaping mouth.

He had to retreat, take a run and jump the awful gap. He stubbed his toes and rocked the displaced flag. He scrambled upright, sprinting for the duty priests' living quarters.

He had no authority whatsoever to try approaching Hapu-seneb, Highest of all High Priests – those of Amun-Ra – nor did he have much hope of finding where this exalted personage might be since, outside of religion, the same was also Vizier to Their co-Majesties and as such, not always within the sacred precincts. Yet something dreadful had gone wrong. Men-amun pelted on, praying disjointedly he might at least reach someone to whom he could rid himself of the problem.

He emerged, panting, into the inner court surrounded by the cells and eating house of the junior priesthood. And surely Amun-Ra had heard him, for seated on a stone bench, glancing through a papyrus roll, was the Third Prophet: the Lord Menkheper-re-sobek.

Men-amun jolted to a halt, making hasty obeisance.

Lord Sobek (he had contracted his name long ago in deference to his royal half-nephew, also Menkheper-re, who was now called King as Tuthmosis III) looked up surprised, halfway to reproof at such lack of dignity. Then he saw sweat, and scented fear, and changed his mind. He frowned, listening to Men-amun's plunging story, snapped his fingers for his steward and sent him instantly to Lord Hapu-seneb bearing a signet ring and a terse message of urgency. He stood up, unfolding his tall, thin figure in one fluent movement.

"Come," he said. "You and I shall see for ourselves."

Men-amun would have done almost anything else rather than go back to the passageway's gloom and that suddenly yawning hole – but he had no choice. When they got there, Lord Sobek peered down into it and grunted. Then he whisked his robes together at the knees and, to Men-amun's great unease, lowered himself over the lip into the dark. At waist height, he paused.

"Since you have knowledge of this, willy-nilly, I would teach you what it is," he said, and, "There is a ladder here. Below, will be rushlights on the walls."

Men-amun was aghast.

"One of the disciplines of priesthood – as you should know – is an ability to walk with fear and come out the further side. You will not progress, else. Follow me," he was bidden.

And undoubtedly, one great difficulty in life is that when a High Priest who is also a Prince of the Blood sets you a task, you may not easily refuse.

Men-amun swallowed convulsively, then – as Sobek steadily descended – offered his own feet, reluctantly, to be guided down the spelky timber treads.

The corridor underground was barely a body's width and led in a different direction to the one above. There were tiny prickets carrying light but it was hard to make much out, though Lord Sobek seemed confident enough.

They walked very straight for more than a hundred paces (Men-amun counted as he kept close to the pale blur that was his superior). Twice they were let through solid doors after Sobek had given a sharp double knock. Those guarding them were armed, going by the creak of leather and tiny metallic chimings of their gear. Nobody said anything. Nor were there other sounds – only an ever-increasing stifling stillness laced with the occasional scrape and slitherings of their progress.

The passage turned an elbow.

Abruptly they came out into a vaulted chamber. Here at least it was possible to see partly by daylight, due to two meagre ventilation shafts high up in the roof. Two other passages branched away on the far side ahead of them. To their right, where the chamber bellied out, a strong-room or cell had been built in, made entirely of smooth, worked stone. The wooden locking bar on its door was split and the keeper it ran into smashed away, but the whole had been jury-rigged fast, by dint of someone wedging a bench obliquely into the stone jambs. Liquid dribbled from the threshold, bringing with it a sour stink.

There were five of them now – the two from the passage having walked behind, heavy spears in hand. A third guard squatting opposite the cell entrance, sword drawn and never moving his eyes from it, was the man with the injured face.

"I have sent to the Lord Hapu-seneb," Sobek informed him.

The man muttered thanks and half pushed himself to his feet.

"No, no, be easy. You have taken enough. He is in there?" Sobek queried.

"He is, Lord Prince."

"What happened?"

The wounded man shook his head, speechless, sliding back down the wall. One of the others set out to explain.

"Beg pardon, sir . . . he got Si-ankh's best mate, see? Me and him –" he pointed at his fellow – "was coming on duty. We'd fetched the supper stuff and water as usual. We'd come from yon side, and got bolted in from behind, like they do. There hadn't been a peep from His Nibs all day, Si-ankh was just saying as Merweh took in his bowl and beaker. There was a pause, like – then all hell broke loose! Si-ankh dashed straight in after – well, you see what he got – but Merweh was blinded and spouting blood. Rolling about and screaming. None of us could get near quick enough to drag him free. You can't hardly believe the mania! We grabbed Si-ankh and His Nibs come hissing and howling after us busting everything he touched, so it was a matter of cobbling the door to before he got out and went rampaging! What happened inside after that don't bear thinking on!"

Sobek nodded and would have answered, but a guard reinforcement appeared from the opposite side escorting Vizier Hapu-seneb and an official of the Queen Regent's household called Senenmut.

There was a brief bustle of activity with people bringing flaring resin torches, brooms and water pots. Si-ankh was taken away for treatment.

Men-amun had to admire Lord Hapu-seneb. He and Sobek stood together, Hapu-seneb with a torch held high. Soldiers made a tight semicircle round them, weapons poised. At Hapu-seneb's command somebody hoisted away the bench and shoved the door smartly inwards.

"Now you rascal!" the Vizier announced into the interior. "You know us. This sort of thing cannot go on!"

Together, the High Priests marched in.

Against the flickering light, Men-amun caught one horrifying glimpse of a creature barely human, crouching toad-like on the lost guard's corpse.

The priests' advance set it off in an unearthly wailing, like a soul in Darkness, but its manic energy was spent.

They bound him, hand and foot, bundling him into a bag made from sewn sheepskins. They pulled his mouth open and made him drink – milk it looked like – but it must have had drug in it to complete quiescence. Four soldiers carried him bodily from the cell and dumped him unceremoniously in a corner.

Merweh's remains came out in pieces – his throat ripped and dripping, the lolling head a red obliteration. There were chunks of gouged flesh, and a wrenched arm separate. Whatever might be retrieved was collected on a sheet of sailcloth.

There was a great deal of brooming and swilling away.

A military joiner arrived to start fitting new locking bars and keepers.

Sheepskins are abomination – ritually unclean – and this prisoner's were particularly rank, yet out of sheer curiosity Men-amun forced himself to go near. He squatted to study the madman covertly.

He had a great mass of unkempt, matted hair and gaunt features – quite a prominent nose and sticking-out upper front teeth. His skin was greyish, from lack of light, perhaps. His eyes flickered, evasive, unnervingly blank. He lay there, keening to himself in some wordless, tuneless monotone. After a bit, wriggling and shifting, he began working his arms up from inside the bag. When he got his hands out, tightly lashed, Men-amun could see his weapons: ten hugely overgrown, horny, thickened nails – honed obsessively, no doubt, in his stark surroundings, to pointed, lethal talons. Blood was drying into them. Worse: an eyeball glistened – white and globular – still impaled on a nail half broken.

Men-amun thrust down revulsion.

Almost by accident he turned a key in the situation, for he joined in the keening sound, making it deftly into a repetitive, childlike tune – then a rhyme – then he built on that by tapping each dreadful finger in turn, going round and round. The creature giggled and flexed them, following his game. In time Men-amun pulled a small trimming knife from his belt and cunningly pared off every talon, short and square. Only when there were no more left did the man grow fretful. So to preserve peace and because he could think of nothing better, Men-amun embarked on telling him a story.

"Remarkable!" was Lord Hapu-seneb's dry comment when he came to oversee the prisoner's return. But by then the man was hardly awake, what with poppy juice and the low hypnotic drone of Men-amun's voice.

Prince Sobek led him back along the underground passage. Workmen came behind to replace the flagstone and remove the wooden steps.

"It wouldn't do to risk this kind of thing again," the Prince explained.

It gratified Men-amun that Lord Sobek saw personally to his repurification, presented him with fine new linen, and – since the refectory evening meal was now long over – insisted Men-amun took supper in his private rooms.

"The First Prophet was impressed with your forethought in trimming our friend's nails," the Prince told him affably, after his steward had served them and retired. "No one else has managed any such thing in years!"

Men-amun looked modestly pleased.

They had roast of goose with salad stuffs, and strong wine imported from islands in the Great Green. The Prince himself broke fresh bread between them.

"Eat, please," he said, "You must be hungry – I am!"

Men-amun ventured some questions.

"Has that man been there long?"

"Not there . . . No."

"How old is he, sir?"

"Approaching thirty perhaps – why?"

"I found that difficult to gauge. Is he always dangerous?" The Prince sighed.

"His condition is intermittent. He might be quiet for

months on end. But the rages strike without warning. That is the problem."

"I see."

Sobek set down his food.

"I must have your undertaking – on your honour as a priest and in writing – that you will never discuss this matter with anyone. Am I plain?"

"Of course, Highness," Men-amun hastened to agree. "Indeed, you have my word."

They spoke of other things but, in the end, Men-amun failed to resist the ultimate, obvious question:

"May I ask – who is that person?"

The Prince's expression turned glacial.

"That," he stated flatly down his fleshy Tuthmosid nose, "can be no concern of yours!"

After a day or two the matter assumed unreality – like some ill dream brought on by too much cheese and garlic late at night. Almost.

Yet, in a day or two also, Men-amun was sent for by Lord Sobek.

"You made an impression," he said, acknowledging Men-amun's bow and watching him sit cross-legged before him, "in regard to the person you may remember. He likes your story-telling."

Men-amun's stomach lurched. He said he found it hard to credit the prisoner had taken any of it in.

"Can Your Highness be sure?"

"Quite sure. Yes. We have consulted. We find it reasonable to try what another tale might achieve. Should you consent, naturally."

("We" – who were "we" – precisely? Men-amun wondered.)

There was an uncertain silence during which he was uncomfortably conscious of minute scrutiny. Then Men-amun prevaricated.

"I hardly know what might hold his interest . . ."

"Oh, come! One doubts if he expects some classic text!"

". . . and if I were missed from duties, sir?"

"If you slip away after refectory supper – might it not seem you had studies given? I shall accompany you to the place – and remain. Any small improvement would help – and be rewarding to yourself, longer term, I might add."

Men-amun argued it in his head. Patronage he was going to need if he were not to be stuck in the lower priesthood all his life. For though his family did middling-well – father retired with honour from the army, and a brother prospering in merchandise – they had no claims to lineage or social influence. But nowadays people could rise to great power. Lord Senenmut was living proof of that.

He bowed his head, consenting.

"I shall try, Prince, as you see fit," he agreed.

They took a different route at such times, skirting kitchens, bread ovens, storage places and down into deep cellars. Again there were guarded doors and another narrow subterranean corridor until they reached the stone chamber from an opposite side. Men-amun often wondered where the third passage led.

The soldiers on duty varied.

In the cell was nothing except a built-in mudbrick sleeping shelf on which, usually, would be the putrid sheepskin bag. A thin litter of straw and rushes scattered the floor, in an effort to sop up filth.

The soldiers would remove Men-amun's knife before he went in, and he would have a bundle of rushes to sit on.

"Daren't make it a stool, sir," one of them apologized. "He could grab it and clobber you!"

Often enough the prisoner would be crouched in a corner, naked, covering his head with one arm.

Men-amun would squat, doing his best to ignore the stench, and begin the counting game on his fingers. The man would watch for a while, unmoving, until he took up the thread of rhyme – then, collecting and dragging the bag, he'd creep close and put himself half inside it. Once he tired of the rhyme, he'd demand, clearly: "Story!"

He liked things about animals. Men-amun invented firstly,

some endless stuff about a cat journeying to find where the Nile was born. Once absorbed, his listener had an obsessional habit of stroking his right earlobe. Often he would seem asleep – or Men-amun's tale would peter out from weariness – but if he stopped too soon or tried, however cautiously, getting to his feet, a bony hand would clamp round his forearm with a speed and force that was frightening.

"More," he would say, "Again! Tell some more!"

Sobek would have to come and intervene with a bowl of whatever-it-was the prisoner drank so greedily, and unlatch the gripping fingers.

"More stories another time," he'd say, "But only if you are good."

It wasn't long before Men-amun came to loathe and fear these occasions.

The return to Temple life afterwards was lengthy – there was always the process of purifying in the sacred pool, not something you could skimp with a High Priest right beside you. The relief, the reward, lay in being rid – in being dry and clean – in taking wine and refreshment in the Prince's quarters.

"I suspect," Sobek told him once, "You think we keep the poor creature badly."

"He is very thin," Men-amun was judicious.

"His diet must be restricted. And often enough he spoils what food he's given."

"Might he not have a loincloth at least?"

"Do you think we haven't tried? He shreds things – or ruins them. Except for the time he twisted his linen thin and strangled someone with it! You yourself are witness to what can happen."

Men-amun said no more. But a question plagued him: if this man was so difficult to keep – why did they persist?

It grew worse. The prisoner would greet Men-amun's arrival with a screech which, given the circumstance, might supposedly be construed as gladness. Like some gigantic vile spider he would scuttle up to sit next to him in his horrid bag – all in a kind of caricature of friendship.

The nails were growing again but this time there was nothing Men-amun could do – no ruse or game which pleased; nor did the guards dare risk leaving Men-amun his knife.

Once, taking advantage of Lord Sobek's temporary absence outside the cell, Men-amun asked the prisoner his name. He had been following the epic adventures of Wepwawet the jackal, stroking his ear. The interruption made him stare, fretting the lobe.

Men-amun repeated his own name and said again: "Who are you?"

"Story!" pleaded the man.

"In a moment. I am M-e-n-a-m-u-n, yes?"

Impatiently the man nodded, poking him sharply in the ribs.

"Tell me: who are you?"

"No name."

Such a thing was inconceivable.

"You cannot – not – have a name!" Men-amun protested, aghast.

A name was the person's unique, essential label. The *ka* and the *ba* of the soul attached to it and all of that carried you forever through Existence. You must be so equipped when it came time for you to go back into the Other; when you had to answer before Thoth, god of Wisdom and Ma'at, goddess of Truth, Justice, Balance, for your deeds. To be unknown, unrecognizable then was to be lost in impenetrable Nothing; to have the lights of your spirit extinguished.

"Wepwawet," the man was repeating anxiously.

"He's in the story. Who are you?"

"No name."

Men-amun tried again. The man looked at him disdainfully – as at an idiot.

"No name," and he shouted, "NO-NAME! No-name IS name! STORY, STORY, STORY!"

He started beating Men-amun with his fists.

Sobek reappeared, alerted by the rise in sound.

Men-amun had no choice but to resume hastily: ". . . so Wepwawet sang to the stars and to his own jackal god, and to

Nut of the night sky before setting off once more across the desert . . ."

Men-amun dreaded these times: the darkness, the dirt, the stink – above all, the ever-present prickling awareness of danger.

Sometimes he had the sensation of being watched – but by whom, how, or for what purpose he couldn't fathom. On leaving once, he could have sworn to a brief drift of perfume in the slack air – sandalwood? – a bizarre note in such surroundings. And having to keep the endless tales going time after time, scoured his mind and imagination dry. It dragged him down, costing him sleep and appetite.

Inevitably, also, after a while his absences from quarters attracted notice. If Men-amun had no great enemies among his fellow lectors, he had no close friendships either. His excuses of extra studies were soon discounted. His colleagues split into two camps: those who pretended mock-sympathy and those who were overtly jealous of him stealing a professional march – for the Third Prophet's interest had not gone unremarked either.

Then as Men-amun sat one night in the cell's dank rushes, he was almost overtaken by disaster. Labouring his way through a life of Nekhbet the Vulture, there came a rustling in the litter somewhere in front of him. He tried ignoring it, but the distraction grew and he detected movement. He could have stomached a rat – possibly even a scorpion – but suddenly a viper reared and surged over the lower end of No-name's bag. Men-amun's voice died. Abruptly, he got to his feet. The thing paused, searching, its tongue flickering. No-name was quickly restive. Seized with fear on both counts, Men-amun could do nothing but stretch a hand and point.

"Ehhchh! Naughty!," screamed the prisoner at the hestitating reptile, "Now Men-storyman upset!"

He leapt from the bag, kicking as he went, dislodging the viper and flinging it some distance but, angered now, it came on again, swarming relentlessly straight for Men-amun's feet and legs. But even as it poised to strike, No-name caught it by the tail, whirling it round in circles so that weight and momentum prevented it from curling or twisting. He cracked it like a whip, and the head flew off, smacking away into a corner.

Galvanized, Men-amun shouted for help. His legs were threatening to fold, but he forced himself to stay upright, for fear this snake was not alone. No-name was peering inside his bag, which he tipped upside down and shook. Nothing fell out.

They came fast, carrying light.

No-name was pleased with himself.

"See!" he told them and presented the long, limp body to Lord Sobek with a flourish, having, as he put it, "Made Men-storyman safe."

The cell was searched meticulously while No-name, back in his bag, demanded a return to Nekhbet. Not unsurprisingly, after a wobbly start, the vulture encountered a huge serpent, fighting and overcoming it – which No-name found highly entertaining, including repeats and embellishment.

Afterwards Men-amun asked Lord Sobek how the viper could have got there, since the cell was all of smooth, close-fitted stone.

"One wonders, true. Yet it happens. There was a cobra once – an enormous thing. He fed it and claimed to play with it a while – but when it annoyed him once he killed it the same way."

Men-amun felt sick. Whatever the cost to his future, he resolved that he had gone as far as he could.

"Lord Prince," he pleaded, being comforted and emboldened by wine, "I beg you to release me from this task! I came on all this by accident. Apart from what just happened, I am dredged empty of stories! I dread the visits. I cannot sleep. And besides, my colleagues grow hostile, by reason of your intervention. I can't fob them off with excuses forever! I'll be bound however you want, but I will not go back!"

Sobek seemed pained.

"But surely you have managed extremely well? Granted, this present shock . . . Can you not see the good you do? Your visits are the only sliver of pleasure this poor man has. He listens. He remembers. He goes over what you tell him for himself – I have heard him! Would he have lifted a finger for you tonight, if he did not cling to that brief reward of your coming?"

Men-amun shook his head, stubbornly, in silence.

The prince refilled his cup, regarding him gravely.

"Very well," he conceded reluctantly, "I do see we cannot ask more than you could honestly give. As for the situation with your colleagues . . . come with me tomorrow afternoon and that shall be remedied."

Never before had Men-amun been in the Royal apartments.

Resplendent in leopard skin, the Prince steered him through sentried, cedarwood doors and pillared halls into a light, airy room with colourful walls, in which were several black and gilt chairs and two tables. One table was empty; the other – a substantial piece in granite – held a large, intricate model of an architectural project.

He'd scarcely had time to look before three people billowed in through fine hangings on the further side: the First and Second Prophets of Amun-Ra, Hapu-seneb and Ipuyemre, and the muscular, rather coarsely severe figure of the architect in person, the Queen-Regent's High Steward, Senenmut.

Ipuyemre also favoured leopard skin. Hapu-seneb was cloaked in night blue sewn with silver stars. Senenmut's pleated white shendyt-kilt was fringed with gold. On his solid shoulders reposed four heavy gold collars of honour.

Men-amun removed his sandals in the presence of superiors. The Lords bowed to one another ceremoniously, pulled up chairs and sat in marvellous unison. Hapu-seneb put down a sheet of papyrus on the empty table. Men-amun stood in front of them and they all leaned back and stared.

It was an interview – more, an examination – like graduating from scribe school, or when he'd done his time as wab-priest learning rites and prayers, before being picked for lector. They knew about him too: the paper on the table – which they referred to now and then – was abstracted from a personal file.

He felt hemmed in.

Dutifully, he confirmed the basics, and that his home was in the suburbs of The City. It seemed to please them that he'd passed out top of his scribal intake, awarded commendations for clarity and style. They liked also the idea of his father's distinctions for military bravery.

Ipuyemre, known for his literary leanings, understood Men-amun was gifted at narrative.

"For what we have in mind, such facility would be an advantage," he asserted ponderously.

Men-amun waited nervously.

Senenmut, silent so far and unmoving – watching him with his arms folded, cleared his throat.

"Do little children put you off?" he asked bluntly. His voice rasped.

Men-amun blinked.

"I cannot imagine so, Lord," he replied, "Though being young and unencumbered I must confess my experience of such isn't wide!"

The priests seemed mildly amused, but Senenmut looked thunder.

"All right – don't be smart! The small princess – Merytre – is aye, maybe six months short of starting education proper. But bright and lively . . . all over the place some days! The Queen is minded for her to be kept occupied of a morning: drawing; simple writing and counting; games; little tales. Nothing formal – more what would interest her happily. You would join the Household – naturally. I'm sure I need not stress the long-term benefits! Your duties would be light enough just now to leave time for some religious work, which Prince Sobek tells me you should. If the Princess takes to you – if your face fits – you could go far. Well?"

It felt like the lifting of some huge oppressive weight.

Men-amun bowed acceptance.

"The Lord High Steward does me great honour," he said.

Senenmut scraped back his chair and stood up.

"I don't," he retorted. "Her Majesty does!"

Since Men-amun was virtually at the end of his current three-month duty, it was agreed he should take some, at least, of his due home leave. Their co-Majesties were travelling in the North.

"You can have ten days," Senenmut told him. "By then they'll be back. Report to my scribes on your return."

"Yes, Lord."

"Her Majesty will, of course, require to have a look at you herself."

They left.

Men-amun retrieved his sandals and lingered, examining the model: platforms, processional stairs, colonnades, chapels, capped by a central pyramidion. All of it was backed by an ingenious rendering in clay and pebbles of a concave cliff face. Quite suddenly, he realized where it was and what it would be. Work on it was already well in hand. He'd seen it from the ferries, across the river from Waset, The City. This was the Queen's intended mortuary temple, next to and rivalling that of King Mentuhotep of antiquity.

A manservant came to escort him superciliously out.

Men-amun caught the first boat he could get, upstream to the southern suburbs. It felt good to be going home and at last he could relax.

His father greeted his arrival with a shout of affection and an arm round the shoulders. His young sister-in-law, Inawt, who ran the household, was minded to make a fuss of him. All his recent difficulties slipped away. Even so, Men-amun waited until his brother Sen-re came home and they assembled for supper, before attempting to break the news of his change in prospects. Sen-re gave him the perfect opening.

"How's the priest business then?" he inquired breezily, pouring beer all round, while Inawt and the servant girl brought dishes.

"Oh . . . fine . . ."

When the activity diminished, he set down his beer and went on, "Actually – I seem to be in line for something new."

"Oh, yes?" Sen-re was dividing up bread and handing it round.

"I've been interviewed. By all three Prophets and the High

Steward Senenmut. What they are offering is the chance to start tutoring little Princess Merytre."

Inawt stared with her mouth open.

"It's a bit tentative, mind you. She's too small for proper schooling just yet, but they have hinted I might secure the permanency if they think I'm right. Also, Prince Sobek reckons I should carry on with religious studies – which is good. I've got liturgy coming out my ears, but I'd like to branch into dream interpretation if I get the chance."

There was a buzz of excitement and congratulations. Inawt asked what age Merytre was, exactly, and impressed on him that he must take her some really nice presents when he went back. Only his father was a mite caustic.

"What have you been doing, then – to get picked out for this?" he wanted to know.

Men-amun shrugged.

"I've submitted some papers lately – maybe Lord Sobek likes my writing! You might remember I left school top of the intake." Well, it was half the truth.

"Watch yourself then, son."

"How do you mean? Oh, come on, Pa, I thought you'd be no end pleased! They recalled your bravery decorations at the interview! This could be a huge step up."

"I'm pleased – of course I am. I can see it as the start of a big career. Didn't Senenmut himself come up by way of tutor to the older girl? All I say is: watch out for yourself. Royal Household – that's a separate world – right? They can suck you dry, then spit you out like a date-pit if anything goes against you. I know. I saw some when I did my stint in the late King's own guard."

But, on the whole, it seemed a very good excuse to celebrate. And a day or two later they threw a big party for family and friends (Inawt was the brothers's second cousin in any case), designed to show off Men-amun in his most glamorous light.

On the last day of his leave, the four of them crossed the river with offerings, food and wine, to visit the maternal tomb.

Men-amun went shaven and purified, and in his proper robe and sash. The whole family had loved their mother. He conducted the rites and read her a Letter to the Dead which he had composed specially. He took pains to do everything with affection and style. Afterwards – with her tomb door open for her spirit to join them – they set up shade awnings, laid mats and picnicked in peace. Through the heat of the day they all dozed. Later, Sen-re and Inawt wandered off on a curiosity tour of other tombs.

"You did that very well," his father complimented Men-amun. "The religious stuff. Your Ma'd be pleased! I hope you'll do the same for me when my time comes . . ."

"Thanks, Pa. I will, of course. You know that, surely?"

After a bit he queried lazily, "How many brothers did the Queen ever have?"

"Which Queen?"

"This one. Hatshepsut."

"Phhhh . . . now you're asking! Quite a bunch. Why?"

"I'm interested. I need a sort of all-round picture consider-ing what I'm going into."

His father scratched equably.

"Well . . . five or six, if I remember rightly. Half-brothers, mostly. There were three very much older, for starters. Wadjmose, Amenmose and Ramose. All of them were from old King Tuthmosis I's previous marriage to Lady Mutnofret. She was a princess, true, but a lesser one. Only when King Amenhotep had him marry the Great Heiress – his daughter Ahmose – did the offspring really count directly."

"Mhhm. And what came out of that?"

"Eh . . . dear me! Ma'at-ka-re Hatshepsut herself . . . Neferubity her sister . . . Amenemes."

Men-amun pricked his ears.

"What happened to him?"

"Who?"

"Amenemes, Pa!"

"Died. Like the sister. That wasting sickness, where they cough. There's a strain of that among them. Oh, and there's your boss of course, Menkheper-re-sobek. He's a half-broth-er. Can't recall who his mother was . . . Then there was the one she married, obviously – Akheperenre – Tuthmosis II as was. He was interesting: the same age as Hatshepsut absolutely – to the day and hour. Odd, that! Also, you couldn't hardly tell them apart as youngsters, they were so alike. They used to play tricks on people, did you know? Little devils . . . !" he chuckled reminiscently.

"Ha! What happened to the first three?"

"Wadjmose was an army man. He commanded my unit once. Killed in action. Amenmose . . . an accident . . . scrunched by a chariot. Ramose was the quiet one – went to be a priest but he had the coughing disease."

"You're sure?"

"I'm not senile! As far as I can be, yes."

There was a pause.

"Anyone else come to mind?" Men-amun asked.

"No. Who else could there be?"

"And when you were in the Guard . . . did you ever have to do – or hear tell of – any special kind of duty?"

"No, I did not! What *is* this?"

"Just trying to build the picture, Pa."

"Well, how about building it back there? You're the one in the Temple. If you doubt my word, go and look things up in Archives, yes? Now – can I please snatch another spot of zizz before those two get back and we all start packing up?"

Like probing pain in a tooth, Men-amun's mind kept touching on the problem of No-name.

At home after supper, with Inawt stitching away at something small in blue imported silk – bending close to lamps augmented by polished metal discs – he remarked obliquely, "I suppose King Tuthmosis II did die?"

Sen-re looked astonished. Their father snorted angrily.

"Are you back on that? Yes – he did! You were at the funeral – in the procession of priests. Hadn't you just been given your lector's sash? I was there. Didn't they call me back to help sort out the Honour Guard? Weren't most of the rest of us there, in the viewing spots along the route I got them? He had twelve good years of rule, and the Queen loved that man! Everyone knew that."

"Sorry, Pa."

But this time his father was not to be put off.

"You were nearer than most. Weren't you lot processed right to the tomb? Didn't you all file right past the bier? Was there any reason at all to think it wasn't a genuine body – albeit wrapped and masked and whatnot?"

"Yes, Pa . . . no, Pa!"

"So then . . . was the Queen not distraught enough for you?"

"Pa . . . honestly . . . I didn't mean . . ."

"Didn't you witness yourself the choosing of the male heir by Amun-Ra in oracle?"

"Yes. Look, I'm sorry . . ."

"I should hope you are! No one in this house goes round insinuating that the Queen faked anything! Understood?"

"Yes, Pa."

Inawt bit off thread.

"There," she said, mystified and anxious to restore harmony, "finished. I swore I would – so you can take it tomorrow."

It was a child's waist-belt neatly edged in bright colours. On the lappet ends, enclosed in gold thread cartouches it read twice: "King's daughter – Merytre."

Men-amun was presented to Their co-Majesties in the Appearance Hall of the Palace, the morning following his return. He had a long wait, being the very last person called to the Presences that day, and there had been a large foreign embassy to receive – the more exotic of whose gifts had rather got out of hand. Meantime, some bossy chamberlain kept lecturing him on what he had to do.

Finally Senenmut pronounced his name in loud, rasping fashion. Men-amun approached barefoot across what felt like a mile of glistening floor, gaze lowered as instructed, cast himself down prone in full obeisance and uttered the correct praise formula: "Life! Health! Prosperity! be to the Lords of the Two Lands."

Someone touched him with a wand, so he could kneel up.

Senenmut relayed to Their Majesties that here was the potential new tutor for the Princess Merytre.

They sat like statues, side by side, the woman and the adolescent boy – aunt/stepmother and nephew/stepson – weighted with gold and regalia – looking down on him from the combined height of dais and elaborate thrones. Behind the eye make-up they were quite startlingly alike: wide foreheads, high cheekbones, straight, fleshy noses, well-cut mouths, small rounded chins. Their top lips didn't quite cover prominent upper teeth. It would be easy to assume, erroneously, that they were on the edge of smiling – when they were not. It was the Queen who wore the double crown of true governance; Menkheperre Tuthmosis III had the irridescent blue War Helmet.

For a moment they regarded him with that sort of baleful hypnotic attention reserved by cats for mice – then the Queen nodded fractionally and Men-amun was free to stand, to bow his thanks, to accept his new Household armring and to back carefully away.

He was allotted rooms to himself. One held a plain but proper bed with headrest – where all his life to date he had been used to sleeping shelves. The other was the schoolroom with a low worktable, two stools – even a chair for his own use. Men-amun's box of personal belongings was sent over from his previous quarters, and a boy servant had been deputed to see to his needs and bring him meals.

The Princess Merytre – when she appeared next morning all by herself – proved to be very lively, articulate and prone to fun.

"Hullo," she said, putting her head cautiously round the schoolroom door-screen, "are you my Teaching Person?"

Men-amun bowed, offered his name, and admitted that he was.

"Can I come in?" she asked – not really waiting for his answer but hopping the rest of herself into view. "I was 'sploring," she confided. "So I could find you first!"

She would not be clothed until her fourth birthday so as yet she trotted about in nothing more than a set of amulets ("Life! Health! Prosperity!"), a pair of tiny gilt sandals and a string of bright beads. Like all royal children, her head was shaven except for the sidelock denoting her rank. This was tightly plaited, tied off with a gold-thread ribbon.

Heeding Inawt's injunction, Men-amun had not come unprovided.

He laid out on the worktable a scroll of best quality papyrus and a new scribe's palette, complete with red and black ink cakes, a reed pen and a brush in their holders.

"These, Highness," he told her, "are my first gift to you. See: they are labelled with your name."

She touched them, curious and shy.

"But I won't know what to do," she said.

"Is it not my job to show you? You shall, quite soon. But we will keep this for your very best work."

He had other things up his sleeve: a splendidly carved and painted wooden duck set on eccentric wheels so that when pulled along by its string it bobbed up and down – as ducks do.

"Ooh!" she exclaimed, entranced.

And after that he unrolled Inawt's blue silk embroidered belt.

"Oo-ooh! Pretty!"

He showed her where it said her name on the ends.

Snatching up the belt and toy, she ran away from him, out of the room. He could hear her voice, eager, diminishing with distance, shouting: "Mama! Mama! See what I have! . . . and the blue thing says its ME!"

He spent an anxious time wondering whether to go after her, but didn't know his bearings yet and feared to put a foot wrong. In a while, Merytre was firmly returned, downcast, and led by a young attractive nursemaid.

"Lady Merytre," the nurse instructed, "You will tell the Tutor, please, exactly what Her Majesty your mother says you must!"

The child took a deep breath, looked him in the eye, and recited in one long rush: "I-must-say-Thank-You-because-your-presents-are-kind-and-I-must-say-Sorry-because-running-off-like-that-is-not-what-princesses-do-and-I-might-have-made-you-cross. There!'' and she added, "You can let go now 'Ty. I won't do it again.''

The nurse told Men-amun she had permission to stay a while until the pupil settled in – and he, beginning with practice slate and sponge and chalk to show his small charge how to set out her name properly inside its Pharaoh House, was rather more than glad.

The little girl was quick-minded, infinitely engaging. Men-amun soon found within himself an ability to teach. He wanted this job. Before too long, the first scratchy entries of "very best work" began to go into the papyrus roll.

They were absorbed in a counting game he had invented – where you stepped along a painted mat from square to square – when, one morning, turning round because his pupil's calculations had abruptly exploded into giggles, he found himself face to face with Queen Hatshepsut. This time, shorn of much formality, she was smiling broadly. He had a job to make his obeisance with proper dignity.

"Forgive me," she said, "I was passing. The mathematics attracted me . . . Please, do carry on."

She dropped in from time to time after that. She was always charming – often complimentary – but she had an astonishing capacity for appearing almost out of nowhere, and in silence. Only a drift of perfume would warn him of her proximity. She often favoured sandalwood. Other things disturbed him.

He had thought up some little tales about a duck called Wek-wek (Merytre's name for the toy he'd given her). Wek-wek got into scrapes and had to be constantly rescued by a small but brave and resourceful princess. These adventures proved sufficiently popular that eventually he wrote them down – not least so that nursemaids might make use of them at princessly bedtimes. He looked up once, in class, from trying out a new one, to find Her Majesty – who had quietly borrowed his chair – sitting enjoying it with them. She was absent-mindedly stroking her earlobe. And she possessed always, an air, however kindly she watched him out of her elegant small-cat's face, of the suppressed danger, the ferocity of Sekhmet, the Lioness.

Uneasily, he remembered No-name.

He tracked down the scribes who were Keepers of the Royal Records and made himself agreeable. Household status had qualified him for limited access and since they were often pushed with work in, say, diplomatic correspondence, his skilful offers of occasional assistance at copying or glossing outdated material was welcome. He located the pigeonholing and labels of the current dynasty. There came an afternoon when sheer press of business combined with some sickness absences had the duty scribe in charge actually asking him to "hold the fort" for the time he was called away to take dictation.

Left alone, Men-amun took down the scroll bearing the labels of Tuthmosis I. Much was as his father had sketched: the Queen's three most senior half-brothers were very much her elders. Their births, careers and deaths were fully documented. Menkheper-re-sobek, the last one living, had a different mother – a lady called Isis, who had also given the King a daughter of that name. Prince Sobek too, was twelve years older than the Queen. Am<u>e</u>memes, her full brother had come and gone, half grown – like Neferubity, her sister. Both were several years her junior. The last of the Lady Mutnofret's sons, Akheperenre, who became Tuthmosis II, must have been a surprise. The gap between him and Ramose was a full ten years. And plainly, in red and black, his birth was recorded as coinciding exactly – to the month, the day, the hour, with that of the Princess Ma'at-ka-re, born to the Great Queen, Ahmose. "His Majesty," ran a marginal note to the text, "was pleased to regard them almost as twins . . ." There was no indication of anyone else.

Akheperenre Tuthmosis II was well accounted for. Being sovereign, he had a scroll to himself: "Prince . . . King . . . slightly wounded in skirmish, fourth regnal year . . . recovered well . . . injured hunting hippopotamus, tenth regnal year . . . persistent grumbling infections from this . . . deteriorating health . . ." For the last two years of his reign, it was tacitly obvious the Queen had carried the burden of government. True to the convolutions of his family, he'd had female children with Hatshepsut; his male heir Menkheperre – now Tuthmosis III – was of the Lady Isis junior.

Men-amun re-examined the first scroll.

Ma'at-ka-re was fifteen when Ahmose, her mother died. Tuthmosis I proclaimed her in co-rule, but died himself a year on. She and Akheperenre were sixteen, barely of age, when they married and were crowned. Sixteen, add twelve and now the two years since his death – made her thirty now . . . just about. Again he scrutinized all the birth entries, but the script was neat and even with no detectable alteration or excision. No-name. Aged thirty . . . just about. But no name.

The Queen was said to be mildly indisposed, but Men-amun soon learned on the Temple grapevine that she had shut herself away in the innermost shrine of Amen-Ra Himself. Only the First Prophet, Hapu-seneb, was in any way permitted to approach.

He ought not have been surprised when Prince Sobek came seeking him, saying, "I need someone I can trust. Will you come?"

He knew what was implied.

Sure enough, the passage they went down – from the royal apartments – penetrated inevitably to the same familiar stony desolation. Only, this time, beyond the first door there was sufficiency of light and there were no guards.

No-name was dead.

He had been carried from the cell and laid down. His hands and feet were bound fast; his mouth stretched wide, seized in a huge rictus which betrayed a terrible and losing fight for breath. His eyelids, not quite closed, showed the dead eyes as white reflective slits.

"Highness! How has this happened?" Men-amun was aghast.

Prince Sobek shrugged.

"I wasn't here. They tell me he began a rage but the guards

pinioned him and tied him up. When they pushed him into his bag, it seems, a cobra had coiled inside.

Death from cobra venom is swift, by means of inexorable paralysis.

"What is it I'm to do?" Men-amun queried.

"Help me sort him out. We'll have him interred tonight."

But whatever No-name was due in the way of burial, by the looks of it, it was to be quite shockingly unorthodox.

Someone had provided new, watersoaked sheepskins, strong twine and needles. They had to set to and stitch the whole thing together with No-name inside it. When these skins dried out they would shrink tight. Men-amun found it grotesque.

"Is he to have no embalming? No proper rites?" he protested.

"No."

Men-amun felt ashamed and uncomfortable.

The head, before its dense crown of matted, crinkly hair disappeared forever, was turned far to one side and had an odd, flattened appearance. No-name might have died of venom – or he might have been subdued and then pressed down into relentless suffocation. There was no way to be certain.

When they finished Prince Sobek sat back on his heels and breathed relief.

"Amen be praised!"

He brought up a rough wooden coffin. Together they lifted in the damp, stiffening bundle. Sobek shut the lid. Inside and out, the coffin was painted plain white. No good spells, no invocations, no name.

Men-amun was enough of a priest to be appalled.

"Have we not just obliterated his Being?" he argued hotly.

"No. I see how it looks to you, but his Being is not here. He has been subsumed."

Men-amun scowled.

"How . . . subsumed?"

He ran a risk, being belligerent, but this mattered to him – or his training, his way of life, his belief-system, would be in doubt. The Prince stayed patient.

"Do we not teach that the soul is unquenchable? That I myself certainly hold! Then it has migrated elsewhere and I assisted it. Now: we shall cleanse ourselves. I would ask you to rest early this evening. In the small hours I shall need you one more time. You will accompany me properly as a priest. I ask you to judge nothing until our task is ended."

In the dense blackness which precedes the end of night, Men-amun was taken to the royal quays. Hapu-seneb was waiting. They boarded the kind of little boat site workmen used. It already held the white coffin. Senenmut alone, was captain and crew. They sculled across the river in silence – making the journey to where the new mortuary temple was building. Once there the coffin was placed on a sledge. They dragged it along what would ultimately be the processional Way, then lifted it up new stone stairs to the great first platform. All of this was recently paved except, in the centre, for an open rectangular pit with a small pile of earth and a single flagstone propped next to it. Using ropes, they lowered the coffin carefully into the hole. Senenmut shovelled and levelled the dirt, manhandling the paving stone to seal the place. He and Hapu-seneb spoke together about getting back.

"There is much to be done," Men-amun overheard Sobek agree, "But he and I remain until the Aten rises."

When they had gone, Sobek hunted about for a workman's mat, batted it vigorously free of grit and spread it on the ground.

"We have quite a wait," he said. "Be easy."

Men-amun sat down beside him, cross-legged.

"No one less than a prince," he stated baldly, "would be buried here. However shabbily it has been done!"

Gazing remotely out into the purple of pre-dawn, Prince Sobek countered drily, "I heard you were busy in the Royal Archives. What did you learn?"

"Nothing, Lord."

"Yet reason and instinct say you are correct. He was my half-brother. Can you not imagine such a burden – such endless sadness? He was the Queen's brother – more – he was her true twin. Yet it was Akheperenre who so resembled her, and whom she loved."

Chastened, Men-amun asked, "Was he always dangerous?"

"Always. But he was never in such hard captivity until these last few years – after he tried, once, to murder the Queen. In youth, she could calm him – but latterly his rages grew until they overtook him altogether."

"I see . . ."

"I wonder if you do!"

After a pause, Men-amun admitted gloomily, "I feel I let him down, all the same. Perhaps I should have gone back."

"I think not. Feel no blame for that. And shortly, now, you and I shall set him free."

The density of night had thinned and greyed.

"I'm not sure, Highness, I understand your meaning in his being subsumed."

"I believe that some part of his Being shall be absorbed elsewhere. I have done rites to that effect. It was his body, surely, that was so wrong – never his soul. The Ka and the Ba are quite other. Is that not what we comprehend as priests?"

"Ah. Yes. But where – absorbed?"

"You shall see. When the Queen emerges from seclusion this day, she will do so renewed, as Pharaoh in her own right, without impediment."

No wonder they hadn't killed him! This inextricable half of the Pharaonic whole. Men-amun's thoughts whirled. . . . Or had they? Finally. Had she? Had she, in the end, taken the risk of overturning Balance in the whole Kingdom by using Wadjet, the cobra, that instrument of royal guardianship, against him? Or worse?

"She has upheld Ma'at – Balance, Truth, Justice – in the Two Lands as it is – since before Akheperenre's death. Redoubled, she can rule now as she should."

"And the young King?" Men-amun queried, astounded – for such a thing was unprecedented.

"Do not imagine her as evil! He will continue as he is. Amun-Ra chose him, and besides, she loves him for his father's sake. He is still two years short of his majority and wishes to pursue a military life – to command, eventually, the whole army. He has nothing to do but wait."

The east was changing – suffusing subtly with colours: violet, rose, the palest aquamarine. They had reached that breathless moment of stillness and expectation.

Prince Sobek stood up, and Men-amun with him, preparing for the return of Amen-Ra in all his glory.

"Did he ever have a name?" Men-amun asked urgently.

"No. The King my father forbade it. His birth was second and a hard one. He was thought dead at the time. Only on the preparation table in the House of Anubis did he suddenly kick and cry. When the embalmers returned him to the Palace my father deemed it unchancy. As it proved. Later, who dared to risk his gaining any understanding of what he truly was?"

"If he had had a name, Highness," Men-amun pursued stubbornly, "What might it have been?"

The Prince half smiled into the coming dawn.

"Is she not Ma'at-ka-re? What is the twin of ka-re?"

"Ba. Ba-re."

"And who is Kheper?"

"The scarab who rolls back the sun daily . . . and Khepri, his deity arising – who is Existence itself!"

"Good. And the prefix 'Established'?"

"Men . . . kheper . . . ba . . . re."

Side by side they raised their arms in prayer, each thereby forming the glyph Ka, commending him to Amen-Ra who made him – this Lost Prince whose flawed body was done with, and whose Ba, also, could now take wing in freedom.

The Aten, his golden chariot poised upon the rim of morning, blazed upward – hastening to receive and refashion him.

"I am Deity," proclaimed Ma'at-ka-re Hatshepsut, Beloved-of-Amun, in her new dual voice as Pharaoh. "I am the Beginning of Existence."

Historical Note

In the 19th century, Gaston Maspero, then Egypt's Director of Antiquities, embarked on a preliminary clearing of Queen Hatshepsut's mortuary temple at Deir el-Bahari.

A plain, white-painted wooden coffin was discovered beneath the paving of the First Platform. It bore neither image, nor label, nor any indication of identity. Inside, sewn into sheepskin wrappings lay the body of an adult male, estimated at death to have been between 25 and 30 years of age. At variance with all custom, no embalming had been done, nor any internal organs removed. The man's wrists and ankles still showed ligature marks, though the bonds had rotted away. Otherwise there was no sign of injury, except what Maspero called "the terrible distortion of the features" – which he thought consistent with the extremity of suffocation. The sheepskin had been sewn up wet and had shrunk on drying out. The white paint was considered to have been deliberate: the creation of a "blind spot" in the Afterlife.

Maspero, who was horrified, called this man "The Unknown Prince". (See: "Everyday Life in Egypt" p. 218, Pierre Montet.)

Pharaoh Hatshepsut's declamatory boast is extant in her mortuary temple. (See: "The Splendour that was Egypt" p. 110, Margaret A. Murray Sidgwick & Jackson 1977.)

"OR YOU CAN DRINK THE WINE . . . ?"

Paul C. Doherty

This story is set at virtually the same time as the previous one. It is also contemporary with the novels by Paul C. Doherty set in ancient Egypt. To date these include The Mask of Ra *(1998),* The Horus Killings *(1999),* The Anubis Slayings *(2000),* The Slayers of Seth *(2001). They all feature Amerotke, the Chief Judge of Egypt. Doherty is renowned for his many historical novels set throughout history, from the time of Alexander the Great to the Middle Ages to the French Revolution. He is also one of the modern masters of the locked-room mystery, and here is one dating from almost 3,500 years ago.*

"The Cavern opens,
Spirits fall within the darkness.
The Eye of Horus makes you holy!
Oh imperishable stars hide her amongst you."

Amerotke, Chief Judge in the Hall of Two Truths in Thebes of A Hundred Gates, whispered his prayer as he stared down at the corpse. It lay on a white-sheeted palliasse; the linen curtains, hanging round the bed to keep away the myriad flies, had been abruptly pulled away. The woman sprawled there, hair splayed out covering either side of the head-rest, had died violently. The corpse was still grotesque despite efforts to prepare the remains before they were taken to the Wabet, the House of Purification for embalming. Lady Tiyea, wife of Meret, looked middle-aged in her long tunic of pure white linen, a blue frieze around the hem and neckline: her ear-studs, rings and necklaces had been removed. The cosmetics which adorned her face carefully cleaned, her thick greying hair combed into some sort of order. The dead eyes peered half-open in a glassy stare, her mouth gaped, tongue still caught between her lips. The muscles of the corpse were rigid, the belly distended.

Amerotke realized he must give the order for the corpse to be removed before the heat of the day increased its putrefaction and polluted the chamber. The mortuary priest, crouched in a corner, was growing impatient. He was dressed in a white kilt, simple reed sandals on his feet: his face and head were hidden behind the black dog mask of the God Anubis, the sharp ears and snout of the mask tipped with gold.

"My Lord." The priest's voice sounded as if from afar off. "The Lady Tiyea must be moved. My servants are waiting. She has been dead for some time!"

Amerotke nodded and stared down at the corpse. The ankles, sticking pathetically out beneath the linen robe, looked swollen. Amerotke shifted his gaze to the face. The ugliness of violent death had contorted it: the greyish cheeks were puffy, folds of fat threatened to hide the eyes. The grotesque expression on the dead woman's face chilled Amerotke's heart and prompted him to invoke further spells from "The Book of the Dead"; the Judge was also struggling against the waves of darkness which threatened to engulf his own heart and soul.

"I am the Lord of Light," he whispered, quoting the canticle to the God Horus. "Death is my detestation. I pray that this woman will not enter into the place of execution. Her Ka must go forth into the Eternal West, to the lush fields of the God Osiris, where she will feast for all eternity."

Another death, Amerotke reflected. Many would die in Thebes today: some violently, some by accident, the bite of a snake, the crushing jaws of a crocodile, a piece of falling masonry, an oil lamp, ill-prepared, bursting into flame . . . Amerotke closed his eyes. What did it matter? Despite his prayers to Osiris and Horus, Amerotke often doubted whether there was anyone beyond the Veil, so what did it matter? A man was born and from that moment onwards he was preparing for death. Across the Nile, the Necropolis, the City of the Dead, was always busy, its embalming shops full of steam and smoke, thick with the stench of corruption and the cloying spices and ointments used to pack the corpses of the dead and prepare them for their journey. Amerotke lifted his head. A journey to what? To the fiery pools of the Am-Duat, the Underworld? Or the Eternal Fields of the Blessed?

Across the room Shufoy, Amerotke's servant, crouched on a stool, legs apart, hands hanging down. The dwarf man's face was puckered in concern which made his features as ugly as those of the God Bes. Shufoy was not only a dwarf but one who had been mutilated, his nose cut off for a crime he did not commit. Shufoy had received a pardon from Lord Amerotke himself and, since then, had vowed to be the Judge's servant, in peace and war. Usually Shufoy would have been full of questions but he sensed his master's moods. They had already clashed over the way Shufoy dressed, in a long tattered robe and battered sandals. Shufoy always loved to depict himself as the poor man, even though his treasure chest contained a small fortune. They'd left Amerotke's house that morning, Shufoy grasping the huge parasol which, when the sun turned threateningly hot, he would open to protect his master's head. Usually he would go before Amerotke, swinging this parasol like a staff of office, loudly boasting and proclaiming:

"Make way for the Lord Amerotke, Chief Judge in the Hall of Two Truths! Trusted member of the Royal Circle! Beloved friend of Pharaoh! The searcher of truths! The champion of Ma'at . . . !"

Amerotke had told him to shut up and, next time, dress more fittingly. Shufoy had stopped swinging the parasol; instead he had trailed sullenly behind Amerotke as they made their way into Thebes, up the Avenue of the Sphinxes and into the Hall of the Golden Lotus. Hatusu, Pharaoh Queen of Egypt, was waiting for Amerotke, deep in conversation with her lover and first minister the Lord Senenmut. Shufoy was left to kick his heels in the antechamber, fingers itching to take down the small alabaster jars which glowed in the niches of the painted walls. Or, perhaps, that pure gold statue of the Goddess Hathor and slip it into his bag? He was glad he hadn't. Raised voices echoed from the audience chamber and Amerotke had come striding out his face as black as a storm cloud.

"I have urgent business," he snapped. "In the Hall of Two Truths. Yet Her Majesty wishes me to go elsewhere!"

Shufoy remained as tactful as he could in their walk back through the city and managed to discover that the Lady Tiyea had once been Pharaoh Hatusu's nurse. A married woman of considerable wealth, Lady Tiyea had apparently become depressed and, according to the accepted story, committed suicide by drinking poisoned wine. Shufoy gazed appreciatively around this lavishly furnished bed chamber. Its floor was of polished wood, the walls whitewashed and decorated with a brilliant frieze at top and bottom, displaying multi-coloured birds nesting in lush green papyrus thickets. A water vase, carved in the shape of a baboon, stood in the far corner. Pottery torches hung on the wall, small alabaster jars glowed from ledges or niches.

Why, Shufoy wondered, did a woman who owned a riverside mansion with high walls and finely decorated door posts, its windows and walls inlaid with lapis-lazuli, commit suicide? Lady Tiyea owned granaries, a fowl yard, aviaries, bee-hives, a breeding pond for geese and other fowl, rich gardens, even pomegranate orchards. Outhouses and pavilions stood near pools of purity with fragrant-smelling lotus blossom nestling on the top. Latticed shutters protected the windows. Furniture of highly polished acacia and sycamore, inlaid with ivory and ebony, was plentiful: it even included a sloping-backed chair for her bedchamber, the end of each ledge carved in the form of Sekhmet the Destroyer. In the far corner stood a beautifully carved cosmetic box, its chest thrown back. Cushions, forming a small divan, were piled beneath the high window. On a table on the far side of the bed, precious collars, ear-studs, rings of amber, gold, silver and faience glistened in the spears of sunlight pouring through the window.

"My Lord." The mortuary priest's grating voice broke the silence. "I must insist. Soon it will be noon. The Lady Tiyea's corpse has to be removed."

Shufoy stared soulfully at his master who now turned round, his long dark face still brooding, his fingers tapping the belt of his fringed and embroidered kilt. Amerotke's long-sleeved tunic of gauffered linen, which fell just over the top of the kilt, was a spotless white. The only jewellery the Chief Judge wore were a neck collar, displaying Ma'at the Goddess of Truth, and rings, bearing the same insignia, on his strong fingers. Amerotke did not wear a wig; his thick black hair was cut short around the nape of his neck, except for a side lock which hung down over his left ear. Shufoy could never understand the reason for that. When a boy became a man the lock was cut; Amerotke, for his own secret reasons, always wore it and Shufoy, despite his best efforts, could never discover why. The Judge's gaze caught Shufoy's. Amerotke's face was taut, the dark eyes seemed more brooding, the nose sharper, his mouth tight-lipped betraying no spark of humour.

"My lord is intrigued?" Shufoy asked.

Amerotke knelt by the bed, gesturing at Shufoy to come to the other side. The manservant did so. Amerotke took a small ivory stick from the wallet which hung from his embroidered belt to open the dead woman's mouth further: her tongue was grey, a streak of black coursed down the centre, dried white froth stained the corner of her chafed, swollen lips.

"Poison, my lord?"

"Undoubtedly."

"And what kind?"

Amerotke laughed, a sharp rasping sound.

"Go down into the markets, Shufoy. Ask your friends the Scorpion Men how many poisons can be bought in Thebes?"

"True, true." The mortuary priest had joined them: he stood at the foot of the bed almost kneeling on the small chest standing there. "The milk of the asp, the venom of the viper, the juice from plants or crushed minerals."

"Enough." Amerotke glanced sharply at the mortuary priest. "You have studied the corpse?"

"My lord, she drank some venom."

Amerotke sighed and got to his feet. He sat on the edge of the bed and grasped the dead woman's hand, holding it gently, stroking the stiffening fingers: a tender gesture, as if the Judge was trying to placate her spirit.

"Why did this woman die?"

The mortuary priest padded across the chamber to a large table which stood on the right side of the window. He brought back a goblet of Calchis green, long-bowled with a fluted stem on a rounded base. He held this gingerly, his fingers tapping the image of the Goddess Hathor carved on the side. He sniffed and handed this to Amerotke who accepted it carefully. He smelt it and recoiled at the sharp acrid odour. The cup was half-full; the stains around the side were dark red, only the odour betrayed the venom.

"I don't know what the poison is, my lord."

"It smells so sharp," Amerotke replied. "Would the woman know that when she drank it?"

The mortuary priest shook his head.

"I am a physician as well as a priest, my lord. Many poisons are colourless and tasteless. Only afterwards does their true nature become apparent."

Amerotke handed the cup back.

"So, the Lady Tiyea, when she drank from this goblet, she'd only taste wine?"

"I think so."

"So, the poison could have been infused secretly?"

"My lord, that's possible. Why do you ask?" The priest's voice became more clipped.

Amerotke gently caressed the dead woman's cheek.

"When you first came here, her face was painted, yes?"

"Agreed. My servants washed the corpse. That is the custom; some attempt to do this had occurred before I arrived."

"And the paint had been removed from her face?"

"Some of it, my lord."

"Her eyeshadow?"

Again the priest nodded.

"Her lips were carmined?"

"Yes, my lord."

Amerotke stared at the small holes in the ear lobes.

"And the Lady Tiyea was wearing jewellery?"

"Ear-studs, a necklace, bangles on her wrists and rings on her fingers."

"Was she in her nightgown?"

"No, my lord, still in the same linen robes she wore when she retired last night."

"Sandals on her feet?"

The priest grunted his assent.

"And how did they say she was lying?"

The priest gestured at the bed. "Half on, half off, as if she had gone to lie down, that's what they told me."

"But in her death agony," Amerotke finished. "She apparently turned and twisted. Was her dress stained?"

"Small traces of vomit here." The priest pointed. "On the collar and chest."

"So." Amerotke got to his feet and stared round the chamber. "Here we have a lady whose husband is absent in the city on business. According to the Divine One . . ."

"May her name be ever-lasting," the mortuary priest interrupted.

"Yes, quite." Amerotke smiled. "According to the Divine One, Lady Tiyea had been withdrawn, secretive, though no one knew the reason. Anyway," he declared, "she came into this chamber yesterday evening and prepared herself for bed. According to you." He playfully tapped the mortuary priest on the tip of the muzzle of the mask. "The Lady Tiyea followed the old custom, a woman who would prepare herself for bed like a bride does for her suitor. She would sit over there." Amerotke gestured at a stool near the perfume chest. "And use the bronze hand mirror to paint her face: green and black kohl around her eyes, paint her cheeks, and carmine her lips?"

"A red ochre," the priest agreed. "As is the fashion for the ladies of Thebes."

"Her bed would be prepared," Amerotke continued as if

talking to himself. "Apparently, according to custom, Lady Tiyea always drank Canaan wine before she retired for the night."

"Perhaps to help her sleep?" the priest added.

"Possibly."

Amerotke recalled how he would do the same, sitting on the roof of his house, cradling a goblet of wine as he savoured the cool night breezes and watched the sun dip in the far west.

"And this cup of wine was always brought by her maid Dedi?" Amerotke whispered. "The daughter of the Lady Tiyea's steward Intef. According to what you have told me, priest, Dedi brought up the cup of wine last night just before sunset and waited outside her lady's chamber. Lady Tiyea was downstairs in the garden cutting flowers." Amerotke pointed to the long wickerwork basket nestling in the corner. The flowers, carefully arranged, were already turning brown though they still exuded a rich perfume. "Lady Tiyea came upstairs with her flower basket and called for her wine. Now, our Dedi, and I have yet to question her, also liked Canaan wine: she took a generous sip from the goblet, then refilled it from a jug kept in the waiting room below." Amerotke held a hand up as a sign for silence. "Dedi brings up the wine. She takes another sip and hands it to Lady Tiyea's page, the young man, Nelet the Kushite."

"Agreed my lord."

"He, too, sipped the wine, whilst waiting for his mistress." Amerotke winked at Shufoy. "A common practice amongst servants." Amerotke closed his eyes. "So, the Lady Tiyea arrives," he continued. "Dedi brings in the wine. Both she and Nelet watch their mistress drink from the cup." Amerotke opened his eyes, the priest nodded in agreement. "She then puts the cup on the bedside table." Amerotke pointed to the round polished table of terebinth wood beside the bed. "She then chats to her servants for a while about going into the market early this morning. They leave. Lady Tiyea closes the door," Amerotke added, "pulling across the wooden bolts at the top and bottom. Dedi goes to her own quarters whilst Nelet sleeps on a reed mattress in the corridor outside."

Amerotke used his fingers to emphasize his points.

"First, we know no one else came into this chamber until early this morning when Lady Tiyea's corpse was found. Secondly, there is no other entrance to this chamber except that window but it's too high in the wall for anyone to enter. Thirdly, you have searched this chamber for the source of any poison but found none. I wish," Amerotke added in exasperation, "you would take that mask off, it's not necessary here."

The priest hurriedly complied, wiping the sweat from his lined, pock-marked cheeks.

"Good!" Amerotke stared into the priest's glittering eyes. "Now I know whom I am talking to. You are Maya, physician-priest in the House of Life at the temple of Anubis."

The judge stretched out his hand which the priest eagerly grasped.

"My lord, I did not realize you knew me?"

"I know of your reputation." Amerotke let go of his hand. "They say you have eyes as sharp as a hawk and wits as nimble as a mongoose."

Maya laughed, a high neighing sound.

"You searched this chamber?" Amerotke insisted.

"My lord, I worked according to the Book of Secrets kept in our temple. I followed the ritual laid down for investigating any mysterious death. I questioned the servants, I searched the chamber. The only poison I found was in that goblet." Maya gestured at the door, half-hanging on its leather hinges, resting against the lintel. "No one came through that door after Lady Tiyea retired. She did not leave." He nodded at the window, its latticed shutters thrown back. "They were closed, the bar across. Lady Tiyea did that herself as protection against the night flies. The outside wall is too steep to climb, whilst servants patrol the grounds. If anyone entered the gardens, or tried to approach the house, the alarm would have been raised."

"So." Amerotke went and sat on the sloping-backed chair, hands resting on his knees. He tapped his sandalled foot. "The Lady Tiyea bolted her door, closed the shutters on her window, perfumed and prepared her face and then, only the Goddess Ma'at knows the reason why, took a deadly poison and poured it into her wine. She must have taken a few gulps and lay down on that bed. She suffered a few convulsions and slipped into death." He glanced sharply at Maya. "Did the page boy hear anything?"

"He heard sounds," the priest confessed. "Footsteps, a loud sigh and some coughs but nothing which alarmed him."

"He was fast asleep?" Amerotke asked, staring teasingly at Shufoy. "Like servants tend to do."

"He slept well and deep'" the priest confirmed. "My lord, you are taking us down a darkened path; where does it lead?"

"Oh, to murder."

"Murder?" Maya exclaimed.

Shufoy watched his master's face, those unblinking eyes, the half-open mouth. You love this, Shufoy reflected, you love to turn things upside down and search out the truth like a woman sifting corn, winnowing away the chaff.

"Murder?" the priest repeated.

Amerotke paused at the sound of footsteps in the passage-way outside. He heard the gruff tones of Asural the chief of his temple police; another voice answered, more a whine than a request.

"Let him through!" Amerotke called.

The door was pushed aside and the thick-set figure of Asural entered, his bald pate gleaming with sweat. Amerotke could never understand why Asural insisted on wearing a quilted jerkin, war kilt and marching boots, a hard leather war-helmet in the crook of his arm, as if preparing for an attack by enemy war chariots.

"The lord of the house." Asural's fat face creased into a smile.

Meret, Lady Tiyea's husband, pushed by him into the room. A much younger man than Amerotke had expected with a thin, lean face and ever blinking eyes, lips pursed as if ready to object. Meret's face was smooth and clean-shaven, his eyes red-rimmed through weeping. He had cast ashes upon his balding head and rent his fine gauffered linen robe as a sign of mourning; his fingers were ink-stained and smudged with ash and dust. Amerotke went forward, grasped Meret's hands and bowed, the usual gesture when conveying condolences.

"The Divine One and the House of A Million Years are grief-stricken at your loss."

"Yes, yes, true." Meret murmured. "May the Divine One's name be ever blessed," he added, remembering protocol.

Amerotke nodded at Asural who left, closing the broken door behind him. Amerotke gestured to the leather sloping-backed chair. Meret took his seat, swaying slightly; Amerotke caught the sweetness of his wine-drenched breath. Meret opened his mouth to speak, eyes fixed on the corpse lying on the bed.

"She should be moved," he protested. "The day draws on."

"She will be moved." Amerotke took a seat on a stool, looking up at Meret. "But tell me what happened?"

"Yesterday afternoon I and three of my servants left. We took pack ponies. I have –" he gestured with his thumb "– a warehouse at the far end of the garden, it's where I keep . . ." Meret's voice stumbled. "The galena and malachite . . ."

"Yes, quite." Amerotke interrupted. "You buy from the Nubian mines as well as those out in the Red Lands?"

"The finest." Meret licked his dry lips. "I have the Divine One's personal warrant."

"Of course you do," Amerotke agreed. "The Divine One held your wife in great affection. You were telling me about the three servants and the pack ponies?"

"We left just after the heat of the day. I own workshops in the southern part of the city . . ."

Amerotke was aware that the mortuary priest had put on his mask and gone to crouch in the corner; Shufoy was gazing enviously at a beautiful ivory figurine of the Goddess Isis suckling the infant Horus.

"I have workshops," Meret repeated. "I stayed there all afternoon and most of the night. I never left. I had accounts to study . . ."

"Yes, yes," Amerotke soothed. "And you came back?"

"As soon as the city gates opened just before dawn; the conch horns were wailing as I passed through."

"And you returned with your servants and the pack ponies?"

"Yes. I have my own chambers at the far end of the house but I always visited my wife. I washed, changed my robes and anointed my head. I went downstairs to ensure all was well and then I came up here. Nelet the Kushite was fast asleep on his paliasse. I knocked on my wife's door."

"Did she always bolt it?" Amerotke asked.

"When I was away," Meret declared. "I became alarmed. I knocked but there was no answer. Nelet woke up. I told him to fetch Dedi and her father, our steward Intef. We all knocked and shouted. Nelet ran downstairs, outside he noticed the shutters were closed over. By now the house was roused, the servants came and we broke down the door." Meret put his face in his hands and sobbed quietly.

Amerotke stared across at a wall painting depicting a Saluki hound chasing an antelope deer. The hound was black as night: the artist had caught the ferocity and savagery of the beast's jaws as it closed on its hapless quarry. Am I like that, Amerotke thought, the Divine One's hound chasing the truth?

"And your wife was dead?"

Amerotke was sharper than he intended and he quietly cursed his own surliness yet that poor woman was dead and he was highly suspicious. Why should a woman adorn herself then commit suicide? Why should a lady make arrangements for the following day when she knew she would never see the sun rise or turn her face north to catch the cooling breath of Amun?

"I came in." Meret wiped his cheeks on the back of his hand, smudging the black kohl round his eyes. "The Lady Tiyea was sprawled half off the bed. The room was undisturbed, a bar across the shutters. I opened them and told the servants not to touch anything."

"Except your wife's corpse?"

"Yes. I couldn't leave her lying like that."

"Did you help?"

"Yes, I think I did. Or I supervised."

"Can you remember if her body was hardening or loose?" Amerotke demanded.

Meret looked at him quizziacally,

"Was your wife's body stiffening?"

Meret gnawed at his lip and nodded.

"So, she must have died many hours previously?"

"She had not donned her night attire," Meret replied.

"What was your wife's routine?" Amerotke asked.

"We would usually dine on the roof. Lady Tiyea often cooked supper. She was very good." Meret smiled. "And could bake the most fragrant-tasting bread, pure flour mingled with fruit juices. Afterwards she would tour the house, talk to our steward and servants and then come up here to her chamber."

"Did she always ask for a goblet of wine?"

"Invariably," Meret replied through his tears. "A goblet of the best Canaan, a small indulgence. She said it soothed her mind and helped her sleep."

"Did she need such help?"

Meret narrowed his eyes. "No, no."

"She took no opiates," Amerotke insisted. "No special powders?"

"Nothing. She was not a wine drinker," Meret added, "but rather sipped and enjoyed its fragrance. I cannot remember her ever finishing a goblet."

"Continue," Amerotke insisted.

"She would wash her hands and face." Meret nodded at the large water jug standing on a table next to a bowl, thick linen napkins folded neatly beside them. "She always prepared herself for bed by . . ." Meret shrugged. "Like many women of the palace, she would beautify herself." He gestured at the ornately carved cosmetic box. "She was always interested in perfumes and creams."

"I know." Amerotke smiled. "I believe she taught the Divine One when she was a girl."

"She would then put on a necklace, ear-studs and rings," Meret continued as if he hadn't heard this interruption. "Sometimes she would play Semet against herself, or do some embroidery or study the accounts. Only then would she change into her night attire."

"But last night she didn't?" Amerotke held up his hand, fingers splayed. "Last night she painted her face and, whilst she did so, drank the wine. Or shall I say the poison?" The Judge allowed the silence to hang heavy. "Now, why should she do that?"

Meret's head went down.

"Was your marriage happy?"

"I loved my wife, my lord; she loved me."

"You had no children?"

"The physicians told her she would never conceive."

"She was considerably older than you?" Amerotke asked.

Meret's head came up. "Yes, we met in the House of Life at the Temple of Osiris. She had gone to consult a manuscript on the making of perfumes. I was there to study the sacred writings, a new form of smelting which the priests had learnt from the Hittites."

"So, your marriage was happy and your business prosperous?"

Meret gestured with his hands. "You have seen our house, my lord, a mansion which anyone would envy."

"But your wife was withdrawn, quiet during the days before her death?"

"She was not happy," Meret confirmed, "with our servants. Dedi the maid had helped herself to some of her perfumes whilst our steward Intef," Meret breathed in noisily, "our steward is a good man with an inordinate passion for wine."

"And the Kushite page?"

"Nelet is as mischievous as a monkey. He was for ever baiting the tame baboon my wife kept in the gardens."

"So, your wife had exchanged harsh words with all three?"

"The Lady Tiyea managed the house." Meret retorted. "She kept the accounts and was vigilant in all she did. She always said —" Meret clicked his tongue, fighting back tears. "She always said people should live in the truth, that the truth would bring them peace."

Amerotke just stared down at the ring displaying the symbol of Ma'at.

"Did she now?" he whispered. "Was your lady devout?"

"She visited the temples. She paid the mortuary priests. We were preparing a tomb across the Nile in the Necropolis."

Amerotke pushed back the stool.

"So, when you came into this room nothing was disturbed?"

"My lord, ask the servants. Nothing was out of place." Meret pointed to the bedside table of polished terebinth. "The wine cup was there; the steward Intef picked it up and sniffed it. I heard him exclaim."

"So, he was the first to detect that the wine was tainted?"

"Yes, my lord."

"Was this immediately – as soon as you entered the chamber?"

"Oh, no, some time later; at first we thought my wife had suffered a seizure."

"So, what made you think otherwise?"

"After we had rearranged the –" Meret broke off. "My wife's corpse, I asked my servants what had happened the previous evening. What my wife had done, what she had ate and drank." He pulled a face. "Eventually we came to the wine."

"Did anyone bring anything into this room, and that includes yourself?"

Meret shook his head. "No, I would have remembered that. Ask my servants. We concentrated on forcing the door."

"Are you sure?" Amerotke insisted.

"My lord, ask the servants."

"Did you see anyone go towards that cup before Intef raised the alarm?"

Again the shake of the head.

"And what happened then?"

"My wife's body was stiffening, very slightly. Her face looked ghastly; the paint she'd put on made it look worse. A white froth stained her lips. I told the servants to look after her. Dedi took a wet rag and wiped her face till I stopped her. I sent couriers to the Temple of Anubis."

Amerotke glanced at the priest. "And you came here?"

"I prepared the corpse, as well as I could," the muffled

voice replied. "My lord, the body must now be taken to the House of Purification."

Amerotke walked back to the bed: he stared pitifully down at this poor woman who had tried to live in the truth.

"But it did not bring you peace," he whispered.

"My lord?" Shufoy rose to his feet.

Amerotke ignored him as he studied the dead woman's face. The discolouration of the skin was progressing; the dark purplish hue staining the cheeks and eyelids had deepened and her lips were cracked and swollen.

"I want to examine the corpse."

He ignored Meret's exclamation. The mortuary priest hurried across and gently removed the linen robe and the loin cloth beneath. Lady Tiyea's corpse was now puffy, the stomach distended and discoloured yet, Amerotke reasoned, when she was young Lady Tiyea must have been beautiful. The priest treated the corpse gently like a mother would a babe, turning it over. Amerotke ignored Meret's half-hearted pleas.

"I have to do it," he explained over his shoulder.

However, apart from the odd spot and pimple, the corpse, despite the effect of the poison, was unmarked.

"It was the wine," the mortuary priest whispered.

"Take it away" Amerotke ordered.

He walked to the window, pulled open the shutters and stared down. Below stretched a cobbled yard and then a high wall which separated the mansion from the gardens beyond. Nelet the Kushite was feeding scraps of food to a greying baboon which squatted like an old man, eagerly snatching the food and tossing it into his mouth. Amerotke remained watching as the mortuary priest's helpers came in, covered the corpse, wrapping it from head to toe in linen bands, then they were gone.

Amerotke turned. Meret still sat slumped in his chair. Shufoy had now picked up the figurine and was examining it carefully. Amerotke walked across to the cosmetic box, picked it up and, carrying it over to the bed, emptied out its contents. There was a leather bag with a wig of human hair with fibre padding, enriched and sweetened with beeswax: alabaster jars of precious unguents and ointments, pouches of powder, creams smelling of fruit and flowers in full bloom: tiny shell caskets containing green and black eye kohl: silver sticks with bulbous ends for the Lady Tiyea to use when painting her face: pots of perfume, as well as small alabaster jars, their caps carved in the shapes of ducks' heads, containing face paints. Finally, small ivory caskets of red ochre for the lips. Amerotke, half-aware of the noises from the house, carefully scrutinised each container.

Lady Tiyea was prudent: she always finished one jar before she opened another. Most of them were sealed and fresh so, by process of elimination, Amerotke could lay out in a row those jars and pots of cosmetics she had used the night before. He sniffed at each carefully and half smiled; their fragrances recalled his own wife Norfret, yet he could find nothing untoward. He then went across to the table and picked up the bronze mirror, highly polished, its handle in the form of a papyrus plant. Amerotke stared into it. He recalled the ancient legend how a mirror, left near a murder victim, if held up and a prayer was invoked, would reflect the assassin's face. Amerotke smiled and put the mirror down. He was sure this was murder yet could not give the reason why or produce a shred of evidence, except a sharp feeling of disquiet, a deep unease.

He went back and sat on the bed and examined the small leather perfume pouches, their necks tied with pieces of silver cord. He opened each of these and sniffed carefully: again the sweet odours of crushed flowers, minerals and fruits. He picked up one pouch embroidered with a symbol of the Goddess Isis. He undid this, sniffed and immediately drew back. Shufoy, alarmed, came hurrying across, still clutching the figurine. Meret also broke from his grief-stricken reverie.

"My lord?"

Amerotke took the figurine from Shufoy's hand, laid it on the bed and handed the pouch to his manservant.

"I suspect that's the poison," Amerotke declared.

Meret came over and snatched the pouch from Shufoy.

"Be careful!" Amerotke warned.

The copper merchant sniffed and thrust the pouch back.

"She must have bought it. She always did that!" Meret exclaimed. "She bought perfume powders from different merchants: she made those pouches herself."

"Did you know she'd bought poison?"

"Of course not!"

"You may leave."

Meret made to object but retreated before Amerotke's stern gaze. The Judge waited until Asural had pulled across the battered door and listened to the footsteps recede.

"Master, you said it was murder? That mortuary priest was intrigued."

"He's not the only one."

Amerotke sat down in the chair vacated by Meret. Shufoy came over and stood looking at him, hands on his hips, shaggy eyebrows pulled together, emphasizing the ugly scar where his nose had been.

"I dreamt last night that I was riding a female hippopotamus. A heset, a dancing girl, sat behind me, her full breasts pressing into my back. I recognized that . . ."

"As the result of too much wine and spiced goose," Amerotke laughed.

Shufoy smiled. Amerotke was a hard taskmaster but he had a gentleness which eventually surfaced and now it had.

"Why murder, master?"

"Some evil spirit out of the west," Amerotke murmured. "That's what murder is, Shufoy. An evil spirit which possesses someone and turns their mind to bloody work but, for what?"

"Very lyrical," Shufoy exclaimed. "But why do you suspect that about the Lady Tiyea? What evidence is there? That's what you are always asking in court."

Amerotke tapped his chest. "We are not just flesh and blood, Shufoy. We have a Ka, a spirit. Perhaps the Lady Tiyea's Ka still remains here. Perhaps she has not begun her journey to the Far Horizon."

Shufoy gazed in astonishment at his master who was usually ever so practical and pragmatic.

"Evidence," Amerotke remarked. "I don't know: Lady Tiyea was beautifying herself for her husband, not for death. She was preparing for today not for the eternal tomorrow. Moreover, Lady Tiyea lived in the truth. She was practical, assertive, according to the Divine One, of indomitable will. Why should she slink into her room, bar the door, pour poison into her wine and slip into eternal night? What reason is there?"

"Very well. Very well." Shufoy tapped his foot, a favourite gesture of Amerotke in court. "If we can't answer the question why, then how? The door was bolted. The wine, when it was brought in here, was untainted. We know that. The door was locked from the inside and never opened until it was forced. No secret entrances exist. No one came through that window. The poison smells disgusting, as did the wine."

Amerotke snapped his fingers. "Oh, mannikin! Oh, my little mongoose! Fetch me a goblet of wine. The best from the black soil of Canaan."

Shufoy, surprised, hurried away. Amerotke sprang to his feet and walked excitedly up and down the chamber. Shufoy came hurrying back; the drinking bowl he carried, slopping with wine, had stained his robe. Amerotke took the pouch of poison and shook out one of its small pellets or cakes: it lay, a dark, sinister bead in the palm of his hand. He took another one and dropped them both into the wine bowl where they quickly dissolved. Amerotke sniffed carefully, so close Shufoy became agitated.

"Nothing!" Amerotke hissed. He thrust the wine bowl at Shufoy. "Would you drink that?"

"If I didn't know what you had poured in!" Shufoy exclaimed. "As you may know, I find it difficult to smell!"

The dwarf went to the window and poured out the wine, ignoring the exclamations of surprise from below.

"Sorry!" the mannikin bellowed, then threw the bowl after it and listened as it smashed on the cobbles beneath. "Well, master." Shufoy's eyes widened. "We know that for a while the poison remains tasteless. You could say that's why Lady Tiyea chose it."

"Or the assassin," Amerotke declared.

Shufoy pulled a face. Amerotke stared at the cosmetic jars on the bed.

"No one brought any poisons in after Lady Tiyea was found . . ."

"What do you mean?" Shufoy asked.

"So she could have been killed by other means yet . . ." Amerotke's voice faltered. "Shufoy, let me speak to the servants."

Amerotke rearranged the room, placing cushions on the floor and pushing the leather-backed chair up before them. His manservant returned, followed by Intef, Dedi and Nelet. The steward was as plump as a plum, his head bald, his fat face heavily oiled: the large kohl rings around his eyes were smudged due to crying. He was dressed in an embroidered robe, rent and stained with ash as a sign of mourning. He was apparently unused to moving quickly for he wheezed and coughed as he plumped himself down on the cushions and glared at Amerotke. Amerotke found it difficult to believe that Dedi was his daughter: she was slim, dark-faced; her hair, parted in the middle, fell down to her shoulders, framing a pretty but sharp face. She was hard-eyed, her generous mouth twisted in a grimace as if she was ready to argue. Amerotke reckoned she must be sixteen or seventeen summers old. Nelet was apparently her friend; the Kushite youth had a cheeky, plump face under a shock of black hair; his dark eyes seemed to regard everything as amusing. Neither he nor Dedi showed any signs of ritual mourning. They stood before Amerotke and waited for his sign to sit then they bowed and did so. Intef kept blowing out his lips like a landed fish.

"You seem troubled, master steward?"

Intef screwed up his eyes in annoyance.

"I have heard the whispers," he rasped.

"What whispers?"

"They say I drove my mistress to suicide and all because I drank too many cups of wine."

"I don't think your mistress committed suicide." Amerotke rearranged his robe and leaned forward, hands resting on his knees. "I believe your mistress was murdered."

All three stared back, eyes rounded in amazement, mouths gaping.

"But that's impossible!" Intef breathed. "My lord," he gabbled, beringed fingers fluttering before his face, "who could have put the poison in the wine?"

"I didn't!" Dedi screeched, one hand going to rest on Nelet's shoulder.

"Hush, now," Amerotke soothed. "Think, why should your mistress commit suicide? True, she had arguments with you, yes?"

They all nodded.

"But she was withdrawn, quiet in the days leading up to her death?"

"Yes," Dedi whispered. "Yes, she was. Yet, before you ask, my lord, we don't know the reasons why."

"And last night?" Amerotke insisted.

Both Dedi and Intef gabbled out their story. How Dedi had brought the wine up and, as customary, had taken a deep sip as she always loved the taste of Canaan wine. Nelet had also taken a drink. Their mistress had then come up and they had taken the cup into the chamber. They had placed the cup on the bedside table and seen Lady Tiyea drink from it.

"And she suffered no ill effects?"

"No," Nelet yelped.

Amerotke watched the maid and page carefully. He suspected they had a great deal to hide but, whether it was relevant to the murder . . . Intef, too, looked discomfited.

"Had your mistress threatened you with dismissal?"

Intef glanced away.

"She had, hadn't she?" Amerotke insisted. "You for your drinking, Intef, and your daughter for helping herself to her mistress's cosmetics. She also informed you that, if you were dismissed, you would be excluded from any inheritance in her will which is lodged in the sacred vessels of a temple in the city."

All three just gazed fearfully back.

"So, why did you believe your mistress committed suicide after she'd sat you down and talked about the arrangements for today?"

Again the silence. Amerotke stared at the latticed window shutters.

"And you, Nelet, you are sure, no one came through that door?"

"My lord, that would have been impossible."

"And, master steward, the outside window?"

"Too high," Intef flustered. "Whilst servants patrol the grounds at night."

"Very good." Amerotke played with the Ma'at ring on his finger. "So, the master comes up, the alarm is raised, the door is forced. All three of you . . . ?"

"And other servants," Intef added.

"Whatever," Amerotke continued. "All of you accompanied your master into the room? What happened then?"

"He went straight to the bed." Intef wiped the sweat from his plump, wrinkled neck. "Meret stared down at his wife and felt her throat for the pulse of life. He started to cry. We all gathered round him."

"Who first looked at the wine cup?"

Both Nelet and Dedi turned to stare at the steward, who shrugged and spread his hands.

"That was some time later. I . . ."

"Did any of you bring anything into the room?"

"Nothing."

"How was your mistress lying?" Amerotke asked.

"Her head was twisted," Nelet replied. "A white froth stained her mouth; her face looked ghastly. I hardly recognized it. Eyes glassy and staring, her skin a strange colour. She looked like a dog snarling."

"And you heard no sounds during the night?"

"I heard my mistress move around. I heard her cough but I thought there was nothing wrong."

"What happened this morning?" Amerotke asked.

"There was a great deal of confusion," Intef declared. "People milling around. I sniffed the wine. It was clearly tainted. My master sent messages into the city and told my daughter to make his wife –" He paused. "Make his wife presentable."

"I washed her hands and face," Dedi explained. "Then the master told me to leave it until the mortuary priest arrived."

"Did Meret love his wife?"

"My lord." Intef drew himself up as if shocked by the question. "They loved each other dearly. They were important people."

"No animosity or quarrels?"

"Not that I know of," Dedi declared weakly.

Amerotke breathed out and stared up at the polished cedarwood ceiling.

"You may go," He whispered.

The Judge sat motionless as all three, whispering amongst themselves, left the bed chamber.

"Will the great Judge share his thoughts?" Shufoy pulled a stool up.

"The great Judge," Amerotke replied drily, "may look wise and solemn but I feel like a bird blown by the wind."

"You didn't ask them about the poison?"

"That's not the problem, Shufoy: the bag of poison was put in the perfume chest after Lady Tiyea died."

"Why?"

"If you are going to commit suicide, Shufoy, do you take a pouch of poison, open it, pour some into the goblet then carefully retie the sack and replace it in the cosmetic box so it's difficult to find? I don't believe that. If Lady Tiyea committed suicide, I suspect the poison would have been found beside the cup. Moreover, if she intended to die, she would have drunk all the wine."

Amerotke got to his feet and walked back to the cosmetic jars lying on the bed.

"Well, you did say she was a tidy lady?"

"Not that tidy."

Amerotke stared at those pots Lady Tiyea must have used the night before: the kohl, the face paint and powders, the red ochre for her lips. He studied the latter carefully; it was blood-red and gave off the most cloying smell. Amerotke dabbed a little on his lips and hastily regretted it; the taste was too rich, like over-sweet honey.

"Shufoy, go downstairs, take Dedi aside. Ask her to find the rags used to clean her mistress's corpse, bring them up here."

"She must have thrown them away."

"I don't think so." Amerotke lifted his head and smiled. "She's all agog with excitement." He pointed across at the water jug. "I think she used some of those napkins. So go, please!"

Shufoy hurried off. Amerotke put his face in his hands and thought.

"Live in the truth," he whispered.

He imagined Lady Tiyea coming in here, a proud but very devout woman: one who would not take her life easily or give it up so readily. "She sits on that stool," Amerotke murmured. "And begins to paint her face." He recalled his wife doing the same and smiled at the thought; the Lady Norfret also prepared her face before retiring for the night and, if she was in a temper, would take longer than usual.

"I can imagine you, Lady Tiyea, getting up, sipping at the wine and the venom." He paused. "The venom courses through your blood; you cough, you splutter. You are too proud to call for help. You think it's something passing so you lie on the bed." Amerotke took his hands away. He had sat long enough in the Hall of Two Truths to recognize that some poisons would act in the space of a few heartbeats. Death came swiftly like a plunging hawk. "But it can't have been the wine?" Amerotke murmured. He picked out one of the poison pellets and began to experiment, keeping his back to the door.

Shufoy burst into the room, carrying a leather bucket.

"I found these. You were right, master. Dedi put them here to be washed later."

Amerotke replaced the pellet and gingerly pulled the cloths out. He laid them over the top of the coffer, three in all; two were dry, one was still wet. The maid must have dipped one cloth into the water to clean the face and neck of her mistress's corpse and used the other two to dry her. Amerotke noted the different colours: the blackish-green of the eye kohl, the cream and powder used on the cheeks and the ochre stains from the lips. He then brought across the cosmetic jars and, ignoring

Shufoy's questions, again studied them most carefully before picking up a fresh napkin and taking a sample from each pot. He placed the fourth napkin on the ground before the coffer.

"Oh, Ma'at be praised!" he murmured, carefully washing his hands. "Shufoy, go downstairs, bring me a fresh cup of wine and ask Dedi to stay outside the door."

Shufoy hastened off whilst Amerotke went back to his studies. He was still staring at the stains on the napkin when Shufoy returned, chattering away to Dedi as if she was a long-lost friend.

"Bring her in!" Amerotke called. "No, on second thoughts." He came and pushed the door aside. "Shufoy, put the wine on the table."

The mannikin did so even as he heard his master quietly questioning Dedi before dismissing her. Amerotke re-entered the room, apparently pleased with himself, smiling and rubbing his hands. He took one of the poisoned pellets, dropped it into the bowl of wine and, grasping Shufoy by the shoulder, made him walk over and tidy the sheets on the bed.

"I have always wanted to be a maid," Shufoy grumbled.

Amerotke straightened up. "Well, there's one ambition realized. Now, Shufoy, bring me the wine." Amerotke squinted across the room. "Not immediately! Count how many pieces of furniture are here and then do so."

Shufoy sighed noisily but obeyed: he went across and brought the wine for Amerotke to sniff.

"Faugh!" He drew away. "Now it smells noxious!"

"Master, what is this about?"

"Ask Meret to join us."

"But . . . ?"

"Ask him to join us," Amerotke repeated quietly.

Shufoy was away for some time; he returned, huffing and puffing, Meret following behind him.

You are arrogant, Amerotke thought, like all assassins. You believe you can wipe away a life as you do a stain on your cloak.

"What is all this?" Meret blustered. "Your servant is running up and down my house like a mouse chased by the cat."

"No, he's the mouse sent down by the cat. Meret, you are my quarry."

The merchant's chin sagged.

"You are a murderer," Amerotke continued. "You murdered your wife!"

"But what . . . ?" Meret flustered.

"Why, sir, the truth!"

Amerotke pushed him on the shoulder, making him sit down on the stool and squatted before him, his face very close. Meret had paled, his breathing was short, panicky.

"How could I murder my wife?"

"Oh, by going to Thebes and pretending that your wife, well –" Amerotke waved a hand "– her humours were so disturbed that she decided to end everything and poured poison into her goblet. Or, if that failed, perhaps one of the servants would be blamed? But unlike you, sir, your servants loved the Lady Tiyea. They had their differences but their souls were not governed by the red-haired Seth; their hearts had not turned to murder, not like you. What was the cause, eh? You married Lady Tiyea for her money and wealth but you have another woman, a heset girl, some courtesan in the city to entertain you during your travels?"

Meret swallowed hard.

"Did the Lady Tiyea find out but she was too proud, too reserved to show her temper, to confront you openly? Nevertheless, she was powerful; things may not have gone well with you so you decided to poison her. You bought some ochre for her lips, a small alabaster pot, as well as pellets of a powerful poison, a deadly venom, little dried cakes which could be sprinkled into the cream. Yes?"

Meret stared bleakly back.

"Yesterday afternoon before you left, you took Lady Tiyea's pot of red ochre and stirred in the poison; the grains are so fine they wouldn't be noticed. I have just done the same myself. Perfumes need oil or fat to absorb the fragrance of flowers, minerals or fruits. This oil or fat works like water does on powder; the fragrance and the poison become one. You crushed one of those pellets, stirring it in until it was fully mingled. Perhaps to ensure it was deadly enough, more was added. Perfumes, especially lip salves, have a very heady fragrance; this would mask any noxious taste, at least until it was too late. Well," Amerotke continued. "Lady Tiyea carmined her lips and what do women do afterwards, Meret? They press their lips together, they wet their mouths, lick their lips. Lady Tiyea would do this as she wiped her fingers clean." Amerotke paused. "Our lips are sensitive: anyone who has been out in the Red Lands, desperate for water, will tell you that. The poison was not only drunk by the Lady Tiyea, it also pierced the thin skin of her lips to wreak its hideous effect."

"But this poisoned dust would smell?" Meret stuttered; he closed his eyes as he realized his mistake.

"You seem to know a lot about this poison," Amerotke retorted. "I have mentioned it but you haven't examined it. How do you know it crumbles to dust so quickly? How do you know the grains dissolve in the wetness of the lip paint, as they do in wine or water? You should know this because you practised. Now, yesterday afternoon, you took that alabaster jar of red lip ochre and laced it with poison, stirring it in with a small stick until the grains crumbled and became one with the lip paint. Lady Tiyea followed her usual routine. She tended to her household but, of course, she was distracted. Her maid brings up the goblet of wine. Lady Tiyea tastes it; of course it's untainted. She then goes over to her cosmetics, coats her lips with that poison and drinks a little more wine; that would only help the venom. Any traces left in her mouth would be washed down her throat. She becomes ill and dies hideously. A quick-acting poison, one that takes its effect in a few heartbeats like the bite of some snake. Perhaps no more time than it would take Shufoy to go downstairs and come back up again. The Kushite page Nelet hears her cough and splutter as she moves across to the bed to lie down. However, Lady Tiyea was past help. A few spasms, convulsions, and she's dead. You return from Thebes where you have been at your workshops, the busy merchant, the loyal husband. No business with any dancing girl or courtesan that night? You want your servants to be able to guarantee where you were and what you did."

Meret began to tremble. Amerotke touched him lightly on the back of his hand; it was ice cold.

"You then acted the concerned husband. The door is forced and you come in with the servants. You are carrying nothing but two small poison pellets in the palm of your hand. Lady Tiyea used that bedside table to place her wine cup on. You simply passed your hand over the cup; in the confusion no one would notice. You yourself said your wife never finished her evening wine. Even if she had, these tiny pellets would easily dissolve in the dregs. Anyway, the poison dissolves whilst you continue to act the grieving husband, distracting the rest. Only some time later does Intef smell the cup; the poison has made itself felt and that would be regarded as the cause of your unfortunate wife's death." Amerotke paused.

"People see and understand what they want to see and understand. A woman lies poisoned on her bed, a cup of tainted wine beside her. You have both cause and effect. Everyone is concerned. How could Lady Tiyea's wine be poisoned by anyone except herself? They will concentrate on that. Lady Tiyea's dead." Amerotke raised his hand to emphasize his points. "Next to a cup of poisoned wine. True, the possibility existed that the servants may have been involved. Yet, and here's a real mystery, how could anyone enter a room which was bolted and barred not to mention guarded?

"The inevitable conclusion is that Lady Tiyea took her own life. They would forget the minor details which surrounded the discovery of her corpse. You order Dedi to prepare your wife's body. She did what any maid would do. The poison had discoloured your wife's face, making it look ghastly; a white froth stained her lips. Dedi takes a napkin, soaks it in water, wipes away the face paint, the carmined lips, the white froth and, in doing so, diminishes the only possible source of an alternative theory. You, of course, master of the house, can come in and out. You pretend to tidy up the cosmetics. You seize the lip cream which you have poisoned and replace it with another, making it look as if that was the one used by

Lady Tiyea before her unfortunate death. You also tell Dedi to leave your wife's corpse. After all, the mortuary priest will be arriving soon and that was his task. No one will remember you doing these little things: the Lady Tiyea is dead and they have the cause so why should anyone recall the minor details? You are her husband, the master of the house; you are full of sadness, moving round the chamber as any grief-stricken husband would.

"You made one mistake. A rather stupid one." Amerotke pointed to the napkins. "I examined the cloths Dedi used. The lip paint she removed, although discoloured by the milky froth from your poor wife's mouth, was a light red, almost pink like the sky just before dawn. However, the pot I examined this morning contained a cream which was blood-red in colour."

"This," Meret stuttered, "is ridiculous!"

"No, it's not." Amerotke shook his head. "My servant Shufoy is an expert rodent-catcher. He'll take that cloth for the one Dedi used and cut out the stains of the lip cream. He'll smear it with cheese or milk, catch a mouse or rat and watch it eat. I am sure enough poison remains to kill the vermin." Amerotke rose to his feet and went across and picked up the corner of the stained napkin between two fingers. "Or, there again, Meret, you could prove your innocence by licking those stains. Why do you object? They have only been used on your dead wife's lips."

Meret lowered his head.

"Or I could call the servants back," Amerotke continued conversationally. "Perhaps I'll ask them to reflect most carefully on what exactly happened when you came into this room? Did anyone of them notice you put your hand over the cup as you approached your wife's corpse? They'll certainly remember you moving round this chamber after you'd sent messengers into the city. Dedi, perhaps, will recall your clearing certain items away. She might begin to wonder, as I did, why you asked her to tend the Lady Tiyea's corpse but later told her to stop."

Amerotke smiled bleakly. "In other words, the petty, aimless gestures of a grieving husband could assume a more sinister significance." Amerotke leaned even closer. "I could also send for the mortuary priest who is busy in the House of Purification. By now the embalming process must be under way. I will ask him to study your wife's lips. I am sure he will discover how blistered and chapped the skin has become. He'll certainly recall the books he studied in the House of Life, how many poisons are very quick-acting, fatal even if held in the mouth and softened by its juices. And then," Amerotke sighed. "I'll become busy. Someone in the city must have sold you such a lethal poison. They'll remember it well. They'll claim they thought they were selling it to keep down vermin in the house: that's the story they'll tell me, in return for the large reward offered. I'll send out criers into the market squares. The Divine One herself will offer rewards and this young lady of yours, and I am sure there is some young lady, will realize that debens of silver and gold are better than your caresses. You are an assassin," Amerotke concluded. "You killed your wife because you were tired of her, because she stood in your way. Lady Tiyea tried to live in the truth; her death cannot be hidden behind a lie. . . ."

"Or there again," Shufoy interrupted briskly, "you could be questioned by the Divine One's interrogators in the House of Death."

Meret's shoulders began to shake.

"I am only beginning," Amerotke hissed. "But in the end, the truth will emerge! You killed Lady Tiyea, didn't you? Her Ka demands the truth!"

Meret nodded.

"What will happen to me?" he bleated.

Amerotke stared back, stony-faced.

"You could make a full confession." He shrugged. "And face the justice of Pharaoh." He picked up the goblet from the table and held it before Meret. "Or you can drink the wine . . .?"

MURDER IN
THE LAND OF WAWAT

Lauren Haney

We are still in the reign of Hatshepsut, but now we are far to the south of Egypt in the fortress town of Buhen, in Nubia, which was then called Wawat. Lauren Haney is the pen name of Betty Winkelman, a former worker in the aerospace industry, who now indulges her interest in ancient Egypt with a highly praised series featuring Lieutenant Bak, head of the Medjay police. The books in the series so far are The Right Hand of Amon *(1997)*, A Face Turned Backward *(1999)*, A Vile Justice *(1999)*, A Curse of Silence *(2000)* and A Place of Darkness *(2001)*.

"**L**ieutenant Bak!"

Bak, officer in charge of the Medjay police, glanced up from the scroll he was reading, the week's compilation of entries taken from the daybook kept by the commandant of the fortress of Buhen.

A boy of 11 or 12 years burst through the opening at the top of the stairs and onto the rooftop of the guardhouse, where the police were quartered and prisoners were kept. The youth was sturdy of body and deeply tanned by the sun; his skin was dusted with fine sand and his kilt stained with sweat and dirt. He bent half over, holding his side. Gasping for breath, he said, "You must . . . come . . . right away . . . sir."

"Go away, Mery." Hori, the police scribe, a pudgy youth a

mere few years older than the boy, waved him away. "Can't you see we're busy?"

Bak took one look at Mery's face, scowled a reprimand. "Silence, Hori."

Clutching his side, breathing hard, Mery hastened to the pavilion beneath which Bak and Hori sat. "A man's been . . . slain, sir."

The shelter, a sturdy affair with a shaggy palm-frond roof, was open on all four sides, allowing the cool early morning breeze to waft through. A quiet, comfortable place to read and write reports before the hot breath of the lord Re reached into the city inside the tall mudbrick walls of the fortress. Painted stark white, towered for strength, the stronghold's crenellated battlements looked down upon an orderly grid of building blocks, barracks, storehouses, and the walled mansion of the lord Horus of Buhen, the local version of the falcon god. The fortress was the largest and most important in Wawat, a land south of Kemet held close in the heart of Maatkare Hatshepsut because of the gold found in its desert wastes.

Muttering an oath, Bak let the ends of the scroll roll together, tossed it into a basket of similar documents, and scrambled to his feet. "Who is he, Mery?" With a permanent population of slightly more than four hundred people, the question was reasonable. Everyone knew everyone else.

"A foreigner, from the looks of him. A man from far to the north."

"A stranger, then. A trader."

The boy shrugged.

"You found him where?" Bak asked, though he could guess easily enough from the brownish yellow dust coating Mery's skin and clothing.

"We were playing in the old tombs, sir. He's in one of them."

Bak summoned his Medjay sergeant Imsiba, a tall, powerfully built man, lithe of gait and sharp of eye. Soon the two of them and Mery were hurrying out of the twin-towered gate, leaving the citadel behind, and striding along the broad, sun-struck thoroughfare that joined the gate behind them to the even larger, desert-facing gate that pierced the massive peripheral wall. Passing the jumble of interconnected houses that formed the outer city, they veered off the street to cross an open stretch of sand to a low shelf of rock that marked the site of an ancient ruined cemetery.

Mounds of rubble and broken mudbrick walls, the tops of low structures built many generations earlier, protruded from sand blown against the face of the shelf. Gaping holes and stairways partially covered with wind-driven grit led to black cavities in the earth. The outer wall of the city loomed over the sandy waste, allowing the sentries on the battlements to look down in idle curiosity.

A half dozen boys close to Mery in age, all as sturdily built as he and as dirty, sat in a cluster on overturned pots and heaps of tumbled bricks. They were the sons of an ever-increasing number of soldiers and scribes who thought the southern frontier safe enough to bring their families. Spotting the newcomers, the boys leaped to their feet and ran to meet them, all chattering at once, the shock of finding a dead man far outweighed by the excitement of discovery.

With Mery leading the way and the rest of the children straggling behind, they walked along the rocky shelf, past broken walls and collapsed roofs, toppled memorial tablets and crushed burial jars, towards a rock-cut stairway enclosed by what looked like a low mudbrick wall of irregular height but which was actually the remains of a vaulted roof. A rectangular black hole at the bottom beckoned.

Imsiba lighted the torch they had brought and they plunged down the dozen rough steps to the low, narrow doorway. Bak ducked down and held the torch inside, examining the walls and ceiling for cracks, the floors for chunks of rock fallen from above, signs that the ceiling was close to collapse. He had suggested more than once that the boys play elsewhere. They had countered by pointing at the sentries atop the walls, who could summon help in an instant.

The tomb was slightly longer than a man was tall, not quite as wide, and barely high enough to stand erect. Chisel marks pocked its rough-cut walls, but it was otherwise unadorned. If a body had been placed inside when newly dug, it had long ago vanished. Now a fresh burial had been made, a casual interment at best.

The fleshy body lay half on its side, arms askew, legs outstretched. The usual smell of hot, dry earth was smothered by the odours of sweat and stale beer, of defecation and the metallic smell of blood. Black hair, held off the man's face by a white band around his head, would have hung nearly to his shoulders when he stood erect. His dark beard had been cut to a point. He wore a long-sleeved, ankle-length white tunic, with a broad wrap of red-fringed white fabric bound around his ample stomach and hips. His seal ring, the torque around his neck, and the bracelets on both arms were of heavy gold. Their presence hinted at a reason for death other than robbery.

A dagger projected just below his breastbone. Blood had spurted out, staining the tunic but not the dust-covered rock floor beneath him. A clear indication that he had been slain elsewhere and carried into the tomb. Sucking in his breath, doing what he had to do, Bak gripped the hilt and pulled the weapon free. The bronze blade was ordinary. Strips of leather, shiny from wear, had been wound around the handle.

Bak examined the floor of the small space. He found many scuffed footprints, but none distinct enough to recognize later should he come upon them. Glimpsing something whitish in a corner, he scooped it up. A knucklebone. Had the boys tired of playing hide and seek or chasing make-believe tribesmen through the tombs and begun to play games of chance?

Imsiba bent closer and stared at the face. "I've seen this man before, my friend. Yesterday evening it was, shortly before nightfall. Entering Nofery's house of pleasure with three other men."

"I remember him," Nofery growled. "How could I forget so vile a man?"

"Who was he?" Bak asked.

The obese old woman, her expression stormy, handed jars

of beer to him and the sergeant. "He was called Ben-Azan. A trader. A man from Retenu, so his name proclaimed, but he'd long ago washed away the remnants of his birth and childhood, thinking himself a man of the world."

Bak settled on one of the dozen or so low stools in the dark, dingy room. Beer vats and baskets piled high with smaller jars lined one wall. A low table held a multitude of drinking bowls, many cracked and chipped. The room reeked of stale beer and sweat, reminding him of the tomb, and a mix of other odours hinting of sex and vomit. Dust motes danced in the slab of light entering through the open doorway. Nofery was his spy, one who enjoyed sly games to gain an advantage. Not this time, he could see.

Imsiba drew a stool close and sat down beside him. "He was passing through Buhen?"

"I thank the lord Amun he had no plans to stay."

Bak broke the dried mud plug from his jar and, taking care not to stir up the gritty sediment, eyed her curiously while he sipped the bitter brew. She usually turned a blind eye to her customers' faults. What had Ben-Azan done to antagonize her? "Was he travelling to north or south, did you hear?"

"Who could not have heard?" she said with a sneer. "He was returning to his homeland, well pleased with himself."

"He'd had a successful trading expedition, I assume."

"From the way he gloated, he left no doubt of his masterful dealings with those poor, ignorant tribesmen in the land of Kush."

Poor and ignorant? Bak doubted the words were hers; she must be quoting Ben-Azan. The river running through Kush and Wawat served as a major trade route along which exotic products highly valued by the royal house of Kemet were transported from far to the south. From what he had heard, many Kushite merchants were men of wealth who could out-barter the wiliest of traders from Kemet and lands beyond. "Where are his wares, do you know?"

Nofery broke the plug from a beer jar, dropped onto a stool that vanished beneath her sagging flesh, and poured a thin stream of brew into her mouth. Bak exchanged a look of long-suffering silence with Imsiba. He knew from experience that the harder he pushed, the more she resisted.

"He came in with a ship's captain, Tjay by name, and two other men," she said. "Traders like him, they were. They'd come north by donkey train, passing down the trail west of the Belly of Stones. Would they not have unloaded the beasts at Kor and reloaded on a vessel bound for Abu?" Abu was the southernmost city in the land of Kemet.

Bak understood her meaning. The Belly of Stones was a long stretch of rapids not navigable much of the year. Merchandise travelling north was transported past the boiling river on the backs of donkeys and unloaded at the small fortress of Kor where the river grew tame. A sensible trader would quickly load his goods onto a northbound ship – such as that of Captain Tjay.

"Who were the other two men?"

She grimaced at a slick-haired yellow dog peering in from the street, but most likely her distaste was directed at the man she held in her memory. "Foreigners, like he was. Friends, he called them."

"You sound doubtful. Did they quarrel?"

Grudgingly, she shook her head. "They behaved like men on the best of terms."

Bak was beginning to lose patience. "Tell me, old woman, what exactly did he do to make you dislike him so?"

"He snapped his fingers and beckoned, as if I was beneath contempt, and treated the women who lay with him as vessels in which to take his pleasure. As for those he called friends, he behaved like a man holding court. I expected them at any moment to get down on their knees and kiss his feet." She screwed up her face in distaste. "Worst of all was the gloating. Smiling expansively, patting his stomach like a man of wealth, bragging of his brilliance as a trader, hinting at some special coup that demonstrated his superiority."

"He sounds like a man asking to be slain," Imsiba said.

They hurried to the harbour, praying Captain Tjay had not yet set sail. If he had left with Ban-Azan's merchandise but without the man himself, he was at best a thief, at worst a slayer.

Their worry proved unfounded. The ship they sought was moored at the near end of one of three long stone quays that reached out into the river. Like many vessels plying the waters between the Belly of Stones and Abu, Captain Tjay's ship looked to be a veteran of the frontier. The wooden hull was gray with age and scarred, but appeared solid and sturdy. Bak noted several neat patches on the faded reddish sail, laid out across the deck so a sailor could repair a fresh tear.

"Dead?" Tjay, standing on the quay near the end of the gangplank, shook his head. "I don't believe it. I was with him just last night. We shared a brew – more than one, if the truth be told – and made merry with congenial companions and a few of that old hag Nofery's women." He was a man of medium height, with broad shoulders and thick, muscular legs. His skin was dark from years of exposure to sun and wind, his eyes almost yellow.

"He was stabbed in the chest sometime during the night," Bak said.

"It can't be true."

Tjay's ship, its fittings and stays creaking, rose and fell on the shallow swells. Brownish silt-laden water lapped the quay, carrying close a duck and her cheeping offspring. Farther out, the river flowed smooth and quiet, with each small ripple like bits of silver, reflections of the bright-white sky.

"How late did you leave him to go your own way?" Bak asked, hoping to avert another denial.

Tjay gave him a sharp look. "You're serious, aren't you?"

"He's even now in the house of death, awaiting the commandant's decision as to what must be done with his mortal remains."

"Ah, yes. What does one do with a foreigner whose home was far away and whose burial customs are different than those of Kemet?"

Bak chose not to respond to the obvious. With the days so hot, the dead man would surely be buried without delay. "You're not grieving, I see."

"I enjoyed his company, yes, but grieve?" Tjay expelled a

humourless little laugh. "I'd never set eyes on the man until two days ago, and not until after midday. When he and his friends came off the desert trail at Kor."

"They asked you to transport their goods to Abu? Or was Ben-Azan the sole man who wished to hire your ship?"

"The three of them, but Ben-Azan did the talking." Tjay scratched his chest, matted with thick, dark hair. "He was a thrifty sort. Though darkness was threatening, he wanted their possessions transferred directly from the donkeys to my ship, saving the price of unloading the poor beasts and leaving the objects where they lay, then hiring men to stow them on board the following morning."

"Such haste must've been irksome."

A hint of irritation touched Tjay's face, quickly supplanted by a smile. "He was thrifty, lieutenant, but not stingy."

Bak noted the stifled emotion, the too quick reassurance. "If he'd not showed up after several days – and he wouldn't have – what would you have done with his wares?"

Tjay did not have to think twice about his answer. "I'd have off-loaded his part of the cargo and taken on board that of someone else. With enough goods on deck to make the journey profitable, I'd have sailed north to Abu."

"You'd not have reported him missing?"

The captain frowned, clearly resenting the question. "I would have, yes. The documents I obtained at Kor list him and his belongings as being on board. We couldn't pass through customs at Abu without an accounting, could we?"

Bak chose to ignore the sarcasm. "Tell me of the two traders who travelled with him."

"Thutnofer and Aper-el."

"I was told they both are foreigners, yet the one . . ." Bak's voice tailed off, inviting an explanation.

"Like many another man who's come from a distant land to make Kemet his home, Thutnofer has taken a name common to his adopted land."

"Where have the two of them gone?"

"They went out in search of Ben-Azan."

*　　*　　*

"Captain Tjay seemed not to care when you laid claim to Ben-Azan's merchandise in the name of our sovereign," Imsiba said.

"The man is dead, his goods forfeit. Tjay's been sailing long enough to know that." Bak eyed the mounds of goods lashed to the deck behind the deckhouse, where the objects were sheltered from spraying waters – unlike the merchandise belonging to Thutnofer and Aper-el, which was stowed on the bow. There was barely room for the oarsmen on either side and for a man at the rudder. "Let's begin at the stern and work our way forwards."

"Can we not look through these objects in a more leisurely fashion after they've been carried into a storehouse?"

Bak called a greeting to two nearly naked fishermen hurrying down the quay, each carrying a long string of silvery fish. Late for the market, they had no time to stop and chat. "We must see all this vessel carries, not merely the wares of Ben-Azan."

"The customs inspector at Kor approved the shipment and authorized their departure. What do you hope to find that he didn't?"

"Why was Ben-Azan slain, Imsiba?"

The Medjay sergeant looked at him with narrowing eyes. "What are you thinking, my friend?"

"Would a man of Buhen think to get rid of a body in one of those old tombs?"

Understanding struck and a hint of a smile touched Imsiba's lips. "All who dwell in this city know of Mery and his friends, of how they play in the cemetery day after day. If you wish to conceal a murder, that's not the place to leave the victim."

"Captain Tjay has been here before, but not often. He might know of the tombs, but not of the boys."

"You believe he slew Ben-Azan?"

Bak knelt before a woven reed chest, broke the seal naming Ben-Azan the owner, and opened the lid, revealing dozens of cloth-wrapped packets. Each gave off the smell of some exotic herb or spice brought from far to the south. "I know only that a man unfamiliar with Buhen left the body in that tomb. A search of this cargo may reveal his name."

"They say he was found in an empty tomb within the walls of this fortress. How can that be?" Thutnofer had been the first of the two traders to return to the ship, carrying word of Ben-Azan's death. As always happened on the frontier, any news of note – in this case, the death of a foreigner – had spread faster than sand in a desert storm.

Bak stood up and arched his back, stretching weary muscles. A detailed search of a ship's cargo could be time-consuming and exhausting. "There's an ancient cemetery near the outer city. You didn't know of it?"

"How could I? I've been here once before and then for no more than an hour. When we travelled south seven months ago, that was. Ben-Azan urged us to hurry on our way, pointing out – and rightfully so – that each day we spent in travel was that much profit lost."

Thutnofer was of medium height and wiry. His black hair had been cropped short and his face was shaven. He wore a knee-length kilt, a string of amulets signifying the gods of Kemet, and a broad beaded collar, bracelets, and armlets. If it was not for his swarthy complexion and long beak of a nose, he could have been taken for a man of Kemet.

"You travelled with him and Aper-el from where?"

"I met them at the harbour in Mennufer. Ben-Azan was my wife's brother, Aper-el his nephew. We thought to travel to Kerma together. For safety's sake and, with luck and the favour of the gods, to increase our profits." Kerma was the largest city in the land of Kush.

Bak watched a small ferry shove off from the next quay. A small boy tended a bleating sheep and her twin lambs in the bow, while several chatting women surrounded by baskets and bundles stood in the shade of a rickety shelter, travelling home from the market. "You don't seem surprised that I've confiscated his wares in the name of our sovereign."

"Someone must've mentioned that such was the law at one time or another. We traders talk among ourselves, you know, especially when we're far from home, surrounded by people whose tongue we don't speak."

"You've travelled often to the land of Kush?"

The trader shook his head. "This was my first journey south. Always before, I've earned my daily bread as a craftsman, a metalsmith."

Bak formed an admiring smile. "Your work must be much in demand to allow you to purchase sufficient wares to make such a long trek worthwhile."

"The objects I make are much admired, yes," Thutnofer said, his chest swelling with pride. "I toil in a workshop of the lord Ptah, and each and every piece is accepted with high praise before it's taken into the god's storehouse."

Noting Imsiba's raised eyebrow, a reflection of his own puzzlement, Bak asked, "If the lord Ptah supports you and your household, where did you get the wealth to invest in trade goods?"

A sudden reticence entered Thutnofer's voice. "Ben-Azan brought to my wife a modest inheritance from their parents. He said I could increase its value ten times over if I accompanied him to the land of Kush."

"And did you return a wealthier man?" Bak asked, pretending not to notice the change in attitude.

"I did well enough," the trader said in a voice bereft of the enthusiasm one would have expected.

"What kind of man was Ben-Azan?"

"A fine man, the truest of friends." Thutnofer's voice shook and he turned away to wipe his eyes with the back of his hand. "One who would give his very life for those he cared for."

Bak glanced at Imsiba, who raised an eyebrow. "You last saw him where?"

Thutnofer cleared the roughness from his throat. "We left him at the door of the place of business in which we celebrated our return to a land less savage than Kush."

"How do you account for his presence in the tomb?"

"Someone lured him there, lieutenant. Probably one of the women he took up with at that house of pleasure, the establishment of that hideous old woman Nofery."

Bak exchanged a look with Imsiba. Both knew Nofery well. She could be greedy, yes, but would never condone murder.

"If Thutnofer hoped his journey into the land of Kush would make him a man of wealth, he was doomed to disappointment." Imsiba dropped onto a mound of soft and supple cowhides and scowled in the general direction of the bags and bundles beyond the deckhouse. "I've no idea what he took south as trade goods, but what he accepted in return is very ordinary. Lengths of ebony and other rare woods, not of the best quality. Many cowhides, none nearly as lovingly cured as these on which I sit. Horns and teeth from animals from far to the south. The best of the lot: ostrich eggs and feathers."

"Ben-Azan certainly wouldn't have gone home a poor man." Bak tapped the edge of a basket filled with lumps of resin, used for incense, and pointed to a chest of spices and a rough linen bag filled with chunks of precious stone.

Imsiba flung a sour look towards the ship's bow. "I'd be willing to bet my newest pair of sandals that I'll find Aper-el's merchandise to be no better than that of Thutnofer."

Bak ran his fingers along the smooth, cool side of an ivory tusk, not large but of exceptional beauty and value. "How could the two of them come north with nothing when Ben-Azan returned a wealthy man? Was he so skilled a trader?"

They sat in silence, mulling over the problem.

Imsiba spoke at last. "I can see Thutnofer and Aper-el slaying him somewhere south of the Belly of Stones, while still in the land of Kush, and taking his trade goods as theirs with no one the wiser. But would they slay him here, knowing full well you'd confiscate these fine objects for the royal house and they'd go home with close to nothing?"

"I've asked myself that question time and time again, Imsiba." Bak eyed a dog loping along the quay, a half-grown rat in its mouth. "We've missed something, but what?"

"I admired him more than any other man."

Aper-el could not seem to stop sniffling, whether saddened by his uncle's death or from some malady carried on the air,

Bak could not begin to guess. No more than 18 years of age, he was of medium height and plump. His beard was black and thick, his curly hair held off his face by a vivid green band. He wore a tunic similar to that of the dead man, but brightly dyed with entwined circles of green, yellow, red, and black. "My father, Ben-Azan's brother, died when I was but a babe, and he took it upon himself to care for my mother and I as if we were his own."

Bak rocked forwards to examine a basket filled with chunks of amethyst. "Is this the first time you've travelled with him?"

"Yes, sir." Aper-el sniffed. "He thought I should make more of my life. I was a merchant, you see, tending the small shop my father left and living with my mother in the rooms above."

"Is she caring for your business while you're away?"

Aper-el shook his head. "Ben-Azan urged me to sell it, to invest everything in the trade goods I took with me to Kush."

Imsiba, sitting nearby, listening, made an unintelligible sound Bak took to be condemnation. He had finished looking through Aper-el's acquisitions and had reported that the young man had fared even worse than Thutnofer in his dealings with the Kushites. Which meant that all he had had in his homeland had been thrown to the four winds. Bak thought of the young man's mother, no doubt dwelling in Ben-Azan's household as scarcely more than a servant, awaiting her son and freedom. Pity filled his heart.

Noticing that the basket containing the amethysts had been placed inside another similar container, Bak picked them up and placed them on his lap. "Your uncle appears to have been a very successful man, his skill as a trader unparalleled."

"Yes, sir." Aper-el wiped his nose with a square of red fabric, then clasped his hands tightly together on his lap. "Would that he'd lived longer so he could pass on to me the knowledge he possessed."

The words were so trite Bak dared not look at Imsiba. "I've been told he was equally able with the ladies."

"He was tireless – and most inventive, so they say."

"Was he also adept at games of chance?"

"Whatever he turned his hand to, he succeeded, sir."

Another banal statement, this delivered with an outward display of pride undermined by a touch of resentment. Bak lifted the inner basket carefully, expecting chunks of rock to drop through a damaged bottom. Nothing happened; the container was in good condition. Why bring along the outer basket, which was clearly not needed? He noted the design, common to a nomadic tribe east of the river, and the seed of an idea entered his heart. Praying the basket would verify the thought, he turned it one way and another, probed it with his fingers. A bright speck fell out from between the woven fibres.

Fervently thanking the gods for smiling upon him, he palmed the tiny granule. "While you were in Kush, Aper-el, did you spend all your time in Kerma?"

"No, sir, we often travelled to towns and villages far from the city, where we traded with headmen and tribal chieftains."

"Such journeys must at times have been long and difficult."

Aper-el nodded, wiped his nose. "A thankless task it was, but Ben-Azan would ignore no opportunity."

Imsiba, walking beside Bak up the quay, asked, "What now, my friend?"

"Make them our prisoners, Imsiba."

"All of them?" the Medjay asked, surprised.

"Tjay, Thutnofer, Aper-el. None must be allowed outside the walls of Buhen."

"Captain Tjay could slay a man, I've no doubt, but resentment for having to quickly transfer goods from donkeys to ship seems too small a reason for taking a man's life. Thutnofer and Aper-el have good reason, but I'm convinced they're both too weak to raise a hand in anger."

Bak nodded at the sentry standing in a thin slice of shade cast by the twin-towered gate at the end of the quay. Holding out his hand, palm open, he revealed the small golden kernel. "We must get some men into the hold of Tjay's ship. I'll wager a jar of the finest wine from northern Kemet that a thorough search will turn up more than ballast down there."

*   *   *

"You can't do this!" Captain Tjay, his hands, like those of his companions, manacled behind his back, glared venomously at Bak. "I'll complain to your commandant, to the viceroy, to the vizier himself."

"Why make me a prisoner?" Aper-el sniffed. "I've done no wrong."

"If you truly seek Ben-Azan's slayer, you'll look closer to home," Thutnofer said. "To that old woman Nofery and the women who toil in her house of pleasure."

Bak rested a shoulder against the doorjamb and eyed the trio his Medjays had brought to the guardhouse. The entry hall seemed full to bursting, with Imsiba and Hori, the prisoners, the four policemen who had brought them in, and the two Medjays currently on duty all crowded together at the near end. The latter pair, their curiosity aroused, had gone so far as to interrupt the never-ending game of knucklebones that went on night and day as the shifts changed.

"I see no need to look any farther than the three of you."

"Why would any of us slay a man we so greatly admired?" Thutnofer scoffed.

"Admired? Or envied. The one oft times supplants the other."

"I'll have your baton of office torn from you," Tjay snarled. "You'll be lucky to remain in the army a common spearman."

Bak signalled the men on duty to return to their game and dismissed two of the Medjays who had brought in the prisoners. Entering the room he used as an office, he ordered the captives to sit on the floor against the wall and the remaining Medjays to stand guard outside. Hori lit three oil lamps to supplement the light coming through the door and sat cross-legged on a floormat facing the bound men, his writing implements close to hand. Imsiba sat on a mudbrick bench built across the back of the room, while Bak dropped onto a low three-legged stool.

"The three of you together slew Ben-Azan." Bak waved off a ribbon of smoke drifting up from a lamp. "One man plunged the dagger into his breast. Tjay, I'd guess – the leather wrapping around the hilt is the mark of a sailor. No less than three men could carry a man so heavy from the place where he was slain to the ancient cemetery." He saw defiance on their faces, added, "We found his blood under a patch of loose sand near the outer city."

"No!" Aper-el cried. "It wasn't my idea."

"Silence, you witless fool!" Tjay snarled.

Bak exchanged a satisfied look with Imsiba. The prisoners would shortly be at each other's throats. "How long ago did he entice you into playing games of chance? After you crossed the border at Semna, I'd guess, and were shown on the records as having returned from Kush. While you travelled north along the Belly of Stones, where he believed he'd be safe."

The three men threw accusatory looks at each other.

"Did he cheat? Or were you so eager to give away all your wares that you made unwise bets?" Bak heard no clatter of knucklebones in the entry hall, no betting. The men were eavesdropping. "And as the days passed I suppose you wagered again and again to recover your losses, only to lose more."

"How did you know?" Aper-el whimpered.

Tjay swung towards him, hissed, "Not another word, you fool!"

Bak eyed the captain. The traders, he suspected, had eliminated one man to take up with another who would in the end have been no more honest or fair than Ben-Azan had been. "What happened last night? Did he constantly boast of his success as a trader, all the while needling you about how stupid you'd been? Ultimately pushing you too far?"

Aper-el opened his mouth to respond, but a harsh grunt from Tjay cut off whatever he intended to say.

"I've never known a trader to come back from the land of Kush impoverished. Nor have I known one to return with enough for three – as did Ben-Azan." Bak bent over and flung a knucklebone, which rattled across the floor and came to rest near Thutnofer's feet. "One of you lost this near his body."

"All right! He stole from us." Thutnofer spat out the words in fury. "But what good would it do us to slay him? We knew all he possessed would go into the coffers of the royal house.

With him alive we might sooner or later get the better of him; dead we're left with nothing."

Bak doubted they would ever have got the better of Ben-Azan. "So you would have us believe." He glanced at Imsiba, who lifted a lumpy, dusty, and obviously heavy leather bag from a basket sitting on the bench beside him. A bag the Medjays had found hidden among the ballast stones.

The three men seated on the floor turned a mottled, sickly grey.

Imsiba untied the knot at the top of the bag and slowly poured out the contents. Rough nuggets, glittering in the light cast by the lamps, clattered into the basket in which Bak had found the golden fragment. Nuggets fused by nomadic tribesmen from granules found in dry watercourses or washed out of quartz dug from the earth. The ragged unformed pieces produced when molten gold is slowly poured into water.

Enough gold to have made the three prisoners wealthy for life.

THE LOCKED
TOMB MYSTERY

Elizabeth Peters

We are still in the Eighteenth Dynasty but have moved on a few kings to the time of Amenhotep III, also called Nebmaatra. He was the father of the renegade king Akhenaten. During his mighty and prosperous reign Amenhotep had a famous namesake, Amenhotep Sa Hapu (meaning son of Hapu), who was the director of all the King's works. He was responsible for many of the major building projects at Thebes, including the famous Colossi of Memnon and the Temple of Luxor. Although he was of relatively common birth, he became the king's favourite and, after a long and much venerated life, was accorded a tomb amongst the royal necropolis. Like Imhotep, a thousand years before him, he was later worshipped as a god.

Elizabeth Peters scarcely needs any introduction. Starting with The Jackal's Head *(1968), which had a contemporary Egyptian setting, she followed in the footsteps of Agatha Christie in developing the archaeological mystery. With* Crocodile on the Sandbank *(1975), set in the late Victorian period, she introduced Lady Amelia Peabody and her future husband, archaeologist Radcliffe Emerson, who meet in Egypt. Later books include* The Curse of the Pharaohs *(1981),* The Mummy Case *(1985),* Lion in the Valley *(1986),* The Deeds of the Disturber *(1988),* The Last Camel Died at Noon *(1991), and others, following through the years and allowing us to watch the Emersons' son, Ramses, grow into a precocious teenager.* Lord of the Silent

*(2001) brings the series up to the First World War. Although
Elizabeth Peters has not written any short stories featuring the
Emersons, she has written the following delightful, and slightly
tongue-in-cheek, ancient mystery.*

S enebtisi's funeral was the talk of southern Thebes. Of
course, it could not compare with the burials of Great
Ones and Pharaohs, whose Houses of Eternity were furnished
with gold and fine linen and precious gems, but ours was not
a quarter where nobles lived; our people were craftsmen and
small merchants, able to afford a chamber-tomb and a coffin
and a few spells to ward off the perils of the Western Road –
no more than that. We had never seen anything like the burial
of the old woman who had been our neighbour for so many
years.

The night after the funeral, the customers of Nehi's tavern
could talk of nothing else. I remember that evening well. For
one thing, I had just won my first appointment as a temple
scribe. I was looking forward to boasting a little, and perhaps
paying for a round of beer, if my friends displayed proper
appreciation of my good fortune. Three of the others were
already at the tavern when I arrived, my linen shawl wrapped
tight around me. The weather was cold even for winter, with a
cruel, dry wind driving sand into every crevice of the body.

"Close the door quickly," said Senu, the carpenter. "What
weather! I wonder if the Western journey will be like this –
cold enough to freeze a man's bones."

This prompted a ribald comment from Rennefer, the weaver, concerning the effects of freezing on certain of Senebtisi's
vital organs. "Not that anyone would notice the difference,"
he added. "There was never any warmth in the old hag. What
sort of mother would take all her possessions to the next world
and leave her only son penniless?"

"Is it true, then?" I asked, signalling Nehi to fetch the beer
jar. "I have heard stories –"

"All true," said the potter, Baenre. "It is a pity you could
not attend the burial, Wadjsen; it was magnificent!"

"You went?" I inquired. "That was good of you, since she ordered none of her funerary equipment from you."

Baenre is a scanty little man with thin hair and sharp bones. It is said that he is a domestic tyrant, and that his wife cowers when he comes roaring home from the tavern, but when he is with us, his voice is almost a whisper. "My rough kitchenware would not be good enough to hold the wine and fine oil she took to the tomb. Wadjsen, you should have seen the boxes and jars and baskets – dozens of them. They say she had a gold mask, like the ones worn by great nobles, and that all her ornaments were of solid gold."

"It is true," said Rennefer. "I know a man who knows one of the servants of Bakenmut, the goldsmith who made the ornaments."

"How is her son taking it?" I asked. I knew Minmose slightly; a shy, serious man, he followed his father's trade of stone carving. His mother had lived with him all his life, greedily scooping up his profits, though she had money of her own, inherited from her parents.

"Why, as you would expect," said Senu, shrugging. "Have you ever heard him speak harshly to anyone, much less his mother? She was an old she-goat who treated him like a boy who has not cut off the side lock; but with him it was always 'Yes, honoured mother,' and 'As you say, honoured mother.' She would not even allow him to take a wife."

"How will he live?"

"Oh, he has the shop and the business, such as it is. He is a hard worker; he will survive."

In the following months I heard occasional news of Minmose. Gossip said he must be doing well, for he had taken to spending his leisure time at a local house of prostitution – a pleasure he never had dared enjoy while his mother lived. Nefertiry, the loveliest and most expensive of the girls, was the object of his desire, and Rennefer remarked that the maiden must have a kind heart, for she could command higher prices than Minmose was able to pay. However, as time passed, I forgot Minmose and Senebtisi, and her rich burial. It was not until almost a year later that the matter was recalled to my attention.

The rumours began in the marketplace, at the end of the time of inundation, when the floodwater lay on the fields and the farmers were idle. They enjoy this time, but the police of the city do not; for idleness leads to crime, and one of the most popular crimes is tomb robbing. This goes on all the time in a small way, but when the Pharaoh is strong and stern, and the laws are strictly enforced, it is a very risky trade. A man stands to lose more than a hand or an ear if he is caught. He also risks damnation after he has entered his own tomb; but some men simply do not have proper respect for the gods.

The king, Nebmaatre (may he live forever!), was then in his prime, so there had been no tomb robbing for some time – or at least none had been detected. But, the rumours said, three men of west Thebes had been caught trying to sell ornaments such as are buried with the dead. The rumours turned out to be correct, for once. The men were questioned on the soles of their feet and confessed to the robbing of several tombs.

Naturally all those who had kin buried on the west bank – which included most of us – were alarmed by this news, and half the nervous matrons in our neighborhood went rushing across the river to make sure the family tombs were safe. I was not surprised to hear that that dutiful son Minmose had also felt obliged to make sure his mother had not been disturbed.

However, I was surprised at the news that greeted me when I paid my next visit to Nehi's tavern. The moment I entered, the others began to talk at once, each eager to be the first to tell the shocking facts.

"Robbed?" I repeated when I had sorted out the babble of voices. "Do you speak truly?"

"I do not know why you should doubt it," said Rennefer. "The richness of her burial was the talk of the city, was it not? Just what the tomb robbers like! They made a clean sweep of all the gold, and ripped the poor old hag's mummy to shreds."

At that point we were joined by another of the habitués, Merusir. He is a pompous, fat man who considers himself superior to the rest of us because he is Fifth Prophet of Amon. We put up with his patronizing ways because sometimes he knows court gossip. On that particular evening it was apparent that he was bursting with excitement. He listened with a supercilious sneer while we told him the sensational news. "I know, I know," he drawled. "I heard it much earlier – and with it, the other news which is known only to those in the confidence of the Palace."

He paused, ostensibly to empty his cup. Of course, we reacted as he had hoped we would, begging him to share the secret. Finally he condescended to inform us.

"Why, the amazing thing is not the robbery itself, but how it was done. The tomb entrance was untouched, the seals of the necropolis were unbroken. The tomb itself is entirely rock-cut, and there was not the slightest break in the walls or floor or ceiling. Yet when Minmose entered the burial chamber, he found the coffin open, the mummy mutilated, and the gold ornaments gone."

We stared at him, open-mouthed.

"It is a most remarkable story," I said.

"Call me a liar if you like," said Merusir, who knows the language of polite insult as well as I do. "There was a witness – two, if you count Minmose himself. The sem-priest Wennefer was with him."

This silenced the critics. Wennefer was known to us all. There was not a man in southern Thebes with a higher reputation. Even Senebtisi had been fond of him, and she was not fond of many people. He had officiated at her funeral.

Pleased at the effect of his announcement, Merusir went on in his most pompous manner. "The king himself has taken an interest in the matter. He has called on Amenhotep Sa Hapu to investigate."

"Amenhotep?" I exclaimed. "But I know him well."

"You do?" Merusir's plump cheeks sagged like bladders punctured by a sharp knife.

Now, at that time Amenhotep's name was not in the mouth of everyone, though he had taken the first steps on that astonishing career that was to make him the intimate friend of Pharaoh. When I first met him, he had been a poor, insignificant priest at a local shrine. I had been sent to fetch him to the house where my master lay dead of a stab wound, presumably murdered. Amenhotep's fame had begun with that matter, for he had discovered the truth and saved an innocent man from execution. Since then he had handled several other cases, with equal success.

My exclamation had taken the wind out of Merusir's sails. He had hoped to impress us by telling us something we did not know. Instead it was I who enlightened the others about Amenhotep's triumphs. But when I finished, Rennefer shook his head.

"If this wise man is all you say, Wadjsen, it will be like inviting a lion to rid the house of mice. He will find there is a simple explanation. No doubt the thieves entered the burial chamber from above or from one side, tunnelling through the rock. Minmose and Wennefer were too shocked to observe the hole in the wall, that is all."

We argued the matter for some time, growing more and more heated as the level of the beer in the jar dropped. It was a foolish argument, for none of us knew the facts; and to argue without knowledge is like trying to weave without thread.

This truth did not occur to me until the cool night breeze had cleared my head, when I was halfway home. I decided to pay Amenhotep a visit. The next time I went to the tavern, I would be the one to tell the latest news, and Merusir would be nothing!

Most of the honest householders had retired, but there were lamps burning in the street of the prostitutes, and in a few taverns. There was a light, as well, in one window of the house where Amenhotep lodged. Like the owl he resembled, with his beaky nose and large, close-set eyes, he preferred to work at night.

The window was on the ground floor, so I knocked on the wooden shutter, which of course was closed to keep out night demons. After a few moments the shutter opened, and the familiar nose appeared. I spoke my name, and Amenhotep went to open the door.

"Wadjsen! It has been a long time," he exclaimed. "Should I ask what brings you here, or shall I display my talents as a seer and tell you?"

"I suppose it requires no great talent," I replied. "The matter of Senebtisi's tomb is already the talk of the district."

"So I had assumed." He gestured me to sit down and hospitably indicated the wine jar that stood in the corner. I shook my head.

"I have already taken too much beer, at the tavern. I am sorry to disturb you so late –"

"I am always happy to see you, Wadjsen." His big dark eyes reflected the light of the lamp, so that they seemed to hold stars in their depths. "I have missed my assistant, who helped me to the truth in my first inquiry."

"I was of little help to you then," I said with a smile. "And in this case I am even more ignorant. The thing is a great mystery, known only to the gods."

"No, no!" He clapped his hands together, as was his habit when annoyed with the stupidity of his hearer. "There is no mystery. I know who robbed the tomb of Senebtisi. The only difficulty is to prove how it was done."

At Amenhotep's suggestion I spent the night at his house so that I could accompany him when he set out next morning to find the proof he needed. I required little urging, for I was afire with curiosity. Though I pressed him, he would say no more, merely remarking piously, "'A man may fall to ruin because of his tongue; if a passing remark is hasty and it is repeated, thou wilt make enemies.'"

I could hardly dispute the wisdom of this adage, but the gleam in Amenhotep's bulging black eyes made me suspect he took a malicious pleasure in my bewilderment.

After our morning bread and beer we went to the temple of Khonsu, where the sem-priest Wennefer worked in the records office. He was copying accounts from pottery ostraca onto a papyrus that was stretched across his lap. All scribes develop bowed shoulders from bending over their writing; Wennefer was folded almost double, his face scant inches from the surface of the papyrus. When Amenhotep cleared his throat, the old man started, smearing the ink. He waved our apologies aside and cleaned the papyrus with a wad of lint.

"No harm was meant, no harm is done," he said in his breathy, chirping voice. "I have heard of you, Amenhotep Sa Hapu; it is an honour to meet you."

"I, too, have looked forward to meeting you, Wennefer. Alas that the occasion should be such a sad one."

Wennefer's smile faded. "Ah, the matter of Senebtisi's tomb. What a tragedy! At least the poor woman can now have a proper reburial. If Minmose had not insisted on opening the tomb, her *ba* would have gone hungry and thirsty through eternity."

"Then the tomb entrance really was sealed and undisturbed?" I asked sceptically.

"I examined it myself," Wennefer said. "Minmose had asked me to meet him after the day's work, and we arrived at the tomb as the sun was setting; but the light was still good. I conducted the funeral service for Senebtisi, you know. I had seen the doorway blocked and mortared and with my own hands had helped to press the seals of the necropolis onto the wet plaster. All was as I had left it that day a year ago."

"Yet Minmose insisted on opening the tomb?" Amenhotep asked.

"Why, we agreed it should be done," the old man said mildly. "As you know, robbers sometimes tunnel in from above or from one side, leaving the entrance undisturbed. Minmose had brought tools. He did most of the work himself, for these old hands of mine are better with a pen than a chisel. When the doorway was clear, Minmose lit a lamp and we entered. We were crossing the hall beyond the entrance corridor when Minmose let out a shriek. 'My mother, my mother,' he cried – oh, it was pitiful to hear! Then I saw it too. The thing – the thing on the floor . . ."

"You speak of the mummy, I presume," said Amenhotep. "The thieves had dragged it from the coffin out into the hall?"

"Where they despoiled it," Wennefer whispered. "The august body was ripped open from throat to groin, through the shroud and the wrappings and the flesh."

"Curious," Amenhotep muttered, as if to himself. "Tell me, Wennefer, what is the plan of the tomb?"

Wennefer rubbed his brush on the ink cake and began to draw on the back surface of one of the ostraca.

"It is a fine tomb, Amenhotep, entirely rock-cut. Beyond the entrance is a flight of stairs and a short corridor, thus leading to a hall broader than it is long, with two pillars. Beyond that, another short corridor; then the burial chamber. The august mummy lay here." And he inked in a neat circle at the beginning of the second corridor.

"Ha," said Amenhotep, studying the plan. "Yes, yes, I see. Go on, Wennefer. What did you do next?"

"I did nothing," the old man said simply. "Minmose's hand shook so violently that he dropped the lamp. Darkness closed in. I felt the presence of the demons who had defiled the dead. My tongue clove to the roof of my mouth and –"

"Dreadful," Amenhotep said. "But you were not far from the tomb entrance; you could find your way out?"

"Yes, yes, it was only a dozen paces; and by Amun, my friend, the sunset light has never appeared so sweet! I went at once to fetch the necropolis guards. When we returned to the tomb, Minmose had rekindled his lamp –"

"I thought you said the lamp was broken."

"Dropped, but fortunately not broken. Minmose had opened one of the jars of oil – Senebtisi had many such in the tomb, all of the finest quality – and had refilled the lamp. He had replaced the mummy in its coffin and was kneeling by it praying. Never was there so pious a son!"

"So then, I suppose, the guards searched the tomb."

"We all searched," Wennefer said. "The tomb chamber was in a dreadful state; boxes and baskets had been broken open and the contents strewn about. Every object of precious metal had been stolen, including the amulets on the body."

"What about the oil, the linen, and the other valuables?" Amenhotep asked.

"The oil and the wine were in large jars, impossible to move easily. About the other things I cannot say; everything was in such confusion – and I do not know what was there to begin with. Even Minmose was not certain; his mother had filled and sealed most of the boxes herself. But I know what was taken from the mummy, for I saw the golden amulets and ornaments placed on it when it was wrapped by the embalmers. I do not like to speak evil of anyone, but you know, Amenhotep, that the embalmers . . ."

"Yes," Amenhotep agreed with a sour face. "I myself watched the wrapping of my father; there is no other way to make certain the ornaments will go on the mummy instead of into the coffers of the embalmers. Minmose did not perform this service for his mother?"

"Of course he did. He asked me to share in the watch, and I was glad to agree. He is the most pious –"

"So I have heard," said Amenhotep. "Tell me again, Wennefer, of the condition of the mummy. You examined it?"

"It was my duty. Oh, Amenhotep, it was a sad sight! The shroud was still tied firmly around the body; the thieves had cut straight through it and through the bandages beneath, baring the body. The arm bones were broken, so roughly had the thieves dragged the heavy gold bracelets from them."

"And the mask?" I asked. "It was said that she had a mask of solid gold."

"It, too, was missing."

"Horrible," Amenhotep said. "Wennefer, we have kept you from your work long enough. Only one more question. How do you think the thieves entered the tomb?"

The old man's eyes fell. "Through me," he whispered.

I gave Amenhotep a startled look. He shook his head warningly.

"It was not your fault," he said, touching Wennefer's bowed shoulder.

"It was. I did my best, but I must have omitted some vital part of the ritual. How else could demons enter the tomb?"

"Oh, I see." Amenhotep stroked his chin. "Demons."

"It could have been nothing else. The seals on the door were intact, the mortar untouched. There was no break of the smallest size in the stone of the walls or ceiling or floor."

"But –" I began.

"And there is this. When the doorway was clear and the light entered, the dust lay undisturbed on the floor. The only marks on it were the strokes of the broom with which Minmose, according to custom, had swept the floor as he left the tomb after the funeral service."

"Amun preserve us," I exclaimed, feeling a chill run through me.

Amenhotep's eyes moved from Wennefer to me, then back to Wennefer. "That is conclusive," he murmured.

"Yes," Wennefer said with a groan. "And I am to blame – I, a priest who failed at his task."

"No," said Amenhotep. "You did not fail. Be of good cheer, my friend. There is another explanation."

Wennefer shook his head despondently. "Minmose said the same, but he was only being kind. Poor man! He was so overcome, he could scarcely walk. The guards had to take him by the arms to lead him from the tomb. I carried his tools. It was the least –"

"The tools," Amenhotep interrupted. "They were in a bag or a sack?"

"Why, no. He had only a chisel and a mallet. I carried them in my hand as he had done."

Amenhotep thanked him again, and we took our leave. As we crossed the courtyard I waited for him to speak, but he remained silent; and after a while I could contain myself no longer.

"Do you still believe you know who robbed the tomb?"

"Yes, yes, it is obvious."

"And it was not demons?"

Amenhotep blinked at me like an owl blinded by sunlight. "Demons are a last resort."

He had the smug look of a man who thinks he has said something clever; but his remark smacked of heresy to me, and I looked at him doubtfully.

"Come, come," he snapped. "Senebtisi was a selfish, greedy old woman, and if there is justice in the next world, as our faith decrees, her path through the Underworld will not be easy. But why would diabolical powers play tricks with her mummy when they could torment her spirit? Demons have no need of gold."

"Well, but –"

"Your wits used not to be so dull. What do you think happened?"

"If it was not demons –"

"It was not."

"Then someone must have broken in."

"Very clever," said Amenhotep, grinning.

"I mean that there must be an opening, in the walls or the floor, that Wennefer failed to see."

"Wennefer, perhaps. The necropolis guards, no. The chambers of the tomb were cut out of solid rock. It would be impossible to disguise a break in such a surface, even if tomb robbers took the trouble to fill it in – which they never have been known to do."

"Then the thieves entered through the doorway and closed it again. A dishonest craftsman could make a copy of the necropolis seal . . ."

"Good." Amenhotep clapped me on the shoulder. "Now you are beginning to think. It is an ingenious idea, but it is wrong. Tomb robbers work in haste, for fear of the necropolis guards. They would not linger to replace stones and mortar and seals."

"Then I do not know how it was done."

"Ah, Wadjsen, you are dense! There is only one person who could have robbed the tomb."

"I thought of that," I said stiffly, hurt by his raillery. "Minmose was the last to leave the tomb and the first to re-enter it. He had good reason to desire the gold his mother should have left to him. But, Amenhotep, he could not have robbed the mummy on either occasion; there was not time. You know the funeral ritual as well as I. When the priests and mourners leave the tomb, they leave together. If Minmose had lingered in the burial chamber, even for a few minutes, his delay would have been noted and remarked upon."

"That is quite true," said Amenhotep.

"Also," I went on, "the gold was heavy as well as bulky. Minmose could not have carried it away without someone noticing."

"Again you speak truly."

"Then unless Wennefer the priest is conspiring with Minmose –"

"That good, simple man? I am surprised at you, Wadjsen. Wennefer is as honest as the Lady of Truth herself."

"Demons –"

Amenhotep interrupted with the hoarse hooting sound that passed for a laugh with him. "Stop babbling of demons. There is one man besides myself who knows how Senebtisi's tomb was violated. Let us go and see him."

He quickened his pace, his sandals slapping in the dust. I followed, trying to think. His taunts were like weights that pulled my mind to its farthest limits. I began to get an inkling of truth, but I could not make sense of it. I said nothing, not even when we turned into the lane south of the temple that led to the house of Minmose.

There was no servant at the door. Minmose himself answered our summons. I greeted him and introduced Amenhotep.

Minmose lifted his hands in surprise. "You honour my house, Amenhotep. Enter and be seated."

Amenhotep shook his head. "I will not stay, Minmose. I came only to tell you who desecrated your mother's tomb."

"What?" Minmose gaped at him. "Already you know? But how? It is a great mystery, beyond –"

"You did it, Minmose."

Minmose turned a shade paler. But that was not out of the way; even the innocent might blanch at such an accusation.

"You are mad," he said. "Forgive me, you are my guest, but –"

"There is no other possible explanation," Amenhotep said. "You stole the gold when you entered the tomb two days ago."

"But, Amenhotep," I exclaimed. "Wennefer was with him, and Wennefer saw the mummy already robbed when –"

"Wennefer did not see the mummy," Amenhotep said, "The tomb was dark; the only light was that of a small lamp, which Minmose promptly dropped. Wennefer has poor sight. Did you not observe how he bent over his writing? He caught only a glimpse of a white shape, the size of a wrapped mummy, before the light went out. When next Wennefer saw the mummy, it was in the coffin, and his view of it then coloured his confused memory of the first supposed sighting of it. Few people are good observers. They see what they expect to see."

"Then what did he see?" I demanded. Minmose might not have been there. Amenhotep avoided looking at him.

"A piece of linen in the rough shape of a human form, arranged on the floor by the last person who left the tomb. It would have taken him only a moment to do this before he snatched up the broom and swept himself out."

"So the tomb was sealed and closed," I exclaimed. "For almost a year he waited —"

"Until the next outbreak of tomb robbing. Minmose could assume this would happen sooner or later; it always does. He thought he was being clever by asking Wennefer to accompany him — a witness of irreproachable character who could testify that the tomb entrance was untouched. In fact, he was too careful to avoid being compromised; that would have made me doubt him, even if the logic of the facts had not pointed directly at him. Asking that same virtuous man to share his supervision of the mummy wrapping, lest he be suspected of connivance with the embalmers; feigning weakness so that the necropolis guards would have to support him, and thus be in a position to swear he could not have concealed the gold on his person. Only a guilty man would be so anxious to appear innocent. Yet there was reason for his precautions. Sometime in the near future, when that loving son Minmose discovers a store of gold hidden in the house, overlooked by his mother — the old do forget sometimes — then, since men have evil minds, it might be necessary for Minmose to prove beyond a shadow of a doubt that he could not have laid hands on his mother's burial equipment."

Minmose remained dumb, his eyes fixed on the ground. It was I who responded as he should have, questioning and objecting.

"But how did he remove the gold? The guards and Wennefer searched the tomb, so it was not hidden there, and there was not time for him to bury it outside."

"No, but there was ample time for him to do what had to be done in the burial chamber after Wennefer had tottered off to fetch the guards. He overturned boxes and baskets, opened the coffin, ripped through the mummy wrappings with his chisel, and took the gold. It would not take long, especially for one who knew exactly where each ornament had been placed."

Minmose's haggard face was as good as an admission of guilt. He did not look up or speak, even when Amenhotep put a hand on his shoulder.

"I pity you, Minmose," Amenhotep said gravely. "After years of devotion and self-denial, to see yourself deprived of your inheritance . . . And there was Nefertiry. You had been visiting her in secret, even before your mother died, had you not? Oh, Minmose, you should have remembered the words of the sage: 'Do not go in to a woman who is a stranger; it is a great crime, worthy of death.' She has brought you to your death, Minmose. You knew she would turn from you if your mother left you nothing."

Minmose's face was grey. "Will you denounce me, then? They will beat me to make me confess."

"Any man will confess when he is beaten," said Amenhotep, with a curl of his lip. "No, Minmose, I will not denounce you. The court of the vizier demands facts, not theories, and you have covered your tracks very neatly. But you will not escape justice. Nefertiry will consume your gold as the desert sands drink water, and then she will cast you off; and all the while Anubis, the Guide of the Dead, and Osiris, the Divine Judge, will be waiting for you. They will eat your heart, Minmose, and your spirit will hunger and thirst through all eternity. I think your punishment has already begun. Do you dream, Minmose? Did you see your mother's face last night, wrinkled and withered, her sunken eyes accusing you, as it looked when you tore the gold mask from it?"

A long shudder ran through Minmose's body. Even his hair seemed to shiver and rise. Amenhotep gestured to me. We went away, leaving Minmose staring after us with a face like death.

After we had gone a short distance, I said, "There is one more thing to tell, Amenhotep."

"There is much to tell." Amenhotep sighed deeply. "Of a good man turned evil; of two women who, in their different ways, drove him to crime; of the narrow line that separates the virtuous man from the sinner . . ."

"I do not speak of that. I do not wish to think of that. It makes me feel strange . . . The gold, Amenhotep – how did Minmose bear away the gold from his mother's burial?"

"He put it in the oil jar," said Amenhotep. "The one he opened to get fresh fuel for his lamp. Who would wonder if, in his agitation, he spilled a quantity of oil on the floor? He has certainly removed it by now. He has had ample opportunity, running back and forth with objects to be repaired or replaced."

"And the piece of linen he had put down to look like the mummy?"

"As you well know," Amenhotep replied, "the amount of linen used to wrap a mummy is prodigious. He could have crumpled that piece and thrown it in among the torn wrappings. But I think he did something else. It was a cool evening, in winter, and Minmose would have worn a linen mantle. He took the cloth out in the same way he had brought it in. Who would notice an extra fold of linen over a man's shoulders?

"I knew immediately that Minmose must be the guilty party, because he was the only one who had the opportunity, but I did not see how he had managed it until Wennefer showed me where the supposed mummy lay. There was no reason for a thief to drag it so far from the coffin and the burial chamber – but Minmose could not afford to have Wennefer catch even a glimpse of that room, which was then undisturbed. I realized then that what the old man had seen was not the mummy at all, but a substitute."

"Then Minmose will go unpunished."

"I said he would be punished. I spoke truly." Again Amenhotep sighed.

"You will not denounce him to Pharaoh?"

"I will tell my lord the truth. But he will not choose to act. There will be no need."

He said no more. But six weeks later Minmose's body was found floating in the river. He had taken to drinking heavily, and people said he drowned by accident. But I knew it was otherwise. Anubis and Osiris had eaten his heart, just as Amenhotep had said.

HERETIC'S DAGGER

Lynda S. Robinson

The best-known of all the pharaohs of ancient Egypt, at least to us today, is the boy-king Tutankhamun, due entirely to Howard Carter's discovery of his tomb in the Valley of the Kings in 1922. He had in fact been a very minor king and one about whom next to nothing was known until Carter's excavation. Today you can't talk about Egypt without mentioning Tutankhamun, even though he ruled for only nine years and died at the age of seventeen. His reign was one of court intrigue and power struggles and is an ideal background for crime fiction. Lynda S. Robinson, who also writes historical romances as Suzanne Robinson, has written a series of novels set during Tutankhamun's reign and featuring the king's mentor and investigator, Lord Meren. The books run Murder in the Palace of Anubis *(1994),* Murder at the God's Gate *(1995),* Murder at the Feast of Rejoicing *(1996),* Eater of Souls *(1997),* Drinker of Blood *(1998) and* Slayer of Gods *(2001).*

Thebes, Year Five of the
Reign of the Pharaoh Tutankhamun

There was a right order to things when one accompanied a living god on military training exercises. The first maxim was not to outpace Pharaoh's chariot. To Meren, confidential inquiry agent and mentor to King Tutankhamun, such rules of conduct were second nature. Thus he reined in his team of thoroughbred chariot horses so that they kept even pace with the 14-year-old boy who rode at the head of a company of Egypt's finest cavalry.

The rumble of wheels over rock, the stamp of hooves and occasional crack of a whip bounced off the high desert cliffs to their right as they rode south from the palace. Meren glanced to his left past the green fields that bordered the Nile and caught sight of the opposite east bank. There, more fields bordered the river with the city districts perched close behind them and, after that, the eastern desert. This was Egypt, a narrow band of luxuriant life hemmed in on the east and west by vast deserts that were the home of sand dwellers, outlaws, and the dead.

The company proceeded at a walk so as not to tire the horses before the training exercises. Pharaoh, who could hardly contain his impatience to attain the status of seasoned warrior, had brought with him an unusual companion. Sa, The Guardian, a black leopard stalked beside the king's chariot, tethered to Pharaoh by a gilded leather leash. Meren smiled as Tutankhamun leaned down to stroke the animal's sleek head. Sa had been with the king almost from birth. Anyone wishing to harm the boy would have to kill Sa to get to him. Sa lifted his giant head and gazed calmly at Meren. Meren bent over the cab of his chariot and made a low trilling noise in the back of his throat, holding his hand out to the big cat.

Sa rubbed his head against the hand, then jerked it away and lifted his muzzle to the sky. Meren heard a loud sniff. Sa dug in his paws. The leash tightened and the king hauled on his reins.

"What ails you, Sa?" the boy asked as the company slowed to a halt behind him.

Meren watched the cat begin to circle, his tail lashing, his nose quivering. Suddenly a low growl made Meren grip the hilt of his scimitar.

"Majesty, he scents something." Meren signalled to the commander of chariots, and scouts broke from the ranks. At the same time orders were shouted. Chariots wheeled and turned, drove ahead and around the king.

Tutankhamun rolled his eyes. "Meren, it's probably a dead animal."

"No doubt, Golden One."

When Meren failed to recall the chariots, Tutankhamun sighed and tugged on the gilded leash. Sa ignored his master. Just then the north breeze picked up, and Sa gave another rumbling growl. Backing up against the leash, Sa gave a hard tug. The king lost his grip, and Sa whirled, springing past horses and chariots alike.

"Sa, return! Sa!"

"Majesty!"

Meren cursed as Tutankhamun launched his vehicle after the leopard. He slapped his own reins and hurtled after the king. Executing a tight turn, Meren followed the king through the ranks of charioteers. In moments he had broken through the lines and was careening after the youth in the golden chariot that gleamed like the solar orb in the early dawn light. They raced across the rock desert after Sa, their wheels sending grit and sharp rocks flying as they headed west towards the wall of limestone cliffs. Here the land undulated towards the base of the escarpment where the cliffs dropped back to form a small bay. Ahead, Meren saw the black streak that was Sa angled sharply to the north and vanish over a small hillock.

Shouting for the king to wait, Meren watched with dread as the boy vanished over the hillock without slowing. This was danger, a young king rushing into the unknown, heedless of peril. For Tutankhamun ruled over a kingdom in disarray. His brother and predecessor, Akhenaten, had almost brought about civil war with his heretical policies. Obsessed with his god of the sun disk called the Aten, Akhenaten had disestablished the old gods of Egypt who had protected the kingdom from the beginning of time. He persecuted those who wouldn't follow his precepts, and Egypt suffered. Only now had order been restored, but there were factions in the land who hated anyone who shared the blood of the heretic, even an innocent boy. Other groups wished to restore the heresy, and others lusted for the power invested in this slim youth with the great dark eyes and compassionate nature. All this flashed through Meren's thoughts as he gained the summit of the hillock. So many lay in wait for a chance to catch this youth alone and unprotected, where a seeming accident could cut short a promising reign.

Meren caught sight of Pharaoh as he plunged down the opposite side of the hillock. The boy was drawing close to Sa, who had stopped at a lump on the desert floor, a smudge of dark brown against the cream of the limestone rock. Vultures flapped their wings and retreated from Sa in an ungainly stumble before they launched into the air. Meren scanned the area for danger as the rest of the charioteers rumbled up behind him. Satisfied that there was no peril lurking nearby, Meren jumped out of his vehicle and walked over to where the king was stooping to grasp Sa's leash.

"Meren, look!"

The big cat was sniffing a bundle of linen covered with flies. As Meren got closer Sa pawed at something – an arm. The king's guardian had scented the blood that smeared the rocks in a trail that originated somewhere at the base of the cliffs.

Meren glanced over his shoulder at the commander of charioteers. "Stay back and deploy the guard."

The body was lying face down and was clothed in a kilt and cloak, both of which were caked with blood. Meren thought briefly of sending the king away, but the boy would see more carnage than this at the head of the army.

"The poor man. Turn him over, Meren."

Complying, Meren beheld a man of middle years, neither a youth nor an elder, with a wound in the abdomen that must have caused a slow and painful death. Quickly Meren noted the short-cropped hair, the swelling, overfed stomach that seemed at odds with work-roughened hands. His clothing was made of ordinary smooth cloth, the quality used by most Egyptians. It was a much thicker grade of textile compared to the fine royal linen worn by Pharaoh and the aristocracy.

"Do you know him?" the king asked as they stared at the corpse.

"No, majesty, but he's most peculiar. He has worked hard

with his hands like a peasant yet had enough food to get a paunch, something one seldom sees in a farmer."

"And his nose is red under all that dirt."

"Yes, majesty, from drink rather than the sun. Do you see those spidery veins?"

"Someone stabbed him, didn't they?"

"Aye, majesty. I'll have the city police investigate."

Tutankhamun handed Sa's leash to a bodyguard. "But we should follow his trail now."

Meren hesitated, knowing the king's curiosity had been aroused. He chafed at the constraints placed upon him by his position, and Meren couldn't blame him. To be a living god was to live surrounded by ritual and formality. To govern an empire required exhaustive training in the ways of Egypt's vast governing bureaucracy, in diplomacy and in military affairs. The boy rarely had a free moment. When he wasn't reading and interpreting reports of the season's harvest he was receiving envoys from foreign kings or studying with his tutors. Most important of all, Pharaoh was the mediator between the gods and his subjects, and through him the balance of the world was maintained. The son of the chief god, Amun, the king propitiated the deities of Egypt to hold at bay the forces of chaos and evil when he celebrated the secret rituals in the temples of the gods. Thus Tutankhamun lived with a great burden for one so young. Meren noted the sympathy in the king's eyes as he gazed at the dead man, and the spark of inquisitiveness. Perhaps this was an opportunity to teach the king something of his methods of investigation and at the same time relieve the tedium of royal duties.

"Thy majesty wishes to follow the dead one's path?"

"Yes. Are you going to let me?"

"Thy majesty's will is accomplished."

Tutankhamun gave him a sceptical look. "Is that so? Then why didn't you let me go on that raid against the sand dwellers last month? Ha! The whole kingdom thinks I rule unchallenged when the truth is I must obey far too many people. Well this time my wishes shall prevail."

"Of course, majesty." Meren bowed before the king.

"Oh, stand up straight, Meren. There's no use pretending you haven't already decided to let me do this."

"As thy majesty wishes."

"Humph."

The trail of blood led straight to the base of the cliffs that rose at least thirty cubits high above the desert floor. They formed undulating vertical shafts like pleats in a linen robe, and the cliff face was riddled with hollows and caves. The trail ended abruptly about thirty paces from the cliff base, but Meren was able to discern dragging footprints that took him to a fan of debris. He climbed over the rocks with the king and his bodyguards close behind only to find nothing but a blank wall with a spray of boulders in front of it. They stared at the area for a few moments before Meren noticed a shadow. Walking between two of the boulders, Meren found the mouth of a small cave, and lying in the sand before it was a dagger. The king stooped, his hand outstretched.

"Majesty, no!" Meren thrust his arm in front of the king. "There is contamination here, and evil. Pharaoh must not touch the blade of a murderer."

Meren explored the small cave and found more footprints and signs of a struggle between two men. Evidently a fight started in the cave and continued outside. Together he and Pharaoh knelt to examine the weapon. The bronze blade was encrusted with blackened blood, but what surprised Meren was the quality of the object.

"Majesty, this isn't the blade of a commoner."

"I know. Look at the engraving on the blade."

The maker had etched a central grove down the blade that ended in a palmette design. The hilt was dusty and smeared with more blood. A bodyguard handed Meren a rag, and he cleaned the weapon as best he could.

"The hilt is ebony," the king said.

"Aye, majesty, and the pommel alabaster that was once carved and stained with black and red ink to bring out the design." Meren held the weapon up to the light. "There may be words engraved in the alabaster."

Meren called for the scribe of charioteers, who provided ink and water. In a short time he was smearing black ink on the alabaster pommel. Holding the dagger to the light again, Meren read, "The good – something – lord – something – valour, Nefer-khep – something." Meren looked at the king, who met his gaze in silence, his eyes wide.

"Meren . . ."

"I know, Golden One."

The king drew closer and lowered his voice. "What is this blade doing here?"

"I know not, majesty."

Meren turned the blade over, but could see no other distinguishing marks. It mattered little, however. The words engraved on the alabaster pommel were fragmentary but more than enough. Both he and the king possessed daggers engraved with similar phrases. In the king's case, almost identical. The alabaster pommel had been carved with the formal phrase, "The good god, lord of valour, Nefer-kheperu-re."

Nefer-kheperu-re was a throne name, the name a king took upon his accession to the throne of Egypt. Tutankhamun's throne name was Neb-kheperu-re. But this name was slightly different, *Nefer*-kheperu-re, and that difference was enough to send dread racing through Meren's body. For Nefer-kheperu-re was the throne name of the king's dead brother, the reviled and cursed heretic, Akhenaten.

On the east bank of the Nile in Thebes lay the massive temples of Amun and his goddess consort, Mut. Protected by high walls and pylon gates, within gold and electrum encrusted doors, rested the statues of the gods. On the west bank, between emerald fields of grain and the barren mountains soared the mortuary temples of Egypt's greatest pharaohs. Within these offerings were made to deceased kings like Thutmose the Conqueror, who had extended Egypt's empire far to the north and south. In the mountains nearby, in a steep-sided valley, was the Place of Truth, the site of the secret burials of the kings of Egypt. Just south of the mortuary temple of Amunhotep III, the king's father, sat the glorious palace of Pharaoh. Surrounding it were lesser palaces of the chief royal wife as well as those of the household of royal women. The dwellings of those who served the king and his family clustered close to the walls of the royal enclosure along with barracks and workshops.

In the royal precinct Meren had just arrived at one of the servants' houses where Kar, the dead man, had lived. He'd seldom had occasion to go into so modest a dwelling, and for Meren the experience was enlightening. He was in the tiny reception area, no more than an empty space before the living room, and he already felt cramped. This place was less than a tenth the size of his town house.

Yesterday after he returned to the palace with the king he'd sent his adopted son Kysen to find out who the dead man was and to investigate the circumstances of his death. It turned out that Kar belonged to a family in service to Pharaoh, one of thousands spread throughout the kingdom. Kysen and Meren's chief aide, Abu, had been investigating all morning. So far no one knew what Kar was doing in the desert last night or how he came to be stabbed with a dagger that had once belonged to the heretic king. Because of the dagger, the death had taken on much more importance that it would ordinarily have had. Meren was by nature suspicious, and the link to the royal family must be followed.

Walking into the deserted living area, Meren examined his surroundings. Along the far wall there was a low platform upon which rested a table with a water jar and clay cups. Reed mats served as rugs, and the roof was supported by a central column. An interior stair probably led to a bedroom. Meren heard voices, and Kysen walked in with Abu from the kitchen that lay beyond the living area.

"Ah, Father. You persuaded Pharaoh not to come," Kysen said.

"Indeed. I explained that his appearance would cause a riot and impede the investigation. The Golden One was most annoyed."

Kysen grinned. "We've talked to Kar's family and friends, what few of them there are. Did you know his brother is assistant to the master of royal unguent makers? What was his name, Abu?"

"Onuris, lord."

"And the parents?" Meren asked.

"The father's name is Wersu, lord. He used to be an unguent maker. The mother is Qedet." Abu nodded towards the kitchen. "They are in there. The woman is weeping, and her husband is staring at her."

"I hope you have something to tell me. All we got from the scene at the cave were imprints of palm sandals, and there are tens of thousands of those in the city."

Kysen leaned against the central column and sighed. "There's not much to be learned. The parents were at home all night, and thought Kar was home sleeping too. Since he was probably killed late last night, he must have slipped out unseen. He was a sweeper and doorkeeper with the royal women's household. The steward had assigned him to watch the garden gate from late afternoon until about three hours past sunset. But the parents say he lost his position there a few weeks ago. Before that he was a tender of animals at the royal menagerie, and before that an assistant to one of the royal unguent makers like his brother."

"And what about the dagger?"

Abu shook his head. "Neither of them know where it came from. They swear they've never seen it before."

"We were going to talk to Onuris," Kysen said. "He's at work in the royal workshops."

"Very well. I'm going back to the palace after I'm through here. I'll talk to the steward who oversaw Kar."

Kysen presented Kar's parents to Meren before he left. Wersu was sitting on the floor in the kitchen at a low table. He was tent-pole thin, with a few wisps of silver hair remaining on his head, and a few brown teeth still left in his head. His wife was younger and retained some of the agreeable features of youth. Her hair was thick and curly, her skin soft from the application of oils. Qedet had a wide face and large, heavy-lidded eyes, and Meren could imagine she had once commanded admiration from many men. At the moment, though, she was squatting on her heels, rocking back and forth and moaning. Her eyes were red, and she kept wiping them with a length of a large piece of linen. Qedet was cleaning the linen by dipping a corner of it in a solution of water and natron salt and rubbing it to get rid of an ink stain.

Wersu shook his head over and over. "He wouldn't listen to me, Lord Meren. He just wouldn't listen. Just wouldn't listen. Paid me no heed at all. Just wouldn't listen."

"About what?"

"Work." Wersu regarded his wife sorrowfully while she rubbed the stained linen furiously "He wouldn't work. He thought it was owed him, his position. He was an unguent maker like I was. Could have been one of the best. He was apprenticed to the royal workshop. How many can say that? But Kar never saw it that way. Ungrateful, lazy. I tried to tell him, but he never listened. Just wouldn't listen."

Meren leaned against a wall beside the archway between the kitchen and living area. "You're saying Kar was too lazy to work."

"Ohhh," Qedet moaned and dabbed her eyes with a dry piece of the linen in her hands.

Wersu rubbed his forehead wearily. "Forgive me, great lord, but that is true."

"What did he do, then?"

"He drank, lord. He ate, drank and slept."

"My poor son," Qedet wailed as she wrung the soaked linen. "You didn't understand him. He was sensitive. Not like other boys."

Wersu scowled at his wife again. "He wasn't a boy. He had almost three decades, and he was a lazy sot."

Qedet shot her husband a venomous look, then saw Meren staring at her and lowered her gaze to the stain in the linen that was almost gone now.

"You told my son you could think of no one who might want to kill your son."

"Everyone liked Kar," Qedet said.

Grunting in disgust, Wersu pursed his lips. Meren lifted a brow, and the old man sighed.

"Kar was annoying, but that is all."

Meren spent a few more unproductive minutes talking to

Wersu and Qedet. Then he went on a tour around the house, leaving the parents grieving in the kitchen. They seemed to be much like other parents, the mother doting, the father stern, both disappointed in their younger son.

He didn't expect to find anything incriminating in this house, but he liked to get a sense of people from their homes and possessions. Kar lived with his brother and parents in this house all his life; it might have something to say to him.

Beginning in the living area, Meren noted the only furniture besides the eating table was a stool made of cheap sycamore wood with a woven seat. The kitchen had baskets of food, but not in any great quantity – bread, onions, dates, leeks and a couple of wrinkled cucumbers. Bread and onions were the staples of the commoner class, Meren knew, as was beer. He'd seen no beer jars, but if Kar was a drinker . . .

Meren took an interior stair down to the cellar. Here he found one jar of dried peas, one of beer and one of fish oil. He opened a small reed basket filled with dates. Onions hung from the ceiling. A dozen or so jars stood empty along with several wicker boxes.

"No spices," Meren muttered. "No dried fish."

Leaving the cellar, he went upstairs and found himself in the main bedroom. Here sat a wooden bed with a plaited rush base and straw-filled mattress. The sheets were askew and looked as if they were seldom straightened. However, they were of good quality, probably the grade called fine thin cloth, almost as good as royal linen. Evidently unlike the linen in the kitchen, Qedet didn't wash these delicate sheets, for they had laundry marks. The portable stool that served as a lavatory stood over a pottery jar filled with sand. It hadn't been emptied. In a corner, rumpled and dirty, were a couple of loincloths and a kilt. Half a dozen empty beer jars stood around the bed. Meren surveyed the room with a frown. It appeared that the drunkard Kar had slept in the large master chamber.

In the remaining room opposite Meren found three sleeping mats, more clothing in a rickety wicker box, and a tarnished bronze hand mirror in a bag along with a comb and cosmetic set. It was peculiar that Wersu and Qedet shared a chamber with their oldest son. This was Wersu's house; he should have occupied the larger, better room.

Mounting the stairs again, Meren went onto the roof where a loom sat under an awning of palm leaves. Nearby he saw a small fireplace over which rested a tripod. Looking over the roof to the courtyard in front of the house Meren saw a beehive-shaped grain bin. One lonely goose pecked at grain scattered on the ground. Beyond the courtyard the street was busy. A herdsman ushered cattle down a narrow road while a man led a donkey loaded with palm fronds the opposite way. A self-important priest wearing a leopard-skin cloak and carrying a walking stick thrashed at a group of boys who danced around and taunted him. Groups of women passed by with laundry in baskets on their heads; some carried water jars. It was a typical busy city street, dirty, noisy and cheerful. Kar's house was barren, deserted, quiet. The family hadn't even hired professional mourners to stand about crying and throwing ashes and rending their garments as people usually did. Meren doubted that Wersu could afford them.

Meren was glad to leave the house. It oppressed his spirits with its air of lost prosperity and strained relationships. The family of Wersu wasn't a happy one, but there seemed to be no undercurrents of violence that could have led to murder. Meren headed for the royal precinct.

The main Theban palace occupied by the royal women's household was called Hathor's Ornament. The steward who oversaw the running of the household, Lord Peya, sent Meren to the master of doorkeepers and porters, a man of foreign descent called Uthi. Uthi was one of those men who glided when he walked. His hands fluttered when he spoke and he talked with a lisp.

"Kar?" Uthi's hands fluttered as he stood before Meren in the lofty reception chamber of the palace. "What would the great Lord Meren want with that lazy donkey?" When Meren didn't answer, Uthi went on. "Kar worked as a doorkeeper here for almost a year, Great One. But he was never satisfactory. He fell asleep on duty, showed up late. Sometimes he left his post but, worst of all, he was drunk most of the time. The other doorkeepers and porters told me that when he received his ration payments he would at once spend them on more drink."

"What finally caused you to get rid of him?"

Uthi sniffed. "I like to think of myself as a tolerant man, O great lord. But three weeks ago when I told Kar his wages would be reduced because he was sleeping on the job, he abused me and tried to strike me. I fended him off with my staff. Luckily my assistant was with me, and he wrestled Kar to the ground. I think all that beer finally pickled his wits. That's the thanks I get for trying to serve the royal ladies so faithfully. Why, I only kept him on because he was in Princess Iaret's favour. If it weren't for her, he would have been cast out long before. And after all, what did he have to do but stand at a garden gate and open it occasionally?"

"Princess Iaret favoured a doorkeeper?"

Uthi must have sensed Meren's scepticism. "Oh, yes, mighty lord. Princess Iaret is a sweet lady, full of kindness and compassion. She is always giving aid to the lowest servants. She even speaks up for slaves accused of stealing. Her reputation for goodness is well known to the royal household."

"Of course."

Meren remembered Iaret now. She the half-royal offspring of the heretic Akhenaten and a lowborn concubine. Had Iaret been a male child, she would have had a chance of becoming Pharaoh, but as a woman, she was just one of many superfluous royal children. Most such half-royal princesses lived uneventful lives in the royal women's household forgotten by the court. Meren asked a few more questions.

Soon Meren dismissed Uthi and started pacing the reception room. He had a murder weapon that had once belonged to Akhenaten, and now he learned that the dead man had been favoured by one of Akhenaten's half-royal daughters. Was there a connection? He couldn't imagine Princess Iaret stabbing a doorkeeper, but perhaps the dagger was an inheritance from her father. Kar might have stolen it. Uthi had denied that

Kar was a thief, saying that the man was too drunk to steal most of the time, and at other times he was asleep.

Meren requested an audience with Princess Iaret, who quickly appeared in the reception chamber carrying her pet cat. Iaret's mother had been beautiful, as was the case with most royal concubines. Unfortunately the 19-year-old princess had inherited Akhenaten's horse-face, hollow shoulders and spindly legs. However, Meren hadn't spent more than a few moments in her company before he understood why Uthi had been so effusive in praise of her.

"Dear Lord Meren, what a surprise. How are your lovely daughters? Isis is the youngest, is she not? And such a beauty."

"All are well, Princess."

"And your fine son Kysen?" she asked as she stroked the cat in her arms. "I have heard that he is becoming a skillful warrior like his father."

"You're kind, my lady."

"I visited Tefnut and Bener at your town house last month, but you were away. Your daughters were kind enough to give me plant cuttings for the garden. Your house is magnificent."

"Thank you, Princess."

Iaret indicated two high-backed chairs of ebony and ivory. "Let us sit, my lord. Why insist on stuffy etiquette, eh?"

Iaret seated herself and settled her cat on her lap. To Meren the creature looked like a miniature Sa – long and lean with shining black fur. This cat's eyes weren't green, though. They were tawny gold and as large as olives. Iaret was holding the cat up to her face.

"My little Miu. You got lost yesterday, didn't you? Mother was frantic. Yes, she was." Iaret turned to Meren. "She went out hunting and got lost in the servants' quarters. She's the first animal I've ever owned, and I love her dearly. I don't know what I'd do if I lost her." Iaret's eyes grew bright with tears. She buried her nose in Miu's black fur. "You will think me foolish, Lord Meren."

"Soft-hearted, Princess, but not foolish. It is never foolish to give one's love."

Iaret looked at him over her cat and grinned. "They say you're the consummate royal courtier, and now I know why."

"Forgive me, my lady," Meren said with a smile. "I have a few questions I would like to ask you."

"Yes?"

"Do you own a bronze dagger with an alabaster pommel?"

"What an odd question. Why do you ask?"

"Please, my lady. Do you own such a dagger?"

"No, I don't think so." Iaret's brow furrowed. "I own a few knives, cosmetic implements such as razors and the like. I've no need of a dagger." She gestured widely. "There are plenty of guards with daggers and spears should I need a weapon."

"I thought perhaps the king, your father . . ."

"No, I don't remember him giving me something like that. I rarely saw him you know." She eyed him. "You're so grave. If it's that important, you should ask the steward for the latest inventory. I think it was done six or seven months ago. It should list everyone's possessions."

"Thank you, Princess. I will." Meren hesitated. "I must also ask you about the garden doorkeeper called Kar."

Iaret was stroking her cat, her head lowered. "The doorkeeper Kar, yes. He's gone, you know."

"He's dead."

The Princess' head jerked up. She stared at him with wide eyes, her mouth open. Moments passed before she spoke.

"Dead? But he was here only a few weeks ago cursing and weaving around drunk. Oh. Did he have some accident while besotted? I was so worried about him. He was drinking himself into ill health."

"No," Meren said softly. "He was murdered. Stabbed to death with a dagger engraved with the name of your father."

Iaret continued to stare at him in horror. "But that can't be. Wait." She narrowed her eyes. "Surely you don't entertain suspicions of me. *Me*? By all the gods, how could you think I would do such a thing?"

"Princess, I am the Eyes and Ears of Pharaoh. When murder touches those near Pharaoh, I pursue the evil one no matter where the trail leads. You know this."

"But *me*. It's ridiculous. I tried to help Kar." Iaret was clutching her cat to her breast as if to protect herself.

"Sometimes there are false trails," Meren said, feeling guilty for upsetting this sweet girl in spite of himself.

"Oh." Iaret sighed. "I see. Then you aren't going to arrest me?"

"Of course not."

"Good. I've never been arrested before. I'm sure I wouldn't like it."

Meren shook his head. Iaret seemed guileless, dangerously so for a member of the imperial court. They talked about Kar, but Iaret had little to add to what Meren already knew. Kar was a wastrel who had been given many chances to reform to no avail. Finally even Iaret had given up on him.

Meren took his leave of the Princess and requested the household inventory from the steward, Lord Peya. The official produced a leather box filled with papyri. Meren located the inventory of the princess only to find that Iaret had been right. She owned no daggers. She had lots of jewels of gold, electrum, lapis lazuli, carnelian and other precious stones. She owned many clothes, and dozens of bolts of royal linen, vessels of alabaster and granite, and a valuable mirror of silver, but no weapons. Several of the foreign princesses who had married into the royal family possessed daggers, but none of the descriptions matched the murder weapon. Looking at the stacks of inventories, Meren considered sending someone else to plough through them. But he was already here. So he read of lists of royal possessions, his fingers tracing the columns in a fruitless search for the engraved dagger. He even sent for the few daggers he located in hopes of finding one similar to the one that killed Kar. A fruitless effort. Finally he thanked Lord Peya and left Hathor's Ornament for his town house.

At home he met Kysen in the large room on the second floor that served as his office. It was late afternoon, and he could smell antelope roasting in the kitchens. Kysen entered the office with a stranger trailing behind him.

"Lord Meren, this is the unguent maker Onuris, brother of Kar. I have brought him to you that you may hear his story."

Meren nodded, taking his seat on his favourite chair on the master's dais at one end of the office. Kysen had been born into the artisan class, the son of a tomb worker in the Place of Truth. His ear was more attuned to the nuances of conduct in commoners. In the past year he'd grown more confident in his position as Meren's heir. Now he could intimidate a reluctant witness almost as well as Meren. They seldom had to resort to physical punishment, which was good in Meren's opinion. Beatings extorted lots of information from people, but often it was useless, given simply to escape pain.

Kysen leaned on Meren's chair and whispered to him. "It was hard going, but I got the truth out of him." Kysen straightened. "Onuris, son of Wersu, tell Lord Meren what you told me."

Onuris was a slim version of his younger brother, with thick hair and a habit of wiping his clammy hands on his kilt. He smelled faintly of myrrh and frankincense. He bowed and cleared his throat.

"Eyes and Ears of Pharaoh, to my great sorrow my younger brother was a dissolute and unworthy man who took it as a great insult that he had to work for his livelihood. I'm afraid my parents doted on him throughout his childhood and youth. They praised him when he made little effort and excused his shortcomings rather than correct them."

"Is this why Kar occupied the master's chamber in your house when it should have been your parents' room?" Meren asked.

Onuris hesitated. "In part, lord. I have explained why Kar behaved as he did, but there came a time when he grew intolerable even to my parents, about a month ago." Swallowing hard, Onuris stuttered before continuing. "I – I have been so worried. I knew something was wrong, but he was my brother, no matter his faults, so I kept silent."

"This isn't the time to keep secrets," Meren said.

"Yes, lord. You see, a couple of months ago Kar began bringing home valuable things – alabaster jars, a gold armband, fine leather sandals. He said he won these things gaming at his favorite tavern. Well, Kar was not the kind of man who won things. He was usually too drunk to concentrate. I thought . . ."

"He stole them," Meren finished.

Onuris hung his head.

Meren glanced at Kysen. "The dagger?"

"No," Kysen said. "It appears he never brought such a thing home."

"No, lord," said Onuris. "I followed him once, thinking to solve the mystery, but Kar only went to his usual tavern and drank until he fell on the floor. Last week I tried again, but he saw me. After that Kar took all the valuable things and hid them. I don't know where."

"The cave," Kysen said.

Meren sighed. "Indeed. Whoever killed Kar must have taken the stolen items."

According to Onuris it was after Kar became wealthy that he demanded the best room and generally became unbearable. He used abusive language to his family and tried to strike Onuris when his brother attempted to persuade their parents to evict Kar. Wersu wanted to toss Kar out of the house then, but Qedet defended her youngest son. She reminded Wersu that Kar's new wealth would provide better for the family than he ever had. In Qedet's view, riches excused almost any evil.

Listening to Onuris, Meren began to get that irritable feeling that meant he'd missed something. There had to be a connection between Kar's death and Hathor's Ornament. Almost certainly that was where the dead man had got the stolen goods, and that meant he had help from someone inside the palace. But why hadn't the thefts been reported? Perhaps Lord Peya was concealing them because such evil doings reflected badly on him. Pharaoh might take Peya's office away from him. Meren dismissed Onuris with a command to report anything else he remembered to Kysen.

When the unguent maker was gone, Kysen sank to the dais beside Meren. "He was stealing from the royal women's palace."

"Yes," Meren said, rubbing his temples. "And someone in a high position was covering it up. Damnation, this is going to be a scandal. More corruption. The high priest of Amun will be delighted to spread stories that the heretic's brother is incompetent and can't even govern the palaces of his women. That old man is riddled with hate for the royal family."

"I can't imagine anyone hated Pharaoh," Kysen said.

"You were a child when Akhenaten did away with the old gods of Egypt. Paranefer and his priests suffered terribly under Akhenaten. Many of them died rather than renounce Amun for the king's new god. Curse it. Thinking of Paranefer has given me a headache."

"What will you do?"

"Try to investigate quickly and quietly, before Paranefer gets wind of the scandal." Meren rose and stepped off the dais. "But tomorrow morning I must first tell Pharaoh."

Meren's town house sheltered behind high walls. Ancient sycamores, tamarisks and willows clustered near the main house with its reflection pools and loggias. Behind the house lay a separate walled garden, service buildings, servants quarters and barracks for the charioteers serving the Eyes and Ears of Pharaoh.

That irritable feeling of having missed something important kept Meren awake when everyone else had gone to bed. Having given up chasing sleep Meren left the house and walked to the stables where his thoroughbreds resided in pampered luxury. The two stallions, Wind Chaser and Star Chaser, greeted him with nickers and tossing heads. Meren fed them handfuls of grain and listened to the low grinding of their teeth as they ate. He had always liked the sound, so peaceful and regular.

He was going back to Hathor's Ornament in the morning, after he spoke with Pharaoh. The scale of his inquiry would increase, and the king must approve. Meren was worried, for what had appeared to be a simple murder of a commoner had become something far more complex. There was no telling how great the scale of corruption was or how high it had spread.

Meren rubbed his face against Star Chaser's dish-shaped

jaw. The horse gently nibbled at his shoulder. Suddenly Star Chaser's head jerked back and his ears flattened.

"What's wrong, old friend?" Meren asked, reaching for Star Chaser's mane.

That was when he felt a tiny current of air against his back. He turned slightly, and pain exploded in his head. Meren fell against the stall door, dazed, clutching his head. Someone grabbed him, and a fist jabbed into his stomach. Meren sank to the ground, trying not to vomit. Before he could recover his attacker yanked him up by the hair. A blade appeared at his throat and pressed into his skin.

"What luck to find you alone so soon," a voice hissed.

Meren was still too stunned to do more than gasp.

"Listen to me, Eyes and Ears of Pharaoh. The doorkeeper was killed by someone he had debts with, a friend or a tavern keeper. Accuse one of them and settle this inquiry. Otherwise you're not so mighty that you can't be dispatched as easily as that drunken sot. Allow me to show you."

Suddenly the blade sliced his throat, but Meren grabbed the arm of his attacker, ramming it backwards and rolling out of his grip at the same time. As he rolled a shadow swooped at him. It fastened hands on his head and jammed it into the hard-packed earth of the stable floor. Blackness took him in less than a beat of his heart.

The uproar over the attack on him caused Meren more pain than his injuries. Kysen stomped around giving orders to the charioteers to track the invader while Meren's daughters tried to put him to bed and called his physician. For his part, Meren was furious. It was humiliating for a king's warrior to be attacked in his own dwelling and beaten like a peasant who had failed to pay enough tax. Thus Meren was in a foul mood late the next morning when he went to Pharaoh's palace to report on his progress sporting a bandage wrapped around his throat. It stuck out above the gold and lapis lazuli broad collar he wore. His head ached beneath the formal wig that fell to his shoulders. When he saw Meren the king wanted to call out the royal guard to arrest someone, anyone. It took all of Meren's persuasive skills to calm the boy down so that he could point out that they had no one to arrest.

Ra's fiery orb was high in the sky before Meren was able to leave the palace and pay another visit to the house of Kar's family. Kysen was already at Hathor's Ornament with a squad of charioteers and scribes. They were going over the accounts and records of the royal women's household in search of inconsistencies. The questioning of the royal women would have to wait until Meren arrived.

Meren now knew he was looking for someone other than a lowborn thief. His attacker had known how to use a blade and had fought like a warrior. That ruled out farmers, craftsmen and many scribes and government officials. And few men in Egypt had the temerity to threaten the Eyes and Ears of Pharaoh and expect to get away with it. The attempt spoke of desperation or a rashness that seemed inconsistent with the careful way in which the murderer had concealed many of his actions.

At Kar's house Meren noticed right away that the family's circumstances had changed. Wall hangings brightened the walls, food was more abundant, and Kar's father appeared almost cheerful.

Wersu greeted him with a sad smile. "You honour us, Lord Meren."

Glancing around the living area, Meren nodded at a large wine jar on a stand. "I see many improvements since I was last here."

"Ah, yes. I am ashamed that I had to conceal many of my possessions from Kar, my lord. He would take things and trade them for beer and wine. His mother had to hide her jewels, her clothing, even her linens."

"Where is Mistress Qedet?"

"I will fetch her.'

Meren shook his head. "We will go to her."

"She is upstairs, lord."

In the master chamber Qedet was busy putting clean sheets on the bed that her son once occupied. When Meren entered she hastily tucked a sheet under the mattress and stuffed more folded linens into a box at the foot of the bed.

"I want to ask you if Kar ever said anything about his work at Hathor's Ornament," Meren said.

Wersu and Qedet glanced at each other.

"Not much, my lord," said Wersu. "He didn't like Uthi, the overseer of doorkeepers and porters. But Kar never liked anyone who had authority over him. That was why he failed as an unguent maker."

"And what about his sudden wealth? The gold bracelet, the other things?"

Wersu flushed, and Qedet burst out, "We were so afraid he'd stolen them. Onuris told you about those things, I know. What were we to do? Give our son to the police? I couldn't bear the shame. Please, my lord, we're old and humble, and have been good subjects all our lives. May the gods witness how we tell the truth. We didn't steal, and Kar didn't tell us anything."

No matter how he approached the matter, Meren couldn't alarm or trick Wersu or his wife into admitting being involved in their son's crimes. Further intimidation would be necessary, and that meant dragging the old couple to the barracks at his house. That could wait until he'd finished with the people at Hathor's Ornament. Then he would send men for Wersu and Qedet. Being summoned at a late hour to appear before him often was enough of a shock to loosen tongues. Meren eyed Wersu as the older man made more excuses for his son's crimes. Qedet added her own litany when Wersu ran out of breath. Losing interest in their justifications, Meren's attention strayed. His gaze drifted from the ceramic lamps distributed about the room to the small alabaster and faience tubes and trays used to hold eye paint and kohl eyeliner.

That nagging irritable feeling was back. He was about to interrupt Qedet when his eye caught the newly made bed. Light streamed in from a window set high in the wall and caught the sheen of the linens on the bed. Such fine cloth, almost the quality of royal linen – soft, smooth, tightly woven. It was then that Meren remembered his first visit to this house. He'd been talking to these two in the kitchen, and Qedet had been scrubbing a spot off a sheet, an ink spot. Only now Meren realized it hadn't been a spot. It had been a laundry mark, and that mark had been from the laundry at Hathor's Ornament. Meren suddenly shoved Wersu aside, walked over to the bed and pulled at the sheets.

Wersu followed him, wringing his hands. "My lord!"

Meren turned to him with the corner of a sheet in his hands. "Your wife couldn't remove the mark entirely. I can still see the name of the owner, Wersu. Your son stole this from Princess Iaret. It's time for the truth, unless you'd rather wait for the attentions of the city police."

"No! No, my lord, please, I'll tell you what I know." Wersu licked his lips and clasped his trembling hands. "Kar brought home a large box of linens, and these are some of them. He – he wasn't stealing –"

"I should have brought my whip," Meren snapped.

"No, please, lord. Kar told me what he was doing one night when he was drunk. He knew a secret, a secret about one of the ladies, and she was giving him valuable things so that he would keep the secret."

"Out with it, Wersu. The woman was Princess Iaret. What was the secret?"

"It was that Princess Iaret had fallen in love with Lord Roma. She met him while performing her duties in the temple as a singer of the great god Amun. Kar saw them meeting secretly late one night in the garden of Hathor's Ornament. He went to the Princess and threatened to expose the affair if she didn't pay him."

Meren's eyes narrowed, but he said nothing. It was worse than he'd imagined. Roma was the grandson of the Paranefer, the high priest of Amun. He had just stumbled onto what could be a plot to take the throne of Egypt. It had been done before. A man of great ambition could marry a royal princess. If he had enough backing from the powerful temples and nobles, he could seize the throne and legitimize his claim through his wife. This was why so many princesses remained within the royal women's household where Pharaoh could keep an eye on them. Iaret was the daughter of Akhenaten. Roma was a young man of great skill as a warrior, having won battles against the wild tribes of Nubia and rebellious Asiatic vassal princes. He had a large following in the army. Together Roma and the Princess could be a real threat to the immature Tutankhamun, especially with the richest temple in Egypt, that of Amun, behind them. Cursing, Meren left Wersu and Qedet pleading for leniency and making excuses for themselves instead of their son. As he stepped out of the house he heard Qedet screeching at Wersu, blaming him for their misery. His last sight was of Wersu, his flaccid skin pale, his eyes watery, staring after Meren like the shade of one without a tomb doomed to wander lost for ever.

Instead of going to Hathor's Ornament, Meren returned home and sent for Kysen and his men. He spent a few hours in preparation before dispatching a messenger with a polite invitation for Lord Roma to visit him. The young man arrived near dusk. Meren received him in the reception hall of his town house, a graceful room with a high ceiling supported by eight slender columns in the form of water lilies. Wearing an intricately pleated robe of royal linen, a gold broad collar set with carnelian and turquoise, and matching armbands, Meren was seated on the master dais in a gilded chair. Kysen and Abu stood beside him.

Roma strolled into the reception hall resplendent in his own jewels and fine linen. He was one of those men who, despite being rather plain, exuded an air of power and confidence. "An invitation from the great Lord Meren. An unexpected honour." He bowed slightly, the salute of one equal to another.

"Welcome, and may the gods bless you, Lord Roma. May I inquire as to the health of your grandfather?"

"He's well, considering his great age." Without being invited Roma sat in a chair near the dais and helped himself from a bowl of dates on a nearby table. "What's the purpose of your invitation, Meren? I'm due at the temple for the evening ritual. I'm a lector priest, you know."

"A learned man and a skilled warrior," Meren said softly. "Admirable accomplishments for one so young. The ladies at court must find you irresistible."

Something flickered in Roma's eyes, but he answered easily. "No more irresistible than you, Meren. You should have remarried by now, if you'll pardon me. You wife has been dead many years."

"True, Roma." Meren rose and stepped down from the dais, ending up beside his guest. He bent down and hissed, "But I don't have a princess besotted with love for me." As he spoke Meren pulled Roma's dagger out of its sheath and rested it against the hollow of his throat. Leaning close, he said, "I don't appreciate being attacked from behind in my own home, Roma. I ought to gut you just for that."

Roma had frozen when Meren drew his dagger. He met Meren's eyes, lifted his chin and spat, "So you know. I've done nothing wrong."

"Corrupting a royal princess, you call that nothing? We shall see what Pharaoh thinks of it." Meren straightened as Kysen and Abu joined him and took up positions on either side of Roma. "You should have made sure Kar was dead before you left him. I'm surprised you didn't take him further out into the desert."

"Kar." Roma's dark eyes flashed with anger. "You think I killed that worthless donkey's arse? I didn't even know he was threatening Iaret until she confessed to me after you came to see her. She kept it from me because she knew I *would* kill him. You can ask her."

"I will, and I'm going to ask her if she gave you a dagger engraved with the name Nefer-kheperu-re."

"Well, she didn't," Roma sneered. "I happen to know that dagger just came in a couple of months ago. It was from a lot of items moved from the royal palace in the Fayyum Oasis. It had been her mother's. If Kar was killed with it, Iaret gave it to him to keep him quiet."

Meren realized with admiration that the sweet-natured and seemingly guileless Iaret had deceived him with great skill. He opened his mouth to reply, but shouting sounded at the front door. Something crashed to the floor in the entry hall, and an old priest charged into the hall followed by several retainers.

"What are you doing here, Paranefer?" Meren demanded.

Paranefer stopped and leaned on his walking stick, his scrawny chest heaving. "What are you doing with my grandson?"

"Don't bore me with this air of injured innocence," Meren said as he walked away from Roma. "I know the plot, Paranefer. You're not going to marry your grandson into the royal family. You'll be lucky to escape this with your life."

"What?" Paranefer squawked. He rounded on Lord Roma. "What's this, boy?"

Meren rolled his eyes, but Roma was staring at the floor and turning red. Curious, Meren remained silent while Paranefer continued.

"Is this true? Answer me, you addled colt!"

"Yes," Roma mumbled.

Paranefer let out a squeal of outrage. "What have you done? Who is it? Who is the woman?" His grandson muttered under his breath. "Who? I didn't hear you."

"It's Princess Iaret," Meren said as he watched Roma shrink under the molten gaze of his grandfather. His swagger and confidence had vanished.

The old priest's jaw dropped. He whacked Roma on the head and took his seat, his hands trembling. "A daughter of the heretic! May Amun protect me." He glared at Roma. "You would taint our blood by allying yourself with the spawn of that great criminal?"

Roma straightened and faced Paranefer. "I love her."

"What?" Paranefer regarded his grandson with horror.

"I love her!"

"Nonsense. No one could fall in love with one of the heretic's brood. You've betrayed me. May the gods witness my anguish." Paranefer moaned and spewed epithets at his grandson.

While the two argued, Meren took Kysen and Abu aside.

"They've forgotten about us," he said ruefully.

"Aye, Father. I believe the old man was ignorant of Roma's doings."

"Indeed," Abu said. "His outrage wasn't feigned."

Meren shook his head. "Love. I never considered it."

"That's what comes of being so jaded," Kysen said with a grin.

Frowning at his son, Meren said, "Nevertheless, Roma has interfered with a royal princess." He thought for a few moments. "However, one could view the liaison differently, as an opportunity to form an alliance with an old enemy."

"Paranefer would hate it," Kysen said with a bigger grin.

"All the more reason to approach Pharaoh with the idea. I shall consider it."

Abu cleared his throat. "And what of the murder, lord?"

"Yes, I'm inclined to believe someone else killed Kar with that dagger he got from the Princess," Meren said. "It's the simplest explanation."

Kysen looked at him inquiringly "Who?"

Meren said nothing for a few moments, toying with Roma's dagger as he thought. "By the mercy of Amun," he breathed.

"What is it, Father?"

"Abu, my chariot, quickly. We may be too late."

Meren paced back and forth. Kysen watched him anxiously while Paranefer and Roma argued, oblivious to their surroundings.

"What's wrong?" Kysen asked.

"I'm probably too late," Meren muttered.

"Father!"

Meren rounded on his son. "You stay here and watch our two guests, but don't keep them. They're not going to flee the city."

"Where are you going?"

Heading for the door, Meren said, "I'll take Abu with me."

Running out of the house, he found Abu careening around the corner of the house driving his chariot. The vehicle swerved so that Meren could jump in, and they rumbled down the tree-lined avenue and out of the gate in the wall that surrounded the estate. Scattering pedestrians, herds of sheep and donkeys, they clattered over the packed earth, down narrow streets and around precipitous corners. They skidded to a halt at a corner occupied by a stall selling fresh beer because the chariot wouldn't fit between it and the opposite house. Meren leaped to the ground with Abu close behind him and raced around the corner. He hurtled down the street and saw Wersu in his courtyard pulling on the tether of a donkey loaded with parcels. Meren stopped just beyond the courtyard wall, but the old man hadn't seen him. Wersu's front door was open, and he was shouting at someone inside.

"Hurry! Leave the rest! I have the valuables already."

Qedet shouted back. "I'm not leaving my linens!"

"Taking a trip, Wersu?" Meren asked softly.

The old man gasped and whirled around. Seeing Meren, he paled and opened his mouth. Nothing came out. Wersu's gaze jumped from Meren to the tall, imposing charioteer at his side.

Meren's fingers ran over the beads of electrum and lapis lazuli in the belt that cinched his robe over his kilt. "How unlike Kar to be so generous as to give you that valuable royal linen. I find myself unable to believe your tale, Wersu. I think Kar kept all his loot to himself. I think you were furious at him for this last and greatest injury. Did Kar threaten to leave and take his wealth with him after all you'd put up with from him?"

Dropping the donkey's tether, Wersu sobbed and dropped to the ground at Meren's feet.

Unmoved, Meren continued. "I think if I look in those carefully wrapped bundles on your donkey I'll find more of Princess Iaret's possessions. What do you think?"

Wersu raised himself, but he spoke to Meren's sandalled feet. "I beg mercy, great lord. Kar wouldn't share anything, not a bead, not a scrap of linen, and Qedet – My wife has always berated me for my lack of ambition and wealth. I thought to myself, at last, here is a chance to please her. She will love me as I've always wished now that I can give her the luxuries she craves. But Kar refused. After all I'd done for him, for years. I couldn't bear it, and Qedet kept complaining and criticizing." Wersu was quivering. "I was so tired and unhappy. I just wanted her to stop telling me what a failure I was, and Kar wouldn't help me."

"So you followed him to his hiding place and confronted him," Meren said.

The old man nodded. "He was in the cave admiring his newest treasure, that d—dagger. I didn't mean to kill him." Wersu was crying now. "He was my son, but he never listened, just never listened. Wouldn't listen to me. I didn't mean to hurt him, but he wouldn't listen."

Meren winced at the way Wersu seemed to disintegrate in front of him. At that moment the front door to Wersu's house banged open, and Qedet backed outside with a long wicker box. She manoeuvred her burden across the threshold, turned and saw Meren. Shrieking, she dropped the box, spilling royal linen into the dusty courtyard.

Glancing at a sheath dress with a hem embroidered in purple and gold, Meren said, "Ah, Mistress Qedet. I think you'll find that those linens have come at a higher price than even you are willing to pay."

SCORPION'S KISS

Anton Gill

The reign of Akhenaten, Tutankhamun's father, had been a turbulent and revolutionary one, and it left in its aftermath, opportunities for others to rise to power, especially during the reign of the young boy-king. Tutankhamun was succeeded by his vizier, Ay, whom some see as a cunning and devious exploiter. Ay may have been Tutankhamun's great uncle and was not young when he came to the throne. He reigned for just four years (1327–23 BC) and was succeeded by Horemheb, a former military general who instigated a wave of reforms, overturning the changes initiated by Akhenaten. Just who Horemheb was, and how he rose to such power, has remained something of a mystery, though it is believed his wife may have been the sister of Queen Nefertiti, the principal wife of Akhenaten.

Anton Gill's background has been in stage and radio drama, including working at times on Waggoner's Walk and The Archers. His first book, Martin Allen is Missing (1984), was a study of missing children in London and he has written on such diverse subjects as croquet, travels in Eastern Europe and the survivors of the German concentration camps. He has also written a series of novels featuring Huy, who was originally a young scribe in the administration of Akhenaten. After Akhenaten's death and disgrace, Huy and his colleagues were dismissed from their services and Huy was forced to earn a living as a private investigator, working unofficially for the crown. Only three novels have been published in England, City of the Horizon (1991), City of Dreams (1993) and City of the Dead (1994).

Three further titles, City of Lies, City of Desire *and* City of the Sea *have so far only been published in mainland Europe.*

Huy survives the reigns of Tutankhamun and Ay and the following story is set early in the reign of Horemheb. Huy is in his early forties, a good age for the time but not necessarily old.

Although there was still something of the old disdain in the face, the agony in which he had died had twisted his mouth in such a way as to make Sonebi seem to plead – an expression which would have been unthinkable in life.

The body, too, was contorted, though it was not maimed: it was whole. The Khaibit could enter the Boat of Night without being forced to wander the world looking for any part that was lacking. Looking down at him, the scribe Huy wondered if the beauticians in the royal Per-nefer hall would be able to restore his dignity as they prepared him for the Fields of Aarru.

One thing was certain: few would miss Sonebi. In his professional life, he had done much to make the reign of the Pharaoh secure; the by-product of that was husbands exiled or dead; families bereft.

"When?" he asked the man standing next to him. Huy was short and, despite advancing years, muscular, though the paunch which was the result of his inability to resist red beer, Dakhla wine, and fig liquor gave the lie to that. (It was getting worse. He would have to do something about it.) Neferhotep, by contrast, though not much younger than Huy, was tall and slim, elegant in a spotless white kilt, his head and body immaculately shaved, new palm-leaf sandals on his feet.

"His Chief Wife sent for me before dawn."

"He died at home?"

"Yes."

They were standing by a cedar-wood bier in the royal Ibu, the first of the four Houses of the Preparation of the Dead, where the Sahu of Sonebi had been brought. It was now towards mid-morning and, despite the steady breeze from the north wind that blew through the hall, the heat was rising. Neferhotep's head shone. They were alone and in the silence

both of them felt Sonebi's Ba hovering, not yet called to the
Fields of Aarru, yet unable to communicate with them. It was
preparing itself for the Judgment and the Boat of Night. The
death of Sonebi no longer interested it. It was one of the eight
parts that had made him a man. Now they were gone in their
separate directions.

Nevertheless for a moment they listened.

"What have the doctors said?"

Neferhotep spread his hands, and Huy glanced from the
body, stiff as a carved and painted statue, to the face of the
Leader of the Black Medjays, trying to catch his eye, to read or
at least glimpse what was in his heart. But Neferhotep's own
eyes remained on the grinning dead face of his former collea-
gue.

Huy persisted. "May I talk to them?"

"I have made all necessary inquiries," said Neferhotep,
turning now to Huy. He was tired. He had been up since
before dawn. It was cool, even cold, at night, for it was Shemu,
the dry season, the quiet spring after the harvest. From
Neferhotep came the scent of dom-palm oil, already stale.

"If I am to help," Huy began, restraining irritation.

"I will tell you what they told me, but you are here to assist,
not lead."

"I can tell no more from this husk." Huy gestured towards
the naked man on the bier, already gaunt and yellow, the
always sharp features sharper, robbing them of the cruel good
looks that had existed in life. Soon, by midday, Sonebi would
be disembowelled, his brain plucked from the skull using
wires on hooks thrust through the nostrils, and laid in a
wooden tub and covered with natron salt, to draw out the
fluids in the Khat, the first step in preparing the Sahu for
eternity.

Huy would not see Sonebi again. There wasn't a mark on
the body; there was only the expression and the racked body to
go by. Now the look on the face seemed less beseeching than
despairing.

"The doctors think poison," said Neferhotep.

"Yes."

Neferhotep was going to give as little information as possible. He did not want Huy to succeed. He did not want Huy to be there any more than Huy wanted to be there himself. Huy looked at his former pupil, and wondered how such a man could have risen so high. Perhaps he had taught him too well, though he had deliberately kept some of the arts of the problem-solver to himself. He had always recognized Neferhotep's ambition and realized that it needed a curb. But if he had trained the man better, Horemheb would not have sent for Huy so soon.

He had not seen the Pharaoh personally for a long time. It was a year at least since Horemheb had taken him from the dreary post in the Archives to which he had been consigned and given him the nebulous position of problem-solver, to be called upon whenever there was need of him. The rest of the time he read and drank, fighting the boredom of his heart, keeping his Khou alive. Horemheb would not allow him to do any other work, and Huy had begun to long for the day when he would be released from the prison his own accidental talent had landed him in. He had no idea how to escape it.

The Black Medjay who had summoned him that morning had arrived at his house as the Sun was rising and taken him to Police Headquarters where Neferhotep kept him waiting just long enough to remind him of his subordinate position. Then they had come here.

"It is a problem I can manage," said Neferhotep. "But in the case of so high an official, no effort must be spared."

Huy said nothing.

"We had better go back. If you have seen all you want."

Huy spread his hands. Despite his reluctance to share what he knew, there was something after all new in Neferhotep's manner – something grudging, as if he were acting against his better judgment. What precisely this was due to, Huy could not guess.

The offices of the Black Medjays were in a wing of Police Headquarters, well-located in the North Quarter of the Palace of the Southern Capital, commanding a vista of the River as it flowed, sluggishly at this season, on its long journey towards the Great Green sea. The elite corps were resented by the ordinary Medjay police, who envied their favoured quarters and regarded them, correctly, as Horemheb's private troop and bodyguard; but Neferhotep was an investigator, and he had responsibility for whatever serious crimes might have a bearing on state security.

King Horemheb had inherited a country in tatters, its northern borders fractured and threatened. A rule as hard as metal was what was needed to steady the Black Land. Huy did not like being linked with this rule, though he knew that Horemheb was as necessary as bitter medicine to a sick man. Huy would have preferred to keep himself to himself. He had seen enough in his life to want to stand apart. He had read somewhere that of every hundred men, ninety were cattle, nine organizers and one wise enough to keep himself to himself. He didn't know if he belonged to the last group. He'd never wholly succeeded in belonging to it.

Neferhotep led Huy into his room and sat at a table piled neatly at one end with rolled documents. Under the window a scribe sat cross-legged, his board on his lap and his palette with its red and black inks and his brushes on a broad low stool at his side. Neferhotep's look told him to get up and leave. Once he had done so, the leader of the Black Medjays unwound a fraction, and poured wine into two ordinary beakers. Huy noted this, and that Neferhotep poured the wine himself. The man hadn't let his position go to his head. That was good: but it showed that he was not a fool. Huy should not underestimate him.

There was a bowl of expensive persea fruit on the table. Huy was not offered one.

"It's Kharga wine."

"Good."

"You prefer Dakhla, as I remember."

Huy said nothing. He knew he would not be asked to sit, but he sat anyway, taking the beaker from the table as he did so. He waited.

"Poison," Neferhotep began. "They could tell that from the

way the body was contorted, and the twisting of the face. But it was not sudden."

"How much has the Chief Wife told you?"

"Senen is very distressed. She told me he came back to his house later than usual. He had visited his mother on the way. He was tired and did not eat. Soon afterwards he went to his room and did not ask her to join him. She heard him cry out in the night and went to him. There was just time for him to take her hand."

"And the room servants?"

"It was not his custom to have servants in his bedroom."

Huy frowned. If Horemheb had known that he would have been furious at the lax security. And yet Sonebi's house was like a fortress.

Neferhotep had fallen silent, holding his beaker in front of him with both hands as it stood on the table in front of him. He had not touched the wine. He was looking inside himself.

"I do not know why Djeserkheprure Horemheb felt it necessary to summon you immediately," he said at last. He raised his eyes to meet Huy's. "It seems you still have great merit in his eyes. Well, I can do nothing about that."

Huy did not know how to answer.

"What is it I am to do?" he said simply.

Neferhotep spread his hands and rose, going to the window and looking out at the opaque River. Outside, the Sun was already high. Few people moved in the maze of narrow streets that spread out from below the walls of the great building. Three falcon ships of the king's navy made their slow way north, their rowers torpid under awnings. There was no other traffic. Beyond the city the farms of the Black Land, their soil now red, straggled along the River's eastern banks. The view to the west, where the royal cemeteries, the Great Place and the Place of Beauty, lay, was blocked by an angle of the outer wall.

"There are no doctors to interview," he said at last, not turning. "Senen sent two body-servants straight to me and two more to Sonebi's personal physician."

Huy understood why. One servant could have gone astray,

made contact with spies from the north. Two meant that they could watch each other.

"They were trusted servants," continued Neferhotep. "Senen will miss them; but the times are dark."

Huy knew what that meant too, and that the other servants of Senen's household would be told that their fellows had been taken into the king's service. Whether they believed it or not was their affair. In any case they could do no more about it than Senen herself.

"And the physician?" he asked.

"He has the ear of Horemheb. He recognized how Sonebi died and told me. He is safe. But no one else must speak to him. He is being watched, of course."

Huy was not surprised. The death of Horemheb's Chief Interrogator at a time when the Black Country's northern borders were broached was something which would have to be investigated discreetly and fast. The Southern Capital would be quietly sealed. But there was no work here involving many of the Pharaoh's ordinary police officers, and the death itself would be kept secret until a successor was appointed, and Sonebi no longer mattered.

Huy reflected that the situation also explained why Horemheb had turned to him: he had not been active for a long time; he had always looked like one of the stevedores who hung around the beerhouses at the quays between jobs. Horemheb knew he was a good problem-solver; but perhaps it was as much for his ability to go unnoticed as for any other that he had been chosen. Perhaps he was one of the cattle after all.

Huy drank some of his wine. It was still cool from the jar, and light.

"What must I do?" he said again.

Neferhotep turned from the window and looked at him. It was clear that Huy's tactical humility did not fool him.

"You are my implement in this, Huy," he said, calling him by his name without ceremony. "You will work alone. If you can find an answer to the question you will be rewarded. We are looking for agents of the north."

"Whom can I talk to?"

"Start with Senen. Be cautious. Tidy yourself up. Get some clean clothes. A white kilt. And discard your wig. Shave your head. You can pass for a priest-administrator." Neferhotep came over to him and Huy rose. Neferhotep stood close. "We will not meet again soon. I have been told to leave you alone. You have five days before a report is required. By then your work must be complete. Do not fail. Do not disappoint me." He paused, looking at Huy, and for a moment it seemed that they were pupil and teacher again. When he spoke it was reluctantly.

"The king has ordered that you are to have full power. No one is above your suspicion. No one's word will stand against yours. Now go."

Huy made his way back to his house near the docks, keeping to the shady sides of the streets and once side-stepping a guard-ape, made angry by the hot Sun and snapping at the end of the leash which anchored it to its stall in a market in one of the small squares he crossed. Once home he washed, dutifully shaved his head, and changed. He wondered what kind of punishments Sonebi had meted out. Greater than the common ones for criminals: none of the men who begged in the Southern Quarter, their ears or their noses cut off, would have been sentenced through him, nor would those who bore the marks of the five open wounds. Few of either sort lived long anyway; the Sun and the flies saw to that. Blinding, impaling, exile: they were the punishments of the great. Horemheb used his power judiciously but without hesitation in order to keep it. Those who worked against him were quickly turned into object lessons for the rest. Sonebi had been good at his job: as useful to his king as an army in the field. And he would have made enemies.

Huy did not relish his task.

The house was a large one, facing north, in its own gardens behind high walls on three sides, while the fourth shared a wall with the palace itself. It was late afternoon, the Sun entering the final hours of the Seqtet Boat, when Huy arrived there, admitted by a body-servant to an arcaded courtyard where a small artificial waterfall ran into a pond filled with pale fish which swam aimlessly and lazily, safe from the attack of white egrets because another servant sat at the pool's edge, constantly on guard.

He didn't have to wait long. Wearing a loose white pleated dress and a wig ritually disarrayed in mourning, a tall woman came towards him unattended. Her long fingers played with a golden ankh suspended from a length of turquoise beads that she held. She wore no other jewellery. Her eyes were so dark it was hard to distinguish the pupils. But they were far from expressionless. They were sad and patient. She had seen perhaps 30 Seasons of the Flood.

"I am Senen."

"I am Huy the scribe."

She motioned him to sit on a bench by the pool and placed herself next to him, though there were chairs nearby. Unbidden, a servant appeared with a dish of dates and a silver ewer of wine. Huy noted the expensive metal: no gold here, but silver: a mark of real wealth.

"I am sorry –" Huy began, but she interrupted him.

"You are sorry to disturb me with questions so soon after my husband's death. I accept that the circumstances must be resolved as soon as possible. But I can tell you no more than I have already told Neferhotep."

"I know that he ate nothing when he came home. Did he drink anything?"

She hesitated for a moment. "Not in my presence."

"Did the servants take anything to him in his room?"

"I am not aware that anyone did." Her manner was courteous, yet her thoughts were elsewhere. "He may have eaten at his mother's house. He sometimes did."

"Did he see her often?"

"He was devoted to her. He visited her frequently."

The dense silences between each exchange weighed heavily on Huy, and beyond them only the gentle plashing of the waterfall relieved the quiet of the house. Huy imagined the great empty rooms beyond the courtyard. It was, after all, a house in mourning. The dates and the wine remained untouched by either of them. Senen had not seemed to notice them. She was extending hospitality with automatic politeness, but she was – what? Not bored. Resigned? Her features were strong and regular, but immobile: Huy could read little for certain in her face, which was more handsome than beautiful, the chin strong, the mouth wide. How much did she know about her husband's work? About what it involved?

"He was poisoned," said Huy, wondering as he spoke if he should have let her know.

But she was unsurprised. "He had enemies. He was aware of the risks he ran, despite the security we live under. He said that it was as well that he had no children. His enemies might have got at him through them."

This seemed to Huy unlikely – an excuse. But he said nothing. He noticed that her voice had faltered slightly. To have no children was a disgrace in the Black Land, and now Senen was close to an age when her last chance would be gone.

"When we met he was a junior priest-administrator. But he was ambitious. When Horemheb ascended the Golden Chair, he saw his chance," she continued. Huy wondered whether this information was some form of apology for having been married to the Chief Interrogator. Huy recalled all the rumours surrounding Sonebi; that he liked to take an active part in the torture. Not that crude violence had ever been mentioned in connection with his name; though hearsay had credited him with one refinement in the interrogation procedure: he would deprive prisoners of water for five days, and then give them vinegar. Had she known anything about what he did when he was not in his house?

"I think his work kept you apart. I know his reputation for hard work," Huy said.

For the first time a look of irony crossed her face, though it was so fleeting that he wasn't sure he had caught it.

"In the past two years he has been less frequently at home." She looked at him. "I thought you were here to ask questions. If you think our private life concerns you, ask questions."

Huy felt increasingly awkward. There were questions he

wanted to ask but could not yet bring himself to: had she been happy? What did she do with her time? Had she wanted children?

"Is there anything?" he asked.

She shrugged. "Little enough. His work took up most of his time."

She was silent for a long moment, and then added: "He had a mistress. You might as well learn that from me."

Huy wondered what she meant by such an abrupt confidence. The fact alone that Sonebi had had a mistress did not surprise him. It was not unusual. In a household like Sonebi's, the junior wives fulfilled the role of housekeepers and senior servants. He would have chosen a mistress of similar standing to his chief wife. And he would have known how to be discreet. Great families were like the houses they lived in: surrounded by high walls to contain secrets.

"Her name is Meryt."

"Did you tell Neferhotep this?"

"No. He was concerned with the immediate circumstances. But I knew there would be more questions. I simply wish to end this so that I may mourn in peace."

"Who is Meryt?"

"The daughter of Pashed, my husband's physician."

"Does Pashed know?" asked Huy, as his heart acknowledged this information.

"Pashed is not a friend. He is close to my husband's family."

Huy sat for a moment without speaking. In the silence, he became aware of the servant guarding the fish, as he discreetly stretched his limbs.

"It is of no importance," said Senen. He felt her retreating from him. He was not at ease with her, yet her sadness embraced him. There was something else that he could not quite identify.

"You have not drunk your wine," she said.

"Nor you yours."

"It does not matter." What she said then surprised him. "You are troubled that I am composed about this. I know what my husband's work was. I know what compromises he made to hold power. I know there were many things about him that earned hatred. But whatever you discover, believe this: I loved him."

Huy realized that for the first time there was absolute truth in her voice.

Darkness fell quickly in the Black Land, and the city was silent as Huy made his dusty way home. He avoided the narrow paved roads which divided the city into its quarters, where there would still be people; instead he used the back alleys which he knew better than the lines on his palms. He was not followed.

Soon after the arrival of the next day's Sun in the Matet Boat, Huy sat in another, less opulent courtyard, belonging to a house outside the vast bounds of the palace. It was a pleasant place, the garden well tended and planted with lotus and palm. Opposite him, the spare old woman – she had seen 60 Seasons of the Flood – leant forwards in her chair. Next to her was another woman, 20 years younger, erect as an egret and as slim and white, though dark lines were incised about her mouth and wrinkled the make up around her eyes. She sat upright and neither her back nor her arms touched her chair. Behind them servants stood, and by them crouched a scribe with his palette and brushes, ready to record what was said. The ritual hospitality had been offered. It was time to begin.

"You have seen my daughter-in-law?" asked the older woman, her mouth tight.

"Yes."

"Before seeing me."

Huy inclined his head. "She is the Chief Wife."

"Yes."

Huy looked at Herya. Sonebi's mother was in the grip, not of grief, but anger. Her body was tense and her eyes keen. It was not long since her own husband had died and she was now in double mourning. Huy had no respect for the old aristocracy whose power had been restored since the death of the great Pharaoh, Akhenaten, but their haughty presence still unsettled him. He knew he would have to pick his way carefully, and had not counted on being joined at the interview by Sonebi's sister, Bakmut. Both women were eager to talk.

"My mother is aware that you have observed the forms," the thin woman said.

"I will be as brief as I can," Huy began cautiously.

"You must not trust Senen. She will do all she can to keep what she has gained through marriage," said Herya immediately. "It is not surprising. Yet she could not in the five Seasons of the Flood that she lived with my son produce one child, not even a girl."

She stopped talking as abruptly as she had started. Huy looked at his feet. He was sitting in the Sun and the hair on his scalp, beginning to grow again, itched. He ran a furtive hand over his head.

"That is why she was jealous," said Bakmut. "It is understandable. But it was hard when he felt he could only visit his family in secret – and so soon after our father's death, when our mother needed comfort."

"He came to you on the night of his own death," said Huy.

The women looked at each other before they looked at Huy, and the scribe sitting nearby suspended his brush.

"Yes."

"Did he eat with you?"

"He ate, yes," said Herya.

"What?"

"Do you usually speak so directly?" she countered imperiously.

"I represent the king in this," Huy said, not to be faced down, and wondering why the old woman should take this tack now.

"He did not dine with us. But he took some duck and onions, and wheat bread, and some wine," said Bakmut. "I served him myself. That is unusual; but he preferred to be quite alone with us when he could."

"He loved us," said Herya. "He should have stayed with us."

"Why should I not trust Senen?" asked Huy, noticing that the scribe had begun to record the conversation again.

"She wanted to rise. She married him to rise. It has brought her a house in the palace compound," said Herya. "I do not know what you are doing here. I shall complain to Neferhotep. You should be talking to that woman, not prodding here with your dirty fingers, ignoring our grief." The old woman's face was hard and bitter. Jealousy would colour everything she said, and Huy saw no reason to prolong the conversation. The scribe had already put down his brush again.

Huy had heard enough, and took his leave. Bakmut, to his surprise, accompanied him to the gate.

"My mother is not herself," she apologized. "The deaths of a husband and a son are hard for her to bear."

"You have suffered the same loss."

"Almost the same. I loved neither man as much as she did." She laid a hand on Huy's arm with a quick, birdlike movement, but with the gesture she smiled. It was an awkward smile, but there was no doubt in Huy's heart that this was an attempt to charm him. And the smile for a moment transformed her face. Huy could see that she had once been beautiful.

"Who might have killed your brother?"

"I do not think his marriage was a happy one," she answered carefully, not looking at him.

"The palace fears he was killed by agents of the north. There will be war with King Suppiluliumas soon."

"Then you are looking in the wrong place here."

"Do you know Senen?"

"Of course."

"But well?"

"No. We have met rarely. My mother never liked her, and we both hoped Sonebi would stay with us always. We are a close family. Senen's father was a priest."

Huy noted the snobbery in her voice. Sonebi should have married an aristocrat. But his career had not been harmed by his choice.

"Why do you think the marriage was unhappy?" he asked.

"It was barren. I was sorry for her, too, but it would have been better for them to part."

Huy looked into his heart before asking his next question. "Do you know Meryt, the daughter of Pashed?"

Bakmut's eyes flashed. "She was Sonebi's mistress."

"Did he speak of her?"

She hesitated before replying. "Sonebi said he could not decide between her and Senen. I do not blame him for that. They were alike. They wanted to use him. But his proper place was here, with us. Now at least he will go to the Fields of Aarru and live in peace."

Hearing the vehemence in her voice, Huy looked at the thin woman, but it was already too late to read her face. She had withdrawn into herself again. The face itself was dry and cold, and the lines that ran from her nose to the corners of her mouth were deeper now than they had appeared before. Her make-up was clumsily, uncaringly applied. Her eyebrows were unplucked; coarse wisps of hair spiralled from them, and one or two more emerged from her nostrils. She had taken her hand away and now stood stiffly by the gate, arms folded across her narrow breast. Remembering Sonebi in death, Huy now imagined how he might have been in life.

The Sun was halfway to its zenith when Huy took his leave. He drew his shawl over his head to protect it. The red earth found its way into his sandals and he had to shake his feet to free them of it. Despite the growing heat he wandered aimlessly for a while. He thought hard about Sonebi and the lack of children. He turned the envy and jealousy of the mother and sister over in his heart. Was their possessiveness as straightforward as it seemed? The old aristocracy had little time for Horemheb, a parvenu who had seized the throne when his predecessor had died without an heir, taking to wife a sister of Akhenaten's Great Wife, Nefertiti. Queen Nezemmut, once Horemheb had persuaded her to marry him, legitimized his claim to the Golden Chair; but there were those who would like to see him fall among the old families. The problem was how to get to them and preserve the discretion imposed on him. And there was another problem: why kill Sonebi? The walls of secrecy that secured the palace were high; and if nothing was lost to the agents of the north – something which the Pharaoh's spies searching through Sonebi's offices would soon establish – Sonebi could go to the crocodiles in peace. He was an implement. No one would miss him, as long as policy was secure. His function was important but he himself was not. As an official he could be replaced. He had been efficient, but there were plenty of efficient administrators eager for advancement in the palace. His removal would inconvenience Horemheb, but do no serious damage otherwise. The only true motivation for such an action was revenge; and what relative, lover or friend of one of Sonebi's victims could ever hope to get close enough to him to destroy him?

Huy called Meryt into his heart, trying to imagine what she must be like. Often men's mistresses were like their wives. Huy had been married twice; but he had never had a mistress. He thought of the lies that would become routine, the excitements that would become dull, the hopes that would become blunted with time. Senen knew about Meryt; so did Sonebi's mother and sister: were they the others to whom Senen had referred? Did anyone else know? It seemed unlikely that it would be common knowledge, and yet in a world as small as that within the encircling walls of the palace it was possible. But Huy rejected the idea: Sonebi would not have been a man to allow weaknesses in the fortifications of his life.

The question was how to see Meryt. Senen knew she had been her dead husband's mistress: but was Meryt aware of that? Huy did not know where Meryt lived; but that was something he could leave to Neferhotep. Within the palace's network of spies there were men who knew much about everyone who lived in the Southern Capital, and Huy's former student had access to them.

He made his way back to the small house near the quays where he had lived since his return from the City of the Sea two Seasons of the Flood earlier. He unpegged the lock and walked through the narrow living room to the dark kitchen beyond, where he drew a beaker of red beer from the urn. It was long since he had kept even one body-servant. He considered his next move: could he trust Neferhotep? Sitting alone in the cool of his house Huy knew that if he applied to Neferhotep for help it would be delayed. It was in his student's interest that Huy should fail. He had been given five days. He partly wanted to fail, in the hope that Horemheb would think him less acute than he had been and let him go; but his heart urged him to succeed, because a direction was emerging, and he knew he had to follow it.

Suddenly he was alert. In the gloom of the house behind him he had heard a noise, so slight that it might have been nothing more than a mouse. He rose cautiously, aware of the noise he himself was making, and made his way back towards the kitchen. The door that led into the yard was ajar and he could see the brush he used to sweep it standing in the corner where the high white walls met. He reached for his knife but the person at his back was quicker. An arm was flung round his head, covering his eyes, and another covered his mouth. He was lifted off his feet and carried, unable to see or breathe, through the house towards his front door. It was the time of day when the Sun was at its height: only the scarab beetles would be abroad. He lashed out and heard a stool fall and be kicked aside. He tried to open his mouth to bite but the salt-tasting arm was clamped too tightly round his face. Outside he was released but there were others there. Someone held his neck firmly where the great artery was. Before he passed out, he saw a heavily-curtained litter, carried by two men, approaching.

When he awoke, Huy was lying on an ornate bed in a large room. His head was clear and his heart felt no grogginess from what had gone before. Only he had no idea of what time of day it was, nor even whether it was the same day. The dim light that came through the windows set high in the wall was that of the late hours of the Seqtet Boat. The room contained little furniture, but the paintings on the walls suggested a place of wealth. A man perhaps ten years older than Huy sat on a chair by the bed, regarding him.

"There is water for you, and honeycomb," he said. "If you wish."

Huy swung his legs over the edge of the bed and sat upright.

"I am Pashed," said the man.

Huy looked at him. "You could have sent a servant. I would have come."

"It was difficult. You have been told not to speak to me. I am being watched. You are not."

Huy let the man's illusion pass. He knew that Neferhotep, in forbidding him to speak to the doctor, had tried to exercise power that he did not have. It had grated with him severely to have to pass on Horemheb's carte blanche to Huy.

"How do you know?" asked Huy.

Pashed spread his hands. "The palace trusts you, they do not want any attention drawn to you; and Neferhotep hopes in his heart that you will fail. It is an irresistible combination."

"And you?"

"I am favoured; but Horemheb trusts no one. Anyone close to Sonebi, however obliquely, is being watched."

"Then what of the men who brought me here?"

"Cousins. Loyal cousins. I cannot guarantee that they were not seen, but I am sure enough to take this risk. The house you are in belongs to them, not me." Pashed stood up and walked to the door. "The evening air will do you good. And walking will clear your heart further. I regret that you were handled roughly. I had no guarantee that you would come. I did not want you to be able to identify this place. I am still uncertain that I can trust you."

"Why take the risk?"

Pashed did not answer immediately. He led Huy into a long gallery, open on one side, that ran along the house on an upper floor. The view to the north was similar to that from Neferhotep's office, except that here one could see across the River to the west bank. The vast red orb of the Sun seemed to rest on the jagged red clifftops there.

"You did not know Sonebi," said Pashed.

"No."

"He was a man whose desires would not let him rest. He would do anything to rise, take any job the king gave him and do it well. But he had no ideas of his own. He was good at climbing ladders to platforms, but once he'd arrived on them, he had to be told what to do. The kind of man Horemheb favours."

"You should not tell me this."

"In the end, Huy, no one would take your word against mine. That must answer your question about risk."

Huy remained silent. Pashed was a man used to being in command. It was not up to Huy to disabuse him. Pashed was taller and more heavily built than Huy, though the fine linen kilt and shawl edged with gold that he wore hid a frame that was more muscular than fat. A heavy necklace of turquoise and gold hung round his neck, a golden Eye of Horus suspended from it. The make-up around his eyes was immaculate, even at this late hour of the day, but his eyes themselves suggested weariness, deep lines cut his face from nose to mouth and across his forehead. Huy could not read his thoughts, but he wondered if Pashed had ever doubted his own invulnerability.

Pashed leaned on the low wall of the gallery's open side, grasping it with strong brown hands, and breathed the warm, dusty air of the evening, smelling the smell of distant spices which you could never escape in the Southern Capital.

Huy wondered if the doctor knew about his daughter's affair.

"Sonebi was successful not just because he was ambitious, but because he was charming," said Pashed. "It was hard for me to be healer to a man whose victims I had seen. It was harder to understand how such a cultivated shell could harbour such cruelty. But the sophistication, as I came to learn, was a veneer. I could see through it, but I could not teach others to. If people do not wish to be persuaded, they cannot be."

"Sonebi was obeying orders. He kept the Black Land secure for Horemheb."

Pashed spread his hand impatiently. "Already there is talk of his successor. There were plans for such a contingency before he died. A post like that cannot be left vacant for a moment under a king like Horemheb. The water will soon close over his head and your investigation will not matter at all." He paused, but when he spoke again it was with intensity. "Sonebi enjoyed what he did. The physical cruelty he left to others, but he loved to manipulate – to turn one suspect against another, to make them so unsure even of themselves that confession and death came as a relief from doubt. And he would promise a man a soft death, but give him a hard one."

Huy did not answer at once. All this may have been true, but he was still interested to see how anyone could have got close enough to kill the man. Something else interested him: Pashed seemed like a man eager to unburden himself. Was he just speaking to Huy because he thought it could go no further? He had gone to great lengths just to have this conversation. Huy would have interviewed him anyway, but he was not to know that.

"Someone like Sonebi is always open to murder," said Huy at last. "However well he is guarded. The work is the enemy, not the man who does it."

Pashed inclined his head.

"Why did you want to see me?"

"To tell you how he was killed."

"Neferhotep has already told me. You told him," said Huy.

Pashed ignored him. "No one close to Sonebi knew what he was like. To his family, to all who knew him privately, he was a civil servant, like any other, but in a delicate and important job. The way he duped people became intolerable to me." Was it Huy's imagination, or did Pashed stumble over his last words?

"When it affected those you loved?"

The doctor looked away towards the River. "I do not know what you are speaking of," he said at last, but his look was shrewd. "I gave Neferhotep no details. It was scorpion's venom in wine, but with a certain herb in it too. It had to be something that ensured he would feel something of the pain he had caused."

Huy thought of the old saying, that when you enter politics you leave conscience at the door. Hadn't this man compromised himself too? Hadn't he done so himself?

He waited in the silence to see what else Pashed would say.

"I am growing old. Meryt's mother was my Chief Wife and she is dead. I have no son."

"You took a great risk."

"The work that had to be done is done."

Huy did not speak. Pashed would not help his daughter by this confession. If he took the information he had just received to Neferhotep, Pashed's family would be disgraced and Meryt would inherit nothing. But Pashed believed that Huy's word could not stand against his own. Nevertheless Huy was not satisfied. Beyond this curious confession, what was there that was made of stone? If Pashed had killed Sonebi, how had he done it?

"Why have you told me?" he asked.

"Because I know of your tenacity," replied the physician simply. "There is no more to know, and there is no need for you to follow paths that lead nowhere."

Huy allowed his eyes and mouth to be bound and his ears to be blocked with wax before they took him from the house. He had no choice, and he did not see the men who took him, but he was resigned. In the litter that carried him away he felt no panic. He was strangely relaxed. He knew this came from him alone: he had eaten and drunk nothing in Pashed's company so he could have taken no concealed drug. He was detached from himself. His heart prompted that nothing could prevent them from killing him; but he did not think they would: Pashed was not a man to kill without need, and believed Huy presented no threat to him.

The route they followed was long, and when the litter stopped and he descended one of the men sat him on the ground and told him to wait. Then there was nothing, though one of the earplugs had worked loose and he could hear them moving away. When all was silent he removed the plugs and the blindfold. It was dark, but he could see that they had left him outside the walls of the city, though not so far that he could not reach them in a short time. It was not good to be outside the walls at night. He hurried towards the nearest gate, which was still open. It was not as late as he had feared.

He made his way home. Someone had pegged both his front and back doors locked. Inside, there was the usual untidiness, but nothing had been disturbed or taken. He lit a lamp and drew a book towards him, unrolling it to where he had left a marker. There was nothing else to do that evening, and he needed to distract his heart. Reading did not work. Soon he set the book aside and sat staring at the lamplight. And it was not until he was sure that he knew how Sonebi had met his end that he grew tired. There were still questions, but they were few, and he knew whom to ask them of.

In the end he slept.

He left it until late the following day before he set off for Sonebi's house again. He had sent no message ahead, but Senen showed no surprise when she saw him. She greeted him in the courtyard of her house, as before. She wore another white dress, and the same jewellery. She looked at him for some time before she spoke.

"You know," she said.

"Yes." He paused. The guardian of the fish crouched by the pool. "Send him away."

She did so.

"What is to be done?" she asked when he had gone.

"Is Meryt here?"

"Yes."

"Which of you did it?"

"Meryt took the poison from her father's room. She knew what was needed. But we did not know how much pain it would cause." Huy knew she did not mean to cry, but now she did, silently.

"No. He prepared the poison specially. He knew whom it was for. He gave it to Meryt. That was Pashed's revenge. For his daughter, and for all Sonebi's victims."

Senen looked away, towards the interior of the house. From its shadows a woman emerged, and as she approached Huy could see that she and Senen might have been sisters, though Meryt was perhaps ten years younger than her rival, and the set of her mouth was stronger. They took each other's hands. "I gave it to him in wine when he came home," Senen continued. "Meryt was already here. We watched him die together. He made no noise. It was too late to help him. We could do nothing about the pain."

Huy turned to Meryt. "Senen has tried to protect your father. There is no need. He tried to protect you. That is how I know."

The women exchanged glances. "It was too much for either of us to bear any more," said Meryt, with defiance in her voice. "Sonebi toyed with us. He wanted neither of us, but he enjoyed the game. And we became so tired of it; but it did not release us from love." She paused. "My father knew. I asked him to give me something that would take Sonebi from us without pain." Her heart was drained. She spoke the last words without expression.

"If we could count the time again," Senen said, "we would not do it. But for five Seasons of the Flood we were tortured. The thorn had to be drawn out at last. It is not something you can live with forever."

"But now you must," said Huy.

He imagined the lives they now faced, and the fear they would be in. And there were no children. Sonebi would never be blamed for that – only the women. No one would take Senen as a wife again; and Meryt would be condemned by Sonebi's mother as soon as she attempted to marry. All they had done was remove somebody loathsome to the Boat of Night. What would happen when Sonebi's heart was weighed in the Hall of Truth? Would Ammit seize him in his teeth? Would Shesmu throw him into the lakes of Fire?

Whatever happened, these women would have punishment enough. Huy would not add to it.

They stood in silence as the waterfall pattered. A fish jumped in the pond. Senen watched it with a look of relief. Everything had been told, and it had taken so little time.

"What will you do now?" Meryt asked Huy.

"Nothing," he said.

The office of the Black Medjays was empty on the evening that Neferhotep finally sent for the scribe. Huy had delivered a report of sorts, and knew that between its reception and this summons it would have been read and considered by Horemheb as well. He expected Neferhotep to be furious, since the Leader of the Black Medjays would have been rebuked because of Huy's failure. Neferhotep's manner was curt, though Huy was not surprised to detect a note of triumph hidden in it.

"This is disappointing," he said.

"Yes."

"It is as well that no activity has been detected among the forces of the north. We are at least satisfied that they had nothing to do with it. But you can take no credit for that."

"No," said Huy.

"Nevertheless, it is a mess," continued Neferhotep. "As far as anyone needs to know officially, Sonebi died of a heart attack. His work was hard. The wife and family have been informed of this decision. Pashed will attest to it in the scroll to be placed in the Archives. Sonebi's successor has already been appointed. He has taken up his post. As far as the world is concerned beyond these walls, there has not been a ripple. Security has not been breached."

"I see."

"But you have failed, Huy." Now there was no mistaking the satisfaction in Neferhotep's voice. "And there is the question of what to do with you."

Huy allowed himself a cautious inward smile. Horemheb would not retain him any longer after this. He would be free. To do what, he did not know; but he was tired of the palace and its ways.

"You must prepare yourself, Huy," continued the Leader of the Black Medjays. "The king wants to see you himself."

"When?"

"Immediately." Neferhotep raised his hand and from somewhere behind him two senior Medjays appeared. "Goodbye, Huy. I am not certain that we shall meet again."

Huy turned without speaking and followed the officers to the broad lane between high walls that led to Horemheb's own quarters. Whatever Neferhotep might think or wish, if Horemheb wanted to destroy Huy, he would not waste time in meeting him. But if the Pharaoh had not been deceived: if somehow he knew that Huy had succeeded–

The scribe could not think of that. But as he stepped into the red sunlight of the First Courtyard of the Palace of the Southern Capital he knew that he had made the right decision.

CLAWS OF THE WIND

Suzanne Frank

With the death of Horemheb in 1295 BC, the eighteenth dynasty came to an end. Horemheb adopted as his heir his vizier. a former soldier, like Horemheb, called Menpehtyra, who came to the throne as Rameses I. He was the first king of the nineteenth dynasty, which is known as the Ramesside period, because most of its kings were called Rameses. The most famous was Rameses II, whose reign of 66 years, from 1279-13 BC, saw one of the most phenomenal building programmes in Egypt. This was the last glow of Egypt's Golden Age.

Suzanne Frank is the author of the Chloe and Cheftu series that began with Reflections in the Nile *(1997). Chloe Kingsley is a Texan archaeologist who, upon entering an ancient chamber in Egypt, is suddenly whisked back in time to the court of Queen Hatshepsut. Later books in the series are set in other ancient civilizations around the Mediterranean. The following story, however, is not a time romance but a straight historical detective mystery set in the time of Rameses the Eternal.*

T he sky was the same shade of dun as the courtyard before me, with the strip of cultivation and the dark green of the Nile laid like a ribbon between them. The grit of sand still clung to my skin and ground between my teeth, but the storm and the evil winds of khamsin were over.

Praise be, I muttered to Shu, god of the air.

"Mistress Nofret," a priest called to me. "The foremen come, from the Village. There has been a murder."

I pushed away from the Hathor-headed column and picked up my cat. She had spent the last hour grooming herself, trying to rid her fur of sand. As I rubbed her ears I envied her. Other than ritual ablutions, I would not see a bath until the water runners arrived. The winds had waylaid them.

The cat deposited in my quarters, I splashed my face and hands in sand-logged water, then changed into my kilt, my jewelled collar and donned my ritual mask, the head of Anubis. Wrapping it in layers and layers of linen had not protected it from the sandstorm. Tiny grains bit into my skin as I adjusted the jackal-head so that I could see out of the slits in the cheeks. An acolyte handed me the symbols of my office, First Prophet of Anubis, the adze and the snake-headed rod. I swept out of the chambers, my heart pounding as it does when I go to meet my god.

We, the priests of the Place of Purification, stood looking southwards, squinting through the dusty air. Though the winds had stopped, the sky, so far from its normal faience blue, seemed ominous. "I would have omens of this event," I announced.

The priests ran to find a rooster. While we waited no one appeared over the ridge that separated the Village from this place, the Most Magnificent. *Guide me*, I asked Anubis. Sweat slicked my cheeks. The weight of Anubis felt especially heavy today. At my feet, the priest killed the rooster and the omen reader whispered to the scribe, who wrote the interpretation on ostraca.

"Prophet?" the priest recalled me. I looked into the blood of the rooster.

What did I see?

The Nile has been red, but it is due to the start of the Inundation. Pharaoh, may his name be glorious for millions of years! dwells in upper Egypt in good health with a happy heart. Nothing unusual.

Then a trickle of blood ran to the south, in the direction of the village.

It split into two channels that ran in opposite directions. I watched their paths, then –

Paneb, next to me, gasped: the two channels rejoined and formed a puddle.

"They come!" the lookout called.

While serfs cleaned the floor, incense was lit and the chants to welcome the body and ka of the deceased swelled. We sang the first of the prayers, pleading for mercy, attesting that the deceased had done nothing, robbed no cow of her milk, deprived no widow of her recompense, taken no life. He was pure.

The Foremen of both Left and Right were accompanied by the scribe of the Village. Two workmen carried the body on a stretcher between them. I could just make out the slow swing of a travelling chair lagging behind. The seeress.

Anubis consumed me in ritual. The body was in its place, the ka resting.

When I came back to myself I was in my chambers, hours later.

"Have some wine, Mistress," Paneb said as he pulled the Anubis head off. "The Villagers await you." I traded my masculine ceremonial robes for the more approachable and human attire of priestess. My gown was white, my wig tipped with gold and my eyes ringed with kohl.

I greeted the Villagers as the daughter of Anubis, and invited them to take refreshment. After we exchanged condolences and blessings I asked the scribe where the water was. Those of us who live in the Redland west of Thebes are brought water and food as partial payment for our service to Pharaoh (living for millions of years!).

"The administrator was waiting for the deliverers when he was killed," the scribe said.

"Who did this thing?" I asked. "What transpired?"

"A painter. We have him," said the Foreman of the Left, Mekhti.

"His grudge against the administrator is well known," User, the Foreman of the Right, said. "He had threatened the administrator countless times. Once, he'd beaten him in his own home."

"A dangerous man," the scribe added.

"We have a witness to the murder," Mekhti said. "She saw the painter push the administrator out of his window."

The seeress Sa'anktet, my sister in both flesh and spirit, said nothing.

"He died in the fall?" I asked them.

They nodded solemnly.

"At what time was this?"

The foremen looked at each other. "No more than an hour before we started our walk here." At a carrying pace, it takes two hours to reach Anubis' temple from the Village. On foot, under an hour; riding, a quarter of an hour.

"Then it has been three hours?" I asked.

Again, they all nodded. I rose, bade them enjoy the fruits of the temple kitchens, and followed the painted halls to the washing chamber.

Anubis' temple was inside a mortuary temple, built hundreds of years ago by a powerful woman who took the title Pharaoh. Myrrh trees flourish still in the courtyards, but only a handful of offerings are made for the benefactor. The temple itself is a wonder, with wide ramps and soaring columns, snuggled against the cliffs, a jewel secure in its setting. It will endure long after Ramessu Eternal goes to Osiris.

It is a beautiful place for my god to reside. I entered the subchambers.

The priests bowed to me and lit lamps. It has often amused me that the god of death and final purification requires the most light to complete his tasks. The scribe took up his position in the corner and together we prayed to Anubis.

"Begin, oh wise one," the priests intoned, filling me with power. "May your eyes be as sharp as Meretseger, may your ears hear the confession of the ka, and may you discern the motive of the hearts and judge the evil of the men who seek to deceive Anubis, Opener of the Way."

I raised my lamp and looked at the deceased.

The administrator was a short, portly man. His light skin betrayed a Libyan heritage. He had shaved this day, and I could still smell sandalwood on his skin. Earrings hung from his lobes, decorated with carnelian and lapis, which matched his necklaces. His face was cut and pieces of limestone gravel were imbedded in his flesh – he had landed face down when he fell. The wounds had clogged with dark blood, my first note to the scribe. "The deceased's eyes are cloudy," I said, my second note. With precise movements the priests washed away the man's make-up, removed his jewellery and closed his eyes.

With prayers and holy waters they took the deceased's linen shirt, stained with sweat and make-up, and his kilt, soiled from his passing. "Turn him over," I said.

A bruise covered his buttocks, the backs of his thighs and the soles of his feet. I pressed the flesh once with my finger and watched the skin. The blood stayed. "Note that too. Bring another lamp." Two more priests lifted lights above me. White creases intersected each other on the deceased's buttocks. "Did you observe The Stiffening?" I asked.

"No, Mistress," Paneb said. "I will watch for it."

Next I checked the deceased's hands and feet for wounds, discolouration, any other signs. *Anubis help me.*

Another lukewarm splashing, and I returned to my guests.

Mekhti was holding forth on some story while User and my sister dozed in their chairs. The scribe was stretched out on the floor, looking half-dead himself. I called for wine and sat.

"Explain what happened," I said.

"Return to the Village with us," my sister said. "We only know what we were told."

"You have the guilty one, the man's widow and the witness?" I asked. "In one place?"

"In anticipation," my sister said. "Come with us."

I gathered my red Cloak of Questioning, my Anubis head, and ordered my priests to wait.

"Mistress," Paneb said, "the body, already it is fly-spotted."

"I know," I said. "I will bring back the truth. Lay the deceased in the Place of Mummification, so no time will be lost." I must work quickly, or the deceased would be impaired in the Afterlife.

*   *   *

The Village is a dreary spot, but the whitewashed walls and red wooden doors camouflage the residences of Egypt's most talented and sought-after artisans and workers. They lived in a wedge, with nothing to see except dusty rock, and no relief offered by either shade or beauty. I grew up there. My nieces and nephews are among those working in the Tomb of Many (which is rumoured to have more chambers and pits of Osiris and storerooms and altars than any other tomb in the Hidden Place).

Pharaoh, be served in glory forever! had already celebrated his third sed-festival – so new tombs have been started for the fledgling Horus and his courtiers and wives. These many projects have brought workers from as far as the Delta and the third cataract. The walls of the Village were fairly bursting with inhabitants.

The workers of the Left are given residences on the east side of the main street, the workers on the Right live on the west side. This late afternoon women were sweeping the sand from their doors, gossiping, complaining about the late delivery of pay (it was already the second of the month; payday was the twenty-eighth) and bargaining.

In truth, the Village is a women's residence. The men, my father among them, are away except for six days a month, and festivals. In these streets laughter rings out, children play and flowers bloom. Everyone is neighbour and anything is for sale.

Birhka makes the flakiest pastries; Nefer-hebit weaves linen so fine that a date weighs more than a whole length of cloth; Ummertani works in gold, hammering the faces of the Magnificent into sheets of the shining metal, with tools no longer than one's finger. They fell silent as I passed.

To them, the girl I was is lost, and they have never known the woman. Sa'anktet, my sister, is their friend. I am Anubis: a face one fears because it means death has come.

The sounds of wailing grew louder as we progressed down the street.

At the gate of the administrator's ostentatious house, I stepped down, the adze in my sweaty hand, the Feather of

Truth, worked in gold, worn on my breast and its image woven into the cloth of my gown. Mourners filled the courtyard of the estate – a property that would have swallowed at least three workmen's houses – and slaves sat in rows, their kilts blue, dust on their heads.

"Show me where he fell," I said to Mekhti.

The house was an Eastern Thebes mansion, in miniature. The main building, (boasting an unheard-of two storeys) with columned porch, looked out over a gravelled driveway and a verdant courtyard with a lotus pool, now empty. Wings spread from each side of the main house, long one-storey rooms with clerestory windows and columned walkways. A coloured cloth fluttered in and out of the second-storey window.

The administrator had left little blood on the gravel. "Has this been cleaned?" I asked.

Mekhti shook his head. "We touched nothing. Your sister said you would want to see it as it was."

I left him and walked up to the administrator's room. Sand had blown in and stood in drifts against scrolls that had fallen off shelves. From here I could see the path coming up from the Nile, hidden, then revealed, by the dancing curtain. The chair was next to the window, close enough to use the sill as a low footstool. A bowl of congealed cucumber salad and a crust of dried bread sat on a tray beside the chair.

"Bring them," I called to the scribe, over my shoulder. Then I knelt, and sniffed and examined.

Downstairs I stood in the doorway. From here I could see the stairwell and foot of the stairs, I could also see into the courtyard.

Anubis, give me your vision.

The foremen chose the widow's threading room for our venue. They seated me then brought the guilty one before me, binding him with oaths.

He fell on his face at the sight of Anubis.

"Have mercy!" he sobbed. His kilt was paint-stained, his face unshaven. He was slightly built and underfed, but I could see wiry muscles beneath his skin.

"Rerari," the seeress said. "A painter of the Left. Husband

and father of four. He was accused of stealing gold leaf from
the tombs of the Magnificent Ones –"

"I didn't!" he cried.

"He was removed from his position and expelled from the
Village."

"Lies," he said to me. "Lies –"

"What has this to do with today?" I asked coldly. Anubis
listened always but did not believe often. "Tell me what
happened."

Rerari sat up and wiped his nose on his arm. "I didn't kill
him. I came merely to converse. He sent a message, he invited
me."

I glanced at my sister; her face was as blank as a mask.

"I wanted the back wages owed me, then I could leave,"
Rerari said. "For months he had put me off, told me the
payment was coming, but it never has. It was supposed to be
today. I thought he would be in good spirits."

"He bade you visit him, and you did," I said. "What
happened then?"

"Nothing!" the man shouted. "He never even acknowledged me. I came during the storm, when the winds were
blowing. The slave girl admitted me and I walked up to his
quarters."

Sweat trickled off the end of my nose, beneath the head of
Anubis. I waited.

"I greeted him, but he ignored me. I spoke, but he didn't
deign to turn around. I wasn't even worthy of his recognition.
But I, I . . . I needed him to listen!"

"And then?"

"The slave girl saw you push him, Rerari," User said.

"Your protestations are for naught here," the scribe said.

I turned Anubis' head to them, and they were quiet.
"Continue."

"Suddenly, I was furious. I ran to him, reached for his
shoulders – I wanted to shake him, to make him listen . . ."
The painter stopped. "I heard a scream, turned and saw the
slave girl standing outside the door. The next thing I know,
the administrator is lying in the garden. I didn't even touch

him." The painter looked into Anubis' face. "The winds did it! Everyone knows they bring madness and –"

"The khamsin pulled the administrator out his window?"

The painter looked at his hands. "Why would I kill him? He was my only chance to getting justice, my only way to petition the vizier." He prostrated himself. "Have mercy. I did not do this thing."

"The administrator jumped out the window," User muttered, "rather than listen to your harping."

I waved the painter away. The witness, a young slave girl with a slithering step, entered. She was shaking, her body bruised and sand-whipped, wearing nothing but beads and smeared kohl. She couldn't have been 12; her body had budded but not yet bloomed.

"What did you see?" I asked.

"I was in the stairwell, going to attend my master," she said, avoiding the gaze of Anubis' obsidian eyes. "I saw this man –" she pointed to the painter "– standing by the window."

"Go on."

"I saw my master, thrown by this man. I think I screamed. I raced down the stairs to find my mistress, to protect her."

"Did he chase you?"

"I don't know, I didn't look and I couldn't hear. The winds were still bad," she said.

The khamsin winds, which blew so hard and loud they could uproot a centuries old palm and deafen one to his own shout.

"In the courtyard, I saw my master. I . . . I called for my mistress and then ran to get a cloth, to cover his body."

"Then what?" I asked her.

"I returned. My mistress had thrown herself on his body, weeping."

"Did you go to find the painter?"

The slave girl shook her head. "I took my lady into her quarters and gave her refreshment, then stood by my master's body and waited for the scribe to arrive."

"When did you last see your master alive?"

"I brought perfume for his mouth, this morning."

"How was he? Did he seem in good health?"

"Yes, he was working." She looked at the foremen. "The payment was to arrive today."

"Why was the window open during the khamsin?"

"It wasn't, my lady; we had affixed a cloth to the wall, to seal it shut. I guess when he was pushed through, it tore free."

"How long have you been a slave, girl?" I asked.

"Since the last Opet festival," she said, staring at her feet. Less than a year. "This is the only master you have known?" She nodded.

The widow was brought in. The first sight of her was startling, for she was quite the loveliest woman I'd ever seen. Tears tend to swell and distend most women's eyes, but they made hers more luminous. She bowed to me, a vision in mourning blue. The foremen and scribe tripped on their sandals to assist her – finding a cushion, a glass of wine, a wrap for her shoulders.

"Condolences to you, daughter," Anubis greeted her.

She bowed to me, then saw the painter. "Murderer!" she screamed. It took all three men and Sa'anktet to pry her off the man. He stayed slumped on the floor, streaming blood from his chest, face and arms. He hadn't defended himself.

"Tell me what happened," I commanded her when she had calmed down. "With control."

She had been in this room, spinning for thread. She had refused both mid-morning and mid-afternoon meals because the winds were making her head ache. At some point in the afternoon she heard a shout and opened the door to see the slave girl running from her husband's corpse.

"After that, I remember little," she said, "I was overcome by grief."

"It was a love match, you and your husband?"

She shrugged, weeping prettily. "We had an understanding."

"Where are your children?" I asked her.

She tore at her hair and fell to her knees. "We were not blessed by the goddess," she said, tears streaming down her cheeks. "Bes has not come to this house."

"Your husband was not a young man," I said. "Was he married previously?"

She nodded. "His first wife died before she could give him a son."

The priests would want to talk to this widow. It was the duty of the sons and daughters to maintain their father's funerary offerings. In the event there were no children, the couple needed to hire a priest to stand in that position. The temple had enlarged its holdings ten-fold through this practice. The other choice was to adopt an adult: certainly less expensive than renting the state's version of offspring.

"You say you heard a shout. Then you saw the slave girl running. How close were those two events?"

She shrugged. "A few moments apart, no more."

"Do you think the shout was your husband?" I asked. "Do you think that is what you heard, his last cry?"

"You couldn't –" the slave girl interrupted.

The girl knew where I was heading.

Her mistress glared at her, then turned to me with wide, tear-filled eyes. "I believe it was. I heard my beloved's last words!"

I dismissed them all. My sister brought refreshments and I took off the Anubis head. "Tell me what you know," I said.

Sa'anktet is a seeress. From childhood she knew things before they happened, saw things that were not there, but would be. She had married a young draughtsman whose life she had saved by telling him not to follow the trail of the lizard that day. His partner had scoffed at the warning and walked into the tomb, just after a lizard had crawled in. No more than a moment later, the ceiling of the tomb caved in and killed the man.

My brother-in-law did not listen so well after they were married, and thus became dinner for a minion of Sobek, the crocodile-god.

"The widow lies," she said.

"She would have never heard his cry," I agreed.

"No," Sa'anktet said, reaching for a thin slice of bread, layered with smoked duck and onions. "The khamsin winds were too loud."

"Also, he was dead long before he fell out of the window."

She sipped some wine and poured me some. It was a northern vintage, well-aged. The administrator had not suffered from the delayed wages. They even had water here.

"If the fall didn't kill him, then what did?" Sa'anktet asked. "And how did he fall out of the window?"

"I cannot fathom it, the method of his death."

"Did the gods come for him, in his time?" she asked.

"There are no marks to indicate otherwise, but my instinct tells me no. The conspirators knew he was dead, because they cleaned up the refuse from his body, though a hint of the odour remains."

She wrinkled her nose and set down her piece of bread. "The wife killed him?"

"You heard her say she was barren. His first wife didn't conceive either. I think perhaps the fault was his, not theirs."

"She killed him because she wants to be a mother?"

"No. She killed him because he wasn't a father. He didn't have any offspring *and* he was wealthy."

I saw the realization on Sa'anktet's face.

"Perhaps he planned to adopt a son," I suggested. " 'If a man dies, he leaves his wife a third of the estate and the rest goes to his children'," I quoted. Inheritance practices are something one learns in the House of Anubis.

"If he has no children," my sister said, "the wife gets it all."

"She's young, could easily marry again . . ." I took a slice of the duck.

"How did the painter get involved?" she asked. "His is such a sad tale. The workers say when he was removed from the Tomb of the Many, from painting, that he upset a jar of paint and the two trails of it circled each other and then met again. The paint won't clean away – it's a sign of his innocence, they say."

The hair on my unshaved head stood on end. "The accusations are false?"

"They were made, but it is more likely that the painter refused User the pleasure of his wife," she said. "That is not the seeress speaking, but the gossip. What are you going to do?"

The image of the two ends of blood meeting together was stark in my mind. "Speak to the slave girl," I said. "The widow has already admitted her guilt, even though she doesn't realize it. With the winds, she could have heard nothing. If she opened the door it was because she anticipated her husband's death. Furthermore," I said, "there are curious marks on the chair's leg."

"Such as?"

"Find the cloak the slave girl claims she covered the body with. I daresay it doesn't exist, but a length of heavy rope does."

My sister knows the weavings of my mind well. "You think they rigged the chair to topple, to throw the administrator out the window?" She chewed for a moment. "How would they know when to do it?"

"Easy enough. If her scream wasn't heard, she could have run down the stairs or thrown something. Anubis cares little for petty tricks. Who killed the man, is his concern."

"So whatever the painter says, whatever his intent, a man can die only once. The administrator was dead, so Rerari is innocent?"

I nodded.

My sister stood and brushed out her linen dress. "Speak to the slave girl, she knows more than she says." She paused. "Her manners are far above her station. And the way she moves – like a snake." She looked at me and quoted. 'Wisdom can be found among slave girls.'"

"A serpent," I murmured. "Yes, she does move as such. Sinuous." I stood, leaving Anubis on the chair. "I'll go walk in the garden. Send her to me."

The storm had torn branches and scattered flowers, and everything lay under a dimming dust. *Anubis, I prayed, help your servant be just and merciful*. I turned at the girl's approach. She was still naked and the evening grew cool.

"What could happen to place a well-educated, well-bred young woman in the slave quarters of a Libyan administrator?" I asked as I inspected an uprooted sycamore. "You are young, and recently have fallen on bad times. I conclude your father must have committed a crime, thus slavery is punishment for his child."

I heard her tiny intake of breath.

"Tell me," I said, turning to look at her. "Was he executed? For what? Treason? Betrayal? –"

"They were lies!" she said. "He was innocent!"

As the First Prophet of Anubis, I hear this refrain as often as the rising cry of the falcon. I know its nuances. The girl spoke what she believed to be the truth. By Ma'at, her father was probably another victim of intrigue and paranoia, no more or no less than Rerari the painter. "Your mother?"

"Executed too," she whispered.

"Brothers and sisters?"

"We were all given into the keeping of the temples," she said. "But, the sem-priest, he . . ." She swallowed. "He made me a woman, and then had no use for me. So he sold me."

I wished I had my mask; hearing of temple misconduct infuriates me, a reaction I cannot control. She shivered under my glare, even though she was not its victim. "He sold you so you could not bear witness against his misdeeds," I stated.

She looked off into the sunset, that last moment before Kemt is plunged into darkness, and I saw the film of tears on her eyes. Deliberately I breathed out myself and inhaled Anubis. I must be relentless. I must have the truth of this matter.

"The painter's children will be sold," I said to her.

"No," she whispered, grabbing my arm. "They are innocent. To punish –"

"You are the witness," I said, pulling away. "Your words are his sole condemnation."

"His wife is pregnant," she said.

"She will be delivered before she is strangled," I said. "The gods are not unmerciful."

"The baby?" the girl asked, stricken.

"It will belong to the temple, to rear as they see fit."

"Oh, mother Isis," she whispered, dropping to her knees. "What about the law?"

"Law? Execution is the law when a life has been taken," I said.

"But during the khamsin? I thought, I was told, I –" She froze, having heard her words.

"What did you think?"

"Crimes of passion during the winds are forgiven, they are accounted as madness brought on by the demons of sand and debris." Her expression pleaded with me, but I needed the truth.

"It *has* been a tradition," I said, "to pardon those who committed such acts, but your painter intended to lay hands on your master. Rerari intended to make the administrator bend to his will. *Intended*. His was not an act of passion."

"What could be more passionate than protecting his family? What greater fire in the belly is there than to provide for one's children?" She wept, but for those children or her own childhood? "He can't be punished for this, he was only doing what he could," she said through sobs. "This is too cruel."

I touched her shoulder and felt the bones beneath her skin, the scabs on her healing flesh. I dropped my voice to a whisper, kneeling in front of her. "Your master was already dead, was he not?"

She hiccuped and looked at me over her fingers.

"Truly, how did your master die?" I asked. "Do you rejoice?" I pressed her shoulder as I spoke. "Did he do this to you?"

"I cannot say," she whispered. "Only death will break my loyalty."

"If you stay, your lady will bring you death."

She looked away. "Then I will see my father much sooner."

Fury burst from me as I got to my feet. "As you will. Serve your lady and court your own martyrdom. Forget those children who will be at the mercy of degenerate priests and unscrupulous owners. Live for yourself." I walked away, calling for my chair and my cloak and Anubis.

I sat alone in the House of Mummification, save for the dozen bodies whose fluids were slowly draining into the pounds of natron we deposited on them daily. Across from me the administrator lay on a low sloped table, naked and washed. Waiting. "Be at peace," I whispered to his ka, and continued to sketch on my ostraca.

What is the sign? I asked Anubis again, as I had asked all through the journey back from the Village, and all the night I had sat here, drawing the curves the blood had followed this morning, the directions the painter's paint was purported to have flowed. After filling in all the pools and drawing the two lines coming together, the amount of ink I had used was almost unconscionable. I sketched the lines again, the bare two meeting, forming a wavering oblong.

I set the flake of stone down and walked to the corpse. "You didn't protect yourself," I said to his ka as I walked around the body. "You were dead before you fell, dead sitting up. Was there poison in the cucumbers? The wine? You have no symptoms, no one stabbed you, nothing bit you and caused swelling. You were not strangled. You did not fight your assailant. Speak to me," I pleaded. "I need you to tell me what happened before putrefaction claims you."

The corpse said nothing; in all my years of speaking to them none have answered. I sighed and rubbed my neck. How long was this day. Out in the desert I heard the lonely cry of the jackal. I glanced over at my empty chair, the ostraca before it.

I gasped.

Upside down, the two lines formed the shape of Edjo, the cobra goddess, the uraeus, the protectress of the Magnificent Ones. Cobras, who leave no outstanding mark. Cobras, who smell like sun-warmed cucumbers. Cobras, who kill with peace and stillness. I called for Djedet and lit all the lamps. The strike mark was there, hidden in a fold of flesh, where two needle-sharp fangs had penetrated straight into the biggest blood channel in the body. A second mark on his thigh.

"Bring me my embalming robes," I commanded, "and double Anubis' offerings this dawn as thanksgiving."

I donned linens that would be buried with the administrator, for they would bear his body matter upon them. The priests chanted as I broke the corpse's nose to extricate the offal in his head. I had already scooped out a lot of it, while my "slitter" sharpened his obsidian blade, when an acolyte interrupted me. He fell on his face, begging for mercy.

One did not interrupt the rites.

"A girl," he cried, "she is bleeding and begs –"

I tore off the linen cloak and foot coverings, the face shield and cloth, and handed the long-handled spoon to Nectanab. Clad in my underdress I ran out of the door and up into the main hallway. The slave girl was leaning against a wall, gasping for air. She turned to me, her skin was ashen and her eyes already glimpsed the Gates of the Gods. No, I prayed to Anubis, not this child, not for years.

"Physician!" I shouted. "A cobra bite!"

Her chest was bandaged, but had bled through. "I cut the strike mark," she said, then laughed. "I fear it is late."

"The same snake?" I questioned as I held her up.

She nodded. "He gave me time to come here and tell you."

I heard a horse whinney outside. "How did your master die?"

"Me," she said. "My mistress, bought me," the girl gasped as I removed the linen on her chest and replaced it with new. "I charm snakes."

"She intended you to kill her husband with a cobra?" I asked. "Is this poison still in there?" I placed my hand on her chest; there was no way to form a tourniquet.

"I tried to suck it out, but –"

With the angle of the strike, she would have had to have been cat-headed Bast to reach it.

"I must tell you," she said, "this morning, while my mistress spoke to my lord, I sneaked up behind him and made the snake strike."

"Your master was seated?"

She nodded her head. The priests washed the wound with wine. Her screams were wrenching, but there was a chance she could live. When she got her breath back she said she and her mistress had arranged the administrator's body immediately and struck him a second time.

"My lady wanted to be sure," she said, her eyes losing focus.

"Why now?" I asked.

"The vizier," she panted. "My master and lady had fought. He was going to adopt a son, the vizier was bringing the documents."

"And the painter?"

"She sent the message. No one would doubt his guilt, for they all knew the enmity between –" The girl breathed deeply as a smile stole across her face. "It doesn't hurt. It feels like falling asleep. He will be saved, won't he?"

"The painter?" I said. She had given her life for his family and I was to blame. "He will be saved."

She nodded, fighting to keep her eyes open. "My name," she mumbled, "so I am not lost in the Afterlife . . ."

I brushed her hair back from her face. "Tell me, child."

"Nofret," she said, and sighed.

Her body was warm still when the priests removed her from my arms. Ra had started his day's journey but I sought the night-blackness of Anubis' chambers. I crawled across the raised obsidian floor to his feet. I said the words for her, for Nofret, the words that she hadn't been able to say in life: "I am pure! I am pure! I am pure!"

Those words I would never be able to say, for I had lied.

The rule of the khamsin was inviolable, a tradition begun by Amenhotep I, patron of the Village. Neither she nor the painter, outsiders both, could have known. Crimes committed during the khamsin were pardoned. Yes the rule had been abused, but it was still upheld. The painter had never been in danger of death.

I had manipulated her. Nofret, a girl who bore my very name.

When I emerged from the temple, day was full upon the land. I entered my chambers, and the girl was there, my cat sniffing her feet. "She breathes?" I said to the attending physician, stunned.

"The venom was weak, if, as you said, it was the third strike of the day. She will live, I think. Should we inform her mistress?" he asked.

I shook my head. "No, her accomplice Nofret died. That is

all she need know. Then execute the widow for murder with intention."

"What about this maid?"

The cat wove between my ankles. "When she wakes, she can choose her own name."

And her own life.

THE WEIGHING
OF THE HEART

F. Gwynplaine MacIntyre

We are now at the end of the twentieth dynasty in the reign of Rameses XI, in the year BC 1073 to be precise. Once again Egypt was heading for another period of decline (what became the Third Intermediate Period) with a rise in the defiant power of the priesthood and increasing strength of Egypt's southern neighbours in Kush. It was a time of unrest with an outbreak of tomb robbing, which meant more work for the courts.

This is the background to F. Gwynplaine MacIntyre's story. MacIntyre is perhaps best known for his science fiction and fantasy, including his novel The Woman Between the Worlds *(1994), but he has a wide knowledge on a vast variety of subjects and has appeared in several of my anthologies. He has a particular fascination for ancient Egypt as the following story shows.*

"A dead man speaks the truth." Khnemes uttered the words of the tongue-twisting proverb that was popular among Egyptian schoolboys and apprentice scribes: "*Medu m'at mai ma'at mety*" . . . or, more formally, "speaks a mummy in straightforward truth." The phrase was merely a writing-exercise, but on many occasions Khnemes had thought that there was wisdom in these words. For a living man may utter falsehoods, but a *m'at* – a corpse, or a mummified man – can only speak the truth.

This was one such occasion. Khnemes had accompanied his employer Perabsah on the journey upriver from Aneb Hetchet to Thebes, along with Perabsah's wife Merytast and a retinue of servants and slaves. While Merytast and her attendants took lodging in Thebes, Perabsah had brought Khnemes and three sledge-bearing slaves across the river, to the Village of Labourers on the western bank of the Nile. As night fell, they made camp here by torchlight. Then, at dawn, they proceeded beyond the workmen's village, into the foothills further west.

Perabsah led his attendants into a landscape stippled with crude mud-brick domes shaped like giant breadloaves. This was a village of the dead. Khnemes had heard of this place: the Plain of the Loaves. Few tomb-robbers ever tarried here, for only lowborn peasants were buried in this place. A few of the domes displayed crude hieroglyphs etched into the clay above their lintels: daubed by a finger when the bricks were still wet from their moulds, and left to bake hard in the Egyptian sun. Now Perabsah pointed to the inscription above the lintel of a dome that seemed no different from its neighbours. Khnemes was unscribed, and could not read, yet above this dome's sealed entrance he recognized the familiar glyphs identifying the ancestral household of his master Perabsah. So *this* dome had been built here by order of one of Perabsah's forefathers.

At a nod from Perabsah, his trio of slaves raised sharpened adzes and broke the mortarwork beneath the lintel. Bricks which had lain undisturbed for a century were now seized, torn loose from their mortar, and flung aside by the slaves.

Khnemes cringed at his employer's sacrilege. Khnemes was Nubian-born, yet he had lived in Egypt long enough to know the customs of this land. To defile a grave was always a serious crime . . . and made even riskier *now*, due to the recent political upheavals caused by the long famine known as the Year of the Hyenas. Officially, this was Year Eight of the Repeating of Births in the reign of the aged king Re's-Abiding-Truth . . . but the old king's power had dwindled, and now Egypt was divided into two kingdoms ruled by rival god-cults. Perabsah owned property and wealth in Aneb Hetchet . . . but that was in *Lower* Egypt, and now here he was across-river from Thebes, defiling a grave in *Upper* Egypt, where Perabsah's titles and estates were too distant to protect him.

Khnemes glanced round nervously as Perabsah's slaves enlarged the hole in the broken dome, and now Perabsah spoke a challenge to Khnemes:

"Most excellent servant, you have often impressed me with your cleverness. Let us see if your wisdom extends into the realm of the dead." Perabsah's three slaves downed their tools and clambered over the heap of shattered bricks, while he continued: "Within that residence sleeps a bondsman of my household, entombed here more than a century ago. I know nothing about him, save the fact of his existence. I challenge you, Khnemes, to unriddle the stranger who is entombed here. Let us see if you can read the pattern of his life . . . or the chapters of his death."

"I accept your challenge, *heri sa'ur*," said Khnemes, flattering his employer. Perabsah preened at this compliment, and daubed himself with a few drops of scented oil from the vanity-phial he always carried. Khnemes often addressed Perabsah as *heri sa'ur*, or "wisdom-master" . . . not because Perabsah was wise enough to deserve this title, but because Khnemes was wise enough to know that there is more than one way to oil a conceited man.

As the slaves emerged from the shattered loaf, Khnemes was astonished to see them bearing an earthenware coffin. The Plain of the Loaves was a burial-ground for paupers: most of the dead in this place were not even properly embalmed. How came this one corpse to possess a coffin? When the grunting slaves set down their load, Khnemes was astonished again: for this was a *child's* coffin in the sands before him. A coffin too small to contain a grown man.

The coffin was oval-shaped, unglazed, with no inlays or inscriptions. "Whoever this coffin contains," observed Khnemes, "he received only the most meagre of death-rites. His mourners were swift to send him on his journey."

Perabsah tucked the small white alabaster vanity-phial back into its pouch on the waistband of his *shent* kilt, and rubbed his hands eagerly. "Because the coffin is unadorned, you mean?"

Khnemes shook his head in the still air, feeling no breeze among the tight rows of echelon curls in his wig. The *Mehut* – the prevailing wind from the north which usually sang through the Nile valley – was strangely absent today. "No, *heri sa'ur*," he told Perabsah. "Even unwealthed peasants can honour their dead. This coffin betrays not only an absence of wealth, but also a poverty of *time*: there are no luck-marks, no death-charms. See? The coffin is boat-shaped, to transport its passenger along the River of the Underworld . . . yet the ritual *utchati* Eyes of Horus are missing from the coffin's prow. If the dead man was too paupered to equip his coffin with golden *utchati*, his mourners could still have applied the sacred Eyes by drawing charcoal images on the coffin's prow. Yet that was not done."

Perabsah's eyes gleamed beneath his headcloth. "Excellent! What else?"

Khnemes circled the earthenware cask. "This is a child's coffin, yet your three strongest bearers exerted themselves whilst carrying it a brief distance, so this coffin contains something heavier than a child." Perabsah stiffened at this, and Khnemes quickly continued: "Mayhap this small coffin's occupant is a *deng*: a dwarf or pygmy, who served as a jester in your ancestors' household."

"Let us see the wisdom of your guesses, my servant." Perabsah beckoned to the tallest and brawniest of his three slaves, who rejoiced in the name Qesf. This man came forwards with his adze. Khnemes saw what was intended, and he raised one arm to protest the sacrilege, but Perabsah anticipated him: "Turn your head aside, then, if it bothers you to see this." Perabsah flung his own hand towards Khnemes, masking the Nubian's eyes while the adze descended. Khnemes heard but did not see the impact of obsidian blade against earthenware. By the time that Perabsah had lowered his hand so that Khnemes could see again, the slaves had picked away the fragments of the coffin's lid. Some sort of pliable material was underneath: this too was pierced now by the slaves, and Perabsah's eager hands tore at this. Only when several pieces of the flexible covering had been ripped away did Perabsah step aside.

A mummy was inside the coffin: a fully-grown man. His arms and legs had been broken, then bent back upon themselves, and the shattered man had been crammed into this too-small coffin. The dead man's face was contorted into an expression of hideous agony.

Khnemes approached the coffin slowly. The mummification was a crude one: the corpse's broken limbs were shrivelled and thin, while the dead man's belly was distended. The mummy's odour was surprisingly pleasant, like a mixture of pickled fish and black pepper. Whoever this dead man was, the embalmers had taken care to preserve him with mummy-resins. Khnemes expected to see the familiar black seepings of bituminous *repnen* oozing from the mummy's shattered limbs, but there was no sign of leakage.

Now Khnemes noticed something. "This man was a slave, or the servant of a cruel master. See? Here and *here* on the shoulders and arms, and across his chest, there are marks where flails and whips have visited his flesh."

Perabsah arched one eyebrow. "Have a care, Nubian. Do you accuse my ancestors of cruelty? No lord of my house would ungentle his servants."

Khnemes frowned, and Perabsah's three slaves looked up sharply. The faithful Qesf was well-treated, but his bond-brothers Huti and Djeb had not been so favoured: their naked backs and shoulders bore testament to their master's cruelty. Khnemes shook his head again. "The flesh of this mummy clearly shows *scars*. They are partially healed, so he received these scars long before his death. Yet look here." Khnemes pointed to some small discolourations near the dead man's nostrils and eyelids. "These are flea-bites . . . in places where a corpse, not yet mummified, would leak the body's natural contents. This man probably died during Shemu, the harvest-season, when fleas are most plentiful. And he was left for some time dead – outdoors, in hot weather – *before* the embalmers worked their craft upon him. If the mummification had come swiftly after his death, the resins used in the embalming process would have repelled the hungering insects."

"Excellent, my servant!" said Perabsah. "What else do you see?"

"It is what I do *not* see that puzzles me," Khnemes confessed. "This coffin contains no death-honours. Even the lowliest citizen of Egypt owns a few delight-beads, or a clay amulet, to bring with him into the afterworld. But I see none here. This man was entombed in a hurry, by someone who had no time to give him the proper death-rituals. Observe his broken limbs: they must have been intact during the embalming process, or else the mummy-salts would have leaked from his body. His arms and legs were deliberately broken *after* his mummification . . . so that his corpse could be compressed into the smallest and cheapest coffin available."

Perabsah raised one hand to his face to adjust his headcloth. "And you discern nothing else of this man, then?"

Khnemes shook his head once more. "I have told all I see, *heri sa'ur*. Only the gods can reveal more."

At that moment a sudden wind sprang up from the north, filling the Plain of the Loaves with a shrill distant howl. The *Mehut* had returned.

The wind snatched several yellowing objects which Perabsah had torn from the coffin and placed aside. Now Perabsah bellowed: "*Kefaythen sen!* Seize them! Capture them all! *Haqythen er cher sen!*" and at once his three slaves hurried to thwart the wind. Something sailed past Khnemes, and he caught it: a large flake of ancient papyrus, torn at its edges, and strangely stiff; the fibres of the papyrus were glutted with a substance which had stiffened the material. Khnemes turned over the papyrus, to see if anyone had written on it. No; it was blank. But . . .

"Give me that!" Perabsah snatched the stiffened flake of papyrus, turned it over, then flung it aside. "Help them, quickly!" Perabsah nodded at his slaves, who were scrabbling to capture other pieces of the wind-torn papyrus. Just then, in the sands near his feet, Khnemes saw a large fragment of papyrus, covered with dark lines of hieratic script from some lost century. He reached for this . . . but the wind from the north snatched the fragment, and swept it whirling away into the deserts beyond. Whatever was written on that page, only the wind knew.

"*Mamu Mehut ma'at*," Khnemes whispered to himself, inventing an impromptu wisdom. "*The north wind knows the truth*."

Now Khnemes learnt why Perabsah had instructed his slaves to bring a sledge with them. "This man served my ancestors faithfully, and I would have him conveyed to a burial-place more dignified than *this*," Perabsah announced, gesturing at the shattered clay loaves on every side.

The child-coffin was grunted onto the sledge by the three slaves, while Khnemes inspected the draught-lines. The brawny slave Qesf had brought along a dozen tarred wine-skins, filled with water. Djeb and Huti had brought a dozen oxen-horns, filled with flaxseed-oil and carefully sealed. Khnemes collected these now, while Qesf and his two bond-brothers manned the sledge's tow-ropes.

They began. Khnemes unstoppered a horn, and poured forth a thick gobbet of its oily contents into the sands in front of the sledge. Before the thirsty sands devoured this offering, Khnemes opened a wineskin and poured a drizzle of water on top of the oil. The two liquids beaded, briefly forming an ooze. Quickly, the three slaves dragged the sledge forwards. It slid across the oiled sand easily. Keeping pace with the slaves, Khnemes continued to pour his oil-carpet ahead of the sledge as their journey progressed: first the oil, then the water on top of it. Khnemes took care to ration both liquids: they had a long distance to go.

They made their way eastward, Perabsah watching from the rear to satisfy himself that his servants gave their full efforts. The sledge-procession reached the Village of Labourers, the work-camp of the tombmakers who lived among the cemeteries of the Nile's western bank. Several workmen left their kiosks to stare at the child-coffin . . . but they saw Perabsah's headcloth and his *shent* kilt of fine linen, and the workmen knew better than to challenge the retinue of a wealthy man.

Beyond the Village of the Labourers, on a hillock to the left as Khnemes trudged eastwards, was the temple Per-Reshtu, erected twelve decades ago by Rameses God-King. Beyond this, two giant figures loomed in the path. Twin sentinels, nearly four times a man's height, had guarded this place for three centuries: the sandstone statues commemorating the reign of Lord-Re's-Truth Amunhotep. Long ago, these two awesome colossi had flanked the largest building ever erected on the west bank of the Nile: now Amunhotep's mortuary temple lay in ruins, yet the sentinels endured. Khnemes was reluctant to approach these silent stones, but he knew that Perabsah would prefer to strut along the wide clear avenue between the twin colossi rather than stumble among the uneven pathways to either side. "Forgive me, centuries," Khnemes whispered as he stepped between the pair of ancient sentinels, and led the way towards Thebes.

At noonday they reached the cane fields on the western bank of the Nile. Here the sledge and its coffin tipped forwards, as if eager to hurtle down the slope. Khnemes helped the slaves hold the sledge *back*, easing it down the riverbank instead of allowing it to tumble headlong.

The Nile's crossing at Thebes is always attended with ferrymen, to transport passengers from the living city of Waset on the eastern bank to the realm of the dead among the cemeteries on the western bank . . . and sometimes back again. Near the marketplace of the burial-hucksters on the western bank, Khnemes hailed a ferryman. Perabsah called out as the ferry approached: "What will you bargain for conveying myself and this sledge? *Akhi!* I have my manservant and these other men as well, but they are only slaves . . . and the manservant is merely a Nubian."

The ferryman made the appropriate gestures: right hand to heart, to demonstrate respect for Perabsah; left hand to knee-cap, to signify submission. "All men are equal aboard my boat, sir," the ferryman answered, "for it tasks me the same effort to convey a living prince or a dead slave." At length it was agreed that the ferryman would be paid one *deben* of copper to transport the lot, if Perabsah's three slaves lent a hand with the bargepoles. The sledge was loaded onto the deck, and the crossing began.

Perabsah seated himself on the ferryman's bench, placing the papyrus fragments in the lap of his kilt. "*Mah'ek!* Behold thee, Khnemes: see what this is."

"I behold, *neb-i*: sovereign-my-lord," said Khnemes, "but I do not comprehend."

Merabsah held up a stiffened shred of papyrus. "This material is *utau*: plastered cartonnage. A century ago, embalmers often used cartonnage to enswathe the mummies they fashioned. Pieces of scrap papyrus, no longer needed by the scribes, would be soaked in wet gypsum plaster to strengthen their fibres, and the plastered sheets glued together to fashion a shroud. The soaked papyrus was moulded round the face and body of the mummy, and sewn together at the back. When the plaster dried, the shroud hardened . . . and the cartonnage formed a protective shell encasing the mummy's remains." Perabsah brandished two more fragments of the stiffened fabric. "Usually the cartonnage was painted by the embalmers, but this one was not. See! There is writing on these *utau*."

Khnemes glanced at the dark lines of hieratic script on the dusty papyrus: cryptic black symbols, randomly speckled with a few symbols in red. For the thousandth time, Khnemes wished that he knew how to read. "These words, *heri sa'ur* . . . they are death-texts for the soul of the dead man?"

"Probably not," said Perabsah. "The embalmers likely used any papyrus at hand, discarded by the archivists. Before we leave Thebes, I must engage a scribe to translate these lines. But I can read a few words myself. See? This word here is 'Rekhseth': the name of my thrice-*tef*."

"Your *tefteftef*?" Khnemes asked. "Your grandfather's father? So we are closer to knowing the year of this man's death. If he was a servant of your great-grandfather Rekhseth, then this man lived during the reign of Amun's-Beloved . . . when Egypt was strong and the throne undivided, and even the lowest people prospered."

From a pouch at his waist, Perabsah took a twist of linen

containing a chunk of spiced natron. He tore off a pinch of this, popped it into his mouth and chewed furiously, talking with his mouth full: "What was it like, do you suppose, to have lived in the golden noon of Egypt's prosperity? I dislike our modern times, with proud Egypt torn into halves."

"Egypt has always been two separate nations: the realm of life and the realm of the dead," said Khnemes. Just now the ferry came abreast of the Isle of Amunhotep, the white lime-stone crag just north of Thebes which marked the midpoint of the Nile's breadth. Beyond the ferry's prow stood the eastern bank of the Nile: the land of fertile soil and swarming cities. Astern of the ferry's rudder lay the Nile's western bank: the land of the dead, where the pyramids stood vigil among the cemeteries which Egyptians of grim humour have nicknamed "the plantations". The few *living* people who dwelt on the Nile's western shore were mostly funeral-workers . . . who sometimes called themselves "farmers" because of the crops which they tended.

"You know my meaning, Nubian," said Perabsah. "For the past three years, Egypt has been sundered north and south, and the parts squabbled over by covetous priests and false kings. There is violence in the provinces, from bands of rebels who would carve Egypt into splinters." Perabsah shuddered, and drew his kilt more closely round his loins. "The sooner my wife and I are gone from Thebes, and we return downriver to our sweet northern home in Lower Egypt, the happier I will be."

"All parts of Egypt are north to me, for I am a Kushite of Nubia," said Khnemes. "But if I remember rightly, you have told me that your forebears were from southern Egypt."

"Your memory speaks truth," said Perabsah as they neared the eastern riverbank. On the quayside, several labourers ran forwards with gaff-hooks, eager to assist the arrivals and hopeful of receiving gratuities. "My grandfather's father Rekhseth was an assistant overseer in the goldfields of Bendet, near the Red Sea. Rekhseth worked long and well, and it was he who built the proud estates which have prospered and grown under the guidance of my grandfather and my father.

Ahai, and I too have done all I can to continue my family's tradition of honour and dignity." Perabsah bent across the ferry's portside strake and spat a gob of natron into the Nile as he spoke. Khnemes shuddered at this vulgarity, but he knew at least that the natron had its benefits. Perabsah had wretched teeth and diseased gums, and he relied on frequent chewings of "holy-mouth" – *netra*, or some other spiced natron – to sweeten the stink of his breath.

Now the ferry was brought to the quay. Khnemes assisted Qesf and the other slaves in the unshipping of the sledge and the coffin, while Perabsah barked orders and acted important.

The eastern bank of the Nile, at its crossing near Thebes, is the place of the Redu ni-Temi: the sixteen-step staircase which serves to measure the Nile's water-level. Just now, the Nile was at low ebb, so the ferry rode low against the riverbank and only the lowermost step of the staircase was underwater. Raising the sledge to their shoulders, Khnemes and the three slaves conveyed their burden uphill to the high redstone pylon arch of Kheft her-en-Nebset, the sentry-gate at the western entrance of Thebes.

It is said that a man can walk across Thebes in an hour. Beneath the weight of the coffin and sledge, this seemed impossible to Khnemes. Even with three strong slaves to assist him, the sledge and its contents tallied a considerable weight.

Perabsah led the way eastwards along the edge of the Kamur, the main canal of Thebes. The western district of Thebes holds the royal temples, and so the pathways here were cobblestoned. But the cobbles dwindled into a rude footpath as Perabsah and his attendants reached the market-district. Here the canal was filled with its usual obstructions: nude bathers, men watering their cattle, and women washing their children and laundry.

The coffin's progress was encumbered by a whim of the calendar. By chance or design, Perabsah had brought his wife and attendants to Thebes just in time for Opet, the festival of the Nile's annual rebirth, lasting 24 days. Today was Arqi Paopi, the first day of the festival, and the revelries were in full cry. As Khnemes proceeded through the greasy streets of

Thebes, his way was repeatedly blocked by masked celebrants, while musicians plucked their harps and rang their ankle-bells. A squadron of acrobatic girls, clad in loin-belts but otherwise naked, flung themselves into handsprings and backward walk-overs directly in Perabsah's path, whilst older women shook rattles and drums, and beckoned for alms. "You see, Khnemes," chuckled Perabsah, "the streets are filled with starveling beggars, and rebellion is everywhere, yet the people are kept happy with drumming and acrobats."

Three attractive young women, with fishnets draped across their nakedness to indicate their profession, and wearing cowrie shells to symbolize their female organs, made gestures of enticement. "Lay down your burden, wanderers," purred the comeliest of the net-maidens. "Come with us, and be refreshed." Qesf growled beneath his corner of the sledge, and the net-wenches withdrew. But now the path was blocked by a crowd of shouting men. Mindful of his duties as Perabsah's bodyguard, Khnemes lowered one hand from the sledge and reached for the dagger in his belt's scabbard. But now he saw that these men were seeking employment. As part of the Opet festivities, a local priest-guild intended to stage a mock battle between the armies of Good and Evil, and strong men would be paid a day's ration of bread and beer to act as soldiers in this counterfeit battle.

And now, thank the gods, Perabsah turned off the main road and down a side-lane, leading into the Padmai district of Thebes. Khnemes was greatly relieved when Perabsah reached the crossroads of the Sedge and the Two Plumes, for here was the lodging-house where Perabsah's wife Mer-ytast and her attendants were waiting.

"*Manu!* Excellent!" said Perabsah as the coffin was set down in the house's antechamber. "Qesf, bring the mummy to my sleeping-quarters. I wish to inspect his person, so that I can deem which anointments and amulets will be suitable for his reburial. Khnemes, I shan't need your services until tomorrow morning. You other lot, help my wife's attendants. Merytast and I will be joining the revels this evening."

* * *

"Can you read hieroglyphics?"

The scribe had been peering at a scroll which he held open to the starlight; now he looked up in reply to this question. He wore a long kilt and was wrapped in an even longer *rhetu* monk-cloak, and the flickering light of the festival-torches gleamed against the top of his bald head: only the top of it, for the scribe wore his hair in a fringe all round his scalp, with his ears exposed and a clean-shaven tonsure above. He sat hunched against the glazed tiles along the threshold of the lodging-house. His Thoth-case of writing-implements was on the tiles beside him, tethered to his waist. A pastille of incense smouldered in a brass tray nearby.

The scribe squinted into the darkness, then saw Khnemes standing over him. "Greetings, Nubian. I nearly failed to see you in the dark: your black skin mingles with the night. Yes, I can read hieroglyphics . . . and I can also read *men*. You are a long way from Kush. What can I do for a former bowman of the King's troops?"

Khnemes was impressed by this deduction, but he sensed the flow of its logic. His service in the Medchay infantry had ended two years ago, yet Khnemes still wore a wig of the *anhu* style favoured by the foot-soldier bowmen of the Medchay: rows of tightly-sewn echelon curls, long at both sides to cover his ears, yet tapering hindwards so that his nape was left bare. The padded *anhu* of brown hair protected an infantryman's scalp from the sun. In the hot weather of Egypt, where it was difficult to keep natural hair clean and free of lice, most men shaved their heads and wore wigs of the same tight-curled style that Khnemes wore . . . but only the archers of the Medchay regiments kept their hairpieces short at the back of the neck, so that the wigs would not catch against a longbow or a bundle of arrows. At this moment, Khnemes carried the leather sling-bag – his *kha'ai* – which he always wore across-shoulder as he had once carried his arrows. As for clues that Khnemes was a *former* infantryman . . . well, he was in civilian garb now, and at 30 years of age he was rather old for active duty.

"So you can translate a man by his haircut?" Khnemes

asked. "Yes, my skin proclaims me as a son of Nubia, and my accent tells you that I am a Kushite, and I boast that I stood eleven years' service in the garrisons of the Medchay. But I have dwelt in Egypt long enough to learn the symbols of its professions . . . and I believe that *your* trade leaves you idle just now."

"*Ehi?*" the scribe's tone was mocking. "This is the first night of the Opet festival. Unless you were blinded by one of your own arrows, archer, you see that I am a priest . . . and even a farmboy from Kush must know that the priests of Thebes are busy during Opet."

Khnemes pointed at the scribe's tonsure. "Your hair is barbered in the *fekhet* style, worn only by priests who serve Hathor and the lesser goddesses. Opet is the festival of Amun-Re and his bride-goddess Mut: even Egyptians who favour other deities will give homage to Amun-Re while there is some chance of receiving Opet-gifts from the sun-god's priests. But the goddess Hathor takes no part in Opet's rituals . . . so you and all the Hathor-monks may be caught idle for the next few days."

"You know much about Hathor, Nubian."

"I should. Under her older name Athrua, she was the war-goddess of Nubia . . . before the priests of Egypt abducted her northwards, changed her name and countenance, and deemed her a goddess of Egypt." Khnemes appraised the monk again. "You are younger than I am, but your kilt is of a length more typical for an older man . . . so you have advanced in your profession, and you are respected. These signs reveal that you are qualified for the task which I offer, and the Opet has not made your time heavy with priest-tasks."

The scribe-priest rose to his feet, passing one hand through the looped cord of his Thoth-case as he stood. His other hand raised the incense-tray towards his nose, and he sniffed the sharp fumes. Khnemes was slightly surprised that the scribe-priest stood nearly as tall as himself; he had seemed shorter. "You intrigue me, Nubian," said the scribe. "I am Nask, a *fekhet*-priest of Hathor."

Khnemes made the traditional Egyptian male's greeting,

touching his hand to his chest and then extending his cupped fingers as if to offer his heart while he introduced himself: "*Enuk Khnemes*."

The priest nodded slightly but did not repeat the gesture of the heart-cup: a subtle reminder that his social rank was above that of Khnemes. "Now give us a look of those hieroglyphics."

From his sling-bag, Khnemes took the fragments of cartonnage. He had taken them from Perabsah's offering-table while Perabsah was busying himself with a skinful of tamarind-wine. "These belong to my sovereign lord, who requires a scribe to decipher them," said Khnemes. Three weeks ago, Perabsah's longtime scribe Seshem had died of river-sweats, in the midst of the long-delayed task of reorganizing Perabsah's family archives. Perabsah – with no assistance from Khnemes – had personally engaged a new scribe for his household in Aneb Hetchet. But Perabsah had chosen not to bring the untested scribe on this long journey upriver to Thebes. Earlier today, Perabsah had declared his intentions to find a scribe in Thebes to translate the cartonnage . . . but Khnemes knew that tomorrow's sunrise would find Perabsah fuddled with wine, and unfit to interview journeymen scribes, so Khnemes had taken it upon himself to engage a scribe. Now he showed Nask the scraps of papyrus. "Can you read these?"

Nask took the fragments, raising them to his face and moving nearer to the portal of the lodging-house so that he could borrow some light from its flickering lantern. "You told me, Nubian, that these were hieroglyphs."

"Are they not?"

"These are not god-words. They are book-words: hieratic text. But they are fragments, not a complete text . . . and the places where red ink was used, to mark the first word of each new passage, have faded badly." Nask squinted at the uppermost flake of papyrus, scanning its marks from right to left. "Here is something: '*The new overseer Rekhseth is cruel to myself and to all of the mine-workers.*'"

"Miners?" Khnemes accepted this as proof of Nask's ability to read the text, for it verified Perabsah's boast: his *tefteftef* Rekhseth had overseen the labourers in the goldfields of

Bendet. "Yes, that must refer to the gold-mine. Continue, please."

Nask gave the translated fragment back to Khnemes, and raised another scrap of cartonnage to his face before speaking again: "'*Each morning, Rekhseth passes through the sentry-posts and brings into the work-camp a birdcage containing . . .*' Hmm! This next word is obscure. It's pronounced '*bai*', and I think it means a brown-necked raven. That's all it says." Nask gave the fragment to Khnemes. "Here's another: '*Every night at sunset, Rekhseth goes alone into the hills beyond the mines. He sacrifices the raven to an unknown god, before returning to us and . . .*' No more there." Nask started to read another piece of cartonnage, but now the *fekhet*-priest suddenly stiffened: "Gods and infidels!" cried Nask. "This speaks of *murder!*"

Khnemes instinctively felt for his dagger as he stepped towards Nask. "You are certain?"

"Indeed." Nask raised his incense-tray again and fortified himself with another draught of its billowing smoke. His other hand thrust the cartonnage towards Khnemes while pointing a forefinger at two hieratic symbols, ligatured together one atop the other in a scrawl resembling a coiled snake. "This word is pronounced '*nik*'."

Khnemes was unimpressed. "Many words of Egypt's tongue have more than one meaning. '*Nik*' has several meanings . . . only one of which is 'murder'."

"Aye, Nubian. But see you this after-mark?" To the left of the coiled snake, Nask indicated a hieratic sign resembling a triangle with three appendages. "This means 'enemy'. The word '*nik*' followed by the enemy-sign means 'murder'." Before Khnemes could examine it closely, Nask passed the papyrus fragment directly underneath his nose as if he was reading its scent. "This says that a man named Teknu was murdered at moonrise."

"By whose hand?" Khnemes asked the monk Nask. "And why?"

"I can't tell. It speaks here '*nik-en'f ma tep Teknu*' . . . so the papyrus says that *he* murdered Teknu, but '*he*' could mean any man. Each of these scraps has several lines of text, but I'm getting only the middle bits of each." Nask turned away from Khnemes towards the light, and read aloud from several papyri: "'. . . *has slain our work-brother unjustly*' . . . '*vengeance of the gods*' . . . '*sacrifice of the raven at sunset* . . .' That's the lot, I think."

"Then I thank you, priest Nask." Khnemes reclaimed the cartonnage. "What barter do you ask for your efforts?"

Nask appraised Khnemes carefully. "You served eleven years in the Medchay, you said? The Medchay are ill-known for never paying their debts."

Khnemes frowned at this familiar accusation. The bowmen of the Medchay had reaped a dark reputation for accumulating long tallies of debts at one outpost, then departing for another garrison without squaring accounts. Gazing steadily into Nask's eyes, Khnemes murmured evenly: "*Smaa-i ma'at shes ma'at.* I pay my debts . . . *always*." From his sling-bag, Khnemes produced a small bar of copper weighing five *qed'tu*, which he tossed towards the priest. Nask lunged to catch the bright ingot. His sandals clattered hollowly against the tiles beneath his feet, and he tottered uncertainly for an instant. Nask was adjusting his long monk-cloak and his tonsure as Khnemes turned and strode into the night.

The next day was Tepi Hathyr, the second day of the Opet festivities. As the rays of dawn touched the portals of the sun-god's temple Opet-Uret in Karnak, the priests of Amun-Re entered their sanctuary to waken the statue of their god. When the statue awakened, the priests would dress their sun-god's effigy in his sacred robes. He would then be anointed and fed, after which the priests would convey the statue of Amun-Re to his seat in the Barque of the Sun. Atop the shoulders of twoscore priests and acolytes, this sacred ship would then be borne through the streets of Thebes to the Nile's quayside, thence towed southward upriver along the Holy Mile to the Temple of Mut, where the sun-god would claim his bride-goddess. This was a day of high sanctity and holiness for all true believers, in which the people of Thebes would devote the hours from dawn until sunset to the sacred task of becoming stinking drunk.

When Khnemes knocked discreetly outside the upstairs sleeping-quarters of his master, the only replies from within were the sounds of Perabsah and Merytast snoring in tandem. Swiftly, Khnemes restored the borrowed fragments of cartonnage to the offering-table outside Perabsah's bedchamber. Then he noticed something strange.

On the surface of the table, and the floor beneath, were several tiny mounds of dark glittering powder. Khnemes touched the nearest mound, then examined his fingertips: the stuff gleamed like gemstones. It seemed valuable, but Khnemes knew his master well enough to suspect otherwise. In recent days, Perabsah's estate had lost much of its value, and Perabsah – who had always been covetous – had lately become more wealth-thirsty than ever. If Perabsah had permitted this glittery sand to pass the night unguarded on his table, then the sparkling dust was clearly worthless. Khnemes shrugged, and transferred several pinches of the stuff to a small drawstring pouch from his *kha'ai*, hoping to learn its nature later.

Downstairs, as Khnemes entered the main hall of the lodging-house, he saw the loyal slave Qesf standing vigil. Several porters and chambermaids, attendant to this lodging-house, were busied with their tasks. Beyond the main hall's outer doors stood the antechamber. By now the sunrise was well past; through the closed outer doors, Khnemes could hear the streets of Thebes ringing loud with cries of revelry.

As Khnemes approached, Qesf gave the traditional greeting which a slave of Egypt offers to a free citizen: he extended both arms, with his wrists crossed as if bound in invisible shackles, his palms upturned and open to show that he carried no weapons. "*Meden-i, emir per,*" Qesf's deep voice rumbled. "I obey thee, steward of my master's house."

Khnemes greeted Qesf with the gesture of the cupped heart, even though Qesf was not a free citizen of Egypt. "Did you sleep well, friend?"

Qesf grunted. "I slept as a slave always sleeps: with one eye open. Djeb and Huti and I took it in turns to guard the house last night, *emir per*. Between vigils, I had a few hours' sleep."

Khnemes brought forth his pouch, and shook some grains of the dark sparkle-dust into his open hand. "Do you know this powder?"

Qesf took a brief glance. "It is *tahn*, sir. That is to say, mica: a glittery dust of no value."

"Has it any purpose?" Khnemes asked.

"Only one, sir, to my knowledge. It is an ingredient in eye-paint. The apothecaries, when blending their wares, sometimes add a bit of mica if the eye-paint is destined for a lady's eyelids. Some women of Egypt believe that a sparkle of mica in their eye-paste will increase their beauty. I am certain that this dust has no other use."

Just then a shout erupted from abovestairs: "*Ahai!* Landlord! Send a eunuch to my wife's room with two portions of breakfast!" With a belch in his voice and a lurch in his step, Perabsah came downstairs and through the inner doorway to the main hall. Perabsah's steps were unsteady, his headcloth was askew and his *shent* apron-kilt was more clumsily knotted than usual. A gold ring glittered in his left ear. Now he belched again, and gestured at a nearby porter. "You there, boy! Give us some air, will you? Open the doors!"

The porter bowed, and flung open the antechamber's doors to reveal the lodging-house's doorkeeper on duty in the vestibule. This servant saw Perabsah, and made haste to open the outer door leading to the Street of Two Plumes. The second day of Opet was in full cry, and as Khnemes looked through the doorways, he could see some portion of the festivities.

Outside the house, a crowd of revellers had assembled. Some of the men and women wore revel-masks of linen and papyrus, painted and shaped to resemble the heads of various animals. At the centre of the crowd, two women were performing a mirror-dance. They stood facing each other, so that Khnemes beheld them both in profile: they were dressed identically and wore matching wigs. While several female minstrels played flutes and six-stringed harps, the two women swayed in unison: approaching each other, then backing away. Each dancer's movements and steps were a perfect copy of the other's, but reversed right and left: as if each woman was her counterpart's reflection in a mirror. Khnemes was vastly impressed: these two women were so skilled in their art, it was impossible for him to tell which was leading the other.

"Do the ladies entice you, Khnemes?" Near his elbow, Khnemes scented Perabsah's foul breath, seasoned with sour tamarind-wine. "Forget those wenches, my servant: their favours grow stale. Let me show you a beauty that is eternal." Perabsah dug into a pouch at his waistband, and brought something forth. "*Mah'ek!* Behold thee!"

Perabsah was clutching a huge emerald, nearly the size of his fist. The emerald was raw and uncut: a bright green six-sided prism, in the shape of a near-perfect cube. Sunlight from the open doorway lit the emerald, filling it with a quiet deep glow like green sea-water. *Green*, the colour of rebirth: the colour of life beyond death. Perabsah smiled proudly, turning the precious stone one way and then another: Khnemes could see no flaws within it. But now he noticed a familiar odour, in unfamiliar quantities: the scented oil from Perabsah's vanity-phial. Was Perabsah anointing himself more liberally than usual?

"I bartered for this in the marketplace last night, from some jackal of a tomb-robber who failed to reckon the worth of his own plunder." Perabsah smugly pouched the green stone as he spoke. "When the fool plucked this bauble from an unknown tomb, he likely thought that he was snatching a pretty piece of coloured glass. Naturally, I indulged his misbelief."

Khnemes was scandalized. "*Heri sa'ur!* That jewel belongs to the dead."

"The dead own nothing except their own dust." Perabsah slapped the bulging pouch at his waist. "Should I search all the tombs of Egypt, and ask the dead to claim their property? If any corpse owns this bauble, I shall keep it safe for him until he meets me in the afterworld."

Suddenly, from the courtyard came the sounds of battle, and Khnemes drew his dagger. There was civil war within the provinces along the border between the two Egypts; had this warfare now reached Thebes?

Khnemes stepped into the antechamber as the women finished their mirror-dance and gathered the trinkets flung to them by the crowd. As the dancers' audience dispersed, Khnemes saw what he had overheard: the mock battle between Good and Evil had begun.

In the public square outside the lodging-house stood two armies, arrayed with wooden swords and leather shields. On one side, their bodies painted red, stood proudly the gallant Companions of Horus. At the far end of the square, hunched and lurking in their yellow-painted stealth, stood the insidious Accomplices of Set. The outcome of this war was pre-ordained, of course . . . but first the crowd would be treated to some spirited fighting. At the edge of the throng stood two tall men, wearing kilts of coarse grey linen, and clutching tipstaffs with heavy bronze knobs. Recognizing their uniforms, Khnemes was grateful that the constables of Thebes were on duty. The Opet festival was notorious for its violence . . . but for now, at least, the violence was counterfeit. With a loud clack-a-kack of wooden swords, the mock battle began.

"Does the battle arouse you, Khnemes?" asked a female voice nearby. Merytast was here, clothed in an elaborate gown and her favourite wig. Perabsah's wife stood by his side in the antechamber, both of them watching Khnemes as he sheathed his dagger and observed the staged battle. At a discreet distance, two of Merytast's handmaidens awaited her command.

"Yes, *neb't-i*: sovereign-my-lady. The battle indeed arouses me," Khnemes answered, carefully studying the eyes of his mistress. Merytast's eyes were brightest green, like smaller versions of Perabsah's stolen emerald. The lady's eyes were rimmed with black *smedyt*, yet her dark eye-paint showed no glitter of *tahn*. Khnemes continued: "I mean of course the *true* war between Good and Evil. Not the struttings of these soldier-dolls." Khnemes gestured scornfully at the counterfeit warriors while he peered over Merytast's shoulder at the faces of her two maidservants. Their eye-paint was plain black as well: it is unwise for a maid to be more gaudy than her mistress.

"We leave for home today, Khnemes," said Perabsah, stepping towards the doorway and spitting a gobbet of natron into the streets, then turning away without bothering to see if his offering had spattered any human target. "You recall the dead man who served my *teftef* Rekhseth? We must convey him and his coffin to my estate, and give him a respectful burial. Summon all the slaves and porters of my retinue, and bid them to prepare for our journey downriver."

Merytast beckoned to her handmaidens. "Attend me, vessels of my whim. Let us go abovestairs, to make ready for the journey home, and leave these men to their busy cleverness." Merytast patted her husband's arm affectionately, then led her attendants away. The obedient Qesf, overhearing his master's words, had already gone off to notify the other slaves.

Khnemes turned towards Perabsah. "Is a river journey wise just now, *neb-i*? The course of the Nile between Thebes and Karnak must be kept clear during the Opet festival, so that the barge of Amun-Re can have free transit through the Holy Mile. Each morning, the god's barge is towed upriver so that Amun-Re can visit his goddess-bride. Then, each evening until the last night of Opet, the barge of Amun-Re goes downriver to Karnak again, and . . ."

"Would you prefer that we journey overland, by camels or chariots?" Perabsah straightened his headcloth. "The borderlands between Egypt's torn halves are filled with bandits and violent factions of the civil war. I would rather see my wife ungentled on the turbulent Nile than place her within range of a bandit's arrows. After we pass downriver from Karnak, the Opet rituals need not concern us. We will . . ."

"Pardon, my sir." A doorkeeper of the lodging-house came pattering towards Perabsah, and made an obsequious gesture. "A visitor asks for you."

"*Ehi!* Yes, that must be the scribe I sent for." The shouts of the mob grew louder as the mock battle neared its climax, while Perabsah turned towards Khnemes: "Did you think, my steward, that I wasted all the first night of Opet in drunken revelry? Last night, after you left, Qesf informed me that a scribe-priest from one of the local guilds was offering his services to anyone who might give a donation to his temple. I wish to have those cartonnage fragments read before we leave Thebes, so . . . *ahai!* Here he comes now."

Khnemes assumed that this scribe must be Nask, and he was about to tell Perabsah that the *fekhet*-priest's services had already been rendered. Yet now a man came through the portals, carrying a Thoth-case on a loop of cord, and Khnemes looked up, expecting to see once again the tall monk of Hathor's temple. But, *nan't*: this was some other man.

This scribe was shorter than Nask, and the pattern of his hair was different from Nask's tonsure as well. This man was a *sem*: above his right ear, he wore the long braided sidelock of the *semu* scribe-priests of Ptah, whose scalps are otherwise shaved bare. This particular *sem* had a week's worth of stubble on his head, and his sidelock was poorly braided: these signs told Khnemes that this *sem* was probably a less scholarly man than Nask. Indeed: the *sem*'s kilt was short, and had no apron, which showed that his priestly rank was not especially high. His face was smudged, too. *Egypt has indeed fallen*, Khnemes thought, *if the priest-guilds of Ptah are recruiting men such as this*.

The *sem* made the heart-cupping gesture of greeting, and introduced himself: "*Enuk Uaf*," he said, with his mouth full, revealing the worst set of teeth Khnemes had ever seen. His breath conveyed the stench of the tombs. This scribe Uaf was chewing a large wad of natron, yet the powerful desiccant failed to perform its traditional task, for the odour emerging from Uaf's diseased gums made Khnemes want to retch. A trickle of black drool formed at the corner of Uaf's mouth; he wiped this away with the back of one hand.

Khnemes was on the brink of telling Perabsah that Uaf's services were unwanted, because the cartonnage-text had already been deciphered by Nask. But this *sem*-scribe might be useful after all. Although Khnemes was illiterate, he knew that hieratic text could conceal many subtle layers of meaning. If Uaf's reading of the cartonnage fragments resembled Nask's version, Khnemes would be confident that both scribes had read the papyri truly. "Wait here, *sem*," he said now to Uaf. "I will go upstairs, and fetch your study-text."

Khnemes stepped past Uaf and towards the staircase. But Uaf stepped forward at the same instant. The two men collided, causing Khnemes to lose his balance and jostle Perabsah. "Take care, sir!" cried Uaf, dropping his scribe-case and reaching forward to catch Perabsah's waist.

"Touch not my master, you of Ptah!" Khnemes doubled his fists, but the slovenly *sem*-priest let go of Perabsah and extended his hands – palms empty and upraised – to show he meant no harm. Uaf's fingertips were stained black from the ink of his scribe-tasks, with a few flecks of red ochre. Uaf stepped away from the outer doors leading to the antechamber, to let more sunlight into the main hall while he shielded his smudged face with one hand and gestured broadly with his other arm. "I only meant to help . . ."

"Really, Khnemes," said Perabsah. "The scribe touched my person, but he did not diminish me. In fact, I . . ." Perabsah's eyes widened in panic. He touched the bulge at his waistband, then he sighed with relief. "Praise be to Osiris, god of green things: my prize is still safe."

A sudden roar of triumph from the courtyard made Khnemes turn. The Companions of Horus were about to defeat the Accomplices of Set. Through the open doors of the antechamber, Khnemes saw one warrior break free of the battle and rush towards the lodging-house. This man wore a revel-mask resembling a bird of prey. It made him seem like a hawk-headed god, and Khnemes had a sudden recognition: *Today is Tepi Hathyr, the first day of the month named Chamber-of-Horus, honouring the hawk-god. This man must be one of the Companions of Horus in the priests' mock battle.*

But something was wrong. The hawk-headed man clutched a longbow, with its arrow already nocked: a strange weapon indeed for a staged battle. Khnemes had just time to shout a warning as the hawk-headed man raised his longbow and let the arrow fly. Something whistled past Khnemes, and then Perabsah screamed and fell, with an arrow piercing his chest.

"*Rehan tu!* Stop, assassin!" With his dagger drawn,

Khnemes ran towards the antechamber. The doorkeeper came forwards, but the hawk-masked slayer swung his bow and sent the doorman sprawling. Khnemes helped this man to his feet while keeping his frantic gaze on the figure of the fleeing bowman. "You! Seal the doors of this hall from within, with yourself inside to guard my master!" Now Qesf came running, and Khnemes shouted to him: 'Qesf! Seal this door from without, and the hall's other entrance as well, and summon a physician! Keep the doors sealed while you stand guard. Hurry!" Khnemes shrugged off his sling-bag and flung it to Qesf, then raced down the steps of the lodging-house, into the street.

The assassin was running into the Street of Two Plumes: this was a wide straight avenue, giving Khnemes a clear view of the archer as he fled. As Khnemes ran into the courtyard with his dagger drawn, suddenly he was surrounded by masked men with swords. They attacked him, and Khnemes had just enough time to see that he had blundered into the mock battle between the forces of Good and Evil: each set of warriors had mistaken Khnemes for a soldier on the *other* side of the battle. The legions of Horus and the legions of Set were all thwacking at Khnemes with their wooden swords, and he had to defend himself without harming these play-warriors who thought this was a game. "*Sebenthen!* Away, fools! Give me room!"

Harp-pluckers and flute-toodlers scattered as Khnemes rushed on down the Street of Two Plumes. He kept one eye towards the fleeing back of his quarry while he searched the crowds for the familiar grey kilts of the city's constables. *There's never a policeman around when I need one*, Khnemes thought angrily. He could see the assassin ahead, running westwards, with his longbow clutched fast in his left hand, and a bundle of arrows slung over his back. The masked bowman had a considerable start, but Khnemes swiftly narrowed the distance until he was close enough to observe a distinctive scar on the right shoulder of the hawk-masked assassin. Suddenly, at a crossroads ahead, the murderer turned leftwards and fled down a side street.

Khnemes cursed as he ran. Now he turned at the same crossing, and was met by two women in fishnets, who blocked his path while gesturing enticingly. "Tarry with us, proud Nubian," said a wigged harlot, beckoning at him with her fingernails dyed in bright henna. "Does your dagger seek a sheath?" Khnemes lowered his weapon, and held his other hand empty to show these harlots that he had nothing to barter for their services. "*Eunuch!*" "*Boy-lover!*" the net-wenches cursed him as Khnemes rushed past.

In a street ahead, the bowman stumbled. His bundle of arrows came loose and scattered. He turned to face his pursuer, and Khnemes saw the eyes of the hawk-mask peering into his soul as the killer raised his weapon and flung it at Khnemes. The longbow fell into a puddle, as from round the corner a crowd of half-naked Egyptians in carnival masks came rushing towards some unseen revel. Up ahead, Khnemes heard distant drumbeats: *Doom! Doom!* The hawk-headed predator changed course, and vanished into the crowd.

Khnemes reached the puddle and snatched the longbow as he ran, hoping it might yield some clue to the killer's identity. The crowd was moving towards the drumbeats. The murderer had vanished in the wave of celebrants . . . but his sudden invisibility meant that he was moving *in the same direction as the crowd*, or else his movements would be seen against the current of the mob. Khnemes ran along the edge of the throng, searching the sea of bright masks.

A face rolled past him in the gutter, and Khnemes recognized the hawk-faced mask of Horus: lost or flung away by the fleeing assassin. Khnemes reached to claim the mask, but a ragged boy snatched it and clapped the mask over his own head, then ran away whooping in triumph: "*Enuk Heru! Mah'ethen!* I am Horus! Behold ye all!" With an oath, Khnemes plunged into the throng, and the drumbeats grew louder as the mob of revellers reached a crossroads.

The crowded streets of Thebes became suddenly empty, and Khnemes felt a dark dread as he saw where he was: the killer had fled directly into the Avenue of Rams, the broad concourse of western Thebes leading to the docks of the Nile.

The central portion of the avenue was clear, for the mobs had stepped back to make way for their god.

Forty chanting priests of Amun-Re came striding towards Khnemes, bearing on their high shoulders the immense golden Ship of the Sun while they intoned in unison the Hymn of Opet. From the prow of the sacred barque, a massive effigy of Amun-Re glowered down at his lowly disciples. *Doom! Doom! Doom!* beat the oncoming drums. At the head of the procession strode a tall man in the robes of a priest, his height made even more imposing by the high bottle-shaped headgear he wore: the *Stethta*, the White Crown of southern Egypt. Khnemes felt his heart turn cold with awe, for this man could only be Piankh-Himself, the High Priest of Thebes who had taken advantage of the civil wars to declare himself king of Egypt's southern lands.

Doom! Doom! Doom!

Nine thousand citizens of Thebes stared at Khnemes, as he stood in the middle of the bare street with his dagger in one hand and a longbow in his other hand, while the Ship of Amun-Re came striding towards him.

"*Seize him!*" shouted someone in the crowd, and Khnemes saw a thousand outstretched hands pointing directly at *him*, while a thousand tongues cried sacrilege. "Seize the Nubian! He seeks to murder Amun-Re!"

The crowd swelled from the gutters on each side of the Avenue of Rams, and came menacingly towards Khnemes. All of them were . . .

No. One man was running *away* from Khnemes, and the sunlight gleamed against bright scar tissue on his right shoulder. Now that his hawk-mask was gone, Khnemes saw that the murderer had long shaggy dark hair: most unusual for an Egyptian. Khnemes turned from the oncoming barge of the sun-god, and ran after this man. Behind him came shoutings and curses, but he dared not turn to see if any of the mob were pursuing him . . .

Ahead loomed a high redstone pylon: the sentry-gate Kheft her-en-Nebset at the west edge of Thebes. "*Seize that murderer!*" Khnemes shouted to the sentries as the killer rushed past them. But the sentries merely stared blankly. The western quarter of Thebes was the temple district, and the Theban priest-guilds paid these sentries a daily wage of bread and beer to guard the western gate and protect the temples from vandals: *those* were their tasks, and none other. No Theban sentry would abandon his post, and leave the portals of the gods unprotected, for the sake of catching a mere *murderer*.

With a sudden inspiration, Khnemes shouted: "*Ehi!* That man attacked the Barque of Amun-Re! Seize him! *Kefaythen ef!*" As Khnemes ran through the gate, three sentries picked up their pikestaffs and joined the pursuit. Now Khnemes glimpsed a familiar kilt of coarse grey linen. He saw the sunlight gleaming on bronze-tipped truncheons, and he knew that several constables had joined the chase.

The sharp-scented tang of the Nile became strong in his nostrils as Khnemes reached the sixteen-step staircase Redu ni-Temi. The annual flooding of the Nile had begun, for already *five steps* were underwater as Khnemes hurried down the Nile-stairs. If the killer had a boat ready for his departure, then Khnemes would never find him. The number of barges and ferries on the Nile must be . . .

No! Thank the gods . . . or thank the calendar, for the stretch of river between Thebes and Karnak had been kept clear today for the Barque of the Sun-God. As Khnemes scanned the riverbank, he saw the entire vast Nile clear of vessels, except . . . *ahai!* . . . just north of the river-stairs, one desperate little washtub of a boat was moving away from the quayside.

"There he is!" Khnemes shouted. Several dockmen with gaff-hooks came forwards. The boatman had cast off, but now a long gaff-pole snaked out from the shore and caught his prow, as several constables arrived.

Khnemes came running up just as the dockmen were hauling their quarry ashore. He was a small rat-like man, with dark hair nearly to his shoulders and a scraggly beard. Yet he was well-dressed, in new-made sandals and a new kilt of white linen. *Who is this man, and who is he to Perabsah?* Khnemes wondered.

Two constables held fast the squirming bowman, while Khnemes sheathed his dagger and straightened his *anhu* wig. "Has this fellow committed a crime, Nubian?" someone asked.

The assassin's bearded face quivered in rage. "*Enuk Atur'meh!*" he protested. "I am a free citizen of Lower Egypt!"

"*Tu ma nikeh*: you are a murderer, that's what you are," said Khnemes.

"One moment, Nubian." From behind Khnemes, a constable strode forwards. He wore an armband displaying a docket of rank – he was a chief constable, then – and his tone was respectful as he examined the echelon curls of the short-naped wig that Khnemes wore. "You wear the wig of the Medchay, yet I have never known their bowmen to wield such a poor weapon." The chief constable pointed: Khnemes was still holding the murderer's discarded longbow. It was a crude weapon, made from several lengths of carved cassia-wood, splinted together and poorly balanced.

"The weapon is not mine: it is evidence," said Khnemes, saluting this man while he unstrung the bow. "And I *was* of the Medchay. *Enuk Khnemes*, master bowman of the Chaut Sefekhnu: the Twenty-Seventh light infantry division, garrisoned at Per Nebes, near the Nile's second cataract. At least, that is where I served longest."

The policeman seemed impressed. "The Twenty-Sevens, you served with? *Enuk Peth*. I was a charioteer, Third Light-foots, the Encirclers. We fought alongside you in the Wauat uprising." Chief Constable Peth saluted Khnemes, then jerked his thumb towards the rat-faced criminal. "Here, now: what's all this, then?"

Khnemes took a deep breath. "This man has slain my lord sovereign, Perabsah. Or he has attacked him, at least: I gave orders for a physician to be summoned." Khnemes scowled at the prisoner. "I would question this man, but first I must see to my master's condition. I pray you: hold this prisoner against my return. He may have committed crimes against Thebes."

"We will hold him for one day, at least . . . but then he must either be charged, or thrown back into whichever gutter spawned him." Peth nodded to his subordinates. One constable seized the prisoner's wrists, yanking them behind his back while another constable stepped forwards with a set of twist-cuffs. The prisoner's hands were shackled, and Peth gestured northeast, towards the central courthouse of Thebes. "Take him away."

Qesf stood at the entrance to the lodging-house. "It is all as you ordered, *emir per*. I sealed the doors with your *khetem*, front and back, while Huti summoned a physician. The doctor's name is Hefren, and he is tending our master even now." Qesf gave Khnemes a long cylindrical object with a handle at each end, like a baker's rolling-pin. This was the *khetem*, the cylinder-seal which Qesf had taken from the sling-bag flung to him by Khnemes.

Khnemes reached the entrance to the lodging-house. The front doors were open, but the doors to the antechamber were tightly shut, and a slathering of clay had been smeared across the join between the doors. Three symbols were deeply pressed into the clay. Uppermost was the image of a man in a nobleman's headcloth. Below this was the rectangular hieroglyph depicting a house. Lowermost was a picture of a bowl emitting rays of sunlight: this was the hieroglyph *nubu*, the symbol of gold. These three glyphs formed the crest of the house of Perabsah, whose family fortune was made in the Bendet goldfields. This unique sequence of symbols was produced only by the *khetem* seal of Khnemes when it was rolled into clay or soft wax. If another cylinder-seal were carved with these same three images, the impression would not be identical, and Khnemes would know it instantly for a counterfeit.

Khnemes inspected the clay seal. There were *two* impressions of Perabsah's house-mark in the clay, one covering the other but not quite precisely aligned. The deeper impression – the one made first – was split at the top and bottom. So these doors had been opened *after* the first seal was made, then closed to receive the second image. "Qesf, you sealed these doors *immediately* after I pursued the murderer?"

The slave nodded. "Indeed, *emir per*. No one entered nor left. I broke the seal to admit the physician, then I resealed the doors. I have stood guard here ever since. Huti came for your *khetem* whilst I stood guard, and he brought it to Djeb at the other door."

Leaving Qesf at his post, Khnemes circled round to the oxen-yard behind the lodging-house, then he entered the inn through the rear entrance. From upstairs came the sounds of female weeping: Merytast was lamenting amid her maidservants. Djeb was on guard at the stairs, and he pointed to the closed doors leading into the main hall. These too were sealed with the unique *khetem*-mark of Perabsah's estate. Khnemes satisfied himself that this mark was unbroken. Now he inserted the blade of his dagger into the join between the doors, and broke the seal. He stepped into the scene of the crime.

Four men were in the central hall. One was the priest-scribe Uaf, squatting in a corner and looking impatient. At the far end of the room was the doorkeeper. In the centre of the room, slumped on the floor, were two men: the man unknown to Khnemes must surely be the physician Hefren.

The other man was Perabsah. The broken shaft of an arrow protruded from his chest. He lay in a puddle of blood, and his breath came in loud hawking gasps. Perabsah's flesh was ash-pale, and his eyes were closed, but he was still alive.

Khnemes ran towards him, and knelt at the edge of the blood. "My lord sovereign! Doctor, how is he? And why do you not remove the arrow?"

Hefren scowled, and reached for a tool from the medical-case on the floor beside him. "If I remove the arrow, his wound will open. This man should be carried on a swift sledge to the nearest healing-house, where I have means to suppress his bleeding. *Ehi*, that reminds me." Hefren gave Khnemes a golden earring. "Your master wore this. He no longer requires it."

"Can I go now?" whined Uaf. "This is nothing to do with me. I only came here to read some cartonnage."

"You will be paid for your time," Khnemes vowed, as he went back to the physician. Perabsah's chest wound was swathed in several strips of bloodied linen, with the arrow still protruding between them. "Can I help?" Khnemes asked.

Hefren shook his head. "Only the gods can help this man now. When your master fell, he struck the back of his head on the floor." Hefren lifted his right hand, with two fingers coated in dark blood. "Your master's *gama* – the temporal bone of his skull – has been fractured, and there is an injury to his brain. You see this?" With his clean left hand, Hefren gently skinned back the lids of Perabsah's right eye, then his left. The pupil of Perabsah's left eye was twice as large as the other. "When the *kem* of one eye is wider than its brother eye, the brain is filling with blood on that side," Hefren explained. "This man's chances are . . ."

"Khnemes!" cried Perabsah, opening both his eyes and trying to sit up.

"I am here, *neb-i*," said Khnemes. "Sir, lie still. You must rest."

"I will have centuries to rest," said Perabsah, in slurred tones. "Khnemes! My wife becomes my heiress now; I die without a son. And I desire . . ." Perabsah coughed up a gobbet of blood, then continued: ". . . I desire that she bring home with her the broken mummy of my great-grandfather's servant, for reburial on my lands."

"It will be done, *neb-i*," said Khnemes, genuinely moved by this dying request. Khnemes had always observed Perabsah to be a selfish man, yet now – on the threshold of death – Perabsah was concerned not only for his wife, but also for the restless soul of the murdered man Teknu: the mummy from the Plain of Loaves.

"Khnemes!" screeched Perabsah, trying to sit up yet restrained by the physician. "I hear the beating of wings: my death comes! But do not let me vanish!"

"'Vanish', my lord?" Khnemes asked.

Perabsah nodded heavily. "My life, my estates, and all the living souls who knew me . . . all of these are in Aneb Hetchet, in northern Egypt. Yet now I die . . ." – he coughed again – ". . . now I die in *southern* Egypt, as a foreigner."

Perabsah was right, and now Khnemes understood the full horrible implications of Perabsah's death in this place . . . in the *wrong* Egypt, where he was unknown.

"*When no one remembers my name, I will vanish*," harshed Perabsah, his voice growing weak. "I will die here in Thebes, among strangers who will swiftly forget me. To die *once* is a certainty, Khnemes . . . but to die and be *forgotten* is *the second death*, the fate of the damned. I had always planned . . . *ahuk!* . . . I had planned to be buried with my father and grandfather, in the tomb on my estate, where those who knew me will see my name after my death." Perabsah trembled now, and he clutched at Khnemes. "Faithful steward, you *must* make certain that . . . *ahauk!* . . . that my body is made ready for the afterworld . . . and then you *must* convey my mummy to my home in northern Egypt."

Do I owe this man so much? Khnemes wondered. *Must I make this last promise, and bind myself to his flesh even after his death?*

"Khnemes!" said Perabsah in a whisper. "Fetch me home . . . *ahuk!* . . . to northern Egypt: the true Egypt of the pharaoh, not this festering cult-nest of the southern priests. Do not let my soul die in this place. *Do not murder my soul!*"

"I will do what must be done, *heri sa'ur*," Khnemes answered. But he was thinking of his duties to the flesh-world, not the afterlife. Silently, Khnemes vowed that he must bring justice to Perabsah's murderer. And, into the bargain, solve the ancient murder of Teknu.

Perabsah's eyes rolled upwards in their sockets, and his eyelids closed. He fell back, with the arrow's broken shaft protruding from the centre of his chest. Hefren caught the dead man, then placed him gently on the floor.

From abovestairs, Khnemes heard the sound of female wailing: the widow Merytast and her maidservants. The mourning had begun.

Perabsah's *shent* kilt was disarrayed at his loins. Khnemes adjusted the garment . . . then he saw that the pouch at Perabsah's waistband hung limp and empty. *The emerald was gone!* "Have you taken anything from my master?" Khnemes asked Hefren.

"Only his headcloth, which I tore into strips to make bandages," said the doctor, calmly repacking his instruments into their case. "Is anything . . ."

"An emerald is missing," said Khnemes. "It was the dead man's property: under Egyptian law, it now belongs to his widow. It is missing. *Djeb! Huti!* Enter this room at once, through the back way."

The two slaves entered, and Khnemes explained. Quickly, the scant items of furniture in the hall were examined: the emerald had not fallen behind any of these.

Qesf entered, as Huti and Djeb herded the physician, the *sem*-priest and the doorkeeper into the centre of the room. "A precious jewel has vanished from this room while the exits were sealed," Khnemes told them. "Whoever took the emerald has probably conspired in my lord's murder. Forgive the indignity, but all three of you must be searched. If you are innocent, you will be compensated for your time and for the liberties which I must take."

"You dare suspect me?" Hefren asked. "I'm a doctor, not a jewel-thief! I gave you back his earring, didn't I?"

"You did," said Khnemes. "But sometimes a large crime is concealed behind a small honesty. The emerald is far more valuable than the earring. Please disrobe."

"Tread carefully, Nubian," said Hefren. "You are in Thebes now. I am more powerful in this city than you are."

"Yes," said Khnemes patiently. "You are a *sunu*, a respected surgeon and healer, whilst I am merely a retired soldier. You are better-known than I am in Thebes. And in the world beyond death, too: you are surely better known in the afterlife than I am, doctor . . . for between us, in our two professions, you have probably killed more men than I did. But in this room, at this moment, I am more powerful than you. Please disrobe."

The doctor glared at Khnemes, while Qesf and Huti and Djeb flexed their arms. "Have your look, then." Hefren took off his headcloth and kilt, and flung these angrily to the floor, keeping only a scrap of linen to wipe Perabsah's death-blood off his fingers while he stood naked in his sandals. "Perhaps you will claim that I *swallowed* this precious stone?"

"The stone was as large as a man's fist," said Khnemes. "You are a *sunu*, not an *unu*: a doctor, not an ostrich. But might I examine your medical case?"

Hefren nodded angrily. With great interest, Khnemes examined the medical kit of an Egyptian surgeon. It was a rectangular cassia-wood case, with a shoulder-cord. Four rows of neat compartments filled the case. The first shelf held several white alabaster pots, with a line of black hieratic scrawled upon each: Khnemes could not read these, but his nostrils told him that these pots contained camphor-root, juniper, meadow-sweet, garlic, henna, liquorice and turmeric. The second shelf held copper knives, an obsidian drill, and a bone-saw. The third shelf contained an incense-lamp, some pastilles, a mortar and pestle. The last shelf held a balance scale, forceps, tweezers, and a pair of shears. Khnemes discovered that the entire set of shelves lifted out of the case to reveal another compartment beneath. This contained several papyri – probably medical texts – as well as linen dressings and a lacquered box slightly larger than a man's fist. Hefren's face reddened as Khnemes hefted this box and raised its hinged lid. Inside the box were a *mes* amulet to assist in childbirth, a bright red Isis-knot to ensure fertility, an *utchat* Horus-eye, a priapic charm and several other talismans.

Hefren looked embarrassed. "I don't put much faith in those trinkets, but my patients expect a bit of magic with their medicines. Are you satisfied?"

Khnemes nodded. "My apologies to you, doctor, and my compliments to the craftsman who fashioned your medical kit." Khnemes turned towards Uaf. "You are next."

The unkempt *sem*-priest had already taken off his garments, proving that the emerald was not on his person. Gesturing at him to clothe himself, Khnemes examined the man's Thoth-case: the proudest possession of an Egyptian scribe.

Uaf's scribe-case was shiny with a bright coat of lacquer: the smudge-faced *sem* neglected his own appearance, yet he clearly took impeccable care of his writing-case. Like Hefren's medical kit, the interior of the Thoth-case had several partitions. There were reed pens of various lengths and diameters, as well as uncut reeds and a flint blade. A drawstring bag contained a piece of sandstone and a scrap of pumice, worn smooth from their frequent use as erasers. The scribe's ink-blocks were next. These consisted of ground pigments mixed into acacia-gum: a small ink-block of red ochre and a much larger one of black charcoal. Khnemes had observed that hieratic script was often written entirely in black letters, with red used only to mark the beginning of key texts, so it made sense that this scribe carried a much larger supply of black ink than of red. A small clay pot, for mixing the pigments in water, was here also. At the bottom of the scribe-case was a long wooden palette with slots and depressions, and a figurine of the ibis-headed god Thoth, inventor of writing.

Khnemes nodded to the scribe Uaf. "My apologies to you, also. Doorkeeper, you are next."

The doorkeeper had already disrobed, revealing that he had only the door-seal of this house and two bronze keys on a chain. "I too should be suspected," Qesf pointed out. "I was in this room after the murderer struck, and I administered the seals."

"But you had time to hide the emerald elsewhere, so there is no point in searching you," said the practical Khnemes. Yet this was very strange. The main hall was on the ground floor, so of course there were no windows. All the doors were sealed immediately after Perabsah was attacked . . . so, the emerald had vanished from this room while all the exits were sealed.

"This riddle must wait a while longer," Khnemes said aloud. "I caught a fish in the river, but he has not been grilled yet. Qesf, give these men some honest barter for their time and their indignities. Gentlemen, please tell Qesf the names of the cross-roads nearest your dwelling-places in Thebes, in case I need to speak with you later. Now I must interview a murderer."

The central police-court of Thebes is where many journeys reach their endings, and where darker journeys begin. This red adobe building adjoins the Kamur, the central canal which runs west-to-east through Thebes . . . in fact, the hind section of the police station overhangs the canal's southern wall. Some criminals of Thebes have speculated that the police-court has a trap door above the canal, so that the Theban police can dispose of inconvenient guests.

Khnemes was sitting on a stool, in a room that was otherwise bare except for two oil-lamps placed in niches in the wall. The lamps were needed for their light, because this room was underground. Above the lamps was a chimney-flue, admitting air from the street level above. The brickwork floor was ramped, tilting slightly southwards to the edge of the room nearest the canal. At this wall, the floor's adobe bricks terminated in a drainage gutter.

Khnemes was facing north. From beyond the red adobe wall directly in front of him, he heard the nearby sounds of screaming, and the irregular rhythm of wood against flesh. Through the wall to his right, he heard someone sharpening a tool. From the room above him, there came through the brickwork the noises of sobbing and prayers to unnamed gods.

A door opened in the wall to his left, and Chief Constable Peth entered with his prisoner. The shaggy bowman's hands were shackled behind his back. The prisoner's linen kilt was stained. His feet were bare, and he walked painfully. In the lamplight, Khnemes saw bruises on the prisoner: clearly, the policemen's batons had forced this man to play the grim-sport which Egyptian criminals have named "smelling the stick". Peth seized the bowman's shoulders and pushed downwards, forcing him to kneel in front of Khnemes.

"Thank you, chief," said Khnemes. "Remove his handcuffs, please."

Peth arched an eyebrow at this breach of procedure. "Softly-softly, Nubian. If you weren't a former Medchay – and serving the interests of a wealthy house – I wouldn't let you see the prisoner at all. Well, it's your lookout if he gets violent." Peth tried to unbuckle the prisoner's handcuffs, but the buckle was snagged on the stiff leather shackles. Peth took his dagger from his scabbard and used this to unbuckle the cuffs.

"We questioned him before you got here," Peth went on, while the prisoner rubbed his chafed wrists. "He says his name's Secheb, a humble fisherman from down north in the Prospering Sceptre district . . . and his accent's northern, right enough. We can't verify the rest."

"Then let us see what *can* be verified." Khnemes appraised the man's beard and unkempt hair. "In Egypt's hot climate, most men keep their heads shaven. Yet this man does not." Khnemes thrust his hand into the bowman's matted locks. "*Ehui!* What's this?" Khnemes withdrew his hand quickly, cracking a sand-louse between his fingertips. More carefully this time, he probed the murderer's greasy tresses again. "Here is something, chief . . . or a *lack* of something. Bring that lamp closer, please." Peth fetched an oil-lamp from its niche, while Khnemes pulled back the bowman's lanky hair.

Secheb's right ear was missing. A thick whitish scar had formed where, long ago, the ear had been neatly sliced off. "So! You have one previous conviction, serious enough to bring a sentence of disfigurement," Khnemes deduced. "But still a minor offence, as you have kept your other ear and your nose."

"He's probably a leg-stretcher," said Peth, using the slang of the criminal world. "Takes his exercise climbing up and down the shafts of tombs. Sooner or later, all the grave-robbers in northern Egypt get word of the riper pickings in the tombs near Thebes, and they slime their way into our precinct. This likely lad must have got himself nicked for selling stolen burial-goods: that's a lesser offence than getting caught in the act of tomb-robbing."

Khnemes glared at the suspect. "Your ear-lack marks you as a thief, so you grow your hair long to conceal it . . . and you wear a beard so that your long hair seems to be the result of neglect rather than intent." Khnemes reached for something on the floor behind his stool. "Here, catch!"

Khnemes flung something at the prisoner's face, and Secheb instinctively raised his left hand to protect himself and catch the object. He found himself holding a cassia-wood longbow.

"That is the murder weapon. You see the *hatrit?*" In the lamplight, Khnemes pointed to the bow's leather handgrip, which also served to support the arrow while it was nocked and aimed by the archer. "This *hatrit* shows a great deal of wear on the left side of the bow, where many arrows have rubbed against the leather, but the right side of the leather is scarcely worn. This longbow has been drawn, and used often, by a *smehi*: a left-handed man."

Secheb had caught the bow with his left hand; now he dropped it as if it had river-plague. He tried to stand up, but Peth kept him kneeling. "All right, I'll admit it: *enuk smehi*," said Secheb. "But just because I'm left-handed doesn't mean I'm an archer. I'm a fisherman, coming up-Nile to Thebes from the delta."

"We found no nets or reed-traps in his boat," Peth told Khnemes. "His boat didn't stink enough to be a fishing-boat. Especially not from the delta, where all those foul marshlands are."

"From the delta, you say?" Khnemes frowned. If this man was indeed from the Prospering Sceptre – the administrative district at the apex of the Nile's delta – then Secheb and Perabsah might have met in northern Egypt. "Did you know my master?" Khnemes asked.

"I don't know anyone in Thebes," Secheb whined, in the flat nasal accent and pinched vowels of northern Egypt. "I'm from downriver. I was just coming up south to Thebes when your men grabbed me, and . . ."

"That's a lie," said Khnemes, leaning forwards. "A mast and a sail were in your boat: I saw them. But the mast was stowed beneath the thwarts, and your sail was furled. So you were travelling north, not south."

This logic was merciless. The Nile's great gift is that it enables transport in both directions. Northbound vessels strike their sails and stow their masts, allowing the Nile's steady current to bear them downriver. Southbound vessels raise their sails, and allow the prevailing northerly wind of the

Mehut to carry them upriver. Caught in his falsehood, Secheb said nothing.

"Why did you kill Perabsah?" Khnemes asked.

"I never met him," said Secheb.

"That is an answer to a different question," said Khnemes. "You are clearly unwealthed, for your speech and your bearing proclaim you are a labourer. Yet, when you were arrested, I saw that you wore expensive sandals, of new leather. Your kilt is new, and made of good white *shent* linen: I would expect a labourer to wear brown muslin. You dress well for a fisherman, especially one who has no nets."

Secheb looked desperate. "Right, Nubian. I'll tell all I know. Yesterday, during the revels, I met a man outside a wine-kiosk near the Street of the Sedge. He offered me three copper *debenu* if I would shoot someone with my longbow. He told me where to find the victim, and he kept a boat ready at the quay for my escape."

Khnemes and Peth exchanged glances. A single *qed't* of copper was an excellent day's pay for an unskilled labourer; three *debenu* would buy many months of comfort. "Who was this man?" Peth asked the prisoner. "Describe his face."

"I can't!" Secheb whimpered. "He wore a revel-costume, with a mask. A bird's face, it had: some sort of carrion-bird. He made a joke about robbing the tombs. He said tomb-robbers were like vultures or carrion-feeders. I think his costume was meant to resemble a *bai*."

Khnemes looked up sharply. "A *bai*? A brown-necked raven?"

Secheb nodded mournfully, and began to weep.

"I'll give you reasons to cry, you bastard," said Peth. "I'll see you go *on the wood* for this." But Secheb was already crying, and Peth's threat of a death-sentence by public impalement on a sharpened stake made no difference.

Khnemes felt hollow inside. This man had clearly slain Perabsah, but he was only an agent of the true murderer: a man in a raven's disguise. One hundred years ago, Perabsah's ancestor Rekhseth had sacrificed a brown-necked raven every night, in the goldfields. The *bai* was a very obscure bird in

Egypt, not a totem in any cult known to Khnemes: surely, the murder of Perabsah and the murder of Teknu – a century apart – were somehow intertwined.

The language of Egypt is subtle, and it comprehends two different forms of time: the momentary, and the infinite. During Secheb's arrest on the quays of the Nile, Khnemes had said to him: "*Tu ma nikeh:* you are a murderer." It was true at that time and that place. Now Khnemes said the same thing, but the rules of Egyptian grammar compelled him to use different words to speak a different truth. "*Netek nikeh:* you are a murderer," he told Secheb, "and this fact is truth for all eternity. It is your shadow now: it will follow you through all your days of life. It will travel with you on your journey to the afterworld, and it will stand alongside you in the Hall of Judgment. No matter where you go, your shadow cries 'murderer'. One million years hence, this truth will endure: *netek nikeh.*"

Khnemes rose from his stool. "I have more questions, but the answers are elsewhere. Please take this killer away, chief constable." Khnemes strode towards the door.

There was a clatter and a shout. Khnemes turned to see Secheb snatching at Peth's dagger. Peth's foot struck the oil-lamp beside him, snuffing the wick, and he cursed as hot oil splashed his leg. Khnemes rushed to aid the constable, just as Secheb broke free with Peth's knife in his left hand and ran across the cellar towards the chimney-flue. The light and shadows in the room swung madly as Secheb snatched the second oil-lamp from its niche with his right hand, and flung this at his pursuers. Khnemes saw Secheb raise the stolen dagger to his own throat . . . then the lamp struck the brick floor, and shattered. The cellar went dark.

"Don't do it, man," said Peth, in the darkness.

Khnemes heard a sharp gasp, then a gubbling sound . . . then a thud.

From somewhere in the dark came a howl through the walls: the voice of a criminal screaming a confession. But it was in another room, another crime. Nothing to do with the murder which Khnemes must solve. In the darkness, he felt his way towards the door.

At the lodging-house, Khnemes found Merytast garbed in mourning. Her finery and wig were put away: now she wore her plainest dress, with its hem torn picturesquely in three places. Her face-paint and *smedyt* were gone: her cheeks and hair were now daubed with a few discreet traces of mud.

When Khnemes entered the upstairs bedchamber where Perabsah and his wife had slept, several of Merytast's attendants were gathering the belongings of their mistress for her journey downriver. Near the door, Khnemes saw the coffin-boat from the Plain of the Loaves. The broken mummy – surely he was the murdered labourer Teknu – was still crammed into his too-small coffin. The mummy looked more at peace now than when Khnemes had last seen him: his face seemed rather less distorted than before, and the distension of his belly had lessened.

"I am surprised, my lady," said Khnemes to Merytast, "to find this mummy cloistered in your private rooms."

"This is a lodging-house, not my boudoir," said Merytast. "My husband desired to bring this mummy home to our estate, to be entombed respectfully. This man served Rekhseth faithfully, and so he merits honour. Perabsah was Rekhseth's *sasasa* – the son of his son of his son – and so he inherited that debt of honour . . . which now passes to me, as his widow and the mother of his son."

"My lady?" asked Khnemes, who knew that Perabsah was childless.

"I had not yet told my husband that I bear his child. You see this vessel?" Merytast beckoned to one of her maids, who fetched a clay pot filled with earth containing brief sproutings of grain. "Here are seeds of barley and wheat. Each day when I awaken, I pass my morning-water over this soil. The barley has languished, but the wheat has prospered . . . so I know that the child in my womb is a son, not a daughter."

This womb-wisdom was of no matter to Khnemes. "*Neb't-i*, can you think of anyone who wished your husband slain? Is there a grudge . . . possibly going back to the time of Rekhseth?"

Merytast shook her head. "My husband had wealth, and such men always have enemies. In recent days, our estate's wealth has dwindled, yet my husband's enemies endure. Beyond that, I know nothing."

Khnemes gestured towards the mummy. "If Perabsah felt a blood-debt to retrieve this mummy, why did he wait so long? Ten years ago, when your husband was wealthy and Egypt was not yet divided, Perabsah might have ventured to Thebes in safety. Why did he make this quest *now?* The civil wars along the border between the two Egypts have made our journey perilous. Why did Perabsah risk his own life and yours to honour a debt to the dead? I knew your husband, *neb't-i.* Perabsah was not inclined to honour his own debts . . . much less the obligations of his ancestors."

"Think you?" Merytast's tone became suddenly less gracious. "Then you knew not my husband at all. Perabsah's heart brimmed with charity and honour. Now he begins his journey to the afterworld. The god Anubis will escort him through the doorway Khersek-Shu and usher him into the Hall of Judgment, the coffin-shaped room where Osiris reigns as Lord of the Underworld, sitting in counsel with the forty-two demons who are the Judges of the Dead. While the demons bear witness, Perabsah must undergo the Weighing of the Heart. Anubis will take my husband's heart from his reborn and transformed body, and place it on the balance scales . . . weighing it against Ma'at, the goddess-feather of Truth. If Perabsah's heart weighs heavy with sins and unpaid debts, then it will be thrown to the monster Amemit, who will devour it and cause Perabsah's damnation. But I tell you, Khnemes, that my husband's heart will be weighed in the balance with Truth, and judged to be feather-light and virtuous . . . and the doors to the afterworld will swing wide to admit him. And now, steward, I have a task for you."

Khnemes nodded. "It is begun, my lady. I seek your husband's murderer."

"What? No; something more important. Perabsah's earthly

remains – his *kha't* – must be conveyed down-Nile for entombment on his family's estate. But the journey to Aneb Hetchet takes three days by barge, and Perabsah's flesh would be corrupted by then. I have arranged for a guild of embalmers here in Thebes to prepare my husband's body for the journey home . . . and for his longer journey to the afterworld. Faithful steward, I require that you tarry here in Thebes and oversee the process of my husband's mummification, whilst I and my retainers go home with the mummy of this servant Teknu. After my husband is properly embalmed, it will be your task to escort Perabsah's mummy homewards to our estate."

To the mind of Khnemes, the task of finding Perabsah's murderer was more urgent than the readying of his mummy. Khnemes began to protest, but Merytast silenced him: "Yes, my steward, I sense your concerns. I lack the wealth to pay your wages during the seventy days of Perabsah's embalming. Fear not, Khnemes: I have arranged for you to enter the priesthood of a local *uabet*, as an apprentice embalmer."

This was not at all to his liking: Khnemes had been suddenly stripped of his livelihood. But a thought occurred to him: by remaining in Thebes, he might perhaps be able to find Perabsah's killer . . . if the villain was still in Thebes.

Khnemes bowed, reluctantly. "It will be done, sovereign-my-lady."

"Excellent. Then report to the *uabet* in the Street of the Four Sons. In six weeks' time, when the embalming-rituals are nearly completed, I shall send a messenger to Thebes with arrangements for your return downriver with my husband's mummy. Have you any questions?"

"Two, my lady." Khnemes studied Merytast's face intently. "Do you know of any sect in Egypt which sacrifices a brown-necked raven?"

"A *bai*?" Merytast frowned. "I am quite certain there is no such cult. The death of a bird is an omen of doom, in all corners of Egypt. Birds are the emissaries between the earth and the heavens. Some cults worship specific birds, and will mummify a bird if it has died a natural death. But to kill a bird wilfully, for the whim of a god?" Merytast shook her head.

"*Non wun mun'et-ef*: there is no such thing. You had another question for me?"

"Aye, my lady," said Khnemes. "When did you learn how to read?"

Merytast gasped. "How did . . ."

Khnemes pointed to the mummy. "You knew that this man's name is Teknu. That name comes from the cartonnage which your husband found, and which he left on the offering-table where you have seen it. But Perabsah could not read the name: he sought to hire a scribe to read the fragments. Perabsah would never have paid a single *deben* of copper for any scribe's hire if he knew that his own wife possessed scribe-wisdom."

Merytast seemed impressed. "You are clever, my steward. You recall that our household's scribe Seshem died recently, midway through his long task of unjumbling the archives of my husband's ancestors? Before his illness, Seshem had taught me some of the scribe-truths, without my husband's knowledge. I have the scribe-wit of a third-year apprentice. Yes, I did read the cartonnage last night. Now, go: prepare my husband for his journey."

The Street of the Four Sons – in the eastern quarter of Thebes, near the canal – was far from the Opet festivities . . . so the streets were nearly deserted when Khnemes came in search of the embalming-house. He was caught unaware by a shout from behind him: "Ho, Nubian!"

Khnemes turned. He was alone, except for a few stray geese. Behind Khnemes stood a bare wall of dressed granite, with four oracle-masks sculpted into the stone. So this place was a temple, then: the temple for which this street was named. The masks depicted a falcon, a jackal, a baboon and a man with a plaited beard . . . the faces of the *mesu-Heru*: the four sons of Horus, the patron gods of embalming who also represented the four quarters of the world. All four faces hung silently with their eyes and mouths closed. The human-faced deity Masety ruled the south, so here in Thebes and in all of southern Egypt he was the most favoured son of Horus. Khnemes stepped towards the man-faced mask: "Did you speak, lord?"

The god's eyes opened, and regarded him, and a deep voice rumbled from within the wall: "I know your mission, Nubian. You served the murdered northerner, and now you are charged to shepherd his remains on their journey."

Khnemes had seen oracle-masks used before, but never so effectively as this. A priest was standing on the far side of the wall, his face within the concave inner surface of Masety's mask. Some trick of indirect lighting – a candle, a mirror – threw a bright glow between the priest and the wall, lighting the oracle-mask from within and making the priest's eyes seem truly to inhabit the eyeholes of the god-mask. Some trick of acoustics magnified the priest's voice, and sent it rumbling from the oracle's mouth. Even Khnemes, who knew this for a priest-trick, felt a shudder of awe as he stood before this artificial god. "Yes, Lord Masety. I was told to offer myself at a *uabet* in this street."

"Then hear me, Nubian. You can trust no one in Thebes except a man named Besek. He will help you find the answers you require." The god-voice spoke in the sibilant accent and broad vowels of southern Egypt: an appropriate choice for an actor depicting the god of the south.

"Are you Besek?" Khnemes asked.

The god's eyes shifted in their eyeholes. "Do not utter Besek's name to any man, for he is shunned. He will proclaim himself to you, within the temple."

The god's eyes went dark, and the god's mouth fell silent.

Khnemes presented himself at the temple's front door, proclaiming his own name in Merytast's service. The tall doorkeeper did not deign to look at him, but made a rude gesture over one shoulder. Khnemes understood, and went round to the rear entrance.

Behind the main temple was the *uabet*: the embalming-house of this particular cult. Khnemes spoke his name again to a less imposing doorman, who permitted him to enter. Two shaven police-priests of Amun-Re stood in the vestibule, flanking a statue of the reigning god of Thebes. "Hold, Nubian," said one police-priest, brandishing the staff of authority which was also his cudgel. "If you soul kindles any spark of rebellion, turn and depart. If you accept the disciplines of Amun-Re, step forth and enter."

I've lost my job, and I have no other prospects, Khnemes thought. *I might as well do this, if it offers the chance to find Perabsah's murderer*. He stepped over the threshold.

"You will remove – here and now – all keepsakes of your former life." The second police-priest pointed to the scabbard Khnemes wore at his belt. "That weapon, to begin with. Your sandals: leather, are they? Animal flesh is unclean, and cannot be purified. And your wig: it is Medchay, I think? Yes, the wig is short-naped: we do not tolerate such military trophies here. Your garments too: come, give them up. When you have surrendered your past life, and been cleansed, you will be given fresh clothes."

An hour later – scrubbed and shaved – Khnemes stood naked before three teacher-priests, who gave him his indoctrination. The temples of Egypt are closed at all times to everyone except for high royalty and the priests themselves. There is one exception: on the feast-days of any specific god or goddess, worshippers may enter the temples consecrated to that particular deity. "It is only because you come to us during the sun-god's festival Opet that we will tolerate your presence in this house of Amun-Re," said one teacher-priest, in a tone suggesting that Khnemes should faint with gratitude.

"You will assist in purifying the temple and the embalming-chamber," said the second teacher-priest. "You will be given vestments suited to your role, and a place to sleep. You may eat of such foods as are rejected by Lord Amun-Re, and disdained by all the priests above you."

"Normally," said the third priest, "applicants to our priesthood must submit to a long period of discipline and education. Yet we know that in seventy days' time you will return to northern Egypt with the mummy of your sovereign. So, you will undertake only such training as required to fulfil your tasks among us. When your employer's mummy is ready, we will give you back your possessions, and send you on your way."

And now it began. Khnemes was required to swear loyalty

to Nebwenen'f, the *heri uab*: the high priest of this mortuary. He was then given a kilt of coarse muslin to wear, and sandals woven from fibres of sedge. Khnemes was assigned to sweeping the floors, scouring the incense-burners, rinsing the toilet-pots of the priests, and other rituals of purification. He was also tasked with expunging the constant flow of messes in the embalming-chamber.

In the embalming-room, Khnemes beheld the dirty underside of Egypt. He learnt, for instance, that most corpses to be mummified were brought to the *uabet* as swiftly as possible . . . *except* for the mortal remains of women and girls who died reasonably intact: these are kept in their families' households, and not brought to the embalming-house until their corpses have begun to moulder. Even the priests of Egypt are known to have profane urges.

Thrice daily, the priests fed the statue of Amun-Re. Banquets of food, supplied by the faithful, were set before the large effigy of the sun-god in the temple's main hall. The god's essence inhabited this graven image whenever it suited Amun-Re's purpose. After the god consumed the essence of the food, the priests were entitled to eat the mortal shell of the food itself. The highest priests ate first, then the acolytes, then lastly the temple's menials. Khnemes ate whatever remained when all the others had eaten. By day, Khnemes was kept busy scrubbing and scouring: this technically made him a "priest" of the lowermost grade. By night, he slept on a pallet in the priest-barracks.

The gods speak to men while they sleep. At night, Khnemes beheld fitful dreams in which he stood naked in front of a high wall inscribed with hieroglyphics . . . god-texts, which he knew not how to read. Carved figures moved across the wall in profile, mocking him through sidelong mouths: Perabsah, the mummy Teknu, the dead bowman Secheb. A weird figure capered before Khnemes, taunting him: a raven's head on a man's body, clutching an emerald. Khnemes awoke, shuddering and perspiring, certain that all the clues to the crime were before him . . . like fragments of papyrus from an incomplete scroll, which could never be rejoined.

Khnemes performed all his tasks in the *uabet*, and learnt all that he could from his fellow priests. At night, in the priest-barracks, his guild-brothers told him of their own experiences before they entered the priesthood. One acolyte of this temple had formerly laboured in Egypt's goldfields. A lector-priest knew some facts about ravens. Another acolyte had some knowledge of gemstones. All of these wisdoms, Khnemes hoarded . . . as the many skeins of the mystery began to form a tapestry.

On the third day after Khnemes began his priesthood, there was a commotion in the *uabet*. Khnemes was cleaning a fouled natron-tub when several embalmer-priests clustered round the table on which was placed a *m'at*: a cadaver made ready for mummification. Khnemes recognized the dead man. Perabsah's corpse had been washed and anointed, but there was a stark wound in the centre of his chest: the dark puncture where the murderer's arrow had struck him.

One priest held a scribe's reed-brush dipped in black ink. The other priests made room as he approached the mummy-table. An acolyte held a basket filled with stones, and several priests selected some of these. Khnemes noticed one priest, dressed more shabbily than his fellows, who stood aside from the rest. This man skulked past Khnemes, and whispered: "*Enuk Besek.*"

The scribe-priest approached Perabsah's corpse. His eyes appraised the dead body while he intoned several ritual prayers, then he extended his brush and painted a black Eye-of-Horus on Perabsah's lower abdomen, to the left of his navel. This priest swiftly withdrew.

Now the man named Besek approached the corpse, and all the priests made a great show of averting their gaze, hissing, and holding their noses. "The shun-priest!" said one man, in tones of contempt. "The ripper!" cried another.

From the folds of his robe, Besek drew a curved obsidian knife. He raised this high, and then . . . *stabbed* the corpse, his blade piercing the eye of Horus.

"*Faugh!* Away!" Shouting curses and insults, the priests flung their stones at Besek, who pulled his robe over his face, then turned and fled. As soon as Besek was gone, the priests gave their full attention to Perabsah's corpse. Swiftly, Khnemes gathered his scouring-implements and went after Besek.

The shun-priest had run to the temple's rear portal. "Away with you, ripper! Never return!" said the doorkeeper, aiming a foot at Besek's backside as he departed. The doorkeeper eyed Khnemes suspiciously, but Khnemes pretended to be scouring the temple's outer wall. When the doorkeeper's back was turned, Khnemes hurried down the Street of the Four Sons.

He found Besek outside a chariot-yard, near the Kamur canal. "Each time, they tell me never to return," said Besek bitterly. "What they mean is, I must never return *until the next time they need me*."

"What is your place in all this?" Khnemes asked.

"I am the shun-priest, the ripper," said Besek. "Nubian, do you not know the taboos of Egypt? To debase a corpse – even for high reasons – is the deepest profanity. When a cadaver is readied for embalming, no priest dares to pierce the corpse's flesh . . . so *I* must make the first incision. The embalmers shun me and stone me for this, and call me unclean. After I make the first cut, the mummy-priests can then hack the corpse to their hearts' content. I have the dirty job that no man wants . . . yet none can fulfil their holy tasks until I first profane the dead."

"My master died with a hole near his heart," Khnemes said. "Perabsah's chest was already penetrated by an arrow; the mummy-priests could have widened that cut without your help."

Besek shook his head. "Never argue with rituals. The first incision into the *m'at* is always made to the left of the navel. The scribe-priest is honoured, for he paints the protective symbol of the Horus-eye on the corpse where the first cut must be made. But then I, the ripper, I am cursed and stoned by the priests . . . because I *make* the necessary cut. Take heed, Khnemes: if you are seen with me, the priests will call you by filth-names, and evict you from their mummy-shop."

"You know me. How?"

"Your name precedes you, Nubian. It is known that you seek a murderer."

Khnemes nodded. "Do you know who hired Perabsah's assassin?"

"I know not, brother."

"Was it you who spoke to me through the face of the god Masety?"

Besek nodded. "I wanted to warn you: the priest-guild which controls this mummy-house is corrupt. On the same day that a servant of your mistress Merytast arranged for your employment in this *uabet*, another man came here with a similar mission. For a small bribe, he persuaded the guild's priests to admit him to their order and apprentice him in the arts of embalming."

"What did he look like? What is his name?"

"I know not," said Besek again. "I stood at the threshold of the *uabet* when I chanced to hear this man conversing with the teacher-priests. I heard his voice, distorted through the wall: he spoke in the accents of northern Egypt, but I would not know his voice if I heard it plainly."

"Thank you, brother," said Khnemes. "Why do you help me in this?"

Besek spat angrily. "Do you know what it is to be a shun-priest? No landlord grants me a lodging-place, no taverner lets me drink beneath his roof. I sleep in a filthy barge in the Kamur canal. The high-nosed embalming-priests sneer at my profane task, yet their own sacred deeds would be impossible if I did not precede them in their procession of the dead."

"Why did you take such a job?" Khnemes asked.

"Someone must always be the shun-priest," said Besek. "I entered this priest-guild with hopes for myself. I did as I was told: I cursed the man who was shun-priest before me, and I helped to throw stones at him. One day, assisting in the mummification of a highborn lady, I overstepped myself. The other embalmers had cut out her liver and lungs, to be cleaned and then placed within ritual urns. In my zeal to assist, I cut out her heart. That was a mistake. As penance for my error, I was offered a choice: expulsion from the priest-guild, or shameful service ever after as the shun-priest."

"I know little of Egypt's mummies," said Khnemes. "When the entrails are removed for embalming, is not the heart also removed with its brethren?"

"In older centuries this was done, but no longer," said Besek. "The heart is the dwelling-place of the soul: it must be kept intact within the *kha't* of the deceased. If the embalmers damage the mummy's heart, it must be repaired before the mummy's chest cavity is closed. The heart of a dead man – or woman, or child – is kept safe within the mummy's body until the deceased has crossed over into the afterworld and reached the Hall of Judgment . . . where the god Anubis then places it in the Scale of Truth, to be reckoned in the Weighing of the Heart."

Khnemes said nothing. He had left the farmlands of Kush long ago, yet many of Egypt's beliefs still seemed alien to him.

"I will help you catch this killer, if I can," Besek told him. "And I am shunned, so any scraps of friendship – even a few *atu* of time spent with a despised Nubian – are like a long cool drink for me. But take care that you are not seen with me, or the shunning will consume you as well."

Besek drew his priest-robe across his face, and hurried away.

Khnemes had many duties in the embalming-chamber: he was the janitor-priest, and this room was the messiest in the *uabet*. He observed the faces of the mummy-priests, wondering which of them was the false acolyte who had bribed his way into this temple. In the constant god-gabble of chants and prayers in the embalming-room, Khnemes strained to hear one voice which spoke in northern accents.

Perabsah's corpse had been cleaned and anointed. The shun-cut – the first incision, leftwards of the dead man's navel – had been widened and enlarged. Khnemes was present when Perabsah's entrails – his liver, gall bladder, lungs, stomach, intestines and colon – were removed. With appropriate rituals, these organs were washed, preserved in mummy-salts and swathed in linen. For many centuries, Egypt's embalmers had traditionally stored their subjects' entrails in four jars, representing the sons of Horus and the four quarters of the earth. Yet in the past three years, because of the schism of Egypt into two separate nations, this custom had changed. Neither half of Egypt comprised both north and south: therefore, it was now deemed dangerous to consign any person's entrails to four separate quarters. The bundled viscera were placed in a trough of natron to become desiccated and purified: later, they would be returned to Perabsah's chest cavity along with figurines of the appropriate gods.

Errors were made in the embalming. Perabsah's *gegtui* – the two large bean-shaped organs in his lower back, which produced his bladder-water – were supposed to remain in his corpse, undisturbed, as was his heart. Khnemes was present in the early morning when an apprentice embalmer – intending to remove Perabsah's lungs – accidentally nicked Perabsah's right kidney with his copper blade. The sliced kidney was stitched shut again with cotton thread, while the priests intoned prayers and god-apologies, and a patch of papyrus was then applied. Late in the forenoon, Khnemes noticed between tasks that similar stitching and patching had now been applied to Perabsah's injured heart, and the arrow-wound in his chest was now cosmetically repaired. Khnemes watched as linen bags, filled with natron, were packed into Perabsah's chest cavity to absorb his body fluids.

In early afternoon, Khnemes contrived to leave the temple without arousing attention, and once again he met Besek at the chariot-yard. Pretending not to know each other, the two men walked between two separate rows of chariots, never meeting each other's eyes while they spoke in hushed tones.

"Are you any closer to catching your criminal?" Besek asked.

"No," said Khnemes. "He was in the temple, I am certain . . . but now he has probably left Thebes. And gone *where?*" Khnemes doubled his fists bitterly. "There are as many hiding-places in Egypt as there are sands in the desert."

"Why do you remain in the *uabet*, then?" asked Besek.

"I have no other livelihood. Since I have failed to catch Perabsah's killer, I should at least give my lord sovereign one final dignity: I will stay in Thebes until Perabsah's mummy is made ready, and then I will convey him northwards to his estate."

"*Ehi.* Of course." Besek's tone implied that he was nodding in agreement, but Khnemes dared not look towards the shun-priest's face. "You are taking him home for the Opening of the Mouth."

"The *what?*" Khnemes very nearly *did* look up. "You mean the Weighing of the Heart."

"No, Nubian. The Weighing of the Heart is a myth, a superstition. It supposedly takes place in the afterworld, under the watchful eyes of Osiris and Anubis in the Hall of Judgment . . . if you believe that sort of thing." Besek's voice suggested that the shun-priest did not believe the rituals of his own temple. "The Opening of the Mouth occurs *here*, in the world of the living. It is a death-ritual, known in Egypt for centuries, but only royalty and wealthy families can arrange it for their deceased. It requires a ritual blade, forged of *bi'a nepet*: iron that fell from the sky in a meteorite. The Opening of the Mouth is so elaborate a god-charade, I do not wonder that you have never witnessed it."

"Describe this Opening of the Mouth," said Khnemes, speaking from the side of his own mouth so that no passing witness might see him conversing with the shun-priest.

"When your master Perabsah has been fully mummified, his mummy must be conveyed to the tomb where his body will rest eternally," Besek explained. "At the tomb's entrance, a priest and a scribe will perform certain rituals. The eyes of the mummy will be opened – symbolically, not truly – and his mouth and ears and nostrils will be symbolically opened as well . . . so that the dead man will be able to speak and retain all his senses in the afterlife. Just before the mummy is entombed, the priest with his knife makes a pretend-cut to a cord above the mummy's navel, as if the dead man were a newborn baby . . . thus betokening his rebirth in the after-world."

Khnemes looked up sharply. In his haste, he forgot not to look at the shun-priest: Khnemes saw Besek's eyes, and now suddenly Khnemes grasped the truth.

"The docks!" Khnemes said. "Quickly! What is the swiftest route to the harbour of Thebes?"

This question caught Besek unawares. "*Ehi?* Well, usually the Avenue of Rams, but today it is thronged with Opet-revellers, and . . ."

"Your barge!" Khnemes seized the shun-priest's arm, no longer caring if anyone witnessed this. "You said you live on the canal? Prepare to cast off your vessel! I must return to the *uabet* for a moment, but I will join you. Be ready!"

A few brief *atu* later, both men were in Besek's quarters: a flat-decked canal barge, with a single enclosed cabin. Khnemes seized a bargepole while Besek cast off, and then the barge drifted west towards the Nile. Only when the craft was underway, with both men poling rapidly, did Khnemes explain himself. While Besek navigated the canal, shouting at bathers and laundry-maids to keep clear, Khnemes described the basic facts of the mystery while he worked his bargepole furiously. After the preliminaries, he continued:

"The wealth of Perabsah's house began a hundred years ago, with his ancestor Rekhseth," Khnemes explained. "But Rekhseth was an overseer in the goldfields. How did a humble overseer become wealthy?"

"Some of the gold stuck to his fingers," suggested Besek.

"No; there were sentries at the work-camps to prevent this. But each day, Rekhseth came into the camp with a raven in a cage. Each night he sacrificed it in a secluded place, and left the work-camp with his cage empty. The next day, another. Did Rekhseth have enough bird-nets to snare a steady supply of brown-necked ravens?"

"*Ahai!*" Besek smacked his forehead. "They were *all the same raven!* Do not ravens steal shining objects? I see it now: each night, Rekhseth gave his raven a gold nugget, and . . ."

"No. Gold nuggets are heavy. But I have learnt something recently: in the goldfields near the Red Sea, *emeralds* have been found. A small uncut emerald is far more precious than a large gold nugget . . . and lighter, too." Khnemes shifted course as a swimmer darted in front of their barge. "Rekhseth used a trained raven to smuggle *emeralds* out of the work-camp. His raven was trained to fly overhead, beyond the sentries, to a secret place outside the work-camp where Rekhseth could accumulate one emerald each night."

"A hoard of emeralds would attract attention," said Besek.

"Indeed. The bandits on Egypt's roads will waylay travellers and search them for valuables. That is why Rekhseth murdered Teknu . . . or arranged his murder. *Rekhseth hid the emeralds in Teknu's corpse.* The insect bites proved that Teknu's corpse was kept unmummified for several days. One of the scribes in the work-camp wrote something on a papyrus: something about Teknu's death, that might incriminate Rekhseth. Plastered papyrus – *utau* – is a cheap way to wrap a mummy, so Rekhseth thought of a scheme to destroy the evidence and use that same evidence to keep anyone from examining Teknu's corpse: he stole the scribe's papyrus, turned it into a shroud of cartonnage, and then stitched the shroud around Teknu's body. After Teknu's corpse was taken out of the work-camp and past the King's sentries, the dead man was cut open and eviscerated, and then his chest cavity was filled with Rekhseth's uncut emeralds. The emeralds were safe inside Teknu's body; few Egyptians would dare to profane a corpse. Even tomb-robbers shun a mummy who seems too poor to possess any death-wealth."

"But if Teknu's corpse was stuffed with emeralds," Besek asked, "why didn't Rekhseth ever reclaim them?"

"He *did* reclaim them," said Khnemes. "Rekhseth's wealth came from the stolen emeralds. Then he arranged for Teknu's burial in the Plain of the Loaves . . . in a labourer's tomb that would attract no attention, yet plainly marked in case Rekhseth needed to return later."

"I don't understand," said Besek, poling faster. "After Rekhseth got the emeralds past the King's sentries and the bandits, why would he still need Teknu's mummy?"

"Let us set that aside for now," said Khnemes. "Think upon this: Perabsah's household contains many papyri, never properly archived. Recently, the household scribe Seshem began to catalogue these documents. He died suddenly, and soon thereafter Perabsah made plans to journey to Thebes. Somewhere in Perabsah's jumbled archives, his scribe Seshem must have found a document which revealed the facts of Teknu's murder . . . and the reason why his mummy was preserved." Khnemes paused. "In the Plain of the Loaves, I mentioned that the child-coffin was strangely heavy, and Perabsah at once became tense when I said this: he knew that *something heavier than a man* was inside the coffin. When his slaves opened the coffin, Perabsah flung his hand in front of my face. There was a reason for that. He did not know precisely what was inside the coffin: he did not want me to look until he had seen for himself. But when his slaves tore the cartonnage, Perabsah knew that something important might be written on its fragments. When the wind scattered the papyri, Perabsah shouted at us to gather all the pieces . . . yet he flung away one scrap when he saw that it was blank. He didn't want the papyrus; he only wanted the *writing* on it."

Now the barge reached a sluice-gate: this quarter of Thebes was far from the Street of the Four Sons, and no resident here would recognize Besek as a shun-priest. He drew his monk-hood away from his face, and he poled more rapidly, while Khnemes took up a new thread:

"I met many people in Thebes. Some of them recognized me for a Medchay when they saw the short nape of my wig. From the front, the *anhu* of the Medchay looks identical to many wigs of Egypt: only the bowman's nape is different. But one man identified me as a Medchay when he saw me only *from the front*. He was a *fekhet*-monk, named Nask."

Besek looked up sharply. "A *fekhet*? A monk of Hathor? He must be quite busy during the Opet festival, then. This year, it falls within Hathyr: the month consecrated to Hathor."

This news startled Khnemes so much that he nearly dropped his bargepole. "No, 'Hathor' is your Egyptian name for our Nubian goddess Athrua. The Egyptian month of Hathyr is named for *Heru*, the hawk-god Horus: 'Hathyr' means 'Chamber-of-Horus'."

"Aye, Nubian," said Besek. "But 'Chamber-of-Horus' is another name for our goddess Hathor. A true *fekhet*-monk would be busy in Hathor's temple all that month."

Khnemes regained his bargepole. There were so many deities in Egypt, no one could know all their intimate secrets. "That fits my evidence," he said. "Nask was no priest of Hathor: he told me that the *fekhet*-monks would be idle during Amun-Re's festival, yet he did not reckon that this year the Opet fell within Hathor's month. But he knew me for a Medchay, without seeing my nape. He *knew* me, and he knew why I had come to Thebes. He knew that Perabsah might find ancient documents – important ones – in Teknu's tomb. Nask was waiting for me outside Perabsah's lodging-house . . . ready to offer scribe-services to a man who had found a papyrus."

"Who is this Nask, and how does he know these secrets?" asked Besek.

Khnemes bent over the side of the barge as he worked his long pole. "Nask is no one: he invented himself. When he stood up, he seemed strangely tall in proportion to his arms and body. Sandals are made of leather or sedge . . . but Nask's sandals made a clattering sound against the tiles, as if his shoes had soles of *wood*. Then he lost his balance, as if unaccustomed to standing so tall . . . and he put his hand to his *fekhet*-tonsure, as if it might fall off."

"The tonsures of the *fekhetu* never fall off," said Besek. "They grow their hair long all round, and shave it bare at the top."

"Nask was a disguise, not a man," said Khnemes. "He wore wooden soles to increase his height, and draped himself in a long kilt and a longer monk-cloak to conceal that his stature was false. His tonsure was a wig: the clean-shaven pate was pigskin, or warm beeswax smoothed over his scalp, or some other falsehood to conceal that his head was not recently shaved. He only needed to deceive me for a few minutes in the dark. But he *had* to deceive me, because he was someone I had seen before . . . or would meet again. Nask only needed to deceive me for a few minutes while he read the cartonnage, and he gained from it one secret which he kept back when he read the papyrus to me: *there were still emeralds inside Teknu's mummy*."

Besek shook his head. "If Rekhseth went to so much trouble to steal emeralds, why would he leave some of them inside a dead man?"

The barge changed course here, to avoid a squadron of washerwomen, and Khnemes gave only an indirect answer: "I have lately learnt that *mica* is found wherever emeralds are mined. Perabsah lied when he said he bought that emerald in the marketplace. He found the emerald – and probably many *more* uncut emeralds – inside Teknu's mummy, with some stray mica among them. Teknu's belly was less distended the second time I saw him, because Perabsah had removed some emeralds from the dead man's body."

They were reaching the westward terminus of the canal now, but Khnemes never slackened the pace of his bargepole as he continued: "On the morning of Perabsah's murder, a scribe came to him named Uaf. He was shorter than Nask. Nask kept a tray of incense burning; when I moved towards him, he held the smoking tray near his face so that I could not see his mouth plainly. I did not realise that the pungent incense was meant to conceal another odour. When Nask read the cartonnage, he held it under his nose to hide his mouth. Uaf, also, kept shielding his face from me. He had not expected me to meet him in *both* his disguises . . . but I saw that he had wretched teeth and foul breath. Uaf claimed to be a *sem*, but the priests of Ptah are not the only men of Egypt who grow a long sidelock. Uaf could have wrapped his sidelock round the back of his head, to tuck it inside the tonsure-wig he wore *when he was Nask*."

Besek gasped. "This grows astonishing, Nubian."

"It grows more so. Uaf was filthy and unshaven: he needed to be, so that Perabsah would not recognize him. Uaf *knew* Perabsah: knew him well enough to expect that Perabsah would be half-drunk on a festival day, drunk enough not to recognize a disguised enemy. Uaf was slovenly, but his Thoth-case was freshly lacquered. Few scribes are wealthy enough to afford two scribe-cases. Uaf and Nask were the same man, with the same Thoth-case: Uaf had to paint his case a new colour, so that it would not be recognized as Nask's."

Khnemes poled a bit harder, then went on: "I paid scant attention to Uaf's face, as his breath was so hideous. He was chewing something black: I saw it dribble from his mouth."

"That cannot be right," said Besek. "If the scribe's breath was foul, he must have been chewing natron. There is *netra* – spiced natron, which is white – or *deshret*: red natron. There is no black natron."

"This wasn't natron, because it failed to cleanse his breath," said Khnemes. "Uaf's fingertips were black: I thought those stains had come from his scribe-ink. They *did* . . . but I had not reckoned *why*."

"Wait a bit," said Besek, nearly dropping his bargepole. "Black ink: are you saying . . ."

Khnemes nodded. "The false monk Nask knew that Perabsah had found a hoard of emeralds . . . might even be carrying one or more on his person. The next day, as Uaf, he deliberately stumbled against Perabsah, touching him at the waist where a man of wealth might keep a treasured acquisition. Then Uaf stepped away from the doorway – so that Perabsah could be seen from the courtyard – and he made a strange gesture. That was the signal for the archer Secheb to strike."

Besek whistled in astonishment. "And then Uaf stole the emerald . . ."

"Uaf stole the emerald while Perabsah was dying," said Khnemes. "Before Secheb fired his arrow, Uaf was chewing beeswax mingled with charcoal: the mixture used by scribes to fashion bricks of black pigment. After the emerald vanished, Uaf's Thoth-case contained a small brick of red pigment, and a very large brick of black pigment. It *had* to be large, because . . ."

"The emerald!" shouted Besek. "The scribe Uaf moulded a small amount of waxed charcoal around the emerald, to disguise it as a scribe's ink-brick! But you still neglect my question: if Rekhseth went to so much grief to hide stolen emeralds, why did he leave them inside Teknu's corpse?"

"A fair question," said Khnemes. "Let us set it aside for now, and consider the murdered man's wife. I suspected Merytast for a time: it is not unknown for a wife to conspire in her husband's death, and Merytast lied to me. Perabsah engaged a new scribe after Seshem's death. The new man is unknown to me, for Perabsah took pride in hiring this man without my assistance. When I tried to meet him, I was told that this new scribe was busy organizing Perabsah's archives, continuing Seshem's task. This scribe must have found a papyrus revealing Rekhseth's secret: namely, that there were still emeralds to be gleaned, in the Plain of the Loaves. The papyrus probably mentioned Rekhseth's brown-necked raven, and this inspired the murderer's revel-disguise. Seshem must have lived long enough to read the same papyrus, and he divulged its contents to Perabsah or Merytast. That is why they came to Thebes: to steal Teknu's mummy and the remaining emeralds. Perabsah could not guard the mummy every moment, so he enlisted the only person who had his full trust: his faithful wife."

It was nearly sunset now as Khnemes shipped his bargepole, and the barge approached the final sluice-gate on the eastern bank of the Nile. "I do not know the murderer's true name, but I know who he is. He is Perabsah's new scribe. He learnt of the emeralds, and came to Thebes on his own, without Perabsah's knowledge. He disguised himself as a monk to offer scribe-services. When I gave him the scraps of the *utau*, he knew that we had found Teknu's tomb . . . and the emeralds. He could have made up a false text when he read aloud to me the words of the cartonnage, but he apparently told me their true contents: out of arrogance, perhaps, or to allay my suspicions. The next day, disguised as a Ptah-scribe named Uaf, he touched the pouch at Perabsah's waist . . . just long enough to verify that something heavy was in it. *One* emerald, of so many, was enough for Uaf to steal. One emerald can buy any Egyptian a long life of comfort . . . and a comfortable afterlife as well."

Now the barge scraped against the retaining wall at the end of the canal. Khnemes clambered off, and danced impatiently while Besek tied up his barge. "Then the murderer is gone," said Besek. "Whoever he was, the scribe took his stolen jewel and ran off to a new life."

"No," said Khnemes. "He may not have escaped yet. Quickly!" Khnemes turned, beckoning Besek to follow him, as he ran west . . . towards the harbour, and the sunset.

Hurrying through the streets, Khnemes explained while he ran: "An emerald might bring a man twenty years' worth of luxury, but it can only do so *all at once* . . . not one day at a time. A single *deben* of gold can be melted down into ten separate *qed'tu*, and each golden *qed't* may be bartered for many *debenu* of copper, and so on down . . . as the wealth is spent gradually. But not so for a gemstone: to break it into smaller pieces is to risk losing all. The murderer needed to keep the whole emerald safe until he could get a fair barter for it. He is from northern Egypt, so he likely intends to return to a place where he would not arouse attention. In a light boat, he can swiftly catch up with the heavy barge which carries Merytast's retinue. He can pass her in the night, and reach Aneb Hetchet before she arrives, and she might never know he was gone. But he dares not keep the emerald on his person for the hazardous journey north from Thebes. A lone traveller would be prey for the robbers in the borderland between the two Egypts." As he spoke, Khnemes put his right hand into the pocket of his kilt. "It is sacrilege, yes, to profane a mummy . . . but I have done so, to avenge Perabsah's murder, while you were readying your barge. Perabsah's chest cavity has not yet been closed by the embalmers. In the *uabet*, I found what I was seeking . . . and then I purified his mummy again, with amulets and incense, after I had tarried within."

Now Khnemes drew forth his hand, clutching something green that caught the last rays of sunlight as he ran. "Earlier today, while Perabsah's chest cavity still lay open, I saw a patch of papyrus on his heart, and stitching to repair a cut: it was placed there this morning, by a man who may still be in Thebes. I thought the injury to Perabsah's heart was caused by Secheb's arrow, when it pierced his chest . . . but an arrow to the heart would have killed Perabsah instantly. No; Perabsah's heart was cut open *after his death* by the false priest who bribed his way into the embalming-room. The murderer knew that Perabsah's mummy would be escorted back to his estate. If looters opened the coffin, and unwrapped the mummy, they would find no jewels . . . *unless they weighed Perabsah's heart.*"

As Khnemes ran westwards, he opened his fist for an instant . . . just long enough to show Besek the emerald. It was large, and a near-perfect cube. But the cube was flawed with cracks and veins. "I recognized the scent of Perabsah's vanity-oil when he showed me this jewel," Khnemes told the shun-priest. "Now here is something else I recently learnt: most emeralds are flawed, but the flaws can be disguised for a few days by soaking the stone in oil. The oil seeps in and conceals the flaws, long enough for a dishonest trader to barter a flawed emerald as a perfect one. Perabsah oiled this emerald; he probably intended to sell it dishonestly. The murderer thought this stone was perfect when he stole it, and when he concealed it inside Perabsah's heart . . . but the natron-bath of the embalming-chamber has absorbed the oil, and exposed the truth."

Khnemes repocketed the stone. "Even a flawed emerald is worth something. Rekhseth knew that too much wealth, acquired too suddenly, might bring him unwelcome attention. So he kept the best emeralds from his hoard, and concealed the flawed ones . . . where they could be found later. He left a scroll in his archives, the scroll that Seshem found. If Rekhseth's descendants squandered his wealth, the scroll would tell them where more emeralds were hidden: in Teknu's tomb, in the Plain of the Loaves."

Besek spat as he ran, following Khnemes towards the red-stone sentry-gate. "Your master was flawed, like his emerald . . . but he must have had some good points, since he earned your loyalty. I am a shun-priest, so I dare not judge anyone. When Perabsah meets his judgment in the afterworld, in the Weighing of the Heart, I do not know if the scales will fall towards innocence or guilt."

"That was the final clue," said Khnemes. Now they reached

the pylon arch at the western border of Thebes. In the torchlight here, the sentries were conversing with three constables – one of them wearing a rank-docket – and Khnemes snatched a torch from its bracket while he beckoned the policemen to follow him. "Before Perabsah's mummy is placed in its tomb, he must first undergo . . ."

". . . the Opening of the Mouth!" cried Besek as he ran. "The household scribe will stand over Perabsah's mummy with a ritual knife. The ritual is conducted before witnesses . . . but the scribe will have some time alone with the mummy beforehand. Time enough to cut into the chest cavity, retrieve the stolen jewel, and then conceal the damage to the mummy-linens."

One of the constables tried to interrupt, but the chief constable gestured with his tipstaff and nodded at Khnemes to continue while they ran: "Perabsah's murder was arranged by his new scribe," panted Khnemes, nearly out of breath now. "I suspected that Merytast conspired with him, but she did not. The flawed emeralds are now Merytast's property: if she and Uaf were partners in crime, she would have shared them with him . . . either willingly, or because he could blackmail her. Yet the scribe – Uaf, or Nask, or whatever his true name – went to great trouble to steal one emerald for himself, and to conceal it in his master's coffin, where only the scribe of Perabsah's household would be able to reclaim it. If he had expected Merytast to share the emeralds with him, he would not have gone to such lengths for one stone. Merytast is innocent."

Now they reached the Nile-steps on the riverbank. The annual inundation was underway; in the torchlight, Khnemes saw that nine steps of the staircase were already underwater. "Our quarry has had a head-start," said Khnemes, peering into the Nile's currents. "But he came here at leisure, not suspecting that we were on his heels. Constable, is that a boat?"

A large hulk loomed in the shadows to the south, upriver. The Barque of Amun-Re had made its daily sojourn to the Temple of Mut, and now the sun-god and his retinue were returning to Karnak. The rest of the Nile had been kept clear of vessels tonight, so the god might proceed without hindrance. To east and west, either side of the Nile, ferries waited in the quays until the sun-god had passed. Now Khnemes swept his torch in the other direction. Just north of Thebes, against the white limestone bulk of the Isle of Amunhotep, a small black shape could be discerned: a single barge, journeying downriver.

The chief constable shook his wooden rattle, and beat his staff against the flagstones. At once, from the docks just north of Thebes, several ferries cast off. The bargeman tried to elude them, but his craft was unwieldy and he showed no river-wisdom. The experienced ferrymen swiftly encircled him, and their bargepoles nudged his unwilling craft towards the eastern shore.

"Do you know what this means, Nubian?" said Besek, as he followed Khnemes and the constables along the riverbank. "Because I have helped you catch a murderer tonight, the gods may favour me enough to lift my shun-burden. I can be a priest again!"

Two ferry-pilots held the struggling bargeman, and snatched away his bundle of provisions. As Khnemes ran forwards, he saw that the man had no weapons, but something dangled from a cord across his shoulder: the Thoth-case of an Egyptian scribe. This scribe looked like Nask but was shorter; he resembled Uaf, but he was cleaner and his scalp was newly shaven. He was dressed as Khnemes was, in sandals of sedge and the garb of an apprentice-priest of the *uabet*. Now the constables closed in, and in the flickering light of the torch which Khnemes held in his right hand, the scribe whimpered.

Khnemes brought his left hand down upon the man's shoulder, and spoke: "*Netek nikeh*. You are a murderer, forever."

CHOSEN OF THE NILE

Mary Reed & Eric Mayer

Six hundred years have passed since the last story, scarcely a season in Egyptian history, but enough to bring us into the Hellenic period. Egypt's civilization has continued to decline until much of its past remains a mystery to many, except perhaps a privileged few in the priesthood. Egypt's past was held in awe by the new civilizations growing around the Mediterranean, not least the Greeks, whose thirst for knowledge took explorers to the boundaries of the known world. The greatest of these was Herodotus, the father of history. Born in Halicarnassus in Asia Minor in about 484 BC, he was in his mid-30s when he travelled through Egypt, exploring as far south as Aswan. By now Egypt was under Persian control but the country's life and tradition continued in much the same way as before. Herodotus is an ideal detective because of his inquiring mind and because, as an outsider, he would take nothing for granted.

Mary Reed and Eric Mayer have written a number of historical whodunnits, and are best known for their series featuring John the Eunuch set during the early years of the Byzantine empire. In addition to several short stories he has appeared in the novels, One for Sorrow *(1999),* Two for Joy *(2000),* Three for a Letter *(2001), with others planned.*

During my travels in Egypt there transpired certain events I would have judged too fantastic to believe, let alone recount in my History, had I not myself participated in them.

It would not be fitting to identify the large village I was visiting at the time, except to say that its inhabitants worship the crocodile. Do not think that the place may be easily discovered from this practice. The scaled god Sobek is sacred to many living along the River Nile. Strange, perhaps, but then the Egyptians are a people whose men crouch to make water while the women stand, or so I have been informed.

As it turned out, the religious procession I had returned to the village to see did not, unfortunately, rival the sacred celebrations of such great centres as Heliopolis or Bubastis. It was brief enough. Shortly after night fell, a number of bald-headed priests dressed in plain linen robes and papyrus sandals bore several mummified crocodiles on elaborately carved wooden litters from the temple to the Nile and then returned the same way, there being only one wide dirt road that did not meander off into some closed way. Certain of these priests chanted prayers, while others jingled sistra and villagers sang loudly, the sound of their rhythmic clapping echoing off mud brick house walls and up into a starry vault which seems of a greater height in those regions than anywhere else in the world.

In truth, however, I believe the onlookers' enthusiasm arose more from consumption of festive barley beer than from their observation of the pious spectacle. From the little I could discern through the thick, smoky veil laid over the proceedings by the priest's few torches, the sacred mummies were rather shabby specimens, even if one could believe the remarkable antiquity the head priest Zemti had attributed to them on my first visit, which I did not.

The most interesting sight was the temple's one living sacred crocodile, borne along in a cage on a donkey cart. But the beast lay so motionless as to resemble a mummy itself and the glittering baubles decorating its leathery body made the creature appear more ludicrous than ferocious. Disappointed, I started back to my lodgings but found my path barred by a man I had not seen before. His aspect was made remarkable by the extreme length of his hair. The gauntness of his features, starkly highlighted by the terracotta lamp he carried, gave his face a passing resemblance to the features of an unwrapped mummy.

"You are Herodotus, are you not?" he asked. "The traveller to whom even our priests reveal their deepest secrets?"

I advised the stranger that he was correct, at least regarding my identity.

"You must help me. I have lost my wife!" was his astonishing reply.

I did not take his meaning at first. Then I recalled that the Egyptians, contrary race that they are, do not cut their hair to signify bereavement but rather allow it to grow. Yet, as I began my commiserations, I noticed that he had not grown a beard, as was also customary in his country when mourning a loved one.

"I am not certain what you mean by lost," I therefore said instead. "For your scalp proclaims one thing, your chin another."

The man smiled, his sunken eyes glittering like torchlight reflected from the bottom of a well. "It is just as they say, you overlook nothing! My appearance is thus because there is a part of me which believes Tahamet still lives in this world while another believes she has passed into the next."

Amasis, for that was his name, began to recount his story as we walked back along the road where the heavy odour of incense hung in the still night air, not quite masking the loamy presence of the unseen river behind us.

Before long I interrupted his account. "You say that anyone whose life is claimed by the Nile, whether by drowning or by the attack of crocodiles, must be treated as more than human and further that such a person may only be buried by your priests? But if your wife suffered such a fate and the rites were properly carried out, why do you seek my assistance?"

"It is true that the head priest told me that Tahamet was found in the River," Amasis answered, "but as I was just telling you, in keeping with custom I was not allowed to touch her body or approach it closely. However, I have good reason to suspect that the woman they buried was not my beloved."

We reached the end of the road but rather than continuing

on to the temple causeway we walked out into the desert. Soon I felt sand shifting beneath my sandals and after a while I made out the indistinct shapes of a squat structure hemmed in by thorny acacia trees.

A torch flared luridly and a figure bearing a lance emerged from between pillars at the front of the low building and challenged us. Amasis quickly trotted forwards and conferred with the guard in an animated fashion.

Finally he called out. "Our friend here knows your reputation for scholarship, Herodotus. Though few are given the privilege, he will permit us to enter the tomb of those whom the River has taken."

Never one to refuse an invitation to visit a forbidden place, I quickly followed Amasis inside. The accommodating guard gave me a wide grin as I went by.

"When you write about these adventures, be certain to mention the name of Montuherkhepeshef," he said.

It is remarkable how often men and women seem to consider ink a better preservative even than natron, aromatic spices and linen wrappings, and just as remarkable what they will offer in return for fame. I remember the men and try to forget the women and their blandishments.

The single chamber to which the guard allowed us admittance was however too commonplace to bear description other than that it was stone-walled with small drifts of sand piled in its corners. The walls were obviously very thick, being punctuated by deep niches holding uncoffined mummies. However, the trembling light of a lamp on a pedestal gave the sacred place an underwater appearance, reminding me that each person resting so peacefully around us had suffered an especially horrible death beneath the Nile's suffocating torrent or in the crushing jaws of a crocodile. Perhaps, I surmised, that was why their bodies had not been interred in the more usual fashion. Since they had already been buried once in the sacred waters of the Nile, it might well have been considered blasphemous to bury them a second time under the sands.

"Here is the one said to be Tahamet." Amasis reached into a

niche and before I could caution him pulled its resident towards him and began to tear at the linen wrappings. He let out a groan. A quick glance revealed the reason for his distress. The embalmer's arts could not conceal the fact that most of the deceased's face had been destroyed. There was no doubt it had been the work of a crocodile.

"I see none of the trinkets I gave her." Amasis' voice verged on a sob. "She deserved adornment fit for a queen. Her hair was lapis-lazuli, her fingers lotus blossoms. I was happy to indulge her. She loved necklaces, hairpins and ivory combs and other such dainty things but she was especially fond of a pair of earrings I had specially made for her. They're yellow topaz in the form of acacia blossoms, and she was wearing them the day she disappeared. Not that the priests can be relied upon to leave such valuables with the deceased, blasphemous though that sounds."

I asked him what had made him suspicious about the head priest's insistence that this was the body of his wife.

"The circumstances." He moved his attention further down the neatly swathed figure and I prayed the guard would not suddenly decide to enter the chamber. "For some time, as a safety precaution I've had my servant Mose follow her about the village. On that day, he swears that she entered the temple at dusk and never emerged."

"How can he be certain?" I asked.

"The temple complex has only one gateway and Mose is a very patient and observant man. Furthermore, he's exceptionally loyal to Tahamet. As you can imagine, when she did not return home that evening, I became extremely alarmed. I searched the streets but she was gone. At dawn I went to the governor, useless lout that he is, and demanded he investigate immediately."

He continued speaking as he freed what remained of an arm which even in the lamp's fitful light displayed further ravages of the ferocious creature this strange people worshipped. "Not two days later this half-consumed body was found in the river. But it's certainly not my Tahamet, Herodotus. She had a pale patch on the back of her right hand where she burnt it while cooking me a duck last year. Look closely and you'll see there's nothing like that here."

Grabbing the now revealed thin arm by the elbow he shook it, causing the dead hand to beckon me. I stepped away, willing to take him at his word.

Because I am always interested in discovering a fascinating tale to recount (and, I will admit, also from simple curiosity) the next morning I visited the temple where Amasis said his wife had last been seen.

Its exterior walls were constructed of the same modest mud-brick as the village houses but here the mud symbolized the marriage of sky and land. As soon as I passed between the unimpressive stone pylons flanking the temple gateway and into the open courtyard beyond, I was approached by a man of such girth that he resembled one of those lumbering beasts the Egyptians call river-horses.

It was Nahkt, attendant to the Sacred One. I had made his acquaintance on my first visit.

"Herodotus! Have you penned your account of our temple and its holy occupant yet?" He gestured towards the large, serene pool in the centre of the courtyard. "I'm sorry to say, however, that the Sacred One has not yet appeared today. He is still resting after last night's exertions."

I explained I had come to speak to the head priest, Zemti. Nahkt chattered breathlessly as he led me through the pillared Hall of the Crocodiles, where the Sacred One's predecessors – the mummified participants in the previous evening's festivities – now again rested on their high pedestals, awaiting worshippers.

After passing though a series of ever smaller and darker chambers, all filled with a thick fog of sickly-sweet incense, I was ushered into the presence of Zemti, who was entirely naked and seated on a three-legged stool beside a stone basin, shaving his legs. He put down his bronze razor and greeted me warmly as Nahkt waddled away.

"I trust you've been enjoying your visit, Herodotus? Wasn't our procession everything I promised? The villagers say they've never seen its equal."

It seemed to me that the villagers obviously did not venture far abroad but tactfully I did not say so.

"Is shaving some ordeal your beliefs require?" I inquired instead.

I could see there was not a hair anywhere on his body, which was considerably fairer of skin than those of his fellow countrymen, many of whom I had seen labouring in the fields, equally naked. Zemti stood to pull on a tunic lying on a sandalwood chest beside him. Several spots of blood immediately bloomed on the white linen garment, revealing where his skin had been cut.

He sighed. "I have to find a keener razor. I imagine this one is as old as the temple. I did mention the great antiquity of the temple during your last visit, didn't I? But to answer your question. Priests must constantly be on guard against uncleanliness, Herodotus. We bathe four times a day, you know. Were lice to be on us as we perform our sacred rituals, it would be an intolerable insult to Sobek."

He dabbed at a small cut on his chin and I offered him the cloth I carry at my belt for similar purposes.

"No, no." He recoiled from it. "It's nothing."

To me there was something incongruous about this fervour for cleanliness in a place where the choking miasma of incense did not entirely disguise the odours emanating from the embalming chambers. But then, other races do not necessarily think as we Hellenes and often attach fanciful notions to the commonest of events. Their priests, for example, cannot bear to so much as glance at a certain type of pulse they regard as grossly unclean, nor will they permit swineherds to set foot in holy places, the pig being considered an abomination.

Tucking the cloth back into my belt I couldn't help but wonder if Zemti had flinched away from my offer because he realized that during my travels I have on occasion been both unclean and unchaste, devourer of pig meat and romantic adventurer that I am.

I questioned him concerning Tahamet. Zemti looked distressed. "A terrible tragedy indeed. Amasis is naturally distraught. He keeps insisting her body wasn't hers and that she was hidden somewhere in the temple. We were not offended, of course, knowing only too well that at times grief deprives men of reason and they grasp at whatever they want to believe. I tried to tell him it would be best to be content that the River had chosen her, but he would not be consoled."

When I expressed my surprise at Amasis' claim that his wife had entered but not emerged from the temple Zemti shrugged.

"He's been saying the same for weeks to anyone who will listen," he replied. "Apparently he bases this astonishing statement on the word of Mose, that servant of his. However, I can assure you that Mose is a disreputable fellow, overly devoted to barley beer and therefore completely unreliable."

"It seems Amasis asked Governor Haphimen for assistance in finding Tahamet?"

The priest's brow furrowed briefly. "Indeed he did," he agreed. "Naturally, the governor ordered the temple searched and thus he also can personally confirm that there is no trace of her here."

I mentioned the temple's single gateway and the high walls around it. Zemti confirmed my suspicions as to the reason for the particular form of construction.

"A single entrance is easiest to guard," he pointed out. "We store many objects of great value, both worldly and spiritual. I have no doubt that Haphimen's search was as much a pretext for him to take note of what we hold here as to assist Amasis."

He paused and then added, "By the way, when you come to write this all down, please ensure your public realizes that women are not allowed to enter the temple itself but may only come as far as the courtyard of the sacred pool."

I would have considered this courtyard to be part of the temple but on reflection supposed that priests may draw the line between sacred and profane areas wherever they please. That was my thought as I left to go to the home of the governor.

Governor Haphimen thrust his hand into one of a row of wide-mouthed pottery jars fastened horizontally to the low wall edging the sunbaked flat roof of his home. He extracted a plump pigeon. "You will stay for the evening meal?"

The man insisted on being addressed by the title of governor, notwithstanding the fact he had no right to demand such treatment. It was, however, entirely in character for the sort of man I judged him to be, for was not his wig glossier than any I had seen in the small settlement, the kohl around his eyes applied more heavily, his wife the most beautiful woman in the village? Fortunately he had not noticed his wife had found me a far more congenial conversationalist than he during my initial visit months before.

Or perhaps he had, for when I declined his offer he did not appear too disappointed at losing the opportunity to later boast of being host to a famous traveller such as myself.

"As to Amasis," he said, "despite the fact that his extraordinary claim is based solely upon the word of a most unreliable servant, I did what I could for him despite our dispute. After all, a governor must carry out his duties regardless of personal animosities. Indeed, if the priests had not known of the woman's disappearance by reason of my inquiries they would probably not have been able to identify the body found a day or so later. The River claims many and they do not always examine the deceased too closely, as you can imagine. Amasis should be grateful to me, for now at least he knows what happened to his wife. Not all men are so fortunate."

At this strange remark I wondered uncomfortably if Haphimen was more observant than I had first thought.

Glancing away, I could see the Nile stretching toward the horizon in both directions. At this time of year it resembled a newly fed snake, sluggish and harmless.

"So you and Amasis have still not resolved your dispute over the farmland?"

The pigeon he was holding cooed softly. Haphimen grasped its head and twisted it quickly. The neck broke with a delicate crack. "He insists that I want what is his but I only wish to obtain what is rightfully mine. Even so, I repeat, I did what I could for him then and there is nothing more I can do for him now."

We made our way downstairs into a room whose geometrically patterned wall-hangings, small rosewood tables and carved wooden chests were illuminated by sunlight streaming through high, securely barred windows.

I asked Haphimen if he thought the missing woman might be concealed somewhere in the temple.

"Absolutely not," he replied. "I ordered the place searched thoroughly and I can assure you that even the tiniest cranny was not neglected. She isn't there."

"Zemti appears to believe you had other reasons for ordering a search," I observed.

Haphimen absently stroked the feathers of the dead bird he held. "The temple's wealth is also the village's fortune, Herodotus. We must be always vigilant. There have been instances where scoundrels have made off with such treasures by means of secret entrances and the like."

His statement was true enough, for as I have related elsewhere in my History I was told of a builder who designed a treasury whose wall incorporated a removable stone used for just such a nefarious purpose.

"But was it not unusual for Tahamet to go walking abroad unaccompanied?"

Haphimen glared at me with kohl-elongated eyes that were, in fact small and unremarkable. "You begin to sound like Amasis. Why shouldn't she visit the temple by herself, or anywhere else she wished for that matter? That is the way of our country. You Hellenes certainly have some strange notions at times."

He glanced down at the pigeon's limp body and his lips pursed, as if he had only just realized he had killed the bird. "Still, Tahamet was a striking woman," he went on, "and a most charming conversationalist. I can certainly understand how even a fool like Amasis is overwrought at losing such a treasure."

"As you say. However, I was wondering rather whether it was safe for her to go out alone," I replied patiently. "Amasis mentioned he thought she needed a guard."

Haphimen grunted. "Perhaps so. You'll have to excuse me,

Herodotus. I must deliver this morsel to my cook. However, I will say that Amasis was always a very suspicious sort, as should be obvious from his conversation with you. As for safety – well, you can easily judge for yourself what danger lurks in our few streets just by strolling around."

The winding, narrow street on which Haphimen's house stood harboured nothing more dangerous than a knot of sun-browned, naked children who paused in their play to gape at my long tunic and full beard. It is a common enough event. I have travelled to the ends of the earth in search of wonders but, if the truth be told, in many places I am more of a wonder to the inhabitants than they are to me.

When I approached Amasis' house I noticed several lintels set in its dark wall but, strange to relate, they were at foot level. As I subsequently learned, strong desert winds oft times blew stinging clouds of sand into the village, forming huge drifts that raised the ground above the height of the lower rooms. New dwellings would then be built using the original houses as foundations, although where drifting was less severe the owners simply constructed higher floors in ground level rooms, inserting new doors and windows at appropriate points.

I mention this unrelated matter to demonstrate that such oddities are the sorts of mysteries I am able to solve simply by observation or by conversing with those who are better informed.

Explaining the disappearance of persons, however, is not something at which I am skilled. Amasis had looked at me eagerly when he answered my knock, but his expression darkened with sorrow when I informed him I had learned nothing further concerning his wife.

He invited me to enter his house but I explained I was only there to ask where Mose resided. "Are you certain you can believe Mose's story?" I went on. "After all, both the governor and Zemti declared most emphatically that what your servant says cannot be trusted."

"Haphimen will say whatever Zemti orders him to say," replied Amasis curtly. "The governor may be nothing more than a common thief with pretensions, but he knows who wields power here. As for Zemti . . . it was in his temple that Tahamet vanished and it was he who lied to me about the identity of the unfortunate woman found in the River."

"Could it be possible that your judgment is clouded by grief?" I suggested as delicately as I could. "And, forgive me, but perhaps might it also have been affected by your dispute with Haphimen?"

"You may call it a dispute, Herodotus, but I call it attempted theft. However, after you have spoken with Mose you will better be able to judge his trustworthiness for yourself."

I paused before leaving. Even standing at the outer doorway I could see that Amasis' furnishings were, if anything, even more lavish than those displayed in the governor's home.

Amasis noticed the direction of my gaze. "Yes, I filled our house with beautiful things," he said sorrowfully. "There was never an itinerant furniture-maker passing through the village who did not receive a commission for something beautiful for my beloved. I know many criticized my indulging her so, sir. But I have always taken note of the wisdom of Ptah-Hotep, who advised keeping a wife well contented so that the chains that hold her to you will be pleasing in their nature and thus doubly binding."

While the trusted servant who had been discreetly guarding the missing wife recounted his tale, I wondered if Tahamet had found marriage to Amasis a pleasing chain.

Mose and I were seated on stools in the small walled courtyard behind Mose's home, a single story house at the end of a narrow, twisting alley of similar dwellings.

He confirmed he had followed her for weeks. Where? Just to the usual places women went. To the market, the temple, to friends' homes. No, she had never noticed him attending at her heels.

"But if she had been threatened, then she would immediately have discovered I was nearby and her attackers would have thought Sobek himself had sprung upon them!"

The statement elicited a muffled laugh from Mose's wife,

who was tending her cooking pots in the corner of the cramped courtyard that served for their kitchen.

Mose bit down hard on the withered piece of dried fish he was eating. He was, perhaps, darker and stockier than average, with bright eyes and slow speech.

"Where did Tahamet go on the day she disappeared?"

"She first called on a woman who's sewing garments for her. Then she went to the governor's house. She's an old friend of his wife's, you see. The governor wouldn't like it if he knew they still visited each other, what with his feud with my employer," Mose replied, "and I think he must have been at home because Tahamet didn't go into the house this time." He took a drink from the jug of beer beside his stool.

I declined his offer of similar refreshment. "She proceeded from there to the temple?"

"No. She went to the market. She never leaves the governor's house without visiting the market."

"Do you remember what she purchased?"

Mose frowned. "Not very well. Nothing important. Vegetables, I think. Then she went to the temple. She usually stopped there to leave an offering for the Sacred One before returning home. Pious? Yes, she was pious indeed but to tell the truth I think the tame crocodile also amused her."

"I understand you remained outside at the temple gate all night, waiting for her?"

He nodded his head vigorously.

The pungent odour of boiling leeks wafted from the corner of the courtyard and with it the voice of Mose's wife. "He wasn't guarding the woman, sir. Just her virtue. Not that she had any left as anyone but my husband would tell you. Detailing her movements to Amasis was what he was really doing."

"Be quiet, Mi! You stupid woman! I'm fortunate to have such a fine man for an employer." He lifted the jug of beer beside his stool and took an even longer drink.

"He should never have married that vulgar woman," said his wife. "Fancied herself a queen, so she did. But the truth of it is, sir, she'd kiss a Hellene on the lips!"

"Mi!" Mose was obviously shocked and furious at his wife's malicious outpouring.

The woman gave her pot of leeks a vigorous stir. "Our visitor needs to know the truth of the matter. Isn't that so, sir? Tahamet was always an ambitious woman, so she was. Not a fit wife at all. And a dreadful cook. Why, one time she burnt a duck so badly that Amasis threw it at her head. My husband saw that personally."

Mose took another gulp from his jug and shook his head. He indicated I should leave. His wife continued muttering to herself as we stepped out into the alley.

"Forgive her, sir. Amasis engaged Mi to carry out household duties but she kept falling out with Tahamet. Finally there was some sort of ugly argument and, well, Mi no longer works there. Tahamet was really just a simple girl. She grew up here in the village. She's a cousin of Mi's, in fact."

"So Tahamet must have led a much more comfortable life after she married Amasis?" I asked the garrulous servant.

"Certainly. It's true, I will admit, that she always had an eye out for something better. Who wouldn't, if their family were merely makers of baskets? I used to see her with a young weaver but then Amasis came along, so now she's risen as high as may be in this village. But she always treated me kindly, sir."

As I departed I assured Mose that I understood perfectly, although in fact I can better grasp those ancient battles between the Amazons and Scythians than I am able to fathom the tiresome, petty squabbles that infect domestic daily life, no matter what the country.

I followed one of many paths leading down to the Nile. Nearer the water the air seemed heavy. Spindly palms towered from the river bank and on the far side of the calm water I could see lush green fields, perhaps the very land over which Amasis and Haphimen were at such odds.

What had I learned? I believe only what I see with my own eyes even though what I am told is usually far more fascinating. Concerning Tahamet I knew only what I had heard. On the other hand, it was my personal observation that Amasis, Haphimen and Zemti were competing in different ways for what little wealth and power might be wrung from life in this wretched outpost.

How reliable was their information? Was Mose more credible? His livelihood depended on Amasis' continued good will. Mi's words had the unpleasantness we tend to associate with truth, perhaps because truth so often is unpleasant. But then she had reason to hold a grudge against the missing woman because of the quarrel Mose had revealed.

Had Mose abandoned his post outside the temple gate at some point and now did not dare admit it? Could the reason for Tahamet's disappearance be that simple, that she had wandered down to the river in his absence and fallen in? It seemed a far more likely explanation than her walking into a temple and vanishing.

I swatted at a cloud of flies that swarmed in my face like a spray of wind-blown sand.

Tahamet interested me. It was quite understandable that a doting husband would praise his wife's beauty but Haphimen had also described her as striking, while Mi had said she had fancied herself a queen.

Could such thoughts be dangerous, even in a village? Ambition, the desire to be more than one is, is a perplexing thing. I have seen strangers flock to me, eager for whatever renown or immortality they imagine my writings might grant them. The Egyptians believe cats will run headlong into any fire they see and in my travels I have met a number of men and women like that. Was Tahamet such a person? What strange fire had drawn her to, possibly, a fatal end?

I had hoped that contemplating the peaceful water of the Nile might serve to calm my thoughts, but instead it seemed to entice them away into fruitless meanderings. Then my concentration was broken completely by a loud splash.

Looking in the direction of the sound I saw an elongated, crocodilian shape gliding in my direction through the murky shallows. It broke the surface in front of me and I realized, with some relief, that it was only a boy, his arms outstretched as he cut rapidly through the water. Taking a step or two forwards I noted a flat rock, hitherto hidden by bushes, from which another boy was just diving.

Further contemplation of the mystery would obviously be futile here. I decided I should again visit the place where Tahamet had vanished.

Nahkt, the Sacred One's attendant, hailed me as I entered the temple courtyard. "The Sacred One is out warming himself, sir," he announced. "You are honoured!"

I followed him to the large sunken pool and squinted over its low wall. The late afternoon sun turned ripples on the water into molten gold. The Sacred One floated there, a half-submerged rough-barked log, regarding us with tiny pig-like eyes.

I remembered my conversation with Mose. "Nahkt, did you know Tahamet, the wife of Amasis? I am told she often made offerings here."

Nahkt gazed down at the crocodile, an expression of affection on his broad face. "I did know her, sir. She used to visit us most days. She liked to watch my friend here – that is, the Sacred One. But now the River has claimed her and she visits us no more. Yet if I may say so, sir, that is how I would choose to go."

My gaze was drawn back to the crocodile and its incongruous adornments – fine gold bangles, gem-studded necklaces and the like.

"Who dared to put such things on this creature?"

"Haven't you noticed all the one-armed beggars in the streets?" Nahkt asked and immediately burst into laughter.

I did not join in his merriment. A particular piece of jewellery had caught my eye. It was one of the Sacred One's earrings. A yellow topaz acacia flower – Tahamet's earring.

Suddenly, with sickening certainty, I knew why Tahamet had disappeared.

"She was fed to the sacred crocodile," I stated.

Nahkt stopped laughing and gaped at me.

"Tahamet, I mean," I went on. "She was killed in the temple and her body fed to the Sacred One. I am not accusing you of anything, Nahkt, but have you observed any — " I broke off, for the man's heavy frame had again begun to shake with amusement.

"Excuse me, sir, but the very notion of my old friend here devouring so much as a human finger . . . well . . . do you suppose this is merely a common crocodile, hiding in the mud and eating what he can catch? No, sir. The Sacred One dines on milk sweetened with honey, specially prepared grains, even wine. He has no taste for human flesh. Besides . . ."

To my horror, Nahkt heaved his bulk over the wall and jumped into the pool with an enormous splash. Waist-deep, he waded towards the crocodile, which gave a lazy shake of its tail and swam straight for him.

My voice caught in my throat as I began to call for help. Then I saw that Nahkt had grasped the monster's jaws and pried them apart, revealing that the ancient Sacred One retained not a single tooth in his elongated snout.

I left the temple shortly thereafter, having decided I would have to inform Amasis that my investigations had ended in failure. I wondered whether I should mention the earring. Were acacia flower earrings such an uncommon ornament? Perhaps it would be kinder not to draw his attention to it, since he had obviously not yet noticed its presence on the sacred crocodile. Yet hadn't he accused the priests of stealing from the dead? It might well be proof of his claim. Or perhaps leaving it and presumably its mate as an offering was a clever way to dispose of things that would immediately implicate the person found possessing them in a terrible crime. However, on the other hand might it be that that his pious wife had offered them to the Sacred One, considering them worthy of the holy beast because Amasis had commissioned them especially – or as a gesture of derision because she did not?

Yet if Tahamet had indeed been murdered, I could not fathom who might be responsible or for what reason. It appeared to me that Mi's insinuations were probably correct and that Amasis' wife had been betraying him. Therefore, despite his claim of being concerned for Tahamet's safety, I believed that Amasis suspected his wife and that was the real reason he had arranged to have her secretly followed by Mose.

Was her infidelity with his rival, Haphimen? After all, the governor was certainly richer and more powerful than her husband. Could Tahamet have been attracted to Haphimen because of that?

The two boys I had seen at the river raced past me. Dust clung to their wet skin, making them appear as if they had been rolled in wheat flour. They stared back over their thin shoulders at me, dark eyes wide at the sight of a stranger.

I recalled seeing the boys diving into the Nile's crocodile-infested waters and admired their courage, although it was born of childish lack of fear.

Then, in an instant, I knew my investigation would end in success.

It was growing dark in the Hall of the Crocodiles when I returned with Amasis, Haphimen and several of the governor's guards. Animated by flickering torchlight, shadows cast by the reptilian mummies appeared to creep stealthily around the pedestals upon which the creatures lay. The eerie sight gave me the distinct sensation that razor-sharp teeth were about to clamp onto my legs and drag me down into oblivion.

"So, Herodotus, thanks to your investigation we will finally discover the truth of the matter." As he spoke, Amasis glared first at Haphimen and than at Zemti, who had reluctantly agreed to receive our party.

"You may not wish to hear the truth, Amasis." I spoke quietly but my voice was magnified by the walls of the great stone chamber. "Even though I believe you already knew that your wife was being unfaithful."

"With Haphimen," Amasis growled. He stepped towards his rival but one of the guards blocked his way with a lance.

"No. In fact, Tahamet had been drawn to the village's wealthiest and most powerful man – Zemti." I pointed at the head priest, whose features betrayed no emotion in the fitful light.

"It was Zemti who murdered her," I went on, "and I know now how he concealed her body."

Zemti's voice was cold. "You may not believe in the might of Sobek, Herodotus, but His wrath will find and strike you down nevertheless. What proof can you offer of this blasphemous lie?"

"The evidence lies in this very hall atop one of these pedestals," was my reply. "You see, I chanced to observe boys playing in the river today and it later occurred to me that the human form, when the arms are stretched out above the head to dive, resembles the shape of a crocodile. Tahamet's body was never found because you immediately wrapped it in imitation of a sacred mummy before the governor's search, which you would surely be expecting. This concealed the crime until later, when you mummified her and placed her in this hall. Perhaps you would point her out to us?"

Zemti paled but said nothing. I glanced towards Haphimen. His face betrayed his struggle to conceal a grim smile. In truth, I was afraid to look in Amasis' direction, for I did not care to see the visage of a man who has just discovered his beloved had been so mistreated.

"Of course, the governor could order his guards to simply begin unwrapping these mummies until we find the right one," I finally suggested.

Zemti remained silent but immediately turned and walked past several pedestals, finally placing his hand on a particular mummy.

"I concealed her thus because I did not wish to bring shame upon the temple of Sobek," he said quietly. "However, I swear that I did not murder her. It's true that we had a bitter argument. She claimed she could do better for herself by going elsewhere. There was a man, a foreigner, she said, who would take her away, to Memphis or to Thebes perhaps. A Hellene. In my rage I pushed her. She fell into the Sacred One's pool. I offered her to Sobek's judgment and walked away. And He let her drown, shallow though the pool is."

He stopped and I could see he was now trembling uncontrollably. He ran his hand convulsively over his immaculately shaved scalp and spat out the rest of his confession. "You see, Herodotus, I lost my temper when . . . when she said she'd kissed a Hellene on the lips!"

From respect for those involved, I will not describe exactly what we found inside the linen wrappings, except that the limbs of Tahamet's body had been arranged much as I surmised. Nor can I reveal anything about the identity of the foreigner about whom she had spoken, for this remains unknown. It's true that I was myself introduced to a number of village women by the governor's wife during my first visit. However, I recall little about them individually for although they were fascinated by me, they had no interesting tales to relate. And though one or two may have made as if to give me a playful kiss, these were never on the lips, unless, perhaps, by accident.

These things that I have related I saw with my own eyes. However, in closing this account I must include certain information that I received some time later while travelling elsewhere in that strange country.

I can hardly lend credence to what I must now record but it was related to me by a priest of a certain temple in Heliopolis, whose denizens I count as among the most learned in Egypt.

When I questioned him concerning Zemti's fate, thinking word of such a scandal would surely have reached his ears, this priest told me that he did not know anything about it. However, he added, the inhabitants of the village of which I have written abandoned the worship of Sobek when they learned of Tahamet's death and its aftermath. Nor, he went on, could he find fault with them, for all unknowingly they had been worshipping not only the sacred crocodile mummies but also the body of a common village woman, and one of no virtue at that.

And as extraordinary as that may seem, there is one last event to recount before my tale is concluded.

In the unrest that resulted, this priest went on, it was discovered that down through the years many of Sobek's priests had shared Zemti's worldly appetites. For when all the sacred mummies were removed from the Hall of the Crocodiles, it was discovered that in fact most of the bodies so carefully preserved there were not of crocodiles, but of women.

THE JUSTICE OF ISIS

Gillian Bradshaw

Another leap, this time of 400 years, brings us to the age of the Ptolemies. The first Ptolemy had been a general under Alexander the Great, who had conquered Egypt in 332 BC. After Alexander's death Ptolemy took control over Egypt and established his own dynasty. Most of them were weak kings and by the time of Ptolemy XII, the legitimate line had become extinct. This Ptolemy was the illegitimate son of Ptolemy IX and so was nicknamed 'Auletes' (the Bastard). He was not a popular ruler and was expelled from Alexandria in BC 58, but was restored with the support of Rome. He thus became a puppet ruler.

The following story has possibly the strangest crime I have ever encountered, but I shall let you discover it for yourself. A classical scholar, and recipient of the Phillips Prize for Classical Greek (in 1975 and 1977), Gillian Bradshaw is a noted writer of both fantasy and historical fiction. Several of her books have Egyptian connections, including The Beacon at Alexandria *(1986) and the recent* Cleopatra's Heir *(2002).*

T he crowd was a complete mix – prosperous citizens in brightly coloured cloaks shouting, women shrieking behind linen veils, angry shopkeepers in leather aprons, a handful of half-naked labourers shaking their fists. In the thick of it was a shaven-headed priest in a long linen tunic, gesticulating wildly. I had been sauntering up the Canopic

Way thinking of nothing more important than what to eat for lunch when I saw it, and instantly recognized trouble.

The mob had formed in the portico on the north side of the Canopic Way, just at the junction with Serapeion Street – the very heart of Alexandria, greatest city in the world. I pushed my way into the middle of it, and saw the focus of attention: a man with a sword. He stood under the portico with his back to the wall of a bronzesmith's shop, and he had the light-coloured hair of a barbarian. A priest and a barbarian: a bad, bad combination.

There were a lot of barbarian soldiers in the city that year – Gabinians, we called them, after their commander Gabinius. Ptolemy the Bastard had come back from Rome the year before with an army of them. You know the reason, don't you? He bought his throne from the Romans with ten thousand talents he borrowed from a Roman moneylender, and the army was the moneylender's, to collect the debt. The Bastard was happy with this, since it prevented the Alexandrians from kicking him out again, and the money stolen and extorted wasn't his. The Alexandrians, of course, felt rather differently. I hated the Gabinians as much as everyone else did, but I knew I had to rescue the sword-toting thug anyway. There would be reprisals if he were lynched, and their inevitable accompaniment, riots. I've had to clear up the streets after riots. Oh, gods, that poor little trampled baby, and that girl with the stake through her belly, and the smell, the smell! It wakes me sweating in the middle of the night. I'd rather die than see it again.

The first trick to imposing order is to sound as if you have the authority to do so. "Right!" I roared to the mob at large. "What's the reason for this disorder?"

The priest turned to me wild-eyed, too furious to question my right to intervene. "Sacrilege!" he shouted. "This savage defiled the altar of our holy mother!" He was a young man, tall and athletic-looking, but he was sweating and out of breath. The cut of his long tunic, which left his right shoulder bare, proclaimed that he served the goddess Isis, whose temple lay just up Serapeion Street. Worse and worse: the barbarian had offended, not just any god, but the most popular divinity in the city.

I groaned, and – to show that I was on the priest's side – picked up a pinch of dust from the street and tossed it over my head. Then I turned my attention to the barbarian. The red tunic and the mail shirt he was wearing were indeed Roman military issue. His hair and his scraggly beard were ginger, and his eyes were a pale blue. He was in his mid-twenties, and his expression was a mixture of bewilderment and panic. Whatever he'd done in the temple, he hadn't expected the result. "You!" I yelled at him. "You speak Greek?"

He blinked, momentarily taken aback, and said "Yes," in a shaking voice. Then he added ferociously, "I am innocent!" He had a strange accent, but he did seem to understand. That was a relief: many of the Gabinians didn't speak a word of any civilized tongue.

"This holy man accuses you of sacrilege!" I barked at him. "What do you have to say for yourself?"

"I am innocent!" he declared again, waving his sword for emphasis. "I wasn't even there when they put the shit on the altar!"

There was a moment of shocked silence as the crowd took in what he'd said, and understood just how crudely the altar of their beloved goddess had been defiled. Then there was a howl of outrage and a surge forwards. The barbarian waved his sword and the surge stopped – but only just. I was aware of somebody on the fringes of the crowd turning aside to look in the street for loose stones. "Liar!" cried the priest furiously. "It was you, you filth: nobody else was there!"

"Let the goddess judge him!" I suggested, raising my voice to drown them out. "Take him back to the temple, and see if he can lie in front of her sacred image!"

It wasn't an outstanding ploy, but it was the best I could come up with on the spur of the moment. In spite of what you in the West may have heard about the bloodthirstiness of Egyptians, our temples are just as much places of sanctuary as anyone else's. Killing him in the temple precincts would double the sacrilege, so if I could get him there, he'd be safe.

Luckily, the crowd were so outraged that they expected Isis to strike the evil-doer dead the moment he crossed her threshold, and they welcomed the suggestion with cheers. The priest, however, was well aware that his goddess was unlikely to be so obliging, and he stared at me in surprised dismay. I hurriedly moved closer and tried an honest appeal in a whisper: "My lord, if this fellow is killed here on the street, without trial, you know as well as I do that his friends will punish the whole city – *and* defile the temple all over again. If you can keep him prisoner at the temple, though, I'll go and inform my master, the market superintendent. He can see to it that the matter is dealt with by the city, instead of by the Romans – that the man is tried for sacrilege, and pays the penalty."

His expression cleared. "You work for the market superintendent?"

I should, perhaps, explain that in Alexandria the market superintendent is a very important man. This is because we don't have a city council – we did once, but it was abolished after it had some disagreements with a king. In consequence, the only elected officials the city has are those it can't manage without, like the superintendent of schools and the market superintendent. These offices thus carry all the honour and respect which in other cities are given to more elevated magistracies.

I pulled out my licence, which I wear on a thong around my neck, but one of the shopkeepers in the crowd had overheard and elbowed his way over to us. All the shopkeepers on the Canopic Way knew me. "That's Peridromon," he informed the priest. "He belongs to the superintendent's office all right; he's their prime pest." I'd fined him once for obstructing the thoroughfare.

The priest considered for a moment. He knew as well as I did that even if we could get the barbarian tried for sacrilege, it would likely end only in a fine and a dishonourable discharge from the army. On the other hand, he also knew what would happen if the fellow were lynched.

"Very well," he agreed reluctantly. "You can bring him to the temple – *if* he surrenders now and hands over his arms!"

That, frankly, was a lot easier for him to ask than for me to deliver. The Gabinian still had his back against the wall and his sword drawn, and he was studying the crowd as though he was only waiting for someone to come close enough to skewer. I couldn't let things take their course, though, and face another heap of bodies. I held up both hands so that the barbarian could see I was unarmed, and stepped forwards. The Gabinian immediately pointed the sword at me. I kept my hands in the air and my eyes on his face and took another step forwards until the sword was almost touching my chest, telling myself meanwhile that I could always fling myself backwards if he lunged. The strange pale eyes bored into mine with an expression of desperate urgency.

"I'm innocent!" the barbarian declared for the third time. I was close enough now to see how heavily he was sweating. The red tunic was damp enough to rust his mail. He stank of armour-grease and fear.

"These good people don't believe you," I replied, keeping my voice calm and steady. "But if you come with me now, they won't take matters into their own hands. Come back to the temple and you'll have a fair trial."

The point of the sword trembled a little. The Gabinian bit his lip.

"The temple is a place of sanctuary," I pointed out. "The Canopic Way isn't. These people are very angry, and it's a long way to your barracks. I'm telling you plainly: unless you give up your sword and come with me now, you won't live another hour."

The Gabinian's lip began to bleed where he'd bitten it. He stared at me a moment longer, then abruptly sheathed the sword.

I let out a breath. I hadn't been aware of holding and took one more step forwards to catch hold of his arm. The Gabinian flinched, but did not resist. He unfastened his sword belt and handed the weapon over. I took it gingerly – the most dangerous weapon I've ever used is a cudgel – and strapped it over my shoulder. Then I waved the mob back. "Out of the way!" I shouted. "This man has surrendered to Isis! The priest and I are going to take him to her temple, to meet her judgment!"

The priest was momentarily surprised to be roped in, but he rose to it, and came forwards to take the Gabinian's other arm. The barbarian allowed us to hustle him up Serapeion Street. I noticed in passing that the man who'd been looking for stones had collected some, and I gave him a steely glare. He looked sullen, but didn't throw any – not because of me, I'm sure, but because he was afraid of hitting a priest.

The temple of Isis, if you're not familiar with it, is part of the Serapeion, the magnificent temple complex constructed by the first Ptolemy in the name of Serapis and Isis. It is the greatest temple in the city, and stands at Alexandria's highest point. The sacred precinct is enclosed within a wall of finely worked stone, and entrance is via a single monumental gateway. That gate lay nearly half a mile from the Canopic Way, unfortunately, uphill along a busy street. The priest and I were eager to get the Gabinian to safety, but we were impeded by the crowd, and the walk seemed to take forever. Most of those who'd witnessed the confrontation abandoned their own business to accompany us – no doubt in the hope of seeing the evil-doer struck dead – and they informed everyone they met of what was going on, so that by the time we finally arrived at the temple we were in the middle of a huge crush of people, all in a very ugly mood. Sacrilege is absolutely guaranteed to spark trouble, and everyone hates the Gabinians. I kept tight hold of the barbarian, occasionally shouting, "This man belongs to Isis!" to keep the stones from flying, but I had no idea how to get him through the gate. The priest, however, let go of the prisoner and plunged into the mob with his arms stretched wide. The crowd respected his robe and shaven head and stood aside, and the barbarian and I managed to jostle through behind him. When we passed under the shadow of the gateway and entered the white paved temple precincts I sighed with relief. So did the Gabinian, which showed that, barbarian though he was, he wasn't stupid.

The temple of Serapis occupies the northern half of the Serapeion complex; the temple of Isis, the southern. Although it was designed by Greeks – like Alexandria itself – the Iseion is laid out in the Egyptian fashion. This means that only the first courtyard of the temple is open to the public: the shrine itself is reserved for the priesthood and initiates of the mysteries. The doors of the shrine, however, are opened at dawn during the morning service, and are kept open until the middle of the afternoon, so that visitors can worship the image of the goddess, which stands just inside them. The public courtyard is large and beautiful, surrounded by a portico and lavishly adorned with stelae and statues. It was crowded when we arrived: people had already heard about the sacrilege, and had rushed to see it for themselves. They were conversing in shocked whispers, but when we appeared, at the front of a flood of excited newcomers, there was uproar.

The Gabinian and I kept close behind the young priest as he made his way through the shouting mob. A small knot of priests was gathered about the main altar, which is a waist-high column of carved porphyry. Behind them the temple doors stood open, and the statue of Isis, dressed in her seven black robes and crowned with a golden serpent, gazed tolerantly down on the mortals who had rushed to her defence.

We were almost at the altar before the temple attendants could even get a look at us. "Theophanes caught him!" shrieked one of them at last, pointing. He was middle-aged, with a thin, pinched face, and he wore the short tunic of a sacristan, rather than the long one of a priest. "That's the brute who did it!"

The priestess beside him covered her face, as though she couldn't even bear to look. The remaining priest in the group – an older man in a magnificent cloak – simply stared. I recognized him as the *pterophoros*, or senior priest, Lord Pachrates. (I've been known to worship Isis, from time to time, and the office had dealings with him every time the Iseion held a procession.)

The Gabinian suddenly straightened and began walking towards the altar with a long stride, pushing past me and the younger priest and forcing us to hurry to keep up with him. The crowd, always willing to enjoy a good scene, pulled aside to let us through. When we reached the altar the barbarian stopped. He glanced at the altar – which had just been washed, by the look of it – then at the statue of the goddess. Then he raised his right hand as though he were taking an oath.

"I swear by Isis and by the gods of my own people that I am innocent!" he proclaimed loudly. He clenched his raised hand and struck himself on the chest, making his mail jingle, then turned to the senior priest. "The goddess saw the one who defiled her altar. She knows that I am innocent. I surrender myself to her judgment!"

There was a murmur around the courtyard. Pachrates stared at the young barbarian for a moment with vast displeasure, then looked accusingly at the priest who'd accompanied me. "Why have you brought the problem back *here*, Theophanes?" he demanded in a whisper.

"I had to," said the young priest defensively. "He'd have been killed if he stayed on the street, my lord, and then there would be reprisals." He glanced at me and added, "This man here belongs to the market supervisor's office: he's promised to see that it's dealt with by the city."

I opened my mouth ready to say "If I can," – then closed it again. It wasn't the time to express doubts.

Pachrates snorted in disgust. The sacristan glared and shrieked, "The city can't do anything! The savage has defiled the altar of our holy lady! Take him out of here, out, out into the street!" No doubt at all what would happen to him there.

"I didn't do it!" the Gabinian shouted back. He crossed his arms and glared around him. "I *honour* the great goddess Isis. I came here this morning because I'd heard her fame, and I wanted to see her for myself. This priestess – this woman here! – told me that I could buy a flask full of holy Nile water to take away with me. I went away to buy the flask, but when I came back with it, there was shit on the altar and everyone started screaming that I'd put it there!"

"There was no one else in the courtyard!" snapped the priestess, dropping her hands to glare at him. "I went to fetch the water, and when I came back, there you were, admiring your handiwork!"

"You put dog-shit on the altar of the holy goddess!" agreed the sacristan, quivering with rage. "A trail of dog-shit from *there* to *here*!" He pointed at the altar to Anubis, which stood just to the right of the main altar. A statue of the god, shown in the Egyptian fashion with the head of a jackal, stood on the temple porch before it.

"No!" protested the Gabinian, before the crowd could catch its breath to curse him. "It wasn't me!"

"Just a moment!" I protested, staring at the old sacristan in bewilderment. "Dog-shit?"

The old man nodded, red with anger to the crown of his shaven scalp.

I know that many Romans do find the idea of a jackal-headed god ridiculous, I could easily imagine a group of soldiers deciding to profane the altar as a joke, but . . . "How do you know it was dog-shit?" I asked uneasily. "How do you know it wasn't the human variety?"

"I had to clean it up, didn't I?" he replied bitterly. "There was a whole frog in it, and . . . and straw, where the dirty creature had been eating manure, all over the altar of our holy lady!" He was almost in tears.

"A frog?" I repeated in disbelief.

"Frog-bones!" cried the sacristan. "Disgusting half-digested frog-skin and a frog skull and little bones mixed with shit! May the man who left such an offering on the altar of our holy goddess perish most miserably!" He glared at the Gabinian.

"You're saying that this man came into the temple with a great big basket full of dog-shit – a smelly thing he must have carted *clear across the city* – and nobody said anything?" I demanded incredulously. "You not only let him into the temple, you left him alone before the altar?"

There was a sudden silence. "He . . . he must have hidden the basket," said the sacristan uncertainly. "Before he came in."

"What do you mean, he must have carted it across the city?" demanded Pachrates the Pterophoros, looking down his nose at me. "Stray dogs do get into the temple precinct. The gates are open."

"Not ones that eat frogs, my lord," I told him flatly. "Oh,

it's the season when the creatures are abundant down at the lakeshore and along the canal, but that's miles from here, and even stray dogs have territories. Shit from a dog that had been eating frogs must have been carted in." I looked at the sacristan. "Do I gather the fellow *didn't* have a basket?"

"He must have hidden it," repeated the sacristan defensively.

"But he was caught while he was standing before the altar, looking at what he'd done," I pointed out. "Where was the basket then?"

The old man sputtered. I turned to the Gabinian. "Let's see your hands," I ordered.

Puzzled, he held them out.

"You cleaned the altar?" I asked the sacristan. "Did you find a handful of dirty leaves lying around it, perhaps? Or a sponge?"

"My hands are clean!" shouted the barbarian, abruptly understanding. "How am I supposed to have put shit on the altar without a basket and without anything to clean my hands afterwards?" He grinned at the sacristan triumphantly. "And why would I have profaned the altar, then cleaned up, put the basket away somewhere, and hung about waiting for the priestess to come back with the holy water?"

Pachrates gave me a very unfriendly look. Important men often do that, and I handled it the way I normally do: bowed deeply and tried to look contrite. He gave a small snort of displeasure, then turned to the crowd, raising his arms.

"People of Alexandria, worshippers of the Holy Isis!" he called loudly. "Have no fear! The great goddess will reveal the truth. I will question this man privately, and soon all will be made plain. In the meantime, the altar of the Lady has been cleaned and washed with the sacred water of the Nile: I urge those of you who love the goddess to cover it with sweet incense, to take away the stink of pollution from her nostrils."

While the crowd was applauding this suggestion he turned back. He looked at me, at the barbarian, at the sacristan, the priestess, and Theophanes. "All of you, come with me!" he commanded, and set off, scowling ferociously.

He led us to the left of the shrine and around behind it, then along a covered walkway and into the part of the temple complex called the *pastophorion*, which provides living quarters for the priests. We went up a flight of stairs into what I guessed was a reception room used by the senior priests – a sumptuous place, with a carpet on the floor, lampstands of gilded bronze, and a window with a view out over the city towards the west. Pachrates sat himself down in a high-backed chair at one side of the room; the sacristan at once hurried over to stand behind him. The rest of us shuffled about uncertainly.

"You," said the pterophoros, looking straight at me. "You work for the market superintendent, do you? Are you Archippos' own man, or do you just belong to his office?"

"To his office, my lord," I admitted, bowing again. "A public slave, my lord, of long standing. My name is Peridromon."

"And you promised Theophanes that your master would prosecute this barbarian for sacrilege? What makes you think Archippos will do anything of the sort? It seems to me that he's far more likely to hand the criminal over to Gabinius with a letter of complaint which nobody will even bother to read."

I winced: he knew Archippos. Our illustrious market superintendent happened to be one of the most useless weak-chinned aristocrats ever to have scrambled into the position, but he had only recently been elected, and I hadn't expected the priests of Isis to know what he was like. "Matters could be arranged otherwise," I murmured.

The senior priest gave me a long hard look. "I see. You are one of those officious public slaves who tries to run the city's affairs behind his masters' backs – an insolent and impertinent meddler in the affairs of free men."

Well, yes, so I am – and very good at it. I set my teeth, put on the contrite look, and bowed. "My lord," I said, in the tone of unctuous respect I can only manage when someone powerful genuinely annoys me." I am heartily sorry if you have found me insolent or impertinent. The city, in its wisdom, has decided that the supervision of shopkeepers and the maintenance of cleanliness and good order on the street is a menial task, more suited to a slave than to a free citizen, so it purchases men like myself. I try do my assigned tasks faithfully and obediently. I admit that I do arrange many of my master's affairs – but he has been in office only six weeks, and he expects such assistance from his staff. I intervened today only because I wanted to help you obtain satisfaction for this foul sacrilege without provoking reprisals from the Gabinians, and I am very sorry if my zeal has offended you."

Pachrates gave me another hard look, as though he understood exactly how much those humble words were worth, then grunted. "And how do you think we can obtain satisfaction?"

I hesitated. "I had been thinking in terms of a hearing convened at once, before Aulus Gabinius even knows what's going on. With a couple of senior priests and a couple of magistrates it should be perfectly lawful, and with luck it could reach a verdict this afternoon. Once there's a legal verdict the criminal could . . ."

"You still think I'm guilty!" objected the Gabinian in dismay. "You yourself just showed that I am innocent, that . . ."

"I did nothing of the sort!" I snapped. "Maybe you came up here with a friend, and the friend was carrying the basket. Maybe you'd agreed that you would distract the priestess while he defiled the altar. Maybe he ran off fast afterwards, thinking you would do the same, and you hung about waiting because you didn't realise he'd already gone."

The barbarian glared. "Why would I go to so much trouble to . . . to commit an ill-omened act of sacrilege against a great and powerful goddess?"

"They make fun of Egyptian gods in your mess hall, don't they?" I asked sourly. " 'Ha, ha, ha, that Anubis looks like a dog, wouldn't it be funny if he shat on the altar of Isis?' A few drinks and a dare in a tavern can account for almost any stupidity in a soldier."

"No!" cried the barbarian, with what seemed to be real indignation. "I don't . . . that is, yes, there are men like that, but I'm not one of them. We have a temple of Isis at home. I'd had a letter . . ." He stopped.

"Yes?" I asked quickly.

He shrugged, then continued resentfully, "I had a letter from my sister in Massalia. She's married, she's expecting her first baby. I thought I could send her a gift from the temple of Alexandrian Isis. For luck and protection, you see, because she's nervous about it."

It was, actually, a respectable and entirely believable reason for a foreign soldier to visit the temple of Isis. I looked at him thoughtfully.

So did Pachrates. "You're from Massalia?" he asked.

The Gabinian nodded. "Quintus Julius Vindex," he identified himself, "a registered foreign resident of Massalia, now of the Fifth *Alaudae*, second century, currently on secondment to Aulus Gabinius."

The priest's eyes narrowed. "A legionary?"

I was staring, too. Most Gabinians were Gaulish and German mercenaries, whose only qualifications were ferocity and greed. Legionaries are altogether a better class of soldier. Vindex was probably an officer of some kind – and the fact that he was from Massalia might well indicate exactly what kind. Although that city lies in Gaul, it was founded as a Greek colony. It is nominally independent – though dominated by Rome and with many Roman residents – and it has more trade with Alexandria than any other city in the West. A Roman from Massalia, who could be expected to speak good Greek and know something about Alexandria, would be an ideal person to liaise between a unit of Gaulish Gabinians and the officials of the Bastard's court. If he had not committed the sacrilege – and I was beginning to believe him that he hadn't – then there were suddenly a lot of very unpleasant possibilities as to who else might have done it, and why.

"Julius Vindex," said Pachrates with distaste. "*Julius* Vindex. Did your family obtain the citizenship from Julius Caesar, perhaps?"

The barbarian hesitated – then nodded.

I suppose that wasn't too surprising. Gabinius was a friend and supporter of that ambitious general; if he asked Caesar for some capable young Greek-speaking legionaries to serve as liaison officers in his army of bailiffs, Caesar would provide them, and pick men he knew. But, oh Lady Isis, this game was getting harder to win by the minute. I groaned, and Pachrates gave me a glance of disgusted agreement.

"Well," said Pachrates heavily. "Quintus Julius Vindex, since you claim to be an innocent man who honours Isis, explain to me how you've come to be accused of sacrilege."

"I told you already," answered Vindex. "I came up here to see the goddess, the priestess there offered to get me some holy water . . ."

"From the beginning," said Pachrates sharply. "When did you receive this letter?"

Vindex had received the letter three days before, off a ship which had arrived from Massalia with a cargo of olive oil. He had told some of his friends about it, but not the men in his unit. Yes, he was indeed a liaison officer for a Gaulish unit, but the rest of the men were from another part of Gaul and a different tribe, and he didn't seem to like them much. His friends were fellow officers, some on Gabinius' staff, one or two attached to royal guard of King Ptolemy Auletes – as Vindex respectfully termed the Bastard. He had told them that he intended to go to the temple of Isis to pray for his sister and buy her a good-luck charm, and he'd informed his commander that he wanted the morning off.

He had walked up from the Gabinian barracks that morning – a long walk; since the barracks lie in the palace area on the Lochias promontory, to the east of the Great Harbour. He had been in no hurry, though, and had arrived in the middle of the morning to find the temple quiet: the public normally come when the shrine is opened at dawn, or when it shuts in the middle of the afternoon. The priestess, however, whose name was Tabzes, had been sitting on the steps sewing a new robe for the goddess' statue, while the sacristan had been busy in the shrine. Vindex had offered the priestess a donation for incense, and had told her about his sister; she'd suggested that he buy a flask of holy water.

"She told me to buy a flask in the outer court," he continued, "and said that while I was buying it, she'd fetch the water. So I went out and found a vendor who sold flasks, and bought one. Then I came back to the shrine. There was nobody around, so I waited. Then I noticed the dog shit – I saw it on the ground first, and I thought a dog had got in, but then I saw it was on the altar as well. I was shocked. I was standing there looking at it, wondering whether I should clean it away, when the priestess came out of the shrine and started screaming sacrilege."

"What about the flask?" I asked.

He looked blank.

"You said you'd bought a flask for the holy water. What happened to it?"

"Oh! I . . . I don't know. I must have dropped it. Everyone was screaming at me, and I . . . I just thought I had to get away."

"He never had a flask!" interjected the priestess, with some venom. "I came out of the shrine, and he was standing there admiring what he'd done!"

"Did he have a basket?"

She was nonplussed. She was a young woman, very pretty with large dark eyes now flashing with anger, and a straight blade of a nose. Her hair was arranged in the latest Greek fashion, piled up behind her head but with a set of black corkscrew curls artfully arranged around her face, and she was wearing a very fine gold necklace and earrings. If I'd seen her without the priestly robes I'd have thought her a Greek, but her name was Egyptian. She looked uncertainly at Pachrates, evidently wondering if she needed to answer me. The Pterophoros nodded.

"I didn't notice," she said. Then she added, "I think there were some leaves lying around the altar, though. He could have had the . . . the foul stuff wrapped up in leaves and tucked into his tunic."

The sacristan looked doubtful. Vindex promptly flung his arms wide with a jingle of mail. "And how did I get it out from under *this*?" he sneered. "Here, I'll take it off, if you like, and you can see if I had shit tucked into my clothing. Leaves or not, it would have squished under armour."

The priestess gave him a look of disgust. "Maybe the slave was right, then," she sniffed. "He must have had an accomplice."

"Leave that aside for the moment," I told her. "I'm puzzled about the water." When that brought another blank look I said, "You told Julius Vindex to buy a flask while you went to fetch some holy water. That's used in the sacred rites every day, isn't it? It must be stored somewhere near the altar."

"At the back of the shrine," supplied the old sacristan. "Leastways, there's an amphora of it kept there, and we have a tank in back. We fill it up from the blessed Nile."

"And may you be blessed for doing so," I said politely. "Do you see why I'm puzzled? It makes no sense to set off to fetch holy water at the same time as Vindex left to buy his flask. After all, you must have known that it would take him some time to find a vendor and make his purchase. The sensible thing to do would be to wait for him to come back, and then fetch the water."

Tabzes flushed slightly. "I . . . well, obviously. But he'd given me some money for incense. I had gone to put that in the strongbox and get the incense, and get it written down in accounts . . ." She cast an anxious glance at Pachrates. "I didn't actually manage to get it written down, sir, I'm sorry. First I had to put away the robe I'd been stitching, and the thread and the needles and everything, and when I'd done that, and put the money away and got the incense, I saw that the barbarian was back, so I went to see to him."

The Pterophoros raised an eyebrow. "Write it down later today," he commanded, and I understood at once that he'd had trouble with the woman over her accounting before, and wondered if it was dishonesty or just laziness.

"That's cleared that up, then," I said politely. I turned to the sacristan. "What about you, sir? From what Julius Vindex has said, you were in the shrine when he arrived, but not when he got back from buying his flask. Is that right?"

He nodded suspiciously. "When he came I was cleaning up the dishes we'd used for the incense and the libations this morning, and setting out the ones for the afternoon. I do it every day."

"I have worshipped here, and noticed how beautiful they are, sir." That mollified him a little. "So you noticed Julius Vindex when he arrived, sir?"

He made a face. "Notice it when a barbarian soldier comes up to our lady's shrine, and there's nobody about in the courtyard but a silly girl? Of course I noticed, and I paid sharp attention to him, at first. He seemed harmless enough. The first part of what he said is true: he did give the girl some money for incense, and act like he wanted to buy holy water to invoke our lady's help for his sister, so I thought he was all right."

"I'm surprised, though, that you felt so confident as to leave him alone in the courtyard, with the doors to the shrine open and valuable sacred vessels set out. In fact, I'm surprised that you *ever* leave the shrine unattended while the doors are open. The house of Isis is full of beautiful things and, while most of us love her, there are always men wicked or desperate enough to steal from the gods."

The old man looked indignant. "Of course I didn't leave the shrine unattended! We never do that, not while the doors are open, like you say. Tabzes was talking to the savage when I finished my work, and I never expected her to go off when nobody else was about!" He scowled at the priestess. "She knows perfectly well we're not supposed to do that!"

She tossed her head. "I didn't!" she snapped. "Theophanes was in the *ekklesiasterion*, if you remember, practising his song. You must have heard him: the door was open! It was safe."

The young priest Theophanes nodded. It emerged that the *ekklesiasterion*, the priests' assembly hall, lay immediately behind the goddess' shrine, and had its own entrance which was used during the ceremonies which were open only to the priests and the initiates. Theophanes agreed that he had been in there, practising a hymn he was to sing at the next festival, all the time between the morning service and the time he heard the shouts of sacrilege. He had, he said, had a good view of the interior of the shrine, though he hadn't been able to see anything in the courtyard. "I like to look at the image of the holy goddess when I sing," he admitted. "Then I can sing for her, and can feel that she's listening."

Tabzes had informed him when she left the shrine to put the robe away. He had noticed her coming back with the incense a little while later. He had not noticed Vindex at all, not until the Gabinian's abrupt departure.

"I wasn't thinking about anything except the praise of the goddess," he said, "until Tabzes started screaming sacrilege. Then I ran out, and I saw what had been done to the altar. I didn't understand it at first, I was too shocked. By the time I did understand that somebody had done that deliberately, the barbarian was already on the other side of the courtyard. I ran after him." He looked pleased and added, "I used to compete in foot races when I was at school. This slowed me down –" he tugged at his tight linen tunic, "– but I still caught him." Then he frowned at Vindex and said uncertainly, "Maybe we made a mistake."

"Did you notice anyone who could have been his accomplice?" I asked. "For example, was he looking around while you were chasing him, or calling out to someone else?"

"No," replied Theophanes, frowning. "He just ran. He looked back at *me* a few times, but that's all." He turned to the priestess and the sacristan. "What about you? Did you notice anyone who might have been his accomplice?"

The old man made a face and shook his head. The priestess said hesitantly, "There was a man in a dark cloak in the great court, near the entrance to the portico. I couldn't see him clearly, but I could see that somebody was there. It must have been the accomplice – waiting there, watching for his chance!"

"I did not have an accomplice!" snapped the Gabinian. "If somebody *was* waiting for a chance to defile the altar, the fact that they took it as soon as they found the courtyard empty isn't my fault, and was nothing to do with me!"

"Do you have enemies?" I asked him.

He gave me a look of surprise. Then his face went white, his eyes widening in an expression of horrified speculation. I found it oddly disconcerting: no Egyptian could ever turn that colour, no matter how shocked he was. I wondered if the barbarian had trouble with sunburn, with skin that clear.

"I . . ." Vindex began – then stopped. The colour came back to his face, this time an angry red. "What are you suggesting?" he demanded furiously. "You can't pin this on me, so you're trying to find another *Roman* who might have done it? Why couldn't it have been some Greek joker, or a member of a rival Egyptian sect, or a Jew? Why do you insist it has to do with me?"

I shrugged. "An officer often has enemies – some common soldier he's disciplined who bears a grudge for it, or a fellow officer who considers him a rival. An enemy who wished you ill might very well try to incriminate you on a charge of sacrilege – particularly since you honour the goddess, and, from what you say, many of your fellows don't. Did you notice anyone following you when you left your barracks?"

"No," said Vindex tightly.

"You're sure?"

"Yes!" he snapped. "You think I don't know how much this city hates us? That I'm not afraid every time I walk along the open street, that I don't watch for people skulking after me? Nobody was following me."

"So," Pachrates broke in repressively, "we have learned all we can of how this crime occurred, and we do not know who defiled the altar." He looked around us forbiddingly, then frowned at the young barbarian. "Julius Vindex, are you content to wait here at the temple while we decide what to do?"

The Gabinian bowed. "I have surrendered to Isis; I am content to wait. I would like to write a note to my commanding officer, however, telling him what has happened. I will tell him that, so far, you have acted fairly and justly."

Pachrates nodded. "I will see that you have writing materials, and that the note is delivered. Theophanes, take Julius Vindex to one of the guest rooms – and stay there with him, to make sure that he is not troubled. Tabzes, Khamwas – I want you to stay close at hand until this matter is cleared up, in case we find more witnesses and need to question you again. Go to the shrine, and pray to the holy goddess, until I send for you. Slave, stay here."

I hate to be addressed as "Slave!" I put on a respectful expression and stood there with my hands clasped behind my back while the others filed out. I felt very uneasy, however. I was aware that I had thrust into that interrogation in a way that probably seemed outrageous to a man who believed that slaves should keep their mouths shut and do as their masters ordered – as Pachrates evidently did. I reminded myself that I wasn't *his* slave, and the worst he could do was complain about me to Archippos.

Pachrates stretched in his chair, then leaned forwards, resting his chin on his fist and his elbow on his knees and looking at me with sharp eyes. "Your thoughts on the matter?" he asked.

I was surprised to be asked. I didn't trust it. I shrugged. "It is possible that it was, as he suggested, nothing to do with him."

"I do not believe that, and neither do you. Your questions were astute. Either he had an accomplice – and I do not believe that, either – or it was done by an enemy of his. You have convinced me that it was a premeditated act – that the excrement had been collected and brought here deliberately from another part of the city. That means that, if it was an enemy of his, it must have been someone who knew he was coming here. He says that he did not tell his men, so it was not a common soldier with a grudge. Come, you saw it as soon as I did: it showed on your face."

I grimaced. "The Gabinians are collecting money to pay the king's debt," I admitted in a low voice. "Where there is a lot of money, there are cheats. When you have two accounts – as you do with Gabinius and the king – the cheats will target the gap between them. A literate, Greek-speaking liaison officer would be ideally placed to spot somebody's profitable little game."

Pachrates nodded. "And a charge of sacrilege could be guaranteed to get rid of him. Even if he escaped the mob, and even if his commander thought the offence trivial, still he would be sent away, for his own safety. Indeed, though I believe him innocent, it's what will happen to him now. If I simply released him, there would be many who said that I did so only through fear of the Gabinians or the king. He would be dead within the month. – He was very disturbed when you asked about his enemies."

I nodded. "He suspects someone, and is either afraid to name him – because it's someone very powerful – or ashamed to admit his suspicions – because it's a man he reckons a friend." I hesitated, considering, knowing that if I went on I was going to offend this man – then went on anyway: "I think he was telling the truth that he noticed no one following him. That doesn't mean, of course, that he couldn't have been followed by someone who knows how to hide on a street – but I do believe him that Gabinians are wary on the streets, and it would be hard."

The Pterophoros watched me with a face that gave nothing away.

"It was very convenient that the courtyard happened to be empty. An outsider planning the act could not have counted on that."

"And?" asked Pachrates, in a flat tone.

"Three of your people were near the shrine when Vindex arrived this morning. Khamwas – that was the name of your sacristan? – seems to me an old, devout, conservative man. Unless he is a very good actor, his distress over the sacrilege was genuine. Theophanes . . . also appears devout. He's a Greek, isn't he? And well-born, with an education at the gymnasium, where he competed in foot-races. The priesthood of Isis isn't the obvious choice for such a man."

"His family opposes it," said Pachrates. "You are right: he is a well-born Greek, and they don't consider the priesthood to be a profession at all – it's something to be dabbled in during one's official career, with a year here officiating at festivals and a year there presiding as a magistrate." He spoke with the incredulous contempt of a man who comes from an old Egyptian priestly family. "Theophanes loves the goddess, and joined us against the wishes of his family."

"So," I concluded, "Theophanes is genuinely devout – and certainly I noticed nothing suspicious in his behaviour. Without his help, I couldn't have brought the barbarian into the safety of this temple, and that can't have served the purpose of Vindex's enemy. Tabzes, however . . ."

Pachrates snorted. "You've already pronounced your verdict, haven't you?"

I shrugged. The priestess had sent Vindex off to buy a flask immediately after the sacristan left, thus ensuring that the courtyard was unobserved. She had gone off, then come back carrying something which Theophanes had believed to be incense. She had been the one to raise the alarm, too, screaming sacrilege when one would have expected a few minutes of shocked and bewildered questions first. She had certainly been trying to incriminate Vindex with her claims to have noticed details – leaves on the pavement; a man hanging about the entrance to the courtyard – which nobody else had remarked on. A pretty Egyptian girl, probably in the priesthood only because she came from a priestly family, who dressed her hair like a Greek and liked expensive jewellery, she did not seem a devout woman. She was slovenly about accounting for donations – which presumably meant she wanted money. Yes, I thought it very likely she had taken a bribe from someone who wanted Vindex out of the way.

Probably somebody had brought her the shit in a covered basket and she'd shaken it out over the altar. I couldn't imagine her touching it: she wouldn't even say the words, "dog-shit", and she certainly would have been too wary, as well as too squeamish, to collect the stuff off the streets around the temple. I wondered what had become of *that* basket – whether it was still concealed inside the shrine, or whether she'd already managed to dispose of it. Probably she disposed of it at once, throwing it down a well or out of a window: otherwise she would have produced it once I started asking about it, as evidence against Vindex.

"It is not your business, Slave," said Pachrates severely.

With a flare of triumph I realised that he, too, thought her guilty. It showed in the grimness of his face. I bowed. "The disciplining of priests is the business of the temple," I agreed. "My concern is the good ordering of the streets and markets of Alexandria." I met his eyes. "That, however, is something that is affected by riots and disorder among the citizens, my lord."

He stared at me in cold offence.

"She may have thrown the basket down a well, or out of a window in the priestly area close to the shrine." I offered helpfully. "There's also the missing flask, if you're looking for proof. The fact that Vindex bought it and came back to the shrine with it is evidence of his good intentions; the fact that it's missing incriminates him. Of course, it wouldn't mean anything if she'd simply picked it up after he dropped it, but if it's found that she concealed it and kept silent while I was asking questions about it – that would be suggestive."

Pachrates gave me a bitter look. "I expect I will find a large sum of money in her room which she is unable to account for," he declared bluntly. "That will be even more 'suggestive'. I will deal with the matter, Slave. I tell you again, it is *not* your concern." He grimaced. "As to disorder in the streets – the barbarian has not been lynched and will not be lynched, so there will be no reprisals and no riots."

"Someone hired that girl to defile the altar," I said angrily. "Someone tried to induce the devout followers of the goddess to lynch an innocent man. Someone has some dirty little game going over the money those Gabinian thugs are extorting from the free citizens of Alexandria, and they're willing to offend against god and man to keep it going."

"I will remind you of something," Pachrates said. "The shrine of Isis is not empty, even if it is unattended. The goddess was there. She saw what was done. Does she need *us* to protect *her*? No: she is a goddess, able to act where we can only wonder. She has brought it about that the man who was falsely accused was *not* lynched: he is safe under her protection, and he will soon depart for his home. There will be no blemish on his record: I will make it clear that we believe him innocent. As for the rest – a king paid his country's enemies for his throne, and handed over his kingdom to its despoilers in recompense. To what tribunal would you bring this criminal, if you caught him – to the king, or the savage who lent him money? Would you call it justice because a stronger robber has deprived a weaker of some of the spoils?

"No. There is no justice among men: only the gods have both the knowledge and the power to judge without error. Whoever this man is, he has offended against Isis. I would not like to dream his dreams or die his death, however it comes to him. Our lady is kind and good, but she is just."

It was one of the very few times in my life when I've been left speechless. After a moment, I bowed. "You are a man of faith," I told him.

Pachrates leaned back in his chair, nodding. "Yes." After a moment, he said, almost gently, "The Gabinian will have written his letter. You may bear it for him, if you wish."

It made me feel . . . no, I was about to say "cynical and faithless", but it wasn't that at all: it was more like being caught red-handed, then let off. He knew I still wanted to find out who had been responsible for the sacrilege, he thought it was foolish, but he was still offering me one more opportunity to find out. He was a very unsettling man, the Pterophoros, and I was glad he wasn't likely to run for market super-intendent. I bowed again, and went off to find Quintus Julius Vindex.

The Gabinian was relaxing in one of the rooms set aside for guests of the Serapeion – a comfortable room, even a luxurious one, with a couch and writing table of polished olive wood. He and the young priest Theophanes were drinking wine together and, as far as I could tell, discussing religious music.

"No, no!" Theophanes was protesting, as I opened the door. "You don't *want* a lot of emotive colouring in a hymn: you want simplicity and dignity, a sense of noble antiquity. The hearer should be moved without . . . oh." He'd noticed me. "Has the Pterophoros given any orders?" he asked anxiously, getting to his feet.

I shook my head, watching Vindex, who'd also risen and was looking at me with a mixture of hope and apprehension.

"We discussed the situation, and agreed that you, sir, were innocent."

At this both men smiled, then grinned with relief.

"Why did the Pterophoros want to consult with you?" asked Theophanes. It was the same question I'd been asking myself. I could think of no answer except that, for all his disdain for slaves, Pachrates was willing to hear wisdom from anyone, and that he actually must have some respect for me. It is shameful, how that pleased me. When you're a slave, the respect of free men is precious.

"If there had been a case to answer, I could have informed my master," I said, to avoid giving any insult to a man who probably felt *he* had more right to be consulted than I did. "I know the city, too: I hoped that I could help. However –" I shrugged unhappily "– we have no clues as to who the real criminal could have been. Lord Pachrates fears that, without that knowledge, he will not be able to convince the public of your innocence, Julius Vindex. As long as you're suspected of having defiled the altar, your life will be in danger if you remain in Alexandria."

Vindex glowered, then sighed. "Well, as long as the temple declares that I am innocent . . . to tell the truth, I'd be glad to leave Alexandria." He snorted. "Your city hates the Gabinians, but have you ever thought what it's like to be in charge of those brutes? To be hated by the men and by the citizens as well, to spend every day in shouting and bullying and anger, and to be afraid to leave the palace quarter at night? No . . ." He began to smile. "If I leave Alexandria, I can go home and reassure my sister in person. Then I can rejoin my legion. Jupiter, who wouldn't rather fight for Caesar than bully a pack of shopkeepers! Your goddess is good!"

I sighed: I'd been hoping that he'd be more forthcoming about his suspicions if he thought it would prevent him from being sent home. Clearly a vain hope.

"Well," I said resignedly, "I am glad that an innocent man won't suffer."

I unbuckled his sword-belt, which I was still wearing over my shoulder, and offered it to him. He came over and took it, then hefted it a moment in his hands, staring at me. "You're a public slave?" he asked.

I nodded. "Of long standing."

"In Massalia public slaves clean the streets," remarked Vindex. "They wouldn't consult with high priests – or walk onto a sword blade to save a man from a lynch mob."

"I have cleaned the streets," I told him. "After riots."

It took a moment, but he understood that, and nodded. Then, unexpectedly, he pulled the sword-belt round so that he could get at the purse, which was clipped to the leather just in front of the scabbard. "On thinking about it, I believe you may have saved my life and reputation, Peridromon," he said, unclipping it. "Here." He handed it to me. "It's not as much as I'd like, but it's all I have with me – and even though you don't seem very servile, you can probably use money as much as any other slave."

I caught myself licking my lips. Oh, yes, like most slaves, I have my little savings-hoard, and my hopes of one day buying my freedom: I can always use money. "Thank you, sir," I said, managing to preserve some dignity, and not pour the contents out to inspect them at once. "I wasn't expecting this. In fact, I came here to see if you'd like me to deliver your letter."

Vindex smiled, went over to the writing table, and picked up a sealed letter. "Here it is. Take it to my commander, and tell him how things stand. Play it right, and he'll tip you."

I nodded, took the letter, and tucked it into the front of my tunic. If I played it right, his commander might give a hint who was guilty. But I'd try one more ploy on Vindex himself first. "Is there anyone else you'd like me to speak to, sir?" I asked innocently.

"Oh . . . my friend Lucius Terentius, if he's around at headquarters. Tall man, brown hair and a scar on his sword hand; he's from Gallia Narbonensis. Nobody else."

That didn't sound like a suspect. I sighed again, then nodded and started for the door.

"Oh," said Vindex again, and the forced-casual note in his voice brought me up short, "you might tell Lord Potheinos that I'm going to have to leave Alexandria. He's one of the king's men, and I was invited to a party at his house a few days from now. It's a big house on the Canopic canal."

"I know it," I told him. "I'll deliver your message."

"Good. Thank you."

I went out, then walked slowly down the covered walkway and around the shrine of Isis into the public courtyard. I could smell the altar even before I reached it, and when I emerged from the portico into the afternoon sun, I could see that it was drenched with perfumed oils and covered with incense. The doors of the shrine were closed now, and the statue of the goddess was hidden. The crowds had done what they could to appease the goddess, then gone.

I sat down on the steps of the shrine and shook the contents of Vindex's purse into my hand. Twenty-nine drachmae. Well. Pretty good for a sum he just happened to have on him, but I wasn't going to be free any time soon. A healthy slave costs about three hundred; more if he can read and write, as I can. Just as well, really: I couldn't imagine what I'd do if I were free. I would miss the streets and markets horribly.

Potheinos. I knew who he was, of course: a royal treasurer with the rank of First Friend to the king. As Vindex had said, he had a big house on the Canopic Canal, and it was something of a landmark in that part of town. Unless I was mistaken, it had a large garden, backing on that canal. Probably there was an ornamental marsh – full of frogs, as they all were at this time of year.

Pachrates was right: there was no tribunal to which I could bring an accusation. It was entirely possible that Potheinos had been acting for the Bastard himself. After all, the Bastard *wanted* the Gabinians in Alexandria. He would find it very inconvenient if they collected their commander's ten thousand talents and went home. If he could take steps to ensure that the sum kept melting away even as it was collected and enrich himself in the process, he'd be very pleased with himself.

I glanced at the closed shrine behind me, then put the money back in the purse. I clipped the purse to the thong around my neck, next to my licence, and tucked it under my tunic so that there would be no misunderstandings when I delivered Vindex's letter. I would deliver the message to Potheinus as well, and leave him to the justice of Isis.

THE WINGS OF ISIS

Marilyn Todd

It would not be a volume about ancient Egypt without at least one story about Cleopatra. The Cleopatra we all know from history was in fact Cleopatra VII, daughter of Ptolemy Auletes. She ruled alongside her brother, Ptolemy XIII, until he expelled her from Egypt in 48 BC and, like her father, she turned to Rome for help.

Marilyn Todd is best known for her series of audacious historical whodunnits featuring the Roman courtesan Claudia Seferius, who first appeared in I, Claudia *(1995).*

"So then."

With two clicks of the imperial fingers, the hand-maidens fell back in a wave, but it took an imperial glare before Kames, Head of the Queen's Bodyguard, retreated his men out of earshot as well. Cleopatra had to lift her head to look into the eyes of her Captain of Archers.

"What are they saying about me this time, Benet? That the Queen speaks nine languages fluently and can't say no in any one of them?"

Spies, deep undercover, kept her abreast of the scheming and plotting among her so-called trusted Council. Feedback from the common people was no less important.

Benet swallowed his smile. "Nothing of the sort, your Royal Highness. Your people are behind you all the way in –" He paused, ostensibly to adjust his swordbelt. "– In Egypt's alliance with Rome."

"Your tact will make you a general some day."

And a good general at that, Cleopatra decided. Benet was a born tactician, intelligent, brave and not too dishonest. Above all, he was that rarest of breeds, he was loyal.

The eagle of Rome was casting a shadow across virtually the whole of the civilized world. Iberia to Asia Minor, Libya to the Black Sea. Now that Julius Caesar had his sights set on the great prize of Egypt, the pickings were rich for, say, an ambitious young Captain of Archers for whom the matter of allegiance rated low on his list of priorities.

So far, Benet had shown no desire to serve himself above his country. But it would be foolish to take such loyalty for granted . . .

Boom, boom, boom-a-doom-a-dum-dum. The pounding of the drums, soft and insistent, cut short the briefing.

"We'll talk later," she told him.

Information could wait.

Mighty Isis could not.

Boom, boom, boom-a-doom-a-dum-dum.

The memory of those lazy drumbeats would stay with Cleopatra for the rest of her life. They encapsulated the point when she walked into the temple a queen – *and walked out a goddess*.

From this moment on, Cleopatra was to be worshipped as Isis incarnate. It was official. She was now the Great Mother, protectress of the Pharaoh, goddess of healing, fertility and magic. Ah, yes. Never underestimate the power of magic, she thought. Rising from the throne of solid gold as the ceremony drew to its close, Cleopatra felt the brush of the goddess' wings on her face. And the wings were beating in triumph.

As she made her way across the cool marble floor of the temple, she passed Yntef the shaven-headed high priest, sweating under his leopard skin, his eyes still unfocussed from his recent trance. Renenutet, the priestess of Bast dressed as the cat-headed goddess, made obeisance. As did Tamar, Hathor's priestess, wearing the ceremonial mask of the cow. Temple musicians lined the aisle, their harps and reed flutes playing the Queen out. The choir sang softly – young women, whose voices had been trained from early childhood to sing as sweetly as the larks which soared above the broad wheatfields of the Nile and lifted the spirits of those who laboured to bring home the harvest.

Glancing back over her shoulder, Cleopatra committed the moment to memory. The temple regalia, the black bowl of divination, the fat sacred cats, the dark ceiling studded with bright silver stars. Flaming torches high on the walls brought brightly painted frescoes to life, made them dance. Acrobats on the north wall, fishermen hauling home their nets on the south, Anubis weighing the heart of Osiris against the ostrich feather of truth on the east. Best of all was the fresh painting on the west wall: Cleopatra as Pharaoh. Let the Council take the bones out of that!

Boom, boom, boom-a-doom-a-dum-dum.

As the mighty cedarwood doors of the temple swung inwards, the Queen suddenly faltered. Priests and priestesses, acolytes, the crowd outside – all would naturally assume she had been blinded by shafts of brilliant white sunshine. They could not possibly know that, for an instant, Cleopatra had forgotten where she was. That, when she stepped into the light, she had been shocked by the alien world into which she had been propelled.

A world which babbled not only too fast, but in Latin.

A world where, in place of the calm, green waters of the life-giving Nile, the Tiber ran, brown and rancid, its lush banks long since vanished under warehouses and wharves. Despite the heat of the sunshine, she shivered. This was a world inhabited by fair-skinned people whose women were chattels, handed over from father to husband without rights, and whose men swaddled themselves in thick woollen togas, even in this merciless heat. There were other differences, too. These barbarians burned their dead. Bent their knee to feeble human gods in devotions which were no better than common horse-trading.

Yet these people ruled the world . . .

It had been easy, while Yntef conducted his ritual divination, the cloudy water swirling in the bowl beneath a film of warm and scented oil, to forget she was no longer in her beloved Alexandria, gazing out from her palace across the Great Sea, feeling its cool breeze brush her lips. Instead Cleopatra was in Rome. A city that, to many, represented the very heart of the enemy . . .

All eyes were upon the Egyptian Queen as she descended the temple steps. Precious stones had been woven into her heavy plaited wig. Amethysts, emeralds, sapphires and pearls, every facet reflecting back sunlight. Bangles and bracelets encircled ankles and arms. Each finger was adorned by a ring, as was each toe, and round her neck hung a shining pectoral of gold. There were times, and this was one of them, when Cleopatra could barely hold herself upright with the weight of the metal but, far from home, her people needed the reassurance of the pomp and the ceremony.

In short, they needed someone to look up to.

Someone to believe in, in these turbulent times.

At the foot of the steps, she held up a hand to stall her bodyguard and beckoned over her Captain of Archers. "You were about to tell me, Benet, what the people of Alexandria really feel about Cleopatra's liaison with the Roman dictator. Do they fear I am selling them out?"

Benet had still not grown accustomed to his Queen's forthright manner. It sat strangely at odds with the long-winded words of her political advisers, and he often wondered how she juggled court etiquette with her compulsion to drive straight to the core.

"Far from it," he replied quietly.

Across the flagged courtyard, shaded with acacias and sacred sycamore trees, Kames scowled his resentment at a mere captain's confidence with the young Queen.

"When Julius Caesar stormed the palace in Alexandria three years ago," Benet said, "your Majesty's people saw hope die in the dust of his four thousand troops."

"Go on," Cleopatra urged.

She was not blind to Kames' scowls. Benet indeed walked a tightrope, but not in the way Kames imagined. Noble from birth, as with everyone else in authority – Kames, included – the Captain of Archers was blessed with the common touch. An ability to tap into the Alexandrians' innermost feelings, secure their trust, assure them their confidences would not be betrayed. Perhaps, she reflected idly, this was because precious little of her own, highly interbred Macedonian blood ran through Benet's veins. Benet was a true-born Egyptian.

"By the time Rome trampled the city," he said, "our own Regency had betrayed its people twice over. First, with the coup which exiled your Majesty in Syria. Then by taking a stand against Rome, a force they could not hope to beat, instead of entering into negotiations. As a result, Egypt believed itself yoked to Rome's plough with no chance of salvation – until, oh munificent Ra! – the Queen smuggles herself to Caesar wrapped in a rug, and overnight the balance of power swings again!"

It hung unsaid that Julius Caesar imagined that, in Cleopatra, he would be manipulating a soft, sweet puppet queen . . .

"From the moment your son was born, your Majesty, the people have embraced Caesarion as Egypt's heir. Nothing, I promise, has changed in the ten months you have been absent."

Cleopatra darted a glance across to the boy who lay cradled in his nurse's arms, his rosebud lips slightly parted in sleep. Caesarion. Little Caesar. She smiled fondly. Who would suspect the child's exquisite public behaviour owed more to a splash of poppy juice on a sweetmeat than a well-trained royal disposition? Caesarion was a lusty two-year-old, with a lusty two-year-old's energy and a lusty two-year-old's lungs. His mother had no intention of curbing either. That boy was the future Pharaoh and his spirit would never be tamed. Indomitable through inheritance, that spirit would soar. *Higher than his father's eagle it would rise. And the breadth of its shadow would be unsurpassed* . . .

"You wouldn't lie to me, Benet?"

Why should the common masses back her, when half her Council rejected Caesarion's claim to royal blood and believed the Queen wielded far too much power as it was. Power, which should rightly be theirs –

The Captain of Archers looked deep into her eyes. "I would never lie to you, your Royal Highness."

He knew full well that the 18-year-old chit who had mounted the throne on Ptolemy's death had not proved the pliable young thing these shadowy figures had hoped. A truth the Roman Dictator had yet to discover . . .

"Good." She flashed Benet a wicked grin. "Because the last man who betrayed me died the Death of One Thousand Cuts, the first slicing off his treacherous tongue."

His eyes smiled. "A point I shall bear in mind in the future – *Holy Ra!*"

Cleopatra's head turned in the direction his and 50 others were turned. For once, she was unable to control her gasp of surprise. Renenutet, still wearing the silver mask of the cat, was standing, arms outstretched, on the roof of the House of Scribes. Her pleated linen gown billowed softly round her ankles in the sticky breeze.

"Renenutet!" The high priest's voice carried its full weight of authority. "Renenutet, in the name of Isis, I command you –"

The screams cut him off.

For a few ghastly seconds, Renenutet seemed to hang in the air. A white pleated cloud frozen against a backdrop of azure.

Then the billowing gown disappeared –

Kames was the first to react. In an instant, his soldiers had surrounded their Queen, tried to hustle her through the nearest doorway for safety.

"Don't be ridiculous," she snapped. "It's not me that needs helping, it's Renenutet. Kames, take some men and see if you can do anything for her. Benet. Go with him, if you will."

The Captain of Archers met her eye and nodded in mute understanding. If Renenutet's fall had proved fatal, it was from him that she wanted to hear it.

As the soldiers trotted off, their bronze helmets and greaves jangling, Cleopatra's instinct was for her child.

"Take Caesarion home," she instructed his nurse.

She must remove him at once from this tainted scene.

"No, wait."

It would not do to have Pharaoh run from a crisis. Even if he was only a babe and fast asleep!

"Tuck this into his clothing instead."

She handed his nurse the amulet Renenutet had given her earlier.

"The sacred amulet of Isis," the priestess had hissed, her voice barely recognizable under the silver cat mask.

Flushed with the priesthood's recognition of the Queen as Isis incarnate, the public attestation of their powerful support, Cleopatra had barely glanced at the tiny object when Renenutet pressed it into her palm.

"Set with carnelian," she'd whispered, "washed in a tincture of ankhamu flowers, fashioned from the trunk of a sacred sycamore tree."

This had been at the very start of today's ceremony, at the moment the priestess was supposed to pay homage to her Queen and nothing else. To cover the delay, Renenutet pretended to disengage the panther tail which hung at her waist from Cleopatra's gold belt, as though the two had become somehow entangled.

"Isis is the goddess from whom all being arose," she murmured, her eyes glittering behind the metal mask. "From her feathers came light. From the brush of her wings came the air. She is the Enchantress, the Speaker of Spells, who protecteth the living and extendeth her protection even beyond, unto eternity."

Oh, Renenutet. You should have kept the amulet, Cleopatra thought, picturing the nightmare vision of Renenutet frozen in space. You should have kept the amulet to protect your own soul from self-destruction.

"Let the wings of Isis cover you instead, little Caesar," she whispered, stroking her son's soft, dark hair. She bent to kiss his cool, dry forehead and wondered how long the effects of the poppy juice would last. As she straightened, Kames and Benet came striding across the shaded courtyard, their white kilts swinging in unison. Their expressions said it all.

"I deeply regret, the priestess Renenutet has already begun her long journey to the West," Benet said softly.

The two men knelt beside the Pool of Purification and allowed the priests to splash their eyes with sacred water to wash away the contamination of having gazed upon a corpse. Cleopatra felt no disrespect. To have deferred the task would have been to taint the Queen with their polluted sight.

Poor Renenutet, she thought. A suicide. Whose imperfect soul was destined to wander the dark paths of the Underworld for ever. "I suppose we shall never know what drove her to take such drastic action," she added sadly.

"On the contrary," Benet said. "I know exactly what drove the poor woman across the Far Horizon."

He hesitated. Pursed his lips.

"Someone else's hands," he said quietly. "Renenutet, I regret to inform you, was murdered."

Whether for business or pleasure, the Field of Mars on which the temple complex stood was arguably one of the busiest places in Rome outside the Forum. Sited on a bend in the Tiber, it was home to seven other temples, as well as a whole host of public baths, theatres, race courses and libraries, offering works of art to admire, tombs to revere, groves to picnic in, trees for the children to climb, steps on which bearded philosophers could debate the meaning of life and open spaces for athletics. The air was never silent. Until now. Snake charmers stopped playing their flutes. Beggars' bowls ceased to rattle. Pedlars stopped hawking. Only the jackdaws continued to chatter.

As the Dictator's concubine, ensconced in the very villa from which his lawful wife had been evicted, Cleopatra was accustomed to being gawped at by the populace. Suddenly, like wasps to honey, they swarmed to the scene of the drama, but their interest, thank Horus, lay not in the dead priestess, rather in the bejewelled Egyptian whore. Cleopatra could handle that standing on her head. No person, living or dead, had ever witnessed a crack in her armour. They certainly would not do so today.

However! As the consort of the most powerful man in the Roman Republic, she was also expecting a different kind of attention. Any minute, Caesar's legionaries would arrive.

She turned to Kames. "I assume from your contemptuous tutting that you disagree with Benet's conclusion?"

"Your Majesty, we *all* saw what happened," Kames replied. "There was no one else or we'd have seen them. With respect, that roof's flatter than the sole of my boot."

The Queen turned to her young Captain of Archers and raised one finely plucked eyebrow in query.

Benet inhaled. Released his breath slowly. "Because of the angle at which the body was lying, because of *where* it was lying, close to the wall, because the blood which had dried round the head wound doesn't correspond with the copious amount of fresh blood inside her mask – all that adds up to only one thing. Renenutet was murdered."

Kames' bluster was shot out of the water. At last, he understood what the Queen saw in Benet. Drawing himself up to his full height, he cleared his throat and squared his shoulders.

"Benet's deductions are correct," he admitted. "Renenutet leapt off with arms outstretched, yet the body was found with one arm pinned beneath it. Likewise, when a person jumps they make a trajectory."

"A trajectory?" she queried.

"Imagine throwing a javelin or spear from that roof, your Highness. This is the same principle. The body lands at the end of that arc. Renenutet, as Benet said, lies close in."

Kames dropped to his knees, his forehead touching the ground.

"Your Majesty, as a soldier I should have recognized the signs –"

How fortunate, Cleopatra thought, to have two such pillars to lean on. Benet, alert to nuances, unafraid to put forward an unpalatable theory. Kames, man enough to admit his mistakes. *Or clever enough to know he could no longer get away with the suicide theory . . .?*

"Don't whip yourself, Kames," she said, bidding him rise.

"You fell into the same trap we all did. You took Renenutet's death at face value."

Hobnail boots echoed on the Via Triumphalis, the rhythmic clink-clink-clink of scale armour, the jangle of bronze medallions as the legionaries drew closer. Grief and shock would no doubt set in later, but Pharaoh was raised to consider emotions an indulgence – never more so in a crisis. As the centurion halted his troops, Cleopatra summarized the points in her mind.

The priestess Renenutet had been murdered.

Renenutet . . . priestess of Bast.

Bast . . . the gentle daughter of Isis.

Isis . . . . Protectress of the Pharaoh.

Cleopatra steepled her fingers. More crimes than murder had been committed today. Sacrilege, for one. The sanctuary of the Great Goddess had been defiled by the spilling of blood. Furthermore, the outrage of Bast had been invoked by the assault on her priestess.

But, worse than that, by embroiling the Queen in this apparent suicide, someone had tried to pull the wool over Cleopatra's almond eyes.

And that was their biggest mistake.

In retrospect, she should have realized Caesar would not let it go at a lowly centurion.

Cleopatra studied the corded muscles of the man dismounting from his pure white stallion, noted the purple stripe on his tunic which pronounced him patrician. He had a strong face, a handsome face, and in spite of herself a shiver of desire rippled the length of her backbone. Contrary to rumours put about by certain viziers, the Queen had only ever taken one lover, and that had been a matter of expediency. The gods do not bestow virginity for it to be taken lightly. The night she had had herself smuggled through enemy lines in a rug, knowing that if she was discovered her own kinsmen would cut her throat like a dog, was the night she had given herself to the Roman Dictator.

Fast-track negotiations, some might say.

The Regency had usurped the throne. Cleopatra was in exile, Alexandria was in the hands of the rioters, the palace in the hands of the Romans. To survive, she had had to act fast. Her first move was to throw her army of Syrian mercenaries behind Caesar. Afterwards –? Well, what greater assurance of Egypt's allegiance than the Queen's precious virginity?

Men. Such fools, she thought. In seducing the young Cleopatra, Caesar believed he was annexing the rich lands of the Nile through the back door, a mission he could not hope to accomplish by force. But with his entrenched Roman attitudes towards women, he had not stopped to contemplate the alternative. That she might be using him . . .

Within days, Cleopatra achieved her first goal. She conceived. In the simple act of giving him an heir, something Caesar was sorely lacking, the tables turned. By the time Caesarion was of an age to rule, his father would be dead. *And Rome would be annexed to Egypt, not the other way around!*

In a journey which had taken her from royal princess to queen to pharaoh to goddess, Cleopatra quite literally held the power of the world in her hands.

The power felt good.

Nothing – and no one – would be allowed to change that.

Which wasn't to say her blood could not be stirred by a lopsided smile here or a bunched muscle there! Benet, although he did not know it, was one such contender. The patrician dismounting from his stallion, another.

"Your Highness," he murmured, making obeisance Egyptian fashion.

"It is good to see you again, Mark Antony."

Nothing would come of these flirtations, of course. Cleopatra was neither stupid nor reckless – she had Caesar in the palm of her hand, and with it the eagle of Rome. But Caesar was old, he was bald and, let's be frank, when it came to the art of love, his was more a quick sketch than an intricate fresco. Other décor could still be admired.

"Caesar salutes you," he said, rising, "and offers his escort to the Queen, that she may return to the villa without incurring unwarranted scrutiny or gossip."

The weight of so much gold jewellery was exhausting her, the heat from the wig almost unbearable. But when Cleopatra smiled at Mark Antony, you would think she had just risen from her bath, calm and refreshed.

"The Queen sends her grateful thanks to the mighty Caesar," she replied.

Heavenly Horus, she would need all her diplomatic skills here! Strictly speaking, she was a foreigner on Roman soil, subject to Roman law. If the most powerful man on earth decreed she must leave the Field of Mars, then leave she must and in the three years they'd been lovers Cleopatra had never gone head-to-head against the Dictator's wishes. Let him think he was in control. Illusion was everything.

"But the Queen has no desire to impinge upon Caesar's generosity," she told Mark Antony. "The Queen shall be remaining at the temple."

The tall patrician blinked. "Is that wise, your Majesty?" Likewise, only a fool would go against *Cleopatra's* wishes. Julius Caesar would not wish to lose his hold on the Nile's treasures just because some clot upset his mistress!

"Wise is a contentious word, Mark Antony."

She linked her arm through his and led him to the shade of the Pool of Peace, where papyrus plants swayed in the hot, sultry breeze. The silvery sound of sistrums filled the air and fragrant incense filtered out from the temple.

"Was it wise of the Queen," she asked, as handmaidens fluttered up with plates of fresh fruit, "to devalue Egypt's currency by one third in order to keep export sales strong? Or a gamble which happened to pay off? Was it wise of her to have her portrait stamped on our coinage, to prove to the world that Egypt's economy was stable in the hands of a woman? Or was it nothing more than female vanity?"

Cleopatra dabbled her hands in the cool, clear water.

"For that matter, was it wise of the Queen to muster an army of mercenaries to fight her own brother? Or simply the banner-waving of a power-mad female with no hope of success?"

"Life, I agree, is entirely a matter of perspective," he said, a twinkle lighting his eyes. "Which is precisely why I am now offering my services to escort you personally to the safety of Caesar's villa."

Cleopatra bit into a peach. "Your concern is touching, Mark Antony. Unfortunately, it would be disrespectful for me to leave until the rites are over."

When the Roman general smiled, the lines round his eyes fell into deep crinkles. "The ceremony finished an hour ago," he pointed out, selecting a cherry.

"To honour Isis, yes, but we have yet to venerate the cobra goddess and sing the hymn to Nut," she replied, and watched as he bought himself time by slicing an apple.

Mark Antony had not bought the lie. True, he was ignorant of the rites conducted here, but he was keenly aware that a surprisingly large number of Roman women made devotions at this shrine. Isis had become popular in Rome, more so since the Queen's arrival last September, when additional aspects had been added. Bast, for instance. Hathor the cow. Plus numerous other female deities who, together, presided over motherhood and love, beauty and healing, all the issues important to women, Roman or otherwise.

Mark Antony might not know the details. But he knew, dammit, when a ceremony was over and done with. Selecting a date, the Roman general changed tack.

"Listen to the baying crowd," he said. "Perhaps the Queen does not appreciate how much resentment her royal presence causes in the city . . .?"

"The Queen knows *exactly* how Republicans view the concubine and her bastard son," she said tartly. "Keep the mistress – flaunt her, even – is the general consensus. After all, the Queen of Egypt is a prize for Caesar to parade, is she not? Just don't play house with the whore."

Another lie. Marital scandal was a minor issue, the cause of gossip rather than resentment. The real fear among the Senate – Mark Anthony included – was for the future of their hard-won Republic. They suspected Cleopatra of dripping poison in the Dictator's ear every night to serve her own ends.

They were not wrong.

Come next March – no later than April – she would have Julius Caesar declare himself King of Rome, with herself crowned as Queen. Upon his death (and who knows how quickly that might come to pass) Caesarion would inherit the title.

Then all of Rome's dominions would belong to Egypt –

The scent of the oil of marjoram drenching her wig wafted in the sultry air. The gems glistened like raindrops.

"As to the mood of the crowd, my answer is this," she said carefully. "Rome likes its spectacles. I say, let the people enjoy this one."

Renenutet was murdered on the sacred soil of Isis wearing the insignia of Bast. Now that Cleopatra was to be venerated as Isis, this comprised a triple sacrilege and the perpetrator must be punished. Pharaoh could not simply walk away this afternoon. It was her duty to stay and see justice served. In any case, she thought sadly, she owed it to Renenutet to find her killer. Renenutet should not journey into the West without the feather of truth on her shoulder. The journey was long enough as it was.

She held out a small, sandalled foot.

The sparring light in the general's eyes died. She inched her foot out further. His expression darkened. There was no mistaking the Queen's message.

Or defying it . . .

As Mark Antony knelt to kiss the royal toe, anger and outrage pulsated from every Roman pore. He! an aristocrat! a general! one of the world's greatest power brokers! had been . . . *dismissed!* There was a very different glint in his eye as he rose.

She watched him stride away, barking orders to the centurion to keep the crowd back. One day, she reflected, this man would return for more of the same. His type always did.

And Cleopatra would be waiting.

Inside the sanctuary, prayers were being said for Renenutet's journey into the Afterlife. Yntef, Tamar and the rest of the attendants had lost no time in shaving their eyebrows. They would have done this had just a temple cat died, much less one of Bast's holy disciples.

The atmosphere inside the sanctuary pulsed with emotion.

Cleopatra glanced at the sky. The sticky, midsummer heat could not last and the first rumble of thunder could be heard in the distance. Excellent. She would be able to interpret the storm as Bast's anger made manifest. Thunder would be the cat goddess' growling, lightning her ferocious spitting. Magic and superstition played a pivotal role in Egyptian life. Only a fool would fail to capitalize.

"Benet. Kames." She beckoned them over. "No one is to suspect this was not a straightforward suicide." If the Romans sniffed murder, this would become a civil investigation. Much better to keep these things in-house. "We will deal with this quietly, between the three of us. Do either of you have any clues as to who killed her?"

"None," Benet admitted. "But we know Renenutet was killed inside the temple."

Cleopatra's eyes flashed. Was there no end to the insult? "How can you be sure?"

"There is only one place on this site where people must bare their feet, even your Majesty. Inside the sanctuary. Renenutet was barefoot."

Cleopatra picked up a sloe-eyed kitten mewing at her feet. The kitten began to rattle like a chariot over cobblestones, snuggling its head into her collarbone.

"Anything else?" she asked.

"Dried blood around the head wound suggests Renenutet died an hour before the simulated suicide —"

"How do you know?"

"Dead bodies don't bleed," Kames explained. "The blood was probably that of a chicken's, poured into the mask at the last moment to make it look fresh. Also, her skin was cool."

Slowly, Cleopatra laid down the kitten. If Renenutet had spoken to her at the beginning of the ceremony, when she passed across the amulet, but had been dead for some time after Benet examined the body, there was only one conclusion.

She died *during* the ritual. Meaning the killer had contrived to use the Queen of Egypt as his alibi.

Another mistake.

Beside the Pool of Peace, with butterflies and bees swarming round the fragrant flowers in the urns and thunderclaps booming ever closer, Cleopatra's memory travelled backwards in time.

It returned her to the soaring temple. Closing her eyes, she saw its star-studded ceiling, just as she had seen it earlier, the dynamic wall paintings flickering beneath the flaming torches. In her mind she once more inhaled the sacred incense, a rich blend of frankincense and myrrh, cedar and gum arabic, juniper, cinnamon and sweet flag. Her ears replayed the lazy beat of the drums – *boom, boom, boom-a-doom-a-dum-dum*. She was mounting the dais again, only everything now moved in slow motion.

"*Homage to thee, Isis,*" the choir sang, "*whose names are manifold and whose forms are holy. Gracious is thy face.*"

At the time, Cleopatra had hardly listened, concerned only that she had won over so powerful a body as the priesthood. With their support, the vipers in her Council could scheme until the sun set in the North and still not get their hands on the throne.

"*You are the north wind that bloweth in our nostrils. Your word is truth.*"

Beside the pool, Cleopatra's head pounded. From the heat, from the weight of the gold, from the hot heavy wig. From wondering how on earth Renenutet could have been killed beneath her very nose. She concentrated on re-living the ceremony . . .

"*O, Isis of a thousand names, who watcheth over us.*"

The nightingales had finished their chant. Silence had descended over the sanctuary. The flames on the torches had been dimmed. From a side door, a score of acolytes entered, each carrying a small gilded cage in reverent, out-stretched hands. Gliding in long pleated skirts, they mounted the steps of the platform. The cages were lined up, side by side on the floor, the eyes of the occupants flashing like fire in the gloom. With a synchronized click, the catches were sprung and twenty temple cats tumbled on to the dais in honour of Bast. Renenutet, Cleopatra remembered, had gone forwards to feed them.

She recalled, too, how Renenutet and Tamar assisted the High Priest in his divination. Supporting him when he fell into his trance. At his side when he pronounced how beneficent Anubis had shown him how the heart of the Pharaoh was happy, how the heart of Osiris was glad, and how the two halves of Egypt would always be one.

"May Isis embrace you in her peace, Yntef," Cleopatra had replied solemnly, using the *ankh* to make the ritual gesture over his head. "For the ka of her High Priest is holy and Anubis has shown him the truth. The heart of Isis is full of joy at her servant's devotion."

Translation: Yntef would be richly rewarded for throwing his support behind the throne.

She pursed her lips in concentration. Remembering how Yntef, unsteady still from his trance, had been helped away by Tamar as Renenutet bestowed upon the imperial wig the sacred crown of Isis, the solar disc cradled between the twin horns of the moon. The priestess' breathing beneath the replica mask had been laboured, Cleopatra recalled. But she was certainly very much alive –

"Your Majesty?" Benet's shadow fell over the pool.

"Ah, Benet, just the man!" The royal headache had vanished. The gold weighed as a pectoral of feathers round her neck, the plaited wig a gossamer veil.

"Have you worked out how the trick was done?"

The Captain of Archers returned the smile. "I have indeed, your Royal Highness."

"Good," she said. "Because if you can tell me how, I can tell you where and when."

Between them, it should tell her who.

The how had been ingenious. The trick as audacious as Cleopatra had ever known.

"The key," Benet explained, "is a metal spike hammered into the brickwork at the junction of the wall of the House of Scribes and its flat roof. Wrapped round the spike were these." He held out a few coarse fibres of hemp from a rope.

An elaborate pantomime had been staged, he explained, which hinged upon no lesser person than the Queen of Egypt witnessing what was supposed to have been a dramatic suicide. Renenutet on the roof, her arms outstretched. Renenutet jumping to her death.

The killer, though, had reckoned without Benet.

Benet was the Queen's spy and spies never take one damn thing at face value.

"The murder was carefully planned," he told her. "During the ceremony, that spike was hammered into the brickwork and a short piece of rope attached to it, with a noose at one end."

Cleopatra's heart twisted. When that first lazy drumbeat began, Renenutet had no idea her thread of life had less than an hour to unravel. Except . . . the priestess of Bast had sensed danger! It had been with force and urgency that the sacred amulet of Isis had been pressed into the Queen's hand. At the time, Cleopatra dismissed it as a token of Renenutet's acceptance of herself as Queen of Earth and Heaven. She should have realized. No priestess, especially one of Renenutet's standing, would need to pretend her sacred panther's tail had become entangled, had the gift been open and above board! Renenutet had passed the amulet in secret.

"Now I shall tell you when and where Renenutet was killed," she said.

After she passed Cleopatra the amulet, the ceremony had continued as scheduled. The choir extolled the virtues of Isis (in other words a public proclamation of the priesthood's support), then the lights dimmed.

That was the moment Renenutet's thread was severed.

As she slipped out of the sanctuary to fetch the procession from the Sacred Cattery, two people were waiting. As one snatched off the silver mask, the other threw a sheet over her head.

"What odds her skull was crushed by her own metal mask?" Cleopatra said. "The sheet would contain any splatters of blood."

The killers had no time to waste cleaning floors. One was already clad in ritual robes. All she had to do was don Renenutet's mask and run swiftly to the Sacred Cattery. Only a few seconds would have been lost and while she was fetching the feline procession, her accomplice carried the body away, arranging it beneath the House of Scribes.

"She?" Benet queried.

"Definitely," Cleopatra confirmed. "The killer had to impersonate Renenutet for the remainder of the ceremony. Only a servant of Bast could possibly have known the routine."

In due course, when the temple cats had been released from their cages on the dais and the lights went up again, who would suspect that Bast's representative was not Renenutet? It was only, thinking back, that Cleopatra remembered how laboured the priestess' breathing had been when she lowered the horned headdress on the royal wig. The killer's hands had shaken slightly as well, she recalled. Not from the heat or exertion. But from nervousness!

"Afterwards," Benet said, "the impersonator climbed up on the roof. She slipped the noose from the rope round her ankle. Waited until her Majesty was looking. And jumped."

No wonder Renenutet seemed to hang in the sky, Cleopatra thought. That was precisely what had happened. The rope suspended the killer in mid air. Dangling like a fish on a line.

"The accomplice at the upstairs window in the House of Scribes threw another noose around her wrist," Benet said, "cut the rope around her ankle and hauled her inside. Then they filled the cat mask with animal blood and stuffed it on Renenutet's head. Plenty of time before anyone else arrived at the scene."

For several moments, Cleopatra listened to the thunder, watched jagged spears of lightning cut through the charcoal sky. Lost in contemplation, she did not even notice as the first heavy drops of rain fell. Finally, she summoned the Head of her Bodyguard and together all three withdrew into the shelter of the painted portico.

"Kames, I want you to observe the priestesses of Bast and, discreetly, mark you, isolate the one with rope burns on her wrist and ankle. I suspect they are covered by bandages."

Cleopatra almost regretted doubting the head of her bodyguard's loyalty. Then again, to make assumptions about even her most trustworthy cohorts was to open herself up to danger.

"Her accomplice will be a priest or a scribe," she added. "Someone with regular access to both buildings, strong enough to heave corpses around and he'll probably have a bloodstained sheet beneath his bed."

The killers would not have expected events to move so swiftly. They would not have needed to take extra precautions at this stage.

In less than an hour, Kames returned. "A novice priestess called Berenice and her lover, Ity, have been quietly removed from their duties," he said. "Shall I send them to the Royal Torturer for confession?"

Cleopatra shook her head. "Have your men smuggle them out of the temple, take them into the hills. Oh, and Kames."

"Your Majesty."

"Be sure they bury the bodies deep." As he left, she turned to her Captain of Archers. "Benet, I want you to remove a few handfuls of silver from the Temple Treasury, also a small but precious statuette. Have it put about that Berenice and Ity stole them and ran off."

Caesar might not agree, but this temple was every bit a part of Egypt as Alexandria itself. Pharaoh's justice would be served – only today it would be served in secret. Only a few hand-picked soldiers would ever know Berenice and Ity had killed Renenutet, and she imagined the ill-fated lovers would be regretting the deed long before Kames' men had finished with them.

"Why?" Benet asked. "Why did they kill Renenutet?"

Cleopatra glanced across at her son, struggling out of his drugged sleep, and pictured the amulet tucked inside his clothing. An amulet set with carnelians, washed in the tincture of ankhamu flowers and fashioned from the trunk of a sacred sycamore tree . . .

"I doubt we shall ever know, Benet," she said, tapping him cheerfully on the arm. "Now, off you go and rob the Treasury, there's a good boy."

She snapped her fingers and two handmaidens scampered forwards. "Fetch my litter," she ordered. "We shall return to Caesar's villa."

I do believe Mark Antony has stood in the pouring rain for long enough.

Five days afterwards, Cleopatra was seated next to Caesar as guest of honour at the games inaugurated to commemorate Rome's victories in Gaul. As befitting the Queen of the Upper and Lower Nile, she wore a gown shot with silver threads, a headdress set with amethysts and enough gold jewellery to turn Midas green with envy. The one hundred thousand Romans crammed into the surrounding tiers ought not to be disappointed, she thought happily.

Syrian lions roared from the pits. Baited bulls bellowed, bears snarled, wolves howled, elephants trumpeted their rage. First in the arena, a half-starved tiger, to be pitted against a trident and net. The human did not stand a chance. After that, beast fight followed beast fight in rapid succession, and Cleopatra's gorge rose at the senseless shedding of blood, the death of so many splendid specimens.

Then it was the turn of the gladiators, their swords and lances gleaming in the sun. She watched, impassive, as steel clashed against steel. Blood spurted, bodies writhed, heels kicked up clouds of sand as Roman fought Roman to the death. From the corner of her almond eye, Cleopatra watched Caesar size up the crowd. How much did they back him? he was wondering. How far they would follow him? Would they accept a monarchy in place of their hard-earned Republic?

As always, Cleopatra pretended not to care. She slipped her small hand into Caesar's. Showed the people – and the Senate – that it was Caesar she loved. Only Caesar . . .

To the backdrop of trumpets, attendants dressed as gods of the Underworld hauled the mangled corpses away in chains, threw fresh sand over the blood. The crowd was insatiable.

Stamping their feet, they bayed for the next treat, the despatching of murderers and rapists by wild animals.

There seemed to be some activity at one of the gates. Guards conferred hastily. Glanced at the Queen. Conferred again. Then one of them made a decision. Marching over to Cleopatra, he pressed his clenched fist to his breast in salute.

"One of the prisoners insists there has been a mistake, my lady. We don't believe this is the case, but – well, he is Egyptian and swears your Majesty will vouch for him."

"Bring him over," she said, in her perfect Latin.

Two guards frogmarched the prisoner across. One eye was closed, his body bruised where he'd put up a fight.

"Your Highness," he gabbled, "tell them they've got the wrong man. Last night some thugs set upon me and the next thing I know, I'm here. In a cage full of murderers awaiting execution."

Whatever did you expect? she wondered silently. You plant seeds of dissension in the minds of two idealistic young lovers and incite them to murder Renenutet under the Queen's nose. She leaned closer, pretending to examine his features. Features that fully expected to kill, get away with it – and then be shown the Queen's mercy.

"I have never seen this man before in my life," she told the guard.

"But your Majesty –! It's me, Yntef! Your High Priest."

Cleopatra smiled pityingly at Caesar. "My High Priest is on a boat bound for Alexandria," she murmured. "To take up his new promotion."

Let's face it, one shaven-headed Egyptian looks the same as another to a disinterested Roman. Only the temple servants would know that Yntef had been replaced. And even they would not know the reason . . .

She watched impassively as Yntef was dragged away, protesting at the top of his voice. The crowd loved it. They would love it more, she thought, if they knew the full story.

Her mind travelled back to the beginning.

Coincidence that it was here, in Rome, that the priesthood chose to throw their support behind Cleopatra? Hardly. Had this happened in Egypt, that would have been different. But it all took place in the back of beyond, and why?

Because the priesthood did not back Cleopatra at all.

That most powerful of organizations had thrown its weight behind the traitors within her own Council. Oh, yes. The bastards planned to have her assassinated in Rome, knowing damn well the finger of blame would point to the Senate, who hated Cleopatra with a vengeance.

Just before the ceremony, Renenutet must have discovered Yntef's treachery. That was the reason she pressed the amulet into her hands. Set with Isis' sacred carnelians, washed in a tincture of the goddess's consecrated ankhamu flowers and fashioned out of the trunk of her sacred sycamore tree, no object was more holy, more sanctified, more precious in Renenutet's eyes than that which invoked the Great Mother's protection.

The amulet had been the warning. That was why she'd passed it in secret. But that loyalty cost Renenutet her life.

Yntef knew she was on to him. Enlisting the help of two sympathizers to the cause (heaven knows how many more vipers there were in the nest, but Benet's skills would root them out and Kames' men would do the rest), the High Priest was forced to eliminate Renenutet in a way that would not arouse suspicion. Set some distance from the temple, the House of Scribes allowed ample time for his accomplices to stage their pantomime then pretend to come rushing up with the others.

Once Cleopatra realized who had killed the priestess of Bast, the motive behind the murder was obvious. Yntef would have known if anyone other than Renenutet had been holding him as he came out of his trance. That meant Yntef was in on it.

Oh, dear Yntef. All those hymns and blessings and public acceptance of the Queen as Isis incarnate, how they backfired. You see, it's all very well to pretend the priesthood backs Cleopatra – provided Cleopatra is dead. Now they've made their support public, the priesthood has no choice but to stand by their decision. The die has been cast. The Queen wins. Best of all, Yntef's failure will have created division among the priesthood and the Council in a way that Cleopatra could only ever have dreamed of. Each would now suspect the others of selling them out. Trust among the conspirators would crumble like sand.

Instinctively, her hand reached for the amulet round her neck. In bestowing Isis's protection, Renenutet had saved the Queen's life at the expense of her own, but she would not go unrewarded. Plans for a sumptuous tomb were already being drawn by the Queen's Architect.

The rewards also extended to the spiritual plane.

Two of Renenutet's killers lay in unmarked graves, where, without proper burial rites, their souls were doomed to wander the Halls of the Lost for eternity. Now the third member of the trio was poised to look retribution square in the face. Kames' men had done well in delivering him to the Roman arena.

With a snarl, a panther bounded into the arena.

Bribes had ensured the beast had been tormented with prods, whips and firebrands, and it had also been starved and denied water. Yntef screamed. Behind her, the crowd cheered and stomped on the wooden boards of the amphitheatre, unaware of what Yntef was seeing.

The figure of Bast incarnate. Leaping to avenge her devoted disciple.

As the panther sat back and licked its bloody lips, Cleopatra felt a brush of soft, white feathers against her cheek. Once again, the wings of Isis were beating in victory.

BRINGING THE FOOT

Kate Ellis

Now we leap a period of some 1,850 years. Had we gone back in time that would take us back to the time of Senusert III, in Keith Taylor's story. But we've come forward to the Napoleonic era and the rediscovery of the treasures of ancient Egypt. The early Egyptologists included Jean-François Champollion and Giovanni Belzoni and it is the latter whose exploits are the basis of the following story.

Kate Ellis is a former drama student and playwright who turned to writing detective novels with The Merchant's House *(1998), which combined her interest in archaeology and crime. So does the following.*

They called my husband The Great Belzoni, and that name described him well. Six foot six and possessing the strength of ten men, Giovanni Belzoni was my world and we held to each other in poverty and riches . . . although for most of our marriage it was the former. When Giovanni Belzoni died the brilliance went from my life and left me with only debts and memories.

I look back now on our years together – on the time Giovanni performed as a strong man in a travelling circus, all the time longing for his hydraulic inventions to come to the notice of some rich patron, then on the years of searing heat and sand that we spent in Egypt – and they seem almost like a play, full of light and colour but seen from the distant darkness.

Giovanni was always careful to record the contents of the tombs he uncovered in Egypt. But one tomb went unmentioned in his writings because of what happened there in December of 1817; events which fill me with horror and sadness whenever I think upon them. The Valley of the Kings is a place of death, and thus it proved those 11 long years ago.

As I think back, I recall again the suffocating air and the fine dust of those forgotten tombs that we entered in dim candle-light. I can smell again the dry stench of mummified bodies which filled our nostrils and in my mind's eye I see the Arab diggers, caked in dust like living mummies, passing baskets of debris from one to the other as they cleared out the underground chambers. Once Giovanni entered a tomb and mistakenly sat down to rest on a pile of rags and bones which he found, to his horror, to be broken mummies. I accompanied him on all his expeditions and became accustomed to such sights. But in the tomb of Hetsut I encountered death in another form.

We were working in the Valley of the Kings, shortly after Giovanni's great discovery of the tomb of Seti I, a monument of such rich decoration that it was rumoured falsely at the time that a great treasure had been found within, when we came upon a small buried tomb which was the last resting place not of a pharaoh or great queen, but of some minor official or courtier. There were many such tombs in the Valley of the Kings but the discovery of each one caused my husband great excitement.

In our party were a dozen or so Arab diggers. But the one I remember best was Ahmut who turned up unexpectedly to help us. We had first met Ahmut in Cairo when Giovanni had demonstrated one of his wonderful hydraulic machines to the Pasha (there was no limit to my late husband's genius). Unfortunately the machine went out of control when Ahmut shouted to his fellows to jump from a great wheel which, relieved of its load, flew back and injured two of our men who became entangled in its workings. Giovanni scolded Ahmut for his carelessness but I suspected at the time that he may have been bribed by my husband's enemies to sabotage the demonstration. However I had no proof of this.

But it seemed that Ahmut now wished to make amends for his actions and Giovanni welcomed his help for he was a strong man and a good worker. But I was still wary of Ahmut and I thought at the time that my Giovanni was far too trusting of others.

Our servant James Curtain also accompanied us, as did Paolo Capeli, a distant cousin of Giovanni's from Padua who had developed a fascination with Egypt's past and seized every opportunity to join us on our explorations of that magical country. Neither James nor Paolo feared hard work and discomfort, although the accident with the Pasha's hydraulic machine had left James scarred and Paolo with a crippled leg and a disfigured face. Both young men were willing workers and I enjoyed their company.

But there was another member of our party who contrived to make himself unpleasant and obstructive. This man was George Pargeter and he was one of the British Consul General's staff – although one can only suppose that Mr Salt, the Consul General, was pleased to be rid of him.

George Pargeter held himself in high esteem, which is more than anybody else did. He lorded it over the diggers, speaking to all the Arabs with disdain, although he habitually dressed in Arab clothing, saying it was more comfortable in the unbearable heat. And it wasn't only the Arabs who resented his arrogant ways: he ordered our servant James about with equal rudeness, although he treated Paolo with some respect as he was Giovanni's kinsman.

My husband, too, disliked Pargeter and I heard him threaten to kill the man on more than one occasion, although I knew Giovanni well enough to be certain that such threats were idle and not to be taken seriously. Or I thought I did. For murder creates such suspicion and fear, even between loved ones, that nobody is sure of the truth until the guilt of the murderer is proved beyond doubt.

As I cast my thoughts back to the day when Hetsut's tomb was discovered, I recall the sights and sounds as I waited to enter the tomb to help Giovanni record its contents. I was in the habit of sketching any paintings that decorated the tombs and copying carefully the strange writing known as hieroglyphics which at that time we could not comprehend.

While I sat in the shade of a rock, I was aware of a voice, braying and self-opinionated. I recognized it as George Pargeter's and I sat still and listened, hoping he wouldn't discover my presence.

"Of course Belzoni has the treasure hidden somewhere," he said loudly. "I don't believe he could have entered a tomb like Seti's and found only painted walls. Not that I blame him for telling everyone he found nothing: I'd probably have done the same in his shoes. But it's rather hard on your men. You'd think he'd have let you have your share of the spoils."

I didn't hear the reply. I was seething with anger. How could this braying jackass of a man cast doubts upon my dear husband's honesty? I knew that Giovanni had found nothing in Seti's tomb; no doubt it had been stripped by robbers some time in antiquity. But rumours and talk are like the floods of the Nile, they spread everywhere and are impossible to stop.

From his words I guessed that Pargeter's companion was one of our Arab diggers. But I knew of only one that spoke good English. I flattened myself against the rock as I saw Ahmut hurrying past towards the entrance of the freshly excavated tomb. I had suspected that it was Ahmut who had received the dubious benefits of George Pargeter's wisdom, although I knew the man had no love for Pargeter. In fact he had seemed to avoid him, as though there was bad blood between them.

I hoped that Ahmut hadn't believed the poison Pargeter had been spouting and that he wouldn't spread dissent amongst the diggers and cause them to demand their fair share of the non existent treasure of Seti I.

Ahmut discarded the distinctive red headgear he habitually wore and folded his outer garments neatly, placing them on a rock before entering the tomb. The dusty interior was no place for heavy desert robes.

When he had disappeared into the tomb I stepped out from

the shadow of the rock, adjusting my hat so that my eyes were shielded from the strength of the sun. Then a voice behind me made me jump.

"Good afternoon, Mrs Belzoni – or may I call you Sarah?"

George Pargeter was standing there in his Arab robes, his head bare and the sun beating down on his sparse greasy curls. He was smiling ingratiatingly and I had to resist the temptation to slap his face.

"Mrs Belzoni would be more correct, sir," I said coldly. I hesitated, but then I decided on the brutal and direct approach, for I doubted if such a man as Pargeter would respond to subtlety. "I should be grateful, sir, if you would refrain from spreading untruths about my husband. He found no treasure in the tomb of Seti and I fear that you may cause resentment and dissent amongst our Arab diggers if you suggest that he has cheated them in any way. Do I make myself clear?" I looked the man boldly in the eye and he had the temerity to smirk.

"Quite clear, dear lady." He turned to go, fanning himself with his hand against the relentless heat. When he had walked a few yards he spotted Ahmut's clothes lying on a rock. With a bold gesture he picked up Ahmut's red headdress and placed it on his own head to keep the sun off his thinning pate. I watched and said nothing: when Ahmut discovered the theft he could deal with it himself.

As Pargeter hurried off towards the tents, I heard a sound behind me. I turned and saw James Curtain, our servant, staring at Pargeter's disappearing back.

"You startled me, James."

The young man looked at me, serious. "I overheard what he said, Ma'am. If he keeps spreading those lies about what we found in Seti's tomb, there'll be unrest. I know you did your best to stop him but I've met his kind before. He likes to make trouble."

"I only hope that Ahmut has the sense not to believe him."

He frowned at the mention of Ahmut: since the incident with the Pasha's machine, James had avoided the man's company. I think that he blamed the accident on Ahmut's recklessness, and not without just cause for I was there on that day and I witnessed all.

"Someone ought to do something about Pargeter," said James suddenly.

"What do you mean?"

He didn't answer my question but excused himself on the grounds that he had to enter the tomb to help my husband. I turned away as he discarded his shirt, unmoved by his nakedness for no man was a match for my Giovanni. But I had noted the livid scars across his back that had been caused when he had become entangled in the machinery of my husband's great invention.

James disappeared into the tomb's small dark entrance. Giovanni and Paolo were already inside and I thought how hard Paolo worked in spite of his lameness which didn't appear to have affected his speed or his strength. I pictured them inside the hot, airless chamber, inhaling the dust of centuries and I was glad that I would not be called upon to enter the place until it was cleared and aired. I had no fear of tombs or the spirits of the dead Egyptians, but I detested dust.

And yet perhaps I should have been more fearful of this particular tomb.

It was two days before the passageway was cleared of the sand and dust that choked it. The Arabs worked from dawn to dusk and my husband too, aided by James and Paolo, dug and toiled until at last they reached the tomb's outer chamber.

I had not seen George Pargeter since I had scolded him for spreading false tales about my husband and I was told that he had gone off to Luxor on some unspecified business. He was not missed. The Arab diggers seemed happier in his absence as he had a habit of standing watching them work, hands on hips, like some great pharaoh overseeing his slaves. No man likes to be treated thus and the Arabs were proud people. Ahmut, I suspected, seemed especially to dislike him but I didn't know why.

So when Pargeter turned up at the tomb near the end of the working day, I was disappointed to see him: I had hoped his absence would be longer. While the men were working in the outer chamber I waited in the shade of the tomb's entrance passage. Suddenly the bright sunlight streaming into the narrow corridor was blocked out by a black shape surrounded by a halo of light. As my eyes adjusted to the darkness I saw it was a large robed figure which I took to be one of the Arab helpers, for all men look the same in those long robes when that light is dim. I uttered a clear greeting in the Arab tongue but the figure spoke back in English.

"Mrs Belzoni. Wherever your husband is, you are never far away."

My heart began to beat fast because George Pargeter made my flesh crawl. There was something in his voice, a veiled threat perhaps, that I did not like.

"My husband is inside the tomb. They have reached the outer chamber."

"But what of the inner chamber? If there are treasures to be found, that's where they will be."

"My husband is no treasure hunter," I said angrily.

He made no reply but entered the passage and the closeness of his body as he edged past me confirmed that he was no true gentleman.

I followed him to the outer chamber of the tomb which was now being cleared and swept. I could see marvellous paintings on the walls that came alive in the flickering torchlight.

"Well, well," Pargeter began, causing the workers to look up.

I saw Paolo give the man a nod of greeting, for he was always a good-natured young man who bore his afflictions bravely. James Curtain scowled at the newcomer and returned to his task of sweeping the debris of years from the sandy floor.

My husband addressed the newcomer, doing his best to conceal his dislike. "Come in, Mr Pargeter, and see how well we progress."

"What have you found?" Pargeter spoke greedily, more interested in wealth than antiquities.

My husband shrugged his great shoulders, shoulders that had supported ten men in his days as a strongman. "Many things, Mr Pargeter." He pointed to Paolo who was carefully packing a statue of a crocodile-headed god into a wooden crate. "I fear this chamber has been robbed of many treasures but the thieves have left us with a few artefacts that will gladden hearts at the British Museum."

"And what of the inner chamber?"

"It is late," my husband replied. "We will enter it tomorrow."

"Where is the entrance?"

My husband pointed to the great slab of plaster that sealed the adjoining chamber. I saw that James Curtain was watching nervously. The Arabs watched also, regarding Pargeter with something between suspicion and hatred. He was not a popular man. Only Paolo continued his work as though he had no wish to be involved in quarrels and unpleasantness. My husband's strong face was a neutral mask. He would avoid trouble if he could.

"Where is Ahmut?" Pargeter asked suddenly.

This was something I could answer for I kept an eye on the Arab diggers and it was I who paid them for the work they had done. "He was here this morning but he hasn't returned this afternoon," I said, wondering why Pargeter was so interested.

"No matter," the man said lightly. He turned to my husband. "Come on, Belzoni, smash that entrance down. I'm sure we're all agog with curiosity to see what lies within."

My husband raised himself to his full height and gazed down on Pargeter's head. "As I have said, Mr Pargeter, the hour is late. The men have worked hard and wish to finish for the day." He looked at me and spoke. "Sarah, my love, please show Mr Pargeter out," he said as though we were in a London drawing room rather than the tomb of an ancient Egyptian.

Pargeter had no option. As I followed him from the tomb I noticed that he looked back longingly at the door to the inner chamber as though he would have smashed it open there and then were it not for the presence of so many people to restrain him.

As he returned to his tent which was pitched some way from

the tomb, I watched him and I thought how like an Arab he looked in his robes; it was only the sickly pallor of his skin that betrayed him as an Englishman. And as I watched I found myself wondering where Ahmut had got to and why Pargeter had been so keen to learn his whereabouts.

But I was not to know that next time I saw George Pargeter he would be dead.

I know now that the owner of the tomb was called Hetsut. And I know her story, thanks to Monsieur Champollion who in 1822, after long examination of the strange granite stone found at Rosetta, gave us the key to the mysterious writing we call hieroglyphics.

If I had been able to decipher the symbols on Hetsut's tomb back in 1817, perhaps I should have guessed the identity of the murderer sooner but as it was, I had only the pictures painted on the wall as a clue to Hetsut's fate. Since then I have learned, by careful translation of the hieroglyphics I copied painstakingly as we explored the tomb, that she was a favoured dancer in the court of Seti I. And I know now how and why she met her terrible death.

But on the night two of our Arab diggers came to our tent saying they had heard noises coming from Hetsut's tomb, we knew nothing of its occupant. The paintings on the walls of the outer chamber had shown a woman apparently dancing before a pharaoh but there were no other clues. My husband's main concern was whether or not we would find the inner chamber disturbed by the robbers who had stripped so many of the tombs we had explored.

Giovanni went out of the tent with the Arabs to look inside the tomb by torchlight and he found that the entrance to the inner chamber had been smashed, leaving a hole large enough for a man to enter. Assuming that robbers were about, he posted guards there for the rest of the night. But all was quiet: whoever had entered the tomb had hopefully left empty-handed.

So it was that we assembled at the tomb the next morning. My husband entered the outer chamber first, towering over the Arab diggers.

"Somebody broke into the inner chamber last night," he announced.

There was a murmuring and Giovanni stood, looking from one face to another for signs of guilt. Even James and Paolo were not spared his fierce gaze but I had my own suspicions. I was certain that George Pargeter had returned the night before to break into the tomb chamber and I feared that he would have taken away any portable treasure he found within. I cursed Pargeter as I thought of his greed and arrogance.

My husband asked James and Paolo to help him enlarge the entrance. Then he called for a torch which he thrust into the dark chamber and I rushed to his side, eager to see the interior.

I could smell the stale air and I could just make out that the walls of the chamber were richly painted with figures that glowed and danced in the flickering light. Women with eyes as wide and mysterious as a cat's watched from the walls as Giovanni stepped carefully inside.

As the light from his blazing torch flooded the chamber, I noted the absence of footprints on the thick dust of the floor: George Pargeter had moved the door aside but had not entered: perhaps he had lost his nerve. A dark Egyptian tomb would be a fearful place for one alone at night.

And yet it looked as though the tomb had been entered at some time in its history. Statues of animal-headed gods stood around but some lay smashed on the ground and the lid of the painted wooden sarcophagus was pushed aside as if the mummy it contained had risen back to life and left its resting place. I watched from the doorway as Giovanni approached the sarcophagus with a blazing torch held high above his head. I saw him bend over the painted chest and when he smiled I guessed that the mummy was still there in its appointed place.

I stepped inside the chamber and the men began to crowd in after me, the Arab diggers chattering excitedly away in their own language. James held back, hovering by the door, but Paolo limped in, as eager as the Arabs to see what lay within.

My husband beamed triumphantly. "My friends, the mummy appears to be intact." Then he leaned into the darkness of the chest and frowned. "There appears to be some cloth beneath the mummy. Help me raise it up."

Two of the Arabs lifted the small, bandaged corpse carefully out of its sarcophagus. Perhaps it had been roughly handled by robbers in the past for I saw that it appeared to have only one leg. For some reason I shuddered although such sights do not as a rule move me.

But as the mummy was placed carefully on the floor, one of the Arab helpers began to shout. I did not understand his words but the meaning was the same in any language. He had seen something that horrified him. Giovanni leaned again into the sarcophagus and I rushed forwards, curious to know what the Arab had seen which had caused such terror.

I stood by my husband's side and looked into the chest. Lying there was what appeared to be a pile of dirty white cloth, stained a deep rusty brown around the middle. It took me a moment to realise that the cloth wasn't ancient: it was one of the loose robes worn by our Arab diggers. The stain I recognized as dried blood and the head was swathed in red cloth, an Arab headdress. There was one man I knew who wore such a headdress and he had gone missing the day before.

I glanced at Giovanni and our eyes met. "Ahmut?" I whispered.

Giovanni said nothing but he lifted the headdress gingerly to reveal the face beneath.

I stepped back in shock, nearly colliding with Paolo who was craning his neck to see what was happening. For it wasn't Ahmut who lay dead before our eyes – it was George Pargeter.

The authorities were satisfied that everything pointed to Ahmut's guilt. He had quarrelled with Pargeter, violently according to one of the Arab diggers who had witnessed the event. The dagger found beside Pargeter's body in the sarcophagus was the type owned by many of the Arabs and then there was the fact that the corpse's face was covered by Ahmut's distinctive headdress: I recounted my tale of Pargeter taking it from Ahmut's pile of clothes but nobody paid me much heed. I was assured that his guilt was certain and the fact that he had absented himself from the camp without explanation confirmed it. Ahmut had murdered George Pargeter – and when he showed his face again he would be arrested.

Pargeter's body was taken to Cairo and buried in haste. Giovanni and I did not make the long journey to attend the ceremony. Later I heard that only three of the Consul General's staff had been present; the only mourners at a sad little funeral for a man who was little loved.

On the evening following Pargeter's burial Giovanni was alone in the tomb examining its structure, for he was concerned about its safety, when he heard a sound and went to investigate.

He was surprised to find Ahmut standing at the tomb's entrance and when challenged, he muttered aggressively in his own tongue, all the time staring at Giovanni with an expression of such hatred that my husband was immediately on his guard.

Now Giovanni had the strength of ten men so when Ahmut produced a knife from his robes and slashed at him, he merely caught the man's arm and carried him out of the tomb over his shoulder like a helpless child. It was all over. Ahmut was to be taken off to Luxor under arrest.

But before he left the Valley of the Kings, Ahmut spoke freely, telling Giovanni of his fury at being cheated of his share of the treasure from Seti's tomb and calling down curses upon him. It seemed that he had believed every word of Pargeter's trouble making lies and had been away planning vengeance with some of the other men who had worked with him on Seti's tomb. Giovanni explained to him patiently that Pargeter was lying, although he wasn't sure if he was believed. Then he broke the news to Ahmut that he was wanted for Pargeter's murder.

Ahmut appeared to be horrified by this turn of events. But as he was taken away, protesting his innocence, the rest of our party resumed work on the tomb in the smug belief that the murderer of George Pargeter was at last safely locked away.

The mummy once more lay in its sarcophagus in which a bandaged piece of wood had been found, carefully carved to resemble a human leg. I guessed that the mummy had lost a limb and that it had been replaced by a wooden one either in life or during the elaborate funeral preparations so beloved of the ancient Egyptians.

My husband was uncharacteristically quiet as he worked and I sensed that Ahmut's accusations had upset him. Nobody likes to be thought guilty of a crime they did not commit.

It is a rare death that touches no one and Pargeter's violent end subdued our party's spirits, even though few people liked the man. Paolo hardly spoke and James Curtain seemed worried, as though he had something on his mind that he could not share with others. The Arabs too worked without their usual chatter. And so I sat on a wooden stool in a hushed tomb, sketching by candlelight and recording every picture and symbol on the wall.

I did not mind being alone now that Ahmut was in custody, although I felt that Ahmut would never have harmed me. Pargeter had been the sort of man who caused men to hate him and I felt, perhaps, that he had reaped what he had sowed. But I was still uncertain of Ahmut's guilt. Surely his grievances had been against my husband rather than the odious Pargeter, unless Pargeter had offended in some way that I was unaware of.

And there were so many others who had good reason to hate Pargeter, one of them being my own beloved husband who had been falsely accused by the murdered man of robbing Seti's tomb. Giovanni had a temper when provoked and I feared that Pargeter might have pushed him too far. But I scolded myself for my disloyalty and told myself that my husband would never stoop to murder whatever the provocation. And yet I was still uneasy for I feared that the puzzle of George Pargeter's death was not as simple as everyone thought.

But I continued my work, sitting in Hetsut's burial chamber copying carefully every image on the walls. One wall was occupied by a depiction of the burial ceremony; the embalming of the body, presided over by Anubis, the jackal-headed god of the dead and the funeral procession. Two figures with what appeared to be sweeping brushes brought up the rear of the strange and colourful procession. I had seen this image before in other tombs and I had always thought it curious that such a mundane task as sweeping a floor could be part of the exotic ceremonies of ancient Egypt. I said as much to my husband when he entered the chamber with James behind him.

Giovanni smiled. "I was told once by a learned Arab, that it was called 'bringing the foot'."

I looked at him curiously, eager to hear more.

"It was the final rite. The footprints of the officiants were erased by dragging a brush along the floor."

I glanced at James. His face was expressionless. I returned to my task but something nagged at the back of my mind, something I knew I had seen but could not quite recall.

James picked up a brush which had been left propped in the corner and began to sweep the sandy dust away from the doorway into the outer chamber and out into the passage. I watched him as he worked and recalled his words – "Someone ought to do something about George Pargeter." I shuddered. James had changed since Pargeter's death. And now, as I watched him sweep, I suspected that I knew why.

"James," I said when my husband was out of earshot in the next chamber. "What did you really think of George Pargeter?"

"I know they say you shouldn't speak ill of the departed, ma'am, but I can't say I'm sorry he's dead. The trouble he caused and the things he said about the master . . ."

"Where were you on the night of his death?" I have always found it best to be forthright and I had always found James to be an honest young man.

He stared at me for a moment. "I was with some of the Arabs that night, teaching them to play cards. Anybody will tell you. I was there until midnight. Do you not remember that I came out to investigate the strange noises from the tomb?"

He hurried from the chamber and resumed his sweeping with determination while I stared at the wall paintings listening to the rhythmic swish of the broom. I did not remember seeing James that night and the noises had been heard at half past midnight. If the noises had been Pargeter breaking into the inner chamber, then James could have killed him. But I was fond of James and I did not want to consider the possibility that he might be a murderer.

I tried to put the matter from my mind and I began to sketch the paintings on the far wall of the chamber, carefully writing down the hieroglyphics in preparation for the day when someone (my husband perhaps, for I had every confidence in his brilliance) would decipher the ancient code. Strange pictures covered the wall and as I stared at them I realized that they told a story.

In the first picture a girl appeared to be dancing before an enthroned pharaoh. Then in the next I can only say that she was cavorting before a man who appeared to be in, how shall I say it, a state of excitement. Modesty forbids me to set down what was in the third picture but, as a married woman, I understood.

All these proceedings were watched by the same female figure who stood at the edge of each picture. Then, in the fourth picture, the figure emerged from the background and appeared to be attacking the dancing girl. The next showed the dancing girl tumbling into water and a huge crocodile approaching as her attacker watched. Then the next one depicted the girl struggling, her leg caught in the crocodile's great jaws. I stared at the wall in horror. I knew that the mummy's leg had been missing and, presumably, these pictures told the story of how she met her death.

But the story continued. Near the bottom of the wall it appeared that the dancing girl was maimed but alive and she was pointing an accusing finger at her attacker. There the tale ended. The dancing girl had obviously survived the crocodile's attack. But there was no clue as to the fate of her tormenter.

I began to make a rough sketch of the paintings and a thought came to me. George Pargeter was dressed in Arab robes and he was wearing the red headdress he had taken from Ahmut a few days before. I had assumed that he had returned the headdress to its owner. But what if the murderer had assumed that too? What if someone had seen Pargeter entering the tomb and had thought that he was Ahmut? The tomb entrance was visible from most of the tents and in the dim moonlight . . .

There was one who had good reason to seek vengeance on Ahmut, the man who had caused the accident in which James had been scarred – and caused it deliberately. There was one who had been maimed for life by Ahmut's reckless stupidity; left with a scarred face and a useless leg. How his resentment must have built up since the incident. What could have been more natural than for that resentment to be released like water from a dam when he found Ahmut alone and defenceless? Only it hadn't been Ahmut. But if Paolo was the killer then he might not have known that at the time.

I had to discover the truth. Ahmut wasn't a good man but I felt that I couldn't let him die for a crime he did not commit. I may have been wrong – I prayed I was – but the more I thought about it, the more I had the uneasy feeling that Paolo had something to hide. I remembered now that he had not emerged from his tent when the rest of us came out in response to the fearsome cries. I had assumed at the time that he was asleep. But then he had said on many occasions that he didn't sleep well.

The outer chamber was quiet. The Arabs, on my husband's instruction, had begun to dig elsewhere in search of yet another tomb and when I stepped across the threshold into the chamber I saw that James had gone and that Paolo was busy packing the statues that we had found in the inner chamber carefully into boxes which would head for the British Museum.

When he saw me he gave a nervous smile. "Paolo," I began. "It is good to know that Pargeter's killer has been caught, is it not? We can all rest easier now."

He nodded and turned away.

"Where were you when George Pargeter died?"

"I was in my tent," he answered quickly. "I came out with the others."

"I didn't see you."

"I was there."

"My husband would never allow Ahmut to die for a crime he did not commit," I said gently.

"And what of the crimes he did commit?" Paolo's voice was bitter.

"You mean the accident with the water wheel?"

"It was no accident. He ordered his men to jump off it and left James and I, not knowing what was going on. He laughed when we became entangled with the machinery. It was deliberate."

"So you killed him?"

Paolo looked shocked and shook his head. "James was injured too. Why don't you accuse him?"

"Your injuries were worse." I spoke gently. "If I or Giovanni were maimed as you have been and the one responsible thought it a joke then perhaps I would be tempted to seek revenge."

Paolo looked at me. His eyes were large and dark. Were it not for his disfigurement, he would have been a good looking young man, beautiful even. "James had good reason to hate Ahmut too. And he detested Pargeter – I had no feelings for the man one way or the other. I am not guilty and there is no proof against me."

Paolo was right. I could prove nothing. As I watched him limp away I told myself that I was probably wrong about him. Wasn't James just as likely to be guilty? He too had good reason to avenge himself on Ahmut. Or if Pargeter had indeed been the intended victim, even my husband himself might have wished to prevent him from spreading his lies – although as a loyal wife, I refused to consider this possibility.

Or perhaps, unknown to me, one of the other Arab diggers may have had some feud with Ahmut or Pargeter. For the moment I dismissed Paolo from my mind. And as to James' guilt, I did not like to think about it.

Two days later we had had no word of Ahmut. But my husband had other concerns.

After a few minor falls of earth from the roof, he feared that the tomb of Hetsut was unsafe. He forbade me to continue my sketches but I assured him that at the first sign of anything untoward I would leave the chamber for the safety of the open air. Giovanni was unhappy but I felt I was in no real danger. And besides, the story of the dancing girl and the crocodile had to be recorded for posterity.

When I returned to the inner chamber one morning to resume my work I found that I had James and Paolo for company. Paolo was still packing the artefacts we had found into boxes to be forwarded to the museum and James was cleaning up the last fall of earth from the passage floor.

I worked as they went about their tasks and after a while my eyes began to ache from drawing in the dim flickering light. I rubbed them and looked round, prepared to make some conversation with Paolo as I felt I needed a rest from my task.

But Paolo had left the chamber to carry a box outside and I found myself alone. Then, as I looked around the room, I noticed something unusual.

Where Paolo had walked his left foot had dragged along the floor, leaving a groove in the sandy dust. A footprint then a groove; a footprint then a groove, repeated wherever he had walked.

I could no longer hear the swish of James's brush in the passage but I could hear the sound of Paolo's dragging footsteps getting nearer.

As he appeared in the doorway I stood up and faced him. "You killed him, didn't you, Paolo? You killed George Pargeter."

Paolo stared at me and said nothing.

"I knew I'd seen something strange and I've been trying to remember what it was. There were no footprints on this floor when my husband first entered this chamber. I recall it clearly."

He shook his head. "You must be mistaken."

"I am not mistaken. I remember it clearly. Whoever killed Pargeter and placed him in the sarcophagus went to the trouble of sweeping the floor. You are the only person who would need to obliterate their footprints because they are quite unique, don't you agree?"

I saw panic on Paolo's face, like a normally docile animal who has been cornered and who must fight for its life. "What will you do?" he whispered.

"I will have to tell Giovanni and seek his advice."

"He does not know of this?"

Foolishly I answered in the negative.

"So you are the only person who harbours these suspicions."

I answered gently, in sorrow. For I felt pity for this unhappy murderer. "They are more than suspicions, Paolo. I fear they are the truth."

He did not reply but stared at me with frightened eyes.

"It is my guess that you were watching from your tent when you saw a man you thought was Ahmut near the tomb entrance. Ahmut who ordered his men to jump from that wheel, leaving you and James in peril – Ahmut who caused your terrible injuries and showed no remorse. When he turned up here, you could bear it no longer. When you saw him entering the tomb alone you thought your chance for revenge had come at last and you followed him. You found him breaking into the inner chamber and you killed him. Then, when you discovered your mistake, you concealed Pargeter's body in the sarcophagus. But you looked down at the ground and saw that you had left the distinctive footprints which would point to your guilt so you had to obliterate them, just as those who had buried the body of the dancing girl had brushed out their footprints during the funeral ceremony."

"Bringing the foot," he muttered. "I have heard of it." He stood for a few moments, considering his next move. Then he looked me in the eye. "I cannot let you tell of my guilt, Sarah. Do you understand? It would bring disgrace to our family: Giovanni would not wish it."

I shook my head. I could not let my good and noble husband shield a murderer. And I knew that, family or not, he would want justice to be done.

As the wife of Giovanni Belzoni who possessed the strength of ten men, I had always thought myself protected and invincible. So I was not prepared for what happened next.

Paolo began to limp towards me but I stood my ground. I could no longer hear James's busy brush in the passage outside but I was not worried. I was certain that Paolo would do me no harm.

I had to speak to Giovanni, to seek his advice. But as I began to walk towards the entrance Paolo grabbed my arm roughly which shocked me, as I had not thought him capable of such an act.

"I can't let you tell, Sarah," he said quietly. I detected a note of desperation in his voice and for the first time I felt afraid.

I broke from him and called out, half-expecting someone to come running to my aid down the passage. But there was nobody about. James must have left to help with the excavation of the new tomb. Paolo made another grab for me and I screamed. Then I heard something fall from the ceiling followed by a trickling sound, like sand.

Paolo held me tightly. I was surprised by his strength as I struggled, fighting with my nails and teeth like a cat. There was a deep rumbling noise from above and Paolo loosed his grip and looked up. Boulders and sand were raining from the ceiling of the tomb. It was collapsing. We had to get out.

I took advantage of the distraction to make my way down the passage. Behind me I heard more rumbling masking the sound of Paolo's dragging footsteps as he gained on me: his lameness had never affected his strength or his speed. My steps felt slow and heavy as I ran and I seemed to make no progress. I had experienced such frustration in dreams but this was reality and if I didn't escape I feared I would face death.

At last I could see the sun at the end of the passage and from the rumblings above I knew that the tomb of Hetsut was collapsing.

Paolo was behind me, breathing heavily, gaining speed. I knew I would only be safe once I was out in the open and I was concerned for Paolo: killer or not, I wanted him to escape the choking tomb.

Then I tripped on a stone which protruded from the wall and fell flat on the sandy floor of the tunnel. I could hear more rumblings and falling rocks. And I could hear Paolo behind me, the dragging of his left leg on the ground. I pushed myself up then there was a crash like thunder overhead as the whole tomb collapsed. I shielded my face and prayed.

A few moments later all was still. It was pitch dark and I put out a hand to feel rubble ahead of me, blocking the passage. Dry dust filled my mouth and when I tried to call Paolo's name the answer was silence. I lay in the darkness, each breath an effort in the hot airless space that I feared would be my tomb.

I formed prayers in my mind and after what seemed like an age those prayers were answered. I heard my husband's anxious voice calling my name and I replied as best I could, choking and coughing on the dust that filled my mouth and nostrils. I tried to take shallow, calm breaths as I listened to the clinking of my rescuers' spades draw nearer. I would be safe soon in my Giovanni's strong arms. But Paolo, I feared, was lost, buried in the tomb of the dancing girl to rest there with her for eternity.

I had not wished to give my dear Giovanni the news that a kinsman of his was a murderer. And yet how could I allow Ahmut to die for a murder he did not commit? I had to tell my story but I told it confidentially so that only Giovanni and the authorities in Luxor knew the truth. The rest, including James, thought that Paolo had died in a tragic accident, as did his unhappy family. An unlucky end for a young man who had had more than his share of bad fortune.

Six years after these events, in 1823, my husband died in Africa on an expedition to Timbuktu and I mourn him as much now as I did when I was first brought the dreadful tidings of his death. After the collapse of Hetsut's tomb he never spoke of Paolo, and the last resting place of the dancing girl was sealed and obliterated from the records we made so painstakingly of our discoveries.

But now I am alone in the world I find myself thinking of Hetsut often. I have translated the hieroglyphics I copied from the wall of her tomb and I have discovered that she was mistress to a great nobleman whose wife was so jealous that she pushed her rival into the Nile where she was attacked by a crocodile and lost her leg. Hetsut died of her injuries several weeks later and the strange painted words on her tomb poured curses down upon her attacker.

Perhaps it is best that such a tale of such bitter hatred and vengeance should never be told. Such things belong in the world of Anubis, god of the dead, lord of the mummy wrappings.

As I sit here in my shabby room, writing by the light of a small candle, I try not to think of Paolo's terrible death. In times of poverty and hardship it is best to think of pleasant things; of my dear, brilliant husband, the Great Belzoni with whom I shared so much.

I shall not allow Anubis to triumph.

UNROLLING THE DEAD

Ian Morson

It was not until Champollion cracked the code of the Egyptian hieroglyphs with the help of the Rosetta Stone in 1822 that light was at last shone on the mysteries of Egyptian antiquity. The following story intriguingly parallels the translation of a papyrus against the actual events at the time of the Tenth Dynasty king Meryakare, four thousand years before.

Ian Morson is best known for his series of novels set in 13th-century Oxford and involving the investigations of Master William Falconer at the fledgling University, starting with Falconer's Crusade *(1994).*

Harkhuf the embalmer woke up in a cold sweat that had nothing to do with the proximity of his new, young wife, Nefre. He thought he had heard a sound, but didn't know whether it was in his dream, or if it had been real. He lay for a long moment, straining to hear anything in the silence, but could hear nothing. For reassurance, he slid a hand under the cool linen sheet, and connected with Nefre's body. It was warm, and smooth, and he could feel the soft down on her back. No, the problem wasn't Nefre – the real problem was the other female. The one who lay on the slab in his workshop.

The magnificent, white-robed figure stepped out from behind the Sphinx. It was preternaturally tall and topped with a cruel, staring jackal's head, ears abnormally pricked. It was the very embodiment of Anubis – God of the Dead, Guide through the Underworld, and Hearer of Prayers. The assembled throng gasped, several ladies recoiling in terror, and having to fan themselves for fear of fainting. The unbearable heat and the anticipation was literally breathtaking. Palm fronds rustled as the god stepped between them. Anubis threw his arms high into the air, and cried out, causing another frisson to run through the witnessing crowd.

> "O Great One who became Sky,
> You are strong, you are mighty,
> You fill every place with your beauty,
> The whole earth is beneath you, you possess it!
> As you enfold earth and all things in your arms,
> So have you taken this great lady to you,
> An indestructible star within you!"

The audience was enraptured. But beneath the mask, beads of sweat were pouring down Il Professore Giuseppe Malinferno's forehead, and stinging his eyes. But he was in no position to wipe them away, and blinked, shaking his head slightly. The mask of Anubis wobbled, and settled at a more uncertain, rather jaunty, angle on his brow. He cursed the Countess for having had that new-fangled steam heating system installed by Sir John Soane. Weren't all English mansions supposed to be icy cold, and draughty? Wasn't it part of their psyche, the English predilection for being uncomfortable at home? He yearned once again for the long, hot summers of Sicily, or even the dry, desiccating heat of Cairo. The sort of heat that made a mummy of anyone buried in the deserts of Egypt. Then he remembered where he was, and invoked the gods once more.

> "Oh Imsety, Hapy, Duamutef, Kebehsenuef,
> Who live by *maat*,
> Who lean on their staffs,
> Who watch over Upper Egypt,
> O Boatman of the boatless just,

Ferryman of the Field of Rushes!
Ferry Ankh-Wadjet to us."

For a moment Malinferno thought the footmen had missed their
cue. Then he heard the creaking groan of the cart on which the
stone sarcophagus was loaded. He hoped the floor of the Countess' ballroom could stand up to the weight. He imagined the
assembled crowd, that included a minor princeling, a sprinkling
of Lords, several Members of Parliament, and Reverend Hilary
Sparling, plunging to the cellars of the house through a hole rent
by the Egyptian queen's coffin. He wryly surmised that most
would not be missed. Least of all the Reverend Sparling, who on
being introduced to Il Professore condemned this "Frenchified
new fad for Egyptian bits and bobs". He roundly castigated
Napoleon, safely dead these three years, then waxed lyrical in the
theme of the English nobility as no better than tomb robbers.

"Indeed, many edifices, having hitherto withstood the
eternal attacks of ancient barbarians, cannot now resist the
speculation of civilized cupidity, virtuosi and antiquarians."

Malinferno, guessing he was included in the latter cate-
gories, chose to ignore Sparling's comment. Especially as the
collector in question here had been the late, somewhat lamen-
ted husband of Countess Rosalind, the very French Count
Amaury de St Tudy. His Egyptian collection, snaffled from
under Napoleon's nose 20 years earlier in 1804, had languished in the cellars of the ancestral home of his English
wife. Until, riding to hounds, he had fallen off his horse,
expired, and the Countess realized unrolling Egyptian mummies had become all the rage.

Which was why Giuseppe Malinferno, civil engineer by
training, amateur Egyptologist and charlatan by inclination,
was standing before the Countess's invited guests in a slightly
cock-eyed jackal mask. He gestured at the footmen to lift the
wooden coffin of Queen Ankh-Wadjet, of the Tenth Dynasty,
out of her sarcophagus, and place it at his feet. The fashionable
entertainment of peeling back the bandages from a mummy,
and revealing its secrets to the overfed, and overstimulated
members of English society was underway.

Malinferno bent over the highly decorated coffin with its images of the gods Geb, Nut, Isis, Thoth and more. He reached across the lid and raised it slowly up. It creaked satisfyingly. At the very moment that all eyes were glued on the dark interior that was being revealed, a wraith appeared as if by magic at the head of the coffin. It was a tall, voluptuous figure wearing the horned mask of Hathor. Not for the first time, Malinferno had cause to revise his description of the figure as wraith-like. The diaphanous robe did little to hide the curvaceous attractions of his mysterious companion, Madam Nefre. She was scandalously nude underneath it, and the audience loved the fact.

"Bleeding 'ot in 'ere," whispered Madam Nefre into Malinferno's jackal ear. "I'm sweating like a pig."

"No, you are a cow."

"I beg your pardon?"

"Hathor is a cow god, hence the horns. Now let's get on with this farrago."

Between them they lifted the mummy from the coffin, and laid the dark, stained bundle on the rosewood table. Malinferno breathed a sigh of relief that it had not stuck to the bottom of the coffin as some mummies did. The linen wrappings were virtually intact, and the unrolling promised to go well. Then Madam Nefre saw a piece of papyrus protruding from the topmost layer of bandages on the mummy's chest. She idly drew it out, and was going to lay it to one side, when she saw there were some hieroglyphs written on it. She read them.

Madam Nefre, known to her old mother as Doll Pucket, ex-street whore, and Malinferno's occasional lover, was proud of her facility to learn anything at remarkable speed. She recalled what Joe Malinferno had called her when first he discovered her abilities. An autodidact, he had called her. She was about to hit him hard where it hurt, on the assumption that it meant something rude. But he had assured her it was a compliment to her self-taught skills. It had all begun one night, after he had availed himself of her services, paid his few shillings, and they were lying back on the rumpled pillows. She had picked up this book at his bedside.

"What's this, Joe? Who's this Champo Lion geezer?"

"Oh, Doll, you will not understand even if I tell you. And it's Champollion." He gave it the correct inflection. "He is French, and he has deciphered the written language of the ancient Egyptians, called hieroglyphics."

It exasperated Doll that Joe could be so patronizing sometimes. So she said no more at the time, but stole his book, and devoured the contents. The next time he brought round one of those bits of Egyptian stone he called a "steelie", she casually translated the inscription on it. It astounded him.

"How did you do that? Have you seen this stele before?"

She smiled enigmatically, and asked him to test her again. He gave her a rubbing he had made himself from a tomb in Thebes. She translated it faultlessly. As she did now with this scrap of papyrus. It read –

"Murder!" yelped Doll.

★

Harkhuf the embalmer thought he heard a whisper, and threw a fearful glance over his shoulder. He had felt an irresistible urge to check on the embalmed body in his workshop, and had left Nefre in the warm pit of their marital bed to venture out into the night. Now, he wasn't sure whether he had imagined the sound that appeared to come from the outer darkness. After all, it might just have been the rustling of the spirits of the dead that had passed through this place. The Pure Place, where the body was made ready for its returning *ka*, scared some people. But Harkhuf was used to living and working at this crossroads for dead spirits. A wandering *ka* held no fears for him. No, he was more fearful that the noise sounded like the scuffling of living, human feet on sand. The sand that now encroached further every day into the streets of the necropolis. Last month, the Priests of Amun-Re had prayed for a normal inundation again, but once again they had failed. Iteru had not burst its banks, and the sands of

Deshret drifted a little further into the Black Land. Kemet was being squeezed out of existence, and so was he. He had had his back to the wall since his terrible discovery. And every little sound made him fear for his life.

He decided it was time for a little insurance cover. He slipped the scrap of papyrus with the tell-tale word on it under the layer of linen bandages he had wrapped Ankh-Wadjet in that very afternoon. The threat of its revelation might delay things a little. He also took one other precaution involving the disposition of the body. But his only hope for a permanent escape was if the scroll on which he had written the full story reached the right hands. The scuffling sound oozed out of the darkness again, and he prayed that the papyrus would be sufficient.

★

The ballroom was silent. Doll's eerie cry had unnerved the assembled worthies, and they had all departed. The ladies sought relief from the unexpected shock in the inhalation of smelling salts, and a comfortable couch on which to swoon. The young princeling, being of a nervous disposition, was also amongst their number. The other gentlemen had, by and large, decided to boost their spirits with some vigorous imbibing. The countess herself had last been seen being consoled in the library by the Reverend Sparling. She could not yet decide if the revelation had made or ruined the unrolling.

In any case, Malinferno was glad to be left alone to carry out the task of examining the mummy. Alone except for Doll Pucket, self-taught genius, of course. Between them they prised open the outer layers of linen cloth, which partially adhered to the topmost inner layers due to being steeped in some sort of resinous gum. Coarser bandages formed the inner layers, and between them Malinferno and Doll Pucket found a pretty floral necklet of lotus petals, and an ornament of red leather, now brittle and broken.

"Look, Doll, you can still make out the impression of various deities on the leather. There's Geb and Nut, and here the jackal god, Anubis."

"Nah! This mummy was dug up in Herakleopolis, wannit?"

Malinferno sighed at the mangling of the English tongue that was Doll's natural inflection, but nodded in agreement.

"Then the jackal god gotta be Wepwawe, eh?"

Doll looked at Malinferno, legs akimbo and her hands on her hips in triumphant pose. He realized she had been reading his books again, and was inclined to cruelly revise his diagnosis from autodidact to *idiot-savant*. But she was right. The jackal god of Herakleopolis, a town many miles south and west of Memphis, indeed regaled in the name of Wepwawe. He returned to their labours, only to be reminded, as he pulled away the bag-like final garment on the mummy, of his desire to strip the semi-transparent robe from Doll's hot body, and fondle her plump charms. Ankh-Wadjet's body, on the other hand, could in no way be said to be adipose.

As he peeled away the final layer of linen, the wonderful odour of cinnamon and cassia wood assailed his nostrils. He never ceased to marvel that the aroma of the spicery used to coat the body some four thousand years earlier could still be so redolent.

"Ahhh. Smell that. That is the odour that would have pervaded the air around the corpse when first it was embalmed."

Doll was not much impressed, being more concerned with discovering why the embalmer should have left such a curious message for them.

"Huh. Wot's this powdery stuff 'ere?" She pointed at the shrivelled appendage that was the queen's nose. Malinferno peered closely, for once glad to be given the opportunity to expound his own knowledge.

"Almost certainly carbonate of soda, with some muriate and sulphate of the same."

"Oh, natron." Doll sniffed in disdain at the traces of the natural dessicant used by the ancient embalmer. Nothing strange in that, then. She began examining the grey skin. "It's soft! And sort of greasy. And look, there's a big slit in 'er side."

"The left side, yes. That is where the ripper would have ritually opened up the body with his obsidian knife."

"The ripper?"

"That was his name. When he had carried out his task, he would then have been ceremonially expelled from the place for defiling the body. Then the viscera – liver, kidneys, lungs and so on – would have been removed, and stored in canopic jars."

Doll pointed at the four earthen jars that stood at the end of the table on which Queen Ankh-Wadjet lay. "That's them."

"Yes. The one with the baboon head holds the lungs. The one with the human head the liver. The jackal-headed one, which curiously is a slightly different shape to the others, guards the stomach, and the falcon-headed one the intestines. They are the four Sons of Horus."

"What about the 'eart?"

Malinferno let a superior smile cross his lips. "Oh, don't you know? The heart, being the seat of the intellect and the emotions, was left in the chest cavity. The brain, on the other hand, was deemed of no importance. It was mushed up, and pulled out through the right nostril with a hook."

If he thought by this lurid description he would cause Doll Pucket to swoon like the rest of the fair sex at the Countess' soiree, then Malinferno was much mistaken. She was already groping through the gash in the mummy's side, her pale alabaster arm contrasting starkly with the livid grey of the body. Before Malinferno could stop her, she was up to her delightful armpit in the mummy's interior.

"I can't feel it. There's nuthin' 'ere."

"Let me try." Malinferno pulled Doll's arm out, feeling the heat of her body as it pressed against him. He rolled back the sleeve of his linen robe, and inserted his arm in the opening. His eyes rolled in his head as he groped around inside the queen.

"You're right – it's not there. That's very odd. Who would have removed it?"

"Mebbe it was the same geezer what did this."

Doll was pointing at a small round hole in the leathery skin of the queen just below her dry and empty left dug. In life, it would have looked no more than a pin-prick. But the natural drying process had tightened the skin and turned the pin-prick

into a small but discernible hole just about where the heart
would have been beating in life.

"Fascinating." Malinferno loved a mystery. *Una tema re-
condita.*

"Where do yer reckon the 'eart is, then?"

"Heart, Doll, heart' " He emphasized the aspirate. "Take a
look in the sarcophagus."

"Wot? You think it might . . . have just fallen out?"

Doll snorted in derision, and raised Malinferno's tem-
perature by flapping the neckline of her diaphanous robe
back and forth to waft cool air over her bosom. The ballroom was decidedly hot thanks to the new-fangled steam
radiators, and her robe was already sticking to her curves.
He tore his gaze away from the clinging material, knowing
there was no point in making any advances now. He recognized one of Doll's intransigent moods coming on. So
Malinferno went over to the stone coffin himself. He had to
climb up on the wheeled bier on which it had been transported before he could reach down inside. And even then he
could not see clearly to the bottom. He felt around blindly,
and his hand encountered all sorts of nasty debris. Some of
which no doubt could have been parts of queen Ankh-
Wadjet. Then something dry and papery rustled under
his probing fingers.

"There's something here, Doll. I think it's a papyrus."

Carefully he got his fingers around the rolled-up bundle and
lifted it from the sarcophagus. It was indeed a papyrus.

"Give it 'ere."

Doll made a grab for the precious document, and Malinferno had to sweep it away from her grasp.

"Careful. It could crumble to dust, if you handle it care-
lessly."

"It'll crumble apart if you keep wafting it around like that
too. Don't fret, I'll treat it as careful as if it were the King's
private orb and sceptre."

She gave Malinferno a coarse wink. It made him wonder,
not for the first time, if Doll had fondled the "Crown Jewels".
Bearing in mind good King George's propensity for dalliance,

and his treatment of poor Queen Caroline, he would not be surprised. Still he was reluctant to give the papyrus wholly over to her. It might be of great value, and without the Countess present to observe their discovery, the principle of finders-keepers was foremost in his mind.

Together, they unrolled the crackling papyrus on to the surface of the rosewood table. Doll peered at it, and began to translate.

"'I, 'arkhuf . . . er . . . Harkhuf the embalmer, do set this record out as a true statement of my discoveries concerning the murder of the old queen Ankh-Wadjet.'"

She looked at Malinferno with sparkling eyes.

"It's a murder tale from four thousand years ago."

"Go on, go on."

"Move yer thumb, then. 'I say murder because of what I found on the embalmed body that was brought to me by Shemai the vizier of the court of Meryakare. Let me start from the beginning . . .'"

★

Harkhuf could not understand why the old huckster Shemai had brought him the queen's mummy to deal with. True, there was a strike of necropolis workers happening at the moment. Who could blame the poor devils – no one had fed them for days. So there were few embalmers available to do the work. Even so.

"I'm doing it for old times' sake," explained the haughty Shemai. "I liked you around at court." He paused. "It was a shame about the king's sister."

"It was all her fault – not mine. I am the aggrieved party here."

Harkhuf's innocent tones sounded strained and false even to himself. Shemai sniffed in that famous way, making full use of that hawk-like, hook nose of his, with its long and ample nostrils.

"Think yourself lucky there was no child, or Great Meryakare, the All-Knowing, the All-Powerful, the Engineer of the Rising Sun, and Lord of This and the Next World, would have suspected you of trying to create your own dynasty. I would not then have been able to prevent him doing what he had wanted to do to you."

Harkhuf gulped, and thought of the eunuchs at court.

"So what does little Mery want?"

"King Meryakare, to you. The All-Knowing, the All-Powerful, the Engineer of the Rising Sun, and Lord of This and the Next World."

Harkhuf waved a hand. "Yeah, and all that. What does he want me to do with his mother?"

Shemai winced. "Repair the damage done, and make sure the grave robbers don't get to her tomb again."

The worst nightmare of all sleeping royalty. Those thieves who steal through the night, and plunder all the goods the king needed to see him through the next life. Shemai hawked and spat on the sandy earth of Harkhuf's workshop. Then for good measure he ground the thick, yellowy gob into the sand with the sole of his elegant leather sandal. Harkhuf felt as though it was grinding him down too.

He sat for some while after Shemai had left, staring at the ornate coffin on its wooden sled that dominated the centre of his workshop. He could feel the icy chill that rolled out from the open top, like the cold and powerful hands of the woman who lay inside. Queen Ankh-Wadjet's tomb had been robbed barely five years after she had been tucked away for all eternity. Now it fell to Harkhuf to put right the damage.

But it still didn't make sense to him. After all, he was a second-rank embalmer, only entering the craft that had been his father's after his short-lived career as a court musician had foundered. Courtesy of King Meryakare, the All-Knowing etc's sister. He had never intended it to get so serious with Sekhmet-her-Sokar. Despite her name – it meant "the face of Sekhmet is beautiful" – she was a dumpy, plain girl. Her only appeal was the frisson of her blood relationship to the king. Plus the fact that he had heard the High Priest of the temple had fancied her. He always did like to irritate Wephopte.

Harkhuf's father had always said he lacked judgement. And the dalliance with Sekhy had proved him right. He had only done it for the fun of it. Still, the abrupt and forced severing of the relationship had provided ample compensations. It had ended up throwing him into his new wife's arms. Which only served to remind him. There was no point worrying why he had been given the work, because there was no doubt he desperately needed it. Suffice it to say that he now had Nefre and her expensive tastes to support.

*

"Nefre!" exclaimed Doll Pucket. "Harkhuf's wife has got the same name you gave me. That's weird."

"Not really, it's a fairly common name. Read on."

"OK, Joe. But I got a funny feeling about this."

A cold shiver ran through Doll, and suddenly she was aware of the gathering gloom in the vast, echoing ballroom. The cold sarcophagus lay empty, and Queen Ankh-Wadjet stared glassily at the lofty ceiling. She ran her finger up the next column of hieroglyphs and read on.

" 'It all went wrong after I unwound the damaged bindings on the body . . . ' "

*

Harkhuf began unwinding the linen bandages which had been slit in places where the robbers had sought to find any jewels bound into the linen. This was going to be a long and fiddly job. But he still had time to admire the work of the previous embalmer. Someone from the old days like his father, who took his calling seriously. The old queen had been given the works – removal of the brain and viscera, natron dehydration, body washing, bandages wrapped and fixed with resinous gum. Nowadays, it was as much as most people could afford to pay for their dear, departed one to have some cheap oil injected up their back passage, and a quick natron treatment if he was lucky. You pay a small reward, you get a cheapskate job. A sign of the times.

Things had gone downhill since old Pepy II had died, and Egypt had fallen apart. There was no one now who could claim to be Lord of the two Kingdoms, and to wear the White Crown and the Red Crown together. Oh, Meryakare liked to consider himself the successor to Pepy, but he was no more than a jumped-up son of a self-aggrandized local nomarch.

No, the world was going to the dogs in a bucket, and even the bucket had a hole in it. The fabled *maat* – the social order – whose praises Harkhuf sang in his ritual incantations over the dead was a myth.

"Oh Imsety, Hapy, Duamutef, Kebehsenuef,
. . . Where are you now?"

Singing softly to himself, Harkhuf uncovered the desiccated body. He ran his hands over the soft, greasy surface of the skin. It was a first-class job indeed, the sort no one bothered with now. It was because of his protracted admiration for the wasted excellence of the old embalmers' work that he saw it. Well, felt it more like.

At first, he thought it was a blemish left over from the living body, then he looked closer. It was a puncture in the skin. To imagine it had been perpetrated by the embalmer, whose work he had been admiring so much, was impossible. The man would not have been so careless with such a corpse. And he too had been extremely careful as he unwrapped the body. It was King Meryakare's mother, after all. So he came to the only conclusion he could.

Murder in the royal household. Worse. It was nothing less than assassination. No one but other members of the royal family, priests and officials, could have been close enough to the old queen to do what that mark suggested had happened. Demanded had happened. Harkhuf felt a constriction of his own heart, as if the hand of the old queen was squeezing the life out of him. It thumped in his chest. Involuntarily, he mumbled the spell that would protect his heart from theft.

"Let not this my heart-case be carried away from me. I make you to ascend his throne, to fetter heart-cases for him in Sekhet-hetep. This my heart-case is devoted to the decrees of the god Tem, who guideth me through the caverns of Suti, but let not this my heart be given away."

Uneasily, Harkhuf removed the beeswax plate that covered the incision in the queen's left side and slid his hand into the abdomen, then up into the chest cavity. He felt the heart, and his finger fumbled around until it poked into a hole. There was no doubt. Someone had violated the queen's heart, the seat of life and all reasoning.

Harkhuf the embalmer did the only thing possible on discovering this awful truth. He went and got drunk.

★

"He must be an ancestor of yours, Joe."

"Just read."

★

Sut's hovel suited Harkhuf's mood. It was dark, grim and smelled of unwashed bodies. The odour was understandable as most of the takers for Sut's barley beer were farm labourers. They had just finished a day of harvesting the pitiful, dried stalks that claimed to be the barley and wheat crop these days. And didn't have the energy to complain. They just wanted some fun, which suited Harkhuf down to the ground. He often escaped the eternal backbiting and incestuous prattle of the royal court and the necropolis village to slum it at this end of town. Most everyone at Sut's knew him, and so there was no reaction when he stooped through the low doorway in his neat, white kilt, and well-groomed and close-cropped black hair. Most of the denizens of Sut's wore no more than a stained loincloth round their hips. And their grooming left much to be desired.

"Ah. Our very own *Hery-Wedjeb*. Welcome."

This was always Sut's gently mocking greeting for Harkhuf. The court official whose title he bestowed on the embalmer distributed donations to temples and cults. Hery-Wedjeb - the Master of Largesse. In the eyes of most of the poor labourers in the room, Harkhuf knew he must seem that way. Rich beyond their wildest dreams. But that didn't stop them letting him mix easily with them. Especially if he dropped some of his possessions in a game of Senet.

There was a table already set up in one corner of the gloomy room with a rush light burning over it. The long board with its thirty squares and disc-shaped counters drew Harkhuf like a magnet. Sut placed a beaker of his best bitter brew in his hand – no honey sweetening here – and motioned Harkhuf over to the table. The others round the board made room for him, and the game began.

It was only later, when he was staggering home through the silent mud huts, that he realized what he had done. He had let slip the most dangerous of secrets. It had been old Sut's fault. He was down on the game, and chasing his losses, when the old man had told him he had had enough. Harkhuf protested.

"You can't stop me now. I need to win back that scarab necklace. Nefre gave it to me for my birthday. Well, I paid for it. But she gave it to me, and I can't go home without it."

Sut looked at the greedy eyes of the other players. They didn't want Harkhuf to stop either. Each was thinking how they could feed their families for a month on just one of his pieces of jewellery. But Sut didn't want to lose the favours of his best customer.

"Time to go home, embalmer, and beg forgiveness from that lovely new wife of yours." He glanced over at the old, wrinkled drab clearing away the remains of the mammoth drinking session. "If I had such a wife as your Nefre, instead of that one, I wouldn't be dallying with this bunch of drunkards. Go home."

"I'm scared to."

He didn't know why he said it, but he did. Of course, the erstwhile band of fellow gamblers took it all wrong, and hooted at this apparent fear of his wife. He had to stop them mocking him.

"No, no, you don't understand. It's not Nefre. It's the old queen herself."

That was when he told them. He told them what he had found, and that the queen had been murdered for sure. And that he had the evidence lying right there on the slab in the Pure Place – his workshop.

That did it for him having any chance of getting his losses back. The superstitious labourers suddenly melted into the night. All they left as proof they had ever existed was the distant sound of mumbled spells, and the after-image of magical signs made in the air to ward off the evil, to which Harkhuf had exposed them.

Sut abruptly pushed him out of the hovel, suddenly not caring whether he had Harkhuf's custom ever again. Harkhuf heard the door being firmly bolted behind him. He was locked out in the darkness with Ankh-Wadjet's restless spirit for company. Suddenly, the grubby, little peasant houses huddled close to each other didn't seem as welcoming as they had done when he arrived. Doors were barred, and the tiny, dark window openings, set high on the otherwise blank walls stared down at him like the dead eyes in a corpse. Then he thought he heard a scuffling sound behind him, and when he looked, he was almost sure he saw a shape melt into the darkness. A large, glistening shape the colour of night that just melted away. Nervously, he realized the shape had come from the west, the abode of the dead, and he scurried off in the opposite direction. He rushed headlong through the narrow warren of alleys, making for the greater familiarity of Ta Djeser – the necropolis village – and home. Where at least the bodies stayed put.

The next morning, his head throbbing from the aftermath of Sut's strong beer, Harkhuf could laugh at his own fears. Since when had he been afraid of the *ka* and *ba* – the spirit and soul – of those that were his stock in trade? His discovery concerning the old queen had certainly unnerved him. Even his hands were trembling slightly as he wrapped the fresh bandages around the body. Though that too might have been due to the beer. Normally he would have bandagers to carry out this mundane task, but they too were striking until all the necropolis workers received their wheat and barley payments. At least the normality and humdrum nature of the wrapping helped to clear his mind.

Until later that afternoon, when Metjen arrived. Metjen was physician to the royal family, a bumbling, self-important old man of 50 years. He feigned to know how to cure every ill by his magic, and in fact could quote a specific for most common ailments. Which is what he proposed to do right now.

"I can see by the tenseness around your eyes that you are suffering from a migraine or the like. I would suggest the use of aloe or catfish oil."

"Thank you Master Metjen, but I will be fine."

Metjen shook his greying locks.

"I can assure you that you are not fine. In fact I would say that you have a life-threatening problem, unless you take some restorative action."

His eyes narrowed, and with a practised flick of his wrist he unrolled his medical kit next to Ankh-Wadjet's body on the slab. Harkhuf's eyes opened wide in horror as he looked over the array of knives, forceps, and pincers, hooks, saws, and bags tied with string. But most of all his fearful eyes lit on the drill. Metjen stood at his shoulder, and whispered in his ear.

"I would recommend a little trepanning for head pain. A hole in the skull goes a long way to relieving the pressure."

Harkhuf felt dizzy, and clutched on to the edge of the slab, his eyes tightly closed. When he opened them again, the tools of Metjen's trade had disappeared, and the old man was exiting his workshop. He did offer one last piece of advice.

"Actually, I think all you need is to take care of your body more. Remember the heart controls the blood, sweat, urine, and sperm. Drink less, and in better company."

It was only when he had gone that Harkhuf understood he had been warned about his blabbing mouth at Sut's the previous night. But if the physician knew, then everyone at court knew. Including the killer of the old queen. Was that Metjen himself? After all, the physician had the tools with which to carry out the gruesome killing. And hadn't he just threatened Harkhuf's life?

It was that very night that he slipped the scrap of papyrus in the fresh linen bindings on the body. If his life was in danger, he would use it as a counter-threat. A hidden means of alerting anyone who handled the body that all was not as it seemed. But he would still need to find out who wanted him dead. So who could he confide in? As he didn't wholly trust Shemai the vizier, he decided he would risk a talk with the temple priest, Wephopte. At least he could speak to him under the guise of arranging the new funerary rites for Ankh-Wadjet.

★

"I wouldn't trust a priest, ancient or modern."

"Really, Doll, that's no way to talk about people who devote their lives to God."

"You've changed yer tune. Remember wot yer said about

bishops not four years ago over the trial of poor old Queen Caroline?"

Malinferno prevaricated.

"That was another matter. I was referring to the House of Lords as a whole."

But Doll was right. The bishops had been the most vociferous critics of King George's wife, Caroline, when Parliament had attempted to have her marriage to the King annulled. The fact that she had, as Bishop Petrie indelicately put it, "romped familiarly" with a number of naval officers, including Admiral Sir Sidney Smith, was irrelevant. Neither was the fact she had appointed one of Malinferno's fellow countrymen, Bartolomeo Pergami, as her secretary. That merely showed good taste in Malinferno's eyes. Pergami was an obscure Italian veteran of Napoleon's Russian campaign. He had encouraged Caroline to buy a villa on the shores of Lake Como, where he became her constant companion. Further outraging the finer sensibilities of Bishop Petrie among others. But the attempt to divorce her had failed, and the establishment satisfied themselves with keeping Caroline away from George's coronation in 1821. On coronation day, she rode to the Abbey, and tried to gain admittance at every door. She was turned away ostensibly because she did not have a ticket.

"A sad occurrence, Doll. But what does our unfortunate queen's life have to do with Ankh-Wadjet?' He waved a hand towards the blackened mummy incongruously laid out on the Countess's finest rosewood dining table like some overcooked joint of beef.

"It was only two weeks after Caroline embarrassed the King, and that snooty Bishop, that she got a belly ache at the Drury Lane theatre. And only a week after taking to her bed that she died. Very convenient for all, wouldn't you say, Joe Malinferno?"

"Are you suggesting the King had her done away with? That's monstrous."

Doll shrugged, and her breasts bounced voluptuously underneath her thin robe.

"I'm not saying Georgy-Porgy arranged it deliberate. But someone near to 'im may have thought they was doing 'im a favour, like. Don't yer think?"

*

"You are distracted, my dear husband."

Harkhuf suddenly realized that Nefre was in the room with him. She was standing over where he lay on the low couch that he had inherited from his father. It had been the old man's prized possession, and he had especially loved the gracefully curved lotus-flower arms at either end. Harkhuf had become so used to it from a boy, that he hardly saw the beauty of it. Until this evening, when he thought of the possibility of imminent death. He stroked the carved arm, smooth from his own father's caressing, and vowed to appreciate everything about this life. He wasn't yet ready to travel to the next.

"Tell me what is worrying you."

Nefre knelt at his feet, and smiled ingenuously. She was clad in a plain white shift that covered her slim body from breasts to ankle, but still managed to enhance her beauty somehow. She began to stroke her husband's manly chin-tuft. Admiring her, Harkhuf wondered how he could burden her with his fears.

His visit to the priest, Wephopte, had been inconclusive. The man had been bathing for the third time that day as required by his priestly duties, and was lounging at the edge of the pool in the temple. He was shaving his body to protect himself from lice, and clearly stroking his every contour with obvious self-pleasure. Not for the first time Harkhuf thought the truculent priest had a most appropriate name. Wephopte meant "the God Wepwawe is satisfied". And no one could exude more self-satisfaction than Wephopte. Harkhuf waited until the priest deigned to notice him.

"Ah, embalmer. You are here to arrange the new rituals for the queen?"

"That and another matter, High Priest."

Wephopte stretched a languid arm, and reached for the long-sleeved, pleated robe that designated his eminent office. Only Shemai, and of course the King, wore anything more elaborate. Wephopte draped it on his body, then gathered up his distinctive leopard-skin, pinning it at his shoulder. This was a modern and, to some at court, an outrageous affectation. Priests traditionally wore linen robes and papyrus sandals to avoid wearing anything from a living animal. Harkhuf didn't object – in fact, he rather envied the man the warrior aura the skin bestowed on him. It beat hands down the jackal's head he had to wear at ritual ceremonies. That only scared the ladies away.

"Another matter, Harkhuf?"

Wephopte seemed unusually genial, and Harkhuf could only assume that he had not heard of his drunken revelations the previous night. He held out the papyrus on which he had scribed all the information he had culled to date, and who he suspected of the murder. He begged the priest to pass it to King Meryakare at the earliest opportunity.

"My life depends on it."

"Oh, I am sure you exaggerate, Harkhuf. Maybe if you drank a little less, and attended to your duties and the gods a little more, you would not have these fancies." He waved Harkhuf's protests aside. "However, I will do as you say as soon as I have the time. Right now the King and I have a ceremony to perform. We must not keep the God Min waiting, or the harvest will be even worse than it threatens to be.'

Harkhuf had to be glad that the priest at least left still clutching the papyrus scroll. It would be sure to draw the murderer from cover.

"Where is the necklace I gave you on your birthday, husband?'

Harkhuf realized Nefre was no longer languidly draped over his legs. She had stiffened, and was facing him, her hands at his neck. And the fingers weren't caressing him, but tightening on his throat. A cry of exasperation wrenched itself from Nefre.

"You have been gaming at Senet again."

"No, I haven't. I promise."

"No. I suppose it was 'Racing-for-home' instead,' said Nefre, naming another gambling game.

"Sort of," mumbled Harkhuf, recalling the previous night, when he did race for home to save his life. Nefre pushed herself to her feet, her pale face a deepening red.

"Well, you can go and gamble away all our wealth, if you like. Only don't expect me to live like a pauper as well."

"If only you did live like a pauper, we might be able to live within our means."

Nefre stormed out, leaving Harkhuf's bitter riposte dying on his lips. Nor did she return that night, and Harkhuf spent it restlessly tossing on the low bed also inherited from his father. He would not have time tomorrow to chase his errant wife, who no doubt had gone to her parents for comfort. They had always criticized their daughter's choice of a husband, and this rift would no doubt delight them. No, the papyrus he had despatched to the King, and the story it told, would be guaranteed to winkle the murderer out. The trap was set, and Harkhuf only had to wait, and pray that he was equal to the task when it was sprung.

*

"He says – 'I have hidden the heart, which is the sole piece of evidence that the queen was murdered. The murderer will give himself away by trying to find and destroy the heart.'"

"Skip to the end, Doll. Tell me who it was killed Queen Ankh-Wadjet. This tale is more exciting than Mistress Shelley's new book about that monster. And a deal more believable. Does he catch the malefactor? Who was it?"

Malinferno was aquiver with anticipation.

"There is no more. There is an end of it."

Malinferno couldn't believe it.

"Now, don't tease me, Doll. I can read the hieroglyphs too. It takes me a while longer, is all. Finish it."

"Look. The end of the papyrus is torn off. If Harkhuf found out who it was, or if he met his end, we will never know."

Malinferno groaned, and looked down at the papyrus spread out before them. It was true – the edge had been deliberately torn. It was not as though it had crumbled over the four thousand years since it was written.

"Maybe the other piece is in the sarcophagus still."

Malinferno clambered on to the bier again, and rifled wildly around the debris in the bottom of the stone tomb. There was no further shred of papyrus. He groaned in despair. It was unbearable to think that the end of the story, that had waited so long to be discovered, would not now be known to them.

Doll shivered.

"It's cold in here. Let's go find some grub, and something warming."

"You're right. I hadn't noticed." Which wasn't exactly true, for Malinferno had watched with growing excitement as Doll's nipples had stood further and further up as the room cooled down. "This damned steam pipe heating must have gone out. Let's find the kitchen, and a good fire. It is the only consolation open to us now."

"Maybe not, Joe Malinferno. Don't give up so easy. We can always try and solve the mystery for ourselves."

"How?"

Doll Pucket snuggled up against Malinferno's warmth, and led him out of the freezing ballroom.

"I'll tell you over a dish of hot chocolate."

★

The ceremonial of reinterment for Queen Ankh-Wadjet began for Harkhuf with a ritual bath. This was a lonely process without the assistance of Nefre, but he concentrated his mind on what was to come. Several people would be present at the ceremony, all of them suspects in the murder of the old queen five years earlier. Whoever it was must have thought he had been safe from apprehension, from even any suspicion that the queen had expired any way other than naturally. It must have been a great shock when the tomb robbers had disturbed the remains, and raised the possibility of the crime being uncovered.

Of course the murderer might well be dead himself by now. Old King Meryathor had died three years ago, and it might have been he who killed his Great Wife of the time. His young concubine, Bener, had been promoted with great alacrity to the position of Great Wife after Ankh-Wadjet's death. Some salacious individuals at court even said Bener had been the cause of Meryathor's later demise. From too much exertion. One thing was certain, Meryakare, the present King, would not have killed his mother. Harkhuf knew from his sister, Sekhmet, that he had doted on her. That was why the embalmer had felt it safe to ask Wephopte to give the papyrus to King Meryakare.

Harkhuf dressed in his long white linen robe, then brushed a layer of sand off the Anubis mask he would wear for the ceremony. As he did so, he went through the list of possible murderers again in his head.

★

"Let me see," opined Doll. "There's King Meryathor himself."

"Yes, but he was dead by the time Harkhuf discovered the murder. You're not going to tell me it was his *ka* spirit Harkhuf set his trap for."

"Hmm. What about Shemai the vizier? He could have done the old King's bidding willingly. And got rid of the old queen to make way for a lustier proposition. Old family servant and all that."

Malinferno stared into the sludgy, brown dregs at the bottom of his cup of chocolate. It reminded him of the turbid waters of the Thames dragging itself through London. Or perhaps the Nile banks after the floodwater receded.

"A bit like the House of Lords with Queen Caroline? Perhaps. Go on."

"Then there's Metjen the quack. He certainly had the tools to do the deed."

"And opportunity. He just had to wait until the ailing queen called for his medical services. Who else?"

"Wephopte, the High Priest. I must say, from Harkhuf's description, I don't care for him."

"Back to the House of Lords and bishops, again. I don't know, Doll. I don't think this is going to work. We don't even know if Harkhuf solved the matter. Or even survived the day."

Doll looked crestfallen, until a sudden thought occurred to her.

"We can find out."

"How?"

Doll banged her dish down on the sturdy oak table, scarred witness to many a meal preparation, and bounced out of the kitchen. She threw her answer over her pretty, naked shoulder.

"Find the heart."

Malinferno scurried after her, back up the echoing servants' stairs and towards the vast ballroom. He grabbed her arm just before she pushed through the grand double doors.

"The heart? What will finding that tell us?"

Doll's beautiful blue eyes blazed.

"If it's still where Harkhuf hid it, then the murderer didn't find it. If he didn't find it, chances are that was because he was caught. It's only if the heart is missing, can we reckon that Harkhuf failed, and was done in himself."

"Very good. The only problem is, we don't know where he hid the heart in the first place."

Doll tweaked Malinferno's long nose.

"Prophet of doom. Always looking on the gloomy side. Just think – if you were Harkhuf, where would you have put the heart to keep it safe?"

"I don't know, Doll. The man is four thousand years dead. I can't imagine what he would have done.'

"Then put yourself in the shoes . . . sandals . . . of the murderer. You're rogue enough for that." Malinferno gave Doll Pucket a hard look, but heard her out. "It's the day of the ceremony to reinter the queen. Everyone is there, and you need to find the heart and destroy it. Where would you look?"

*

Predictably, as the day had dawned, Shemai was the first to arrive, dressed in a long white robe, clasped at the shoulders. As ever, he was shadowed by two dark-skinned Nubians, denizens of the night. They scared Harkhuf. Shemai had proceeded to fuss over the process of returning the queen to her ornate coffin. And had asked Harkhuf whether everything had gone smoothly.

"You did not have any . . . er, problems with the body?"

"Should I have, Vizier?" If Shemai now asked about the heart, or the condition of the body, Harkhuf would have him.

"No, no. I just wished to be reassured that the tomb robbers . . ." again he hawked, and spat in the sand. ". . . that they didn't damage the queen in any way."

Harkhuf was just about to draw Shemai out further, when both men received a surprise. Sekhmet-her-Sokar appeared in the doorway to the Pure Place. She was garbed in a long white linen robe that was cut to artfully reveal the swell of her bosoms, while still covering the rolls of fat on her hips and thighs. A long, black wig covered her head, from under which runnels of sweat were already dribbling down her chubby face. A multi-coloured necklace of faience beads swathed the folds of her double chin. She was even fatter than when Harkhuf had romped with her through the palace gardens. A sort of self-satisfied corpulence that brooded no comment. Harkhuf gulped, and hastily donned his jackal mask, as though it would protect him from discovery.

He needn't have worried. Wephopte now appeared, and Sekhmet began making cow-eyes at him, ignoring Harkhuf completely. The priest for his part returned the sentiment, and positively drooled over the king's sister. The next surprise was the arrival of Bener, the old king's second Great Wife, and successor to Ankh-Wadjet. She was now a sort of redundant senior queen at the court, stepmother to Meryakare, but serving no proper purpose. Still only 22 years old, her relegation had not spoiled her looks, however. Harkhuf's heart beat faster at the sight of the yellowish-red tinge of the henna in her luxuriant, natural hair, and the dark pool of her eyes accented by the lines of kohl and red ochre. She swept in, and took Harkhuf's hand in hers in silent obeisance. Close to, he could detect the faint scent of oil of fenugreek on her. It was used to smooth wrinkles, but Harkhuf could detect none. Obviously it worked.

"Overseer of the Mysteries, I am nothing more than a poor seamstress now." She toyed with a pair of copper scissors that hung from her belt. "But I thought I may be allowed to attend the interment of the old Great Wife."

Her voice was sultry, and the emphasis laid on the word "old" was not lost on Harkhuf. Nor could he help but notice that the long blades of the ornamental scissors were innocent of the scars of daily usage. But lethal nonetheless. And that the belt they hung from was inlaid with butterflies of turquoise and lapis lazuli. A very rich seamstress, if so she was. With the means of stabbing someone, and piercing them to the heart. Her name was of course that of the sweet date that was an Egyptian's pleasure. And the connotation was not lost on those who met her. All men in her presence licked their lips with pleasurable anticipation.

She had obviously come to see her old rival safely entombed once again. But had Bener had anything to do with her murder? Harkhuf had no time to think on this new possibility. Wephopte began the ritual incantation, and the ceremony got under way.

> "O Ankh-Wadjet,
> Nut, your mother, spreads herself above you,
> She conceals you from all evil,
> Nut protects you from all evil,
> You, the greatest of her children!"

Harkhuf, in his jackal-guise as Overseer of the Mysteries, led the procession into the Pure Place. Behind him paced God's Seal-Bearer. This made him somewhat nervous, as the role was a physician's, and Metjen was fulfilling it at present. The vulnerable space between Harkhuf's shoulder-blades prickled. Wephopte was the next in line as Lector Priest. They made their way through to the inner room, where reposed the queen's ornate coffin.

Ankh-Wadjet had been returned to it the previous night, and now lay inside with only the lid left to replace. Those present murmured in approval at the scenes on the sides of the coffin depicting the deceased making offerings to various deities. Every scene was brightly coloured in reds and blues on a yellow background. At the foot of the coffin, facing everyone, were depictions of the Gods Amun, Tefnut, Ne-

fertem and Bennu. All providing the protection of magic for
the Day of Judgment to the body within. Harkhuf fervently
prayed for the same sort of protection for himself.

Wephopte intoned the final incantation, as Harkhuf anointed the bandaged body with a mixture of myrrh, cassia,
gelatine and resin.

> "If you love life, O Horus, upon his life staff of truth,
> Do not lock the gates of heaven,
> Do not bolt its bars,
> After you have taken Ankh-Wadjet's *ka* into heaven,
> Clad in red linen,
> Living on figs,
> Drinking wine,
> Anointed with unguent,
> That it may speak for her to the great god
> Let Ankh-Wadjet ascend to the great god!"

The two Nubians were induced to lift the heavy lid into
place, which they did with rippling muscles and stunning ease.
Suddenly, the ceremony was over, and for Harkhuf, expecting
the killer to give himself – or herself – away, all was anticlimax.
Wephopte left first with Sekhmet simpering on his arm.
Metjen was deep in conversation with the beautiful Bener,
who still had time to cast a languid look over Metjen's
shoulder at Harkhuf. She looked bored stiff by the physician's
droning conversation. And her eyes made it clear she was keen
to seek out the company of Harkhuf. His heart thumped a little
faster in his chest. He was on the verge of going over to save
her from a conversation about cures for constipation – a
favourite of Metjen's – when he felt a hand on his own
shoulder. It was Shemai.

"I will arrange for the *medjoi* – the Nubians – to return the
coffin to the vault now your work is complete."

Harkhuf nodded, and agreed with Shemai a time for the
coffin to be removed on its sled. He noted that the vizier was
getting very pernickety about the detail of the coffin's return
to its sarcophagus. Almost over-anxious to get the job done.

Did he have good reason to want everything sorted out, and returned to the state it was before? It seemed very much like it. Unfortunately, when Shemai had finished with him, Harkhuf turned to see that Bener had left, and Shemai was also hurrying away with his Nubian escort, before Metjen could trap him. Unfortunately Harkhuf could not escape.

"Ah, Harkhuf. You look pale and I can see the strain on your face. I diagnose constipation. I recommend that you take half an onion in the froth of beer. It is an excellent specific, and is also a remedy against death."

Before Harkhuf could construe whether the comment was another threat, Metjen turned on his heels and left. Harkhuf was alone, and still uncertain as to the identity of the murderer. Though he now had his suspicions. As darkness fell outside, he began to tidy up his workshop. By the light of the flickering oil lamps, he carefully transferred the four canopic jars with their contents on to the sled next to the coffin.

*

"It's no good. I give in, Doll."

"The pickle jars! That's where I would have put the heart."

"Pickle? Oh, you mean the canopic jars. On the basis that hiding one organ amongst a load of other organs makes it disappear. You may well be right."

Malinferno began to grope his way forwards in the now darkened ballroom. Now, where were the four jars when last he saw them? On the end of the rosewood table, wasn't it?

"Wait for me," hissed Doll, and grabbed his arm. Together they moved cautiously ahead, hoping not to bump into anything. A ghastly, groaning sound brought Malinferno's progress to an abrupt halt. He felt Doll's pneumatic breasts squashing against his back.

"Oi! Next time, tell me when you're going to stop."

"Sorry." Another groan rent the air.

"Joe, what is that noise?" Her grip on his arm tightened. He tried to sound calm, but feared his voice was trembling as much as he was.

"Just the old house creaking as it cools down. That heating

system will ruin the timbers. I don't doubt that in a few years it will come crashing down around the Countess' ears."

They took a few more steps forwards when a double groan echoed round the room.

"That didn't sound like wood creaking, Joe. It was positively ghostly – inhuman even. You don't reckon the old queen has come to life, do you?"

The groans became louder, and more regular. Suddenly, Doll stifled a snigger, and edged over to the wooden bier on which lay the massive sarcophagus of Ankh-Wadjet. She peered in, then beckoned Malinferno over, a finger to her lips. Fearfully, he boosted himself up, and peeped over the broken edge of the sarcophagus.

A pair of naked, white male buttocks rose and fell on to a froth of red silk and white lace from which protruded two scrawny, white legs. Malinferno recognized the dress the Countess had been wearing an hour or two earlier. But from the section of anatomy on display, he was temporarily at a loss to recognize the gentleman rogering her Ladyship. He felt a tugging at his long white robe, and dropped down to sit on the floor next to Doll.

"Leave them to it, Joe. We've got a murder to solve."

"But . . . in the queen's sarcophagus?"

"It's the closest either of them will get to romping with royalty, I suppose. Look, there are the jars. On the table."

They crawled on their hands and knees towards the table, and sat staring at the four jars. They were all sealed, and the animal heads on the stoppers stared enigmatically back at them.

"Hapi, Imsety, Duamutef, or Kebehsenuef?"

"My money's on the jackal, Joe. Though the baboon face does put me in mind of you."

"It looks more like that arse we saw in the coffin."

Doll began to titter uncontrollably, and pressed her face into Malinferno's chest to stifle her laughter. Malinferno liked the sensation.

"Doll, do you think there's something in this?"

"In what?"

"Congress in the presence of a queen."

"Geroff!" Doll swatted away Malinferno's groping hands, and he toppled backwards. Reaching behind to save himself, his arm swept across the table top. One of the jars slid across the polished surface, and teetered on the edge. Malinferno fumbled for it, but it slipped through his fingers, and fell towards the floor. He noticed it was the jackal-headed one – Duamutef. The one that was a slightly different shape to the others.

*

"Harkhuf."

The embalmer spun round in alarm. The priest, Wephopte, stood in the doorway to the Pure Place.

"Thank goodness it's only you, Wephopte. I thought it was someone else."

"Shemai, you mean?"

Harkhuf looked at him with curiosity. "Or Metjen, or Bener . . . or Sekhmet, come back for some reason. Why did you specifically mention Shemai?"

The priest cast his eyes to the floor. "The papyrus. I didn't deliver it."

"Why not?"

"I read it. Do you realize you accuse virtually everyone at court of potentially being a murderer? It would have been a scandal. And Shemai would have got his hands on it first, anyway. He reads everything that is presented for Meraya-kare's attention. And that would have been the end of you."

"You think it was Shemai killed the queen?"

"Who else? Meryathor was hopelessly enamoured of Bener, and wanted her for his Great Wife. Bener wasn't content to remain secondary to some scrawny old witch who would have made her life a misery, if she had been set aside."

"And Meryathor asked Shemai to get rid of Ankh-Wadjet?"

"The King, or Bener – does it matter who? You know how protective Shemai is of the family, preventing outsiders worming their way in." Harkhuf thought of himself and Sekhmet, and blushed. It was true that the vizier's Nubians had tossed him out of the palace with hardly a by-your-leave when he was found naked with Sekhmet. Wephopte stared him in the eye, and went on. "Here's the papyrus. Destroy it, for the gods' sake. Look, I'll tear the bottom off myself. Where you name names. I'll make sure it's burned."

Harkhuf took the ripped papyrus from Wephopte's outstretched hand, and tossed it on the sled.

★

The jackal-headed jar landed in Doll Pucket's ample lap, saving it from being smashed on the ballroom floor. But the lid, whose seal had been tampered with at some point, popped open. A blackened lump the size of an orange rolled out and dropped on to the floor. Doll grabbed it before it rolled away under the table, and turned it around in her palm. She hissed at Malinferno.

"Look, it's the queen's heart. And there's the wound. No more than a pin prick." She paused. "You know what this means, don't you?"

Doll's voice was rising with excitement.

"No. What?" Malinferno did not follow Doll's *idiot-savant* logic at the best of times.

"It was the priest, you idiot," she yelled.

★

A voice in Harkhuf's ear made him flinch, and he felt a stinging sensation in his left arm. Ridiculously, he thought at first he had been bitten by a marsh fly, and swatted at the offending insect. A metal clasp with a long, long pin clattered on to the coffin that he was leaning over. He gazed in stupefaction, wondering how the fly had turned itself into a glittering, gold scarab. A scarab like the one that held the edges of Wephopte's leopard-skin together at his shoulder.

Then he knew he had been right, and his blood ran cold as he realized he had flushed the murderer out after all. He wasn't so glad now that he had succeeded. He felt something heavy make contact with the back of his head. There was the sound of something shattering - his skull, no doubt. Harkhuf uttered a prayer for a swift, and painless journey to the next life.

★

"It's the priest," repeated Doll in triumph, dancing around the ballroom floor.

The Reverend Sparling's head popped up over the edge of the sarcophagus. He looked red and startled. He saw Doll dancing, and Malinferno sitting on the floor amidst the spilled contents of a jar, and disappeared below the lip again. Only to reappear hoisting his breeches up, and attempting to button their flap as he scrambled over the broken edge of the sarcophagus.

"No, no. You have the wrong impression. We were examining the tomb for . . . er . . . evidence."

He stood for a moment in his stocking feet, transfixed. Then Reverend Sparling offered up a wild prayer to the heavens, and fled. From the depths of the coffin came a hollow and desperate wailing.

"Reverend . . . reverend . . . where are you? Don't stop now, I pray you."

★

Harkhuf awoke to the sweet scent of coriander, juniper and honey. Better still he could feel the soft hand of a woman spreading unguents on his forehead. But for a splitting headache, he would have thought he had crossed over to the afterlife.

"I prepared the concoction for a headache – equal parts of the berry of the coriander, the berry of the poppy-plant, wormwood, berry of the sames-plant, berry of the juniper-plant, and honey. I hope it works."

"Just keep rubbing my brow, Nefre, and it will work."

"Hmm. Maybe I should have used the remedy against death, the state you were in last night."

Harkhuf grimaced, and prised open his eyes. The bright, morning sunlight lanced through his brain, and he twisted away from it. He wished he hadn't. His neck screamed as though he had been carrying the whole weight of the great pyramid of Khufu on it He remembered what had happened to him.

"How did I get here? The last thing I remember was being smitten to death."

"Some gorgeous Nubian keeper of the peace carried you in. Over his shoulder, as if you weighed nothing."

Harkhuf didn't like the faraway look in his young wife's eyes. How could she drool over a dark-skinned *medjoi* – a Nubian as dark as the night – when her husband was near to death? He struggled to sit up.

"I was attacked. Nearly killed."

"Pianki – the Nubian – said you were never in danger. That he and his companion had been following you wherever you went for days."

Pianki. So now she had his name as well. He would have to watch his young wife.

"They have arrested Wephopte, and Shemai will pass judgement on him soon. Pianki apologized that they didn't reach the priest before he had broken one of the canopic jars over your head."

"So that's why I kept seeing dark shapes always disappearing out of sight. The *medjoi* were following me. Who told them to?" He thought he knew, even as he said it.

"Why, their boss, of course. Shemai. Pianki said he knew about Ankh-Wadjet's murder all along, but no one would listen to him. When the tomb was damaged, he arranged for you to do the work on the queen, because he wanted someone independent to find the signs of murder. He knew you would see them, because they were so obvious, and because . . ."

Nefre looked at the floor, a smirk on her face. Harkhuf stared at her with what he fondly imagined was a stern gaze.

"And because?"

"Oh, Shemai knows you so well. He said it was because he could guarantee that you would get drunk when you found the wound, and blab in your cups to all and sundry. That way he would draw out the killer."

Harkhuf sat up, his sore head forgotten in his indignation.

"Shemai and Meryakare used me as a sacrificial lamb to winkle out his mother's killer. I might have been killed, myself."

Nefre nodded, more solemn of a sudden.

"Pianki also passed on the message that, if you were inclined to complain, you were to be reminded you deserved it. Something to do with the King's sister. What did he mean, Harkhuf?"

Harkhuf looked sheepish, and clutched his head.

"I feel giddy, darling. Maybe some more of that ointment?"

*

Malinferno hugged Doll with pure delight at the sight of the Reverend's discomfiture.

"So, priests both ancient and modern were guilty of social climbing. I suppose Wephopte had eyes for Sekhmet, and for founding a new dynasty. Do you think he would have murdered Meryakare too?"

"I don't know, Joe. And I don't care. I'm freezing, and I fancy a bit more than a dish of chocolate to warm me up."

Malinferno glowed at the ravenous look in Madam Nefre's eyes.

*

Harkhuf turned to his wife as they lay together on the old couch.

"I want to thank you for shouting out that warning. It saved my life."

"What warning? I was still at my parents' when Shemai told me you had been hurt."

Harkhuf frowned, then sighed. He must have imagined Nefre's voice calling out a warning about the priest. Maybe the bang on the head had been more severe than he thought.

"Goat."

"What?"

Nefre smiled knowingly. "I think of you more as a sacrificial goat than a lamb."

Harkhuf grinned, and yanked at Nefre's robe. "I'll show you what sort of goat I am."

As he plunged on to the naked, pliant body of his young wife, he made sure her brooch pin was well out of the way.

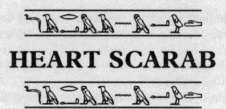

HEART SCARAB

Gillian Linscott

We have now reached the start of the 20th century during the heyday of the British Egypt Exploration Society. This had been founded in 1882 (as the Egypt Exploration Fund) mostly due to the enthusiasm of writer Amelia B. Edwards. It helped finance the work of Flinders Petrie, one of the most important of Victorian and Edwardian Egyptologists, but it also helped preserve and protect Egyptian antiquities. Thanks to the Society the science of Egyptology moved forward significantly.

Gillian Linscott is the author of the award-winning series about Nell Bray, suffragette and occasional amateur sleuth, whose adventures began in Sister Beneath the Sheet *(1991).*

I t was like being inside a one-eyed skull, a dark dome above, rock floor where the jawbone would be, one round opening with a little light coming through. The air in the tomb smelled mostly of old resinous dust, with a tang of something acrid underneath. There were five men to breathe it. Three of them were Arab workmen, waiting near the entrance with a plate camera, measuring rods, sketch pads, impassive because this was their work, like any other work. The other two were Europeans. The younger one stood back a little from the stone sarcophagus, holding a paraffin lamp. He was so nervous that the light from it swung up and down the rock walls and the face of his older companion was sometimes in shadow, sometimes flooded with light like a character in a pantomime. Even without the lighting effect the older man had a striking face, like a philosophical pirate with a beak of a nose, bright eyes, grizzled beard and jutting eyebrows. Some of the more conventional members of the British Egypt Exploration Society even called him The Buccaneer because of his disdain for all rules but those of scholarship. His real name was Professor Brightsea.

"Well, Thomas, we know what we're going to find inside, don't we?"

His deep voice rolled round the cave. His assistant made a pleading gesture that set the lamp swinging more wildly. The professor laughed.

"Not sure? Well, in that case, you may have the honour of discovery."

Looking sick, Thomas put the lamp down on the floor and advanced to the head end of the sarcophagus. It was already open, the stone lid lodged against the rock wall. As he got nearer, the acrid smell increased and his nose wrinkled.

Brightsea laughed harshly. "You should be used to it by now."

Thomas made a choking sound and fell on his knees, arms hooked over the stone rim. Brightsea strolled over, reached into the sarcophagus and straightened up with something white and cylindrical between his fingers.

"Just as I predicted. See?"

He waited while his assistant got to his feet and came, shoulders hunched, into the circle of lamplight.

"So, Thomas, would you care to put a date to this artefact?" Thomas wouldn't or couldn't speak. "Well, then, hazard a scholarly guess. This year's, would you say, or possibly last year's? The fifth year or the sixth of the reign of Pharaoh Edward the Seventh?" Then, impatiently, tiring of his bitter joke, wafting the smell of it under his nose, "Come on, man, is this a cigarette butt from 1906 or 1907?"

Back in Cairo, Tutty Brightsea was profiting from his father's absence on a field trip to follow his own studies into Egyptology. He and a friend were in a room in a small white cube of a house near the bazaar, watching a man unwrapping a mummy. Her feet were the first things revealed – sticking up at right angles to the narrow trestle table under yellow lamplight. Smells of resins and spices mingled with sweat from the small crowd pressing round the platform. There were a few middle aged Egyptians present, but the audience was the usual cosmopolitan mix of Cairo, with British predominating. An Egyptian man in the black robe looped the stained bandages carefully over his arm and stood back so that everybody could see.

"It's all wrong, of course," said Tutty cheerfully. He was large, pink-complexioned and fair-haired, taking after his late mother rather than his piratical father, 22 years old but alternating like a schoolboy between over-confidence and self-consciousness.

"I suppose it's the inside that matters," the friend said.

The man put down his armful of bandages, resumed unwrapping. There was a general intake of breath as ankles then calves appeared, the outline of them clear under a thin gold drape. The man beckoned his young assistant to prop up the figure so that he could unbandage the lower torso. A jut of hip bones emerged under their gold chemise-shroud, then a gently rounded stomach. The trail of Tutty's cigar smoke made a wavering line in the air and he gave a little groan.

"Oh, I say."

His face was red and sweating. The unspooling bandages made regular little flip flop sounds against the trestle. Elbows were revealed, folded close against the rib cage like wings of a trussed chicken. Flip flop. Brown arms, wrists then hands clasped together over where a heart should be. Flip flop flip flop. The smooth swell of gold-shrouded breasts, ornamented with beaten-gold leaves and blue beads of lapis lazuli. Tutty stared in a trance of desire, pushing against the men in front to get a better view. Only the shoulders and neck were still bandaged and, presumably, the head under its blue and gold painted funerary mask with the rearing royal cobra over the forehead. The painted eyes, eternally open, stared up at the low ceiling. The hands clasped on the golden breast looked as brown and plump as a young child's.

"She moved. Her leg moved." Tutty's triumphant bray rang out across the room. When heads turned towards him his face went even more red. It had seemed the only safe way to release the desire building up in him and he'd said it – as he did so many things – without thinking. From the platform, the black-robed man gave him a poisonous look. His eyes, naturally dark and large but accentuated further with kohl, looked as unearthly as those on the funeral mask. Tutty went quiet. The man turned slowly, put his hand to the painted mask. The minute he touched it, the thing happened. A sneeze exploded from under the mask, a sneeze blowing out two thousand years of sand and dust or perhaps 20 minutes of burnt resin, dried sweat and cigar smoke. The mask slipped and brown hands unclasped themselves and rose up from the gold breasts, tearing at the head bandages. Tutty made a move towards the platform.

"She's choking. It's not a joke. Undo her, somebody."

Peter grabbed his arm.

"Don't make an exhibition of yourself. She's all right."

The young assistant too had moved forwards, but the black-robed man pushed him away. Less ceremoniously than before he spun the loose covering of bandages away from the head, one hand firmly on the girl's chest to stop her writhing. The face revealed was red and gleaming with sweat and snot, eyes screwed up. The man and his assistant each took one of the girl's hands and helped her off the trestle to her feet. The assistant produced a flute from his robe and as the thin notes from it wavered into the air the girl began to dance, slowly at first as if dazed, bare feet padding on the platform, upper body moving from side to side. The flute player followed her every move with big, sad eyes. She used her hands to wipe her face, trying to make it look like part of the dance. The man in black hissed something at her and the movements became more inviting. Her rouged lips smiled mechanically, black-rimmed eyes throwing flirtatious looks out over the audience, but at random, not caring if they hit a target or not. Another hissed instruction from the man in black and her hands came down, fingers massaging the gold-draped breasts. Tutty's face was pouring sweat.

"You'd better come out and get some air," the friend said.

Tutty followed him obediently through a curtain and into the street, with a last glance back at the girl, now miming a shuddering climax with her upper body thrown back and her legs apart. Outside it was a golden evening, with the smell of the Nile in the air. There was a cafe opposite, with tables under an awning. They made their way there and Tutty clicked his fingers for a waiter, ordered whisky and coffee. He was trying to get back his composure, lounging in his chair like a man of the world.

"I don't think my respected father would have cared for it, do you?"

"Won't he be shirty if he knows you've been there?"

"He won't. My father takes no interest whatever in anything less than two thousand years old. I swear the night he begot me he was thinking more about Queen Hatshepsut than he ever did of my poor mother."

"Tutty, people will hear."

"Let them. There's another thing, what do you think it does to a boy to go through prep school called Thutmose? I was conceived in ancient Egyptian, swaddled in mummy clothes, cut my milk teeth on a chip of the Rosetta stone."

"I'm sure not literally."

"Near enough, though. I hate Egypt. All I want to do is get back to London, find a job in a bank and marry a good-tempered girl who thinks Ptolemaic is something you take for colic."

"I hope you haven't told your father that."

"I'd have to write it down in hieroglyphics before he'd take any notice."

"You were making a bit of an exhibition in there.'"

"I thought the poor girl was choking."

"You didn't do her a favour. You saw that man's face when she sneezed. I shouldn't be surprised if he isn't giving her a bruise or two to remind her not to do it again."

Tutty gaped. "He wouldn't, would he? She couldn't help it."

"It was probably from trying not to laugh when you yelled out that she was moving. Did you notice the language, by way, when he whispered to her?"

"No."

"I only caught a few words, but I'd swear he was talking English."

Tutty was caught childlike, between guilt and self-defence. "You're saying the brute's hitting a girl – an English girl - and it's my fault."

"I don't know. Forget I said it. Drink up and let's go and have dinner."

But Tutty was staring at the little white cube of a house on the other side of the road with the dark curtain over its doorway.

"You go ahead. I want another drink."

Still staring at the house, he clicked his fingers for the waiter. His friend gave him an exasperated look and left.

Professor Brightsea and Thomas travelled back to Cairo on a horse-drawn wagon, empty except for the unused camera and measuring rods. The Egyptian foreman who always accompanied the professor on his excavations sat disconsolately with his legs hanging over the back of the cart, aware of loss of money for him and loss of face for them all. The sunset was a red flare of sand particles, the air full of the scent of thorn fires and camel dung. The professor's mockery had turned to bitter anger.

"The fifth time, Thomas. The fifth time and the worst. You know where the mummy and mummy case will be now? In the hold of a ship en route for New York or Hamburg, whoever bid higher."

"Couldn't the police . . . ?"

The professor made a contemptuous sound, mimed the counting out of bribe money. "Besides, even if they could be brought back - which they can't – the damage is done. The whole point of what we do is finding burials undisturbed and recording them. Every little detail, the very faintest trace in the dust, has got something new to tell us. Imagine seeing a handprint and knowing that the person who made that print might have looked on the living faces of Amenhotep and Queen Tiy. And for profit, for simple financial profit, this . . . this creature, this worse than murderer, destroys irreplaceable evidence of the most fascinating civilization that every existed on earth. The smallest particle of dust from the bandages of the meanest mummy is worth more to the world than the whole of his contaminated, disease-ridden body."

Miserable at the professor's disappointment and anger, Thomas murmured, "They say he does other things too. Brothels and so on. Drugs and dancing girls. Anything to make money."

Brightsea shrugged, as if to say that these things were only to be expected, but were insignificant compared to tomb robbery.

"And the sickening thing is, Thomas, that this corpse-maggot, this smear of slime is one of our own fellow country-men."

The cart rolled on towards Cairo.

Tutty was staring at a bare white arm, still streaked here and there with greasepaint, pitted with five red marks of fingers and a thumb.

"It'll be black and blue by tomorrow," she said. "I'll have to put the stuff on thicker to hide it." Her voice was Cockney and choked up with a cold. She sneezed again. "And then he gives me what-for if I use up the grease paint too thick. Whatever I do he belts me, doesn't matter what."

They were sitting on either side of the table in a little back room. The table was covered with unrolled bandages. As she talked the girl was rolling them up again, methodical as a nurse.

"I'm sorry," he said. "I'm sorry I made you sneeze."

She was still wearing her thin golden costume. Seen close to, you could tell it for the cheap dyed muslin it was, and the beads on her breasts were painted clay, not lapis lazuli. He could hardly take his eyes off them. When he did manage to look up her eyes were blue too. He found that so disturbing that he looked down again at the beads, but they were no help.

"Ain't your fault. I'd probably have done it anyway. Back in London, when a man said did I want to travel with him to Egypt I thought, well, that's supposed to be hot, isn't it, so at least I won't get colds there like I always do here, only it's worse. Must be all that dust from the dead people."

"Why don't you go back home?" he said.

"Home?" She made a little huffing sound, finished rolling a bandage and tucked the end in, threw it into a basket by her bare feet and started on another.

"Why not? I could pay your fare. I've got a bit of money saved up."

Wildly he imagined himself sailing back to England with her, delivering her to friends and family, her aged parents blessing him.

"I can't get away."

"Why not, if he beats you?" A thought struck him. "You're not *married* to the fellow, are you?"

She shook her head. "Worse than that."

"What could be worse than being married to a brute like that?"

"Somebody's put a curse on me so I have to stay here and do as I'm told."

"What?" The surprise of it jerked his gaze up from the beads to her eyes again. They were scared, brimming with tears.

"An old Egyptian curse. There's this man who brought me here. He was a priest in another life, hundreds of years ago, that's how he knows all about mummies and so on. He said all these words over me like prayers in a foreign language, only they were curses. And he had this special old dead beetle the priests used for cursing people."

"A scarab?"

"Nothing to do with scabs. A dead beetle, like I said. So he put this curse on me, then he took me to meet this man Abdul I do the mummy act with and said I was Abdul's slave until he came and released me. If I go away without the priest man saying I can go, I'll be dead in agony before the next sun rises. That's what the curse is."

He laughed, unbelieving. "You don't believe that nonsense?"

"It's true. I tried it and its true. One day when Abdul beat me worse than usual I thought, well, anything's better than this, so I ran off. I hadn't got no further than the end of the street when this dog came out of nowhere and bit me. Look, I've got the marks." Still rolling bandages, she shot out her leg towards him, almost touching his knee with her toes. Just above the ankle he saw a crescent of white marks.

"I thought it had rabies and I'd be dead in agony by morning, like he said."

"But it hadn't. I mean, you're still here."

He was stammering, not able to take his eyes off the leg she was presenting to him.

"He says next time it will be rabies, or something even worse. It was a warning to me."

"But don't you see, it's just a lot of hocus pocus to scare you? You could walk out and nothing would happen to you."

She shook her head, sulky with him for doubting her misery.

"This man, the one who makes out he's a priest, is he an Egyptian?"

"No, he's English, just like you and me."

"What? Oh, look, this is ridiculous. He's no more a . . ." Then the idea hit him, just at the point where his eyes, travelling up from her ankle, had got as far as a pink and rounded knee, streaked with brown like a sugared almond dropped in mud. He paused, realizing that his hated education hadn't been a waste of time after all, had been leading up to this moment. "Well, if your Englishman was only a priest in ancient Egypt, I outrank him by miles. I was a pharaoh."

It fell flat. "A what?"

His heart bounded at her ignorance. He could have kissed her, almost did.

"A kind of king. If he can put curses on people, I can lift them, just like that."

He clicked his fingers. She looked puzzled.

"There," he said. "I've just lifted the curse. You can go where you like."

"It's not right to laugh about it."

She snatched her leg away, placed it sedately beside the other one.

"I'm not laughing. I tell you, I've lifted his curse."

But she gave him a hurt look and started rolling another bandage. He stared at her, like a willing horse face to face with an unjumpable fence. But there was a way round it, there had to be. The feeling in him was as strong as if the rest of his life depended on getting this right.

"All right, I'll come back tomorrow and bring you something to protect you, something that will keep you safe against any curse."

"What?"

"A scar . . . I mean a beetle of your own, only a lot more powerful than his beetle. You can wear it round your neck and it will protect you."

He saw from the look in her eyes that he had her. Something to touch, something to hold was what she wanted. An amulet. Any ancient Egyptian would have understood.

Tutty hadn't expected to find his father and Thomas back home already. He gathered from the atmosphere in the house that their field trip had not gone well, but was too full of his own affair to take much interest. He said he wasn't hungry, fended off questions from Thomas about whether he'd got a touch of sunstroke and went straight upstairs to his room.

He lay on his bed with the window open and the breeze coming off the river. His father's study was directly below. With both windows open he could hear the murmuring voices of him and Thomas, the rustle of papers. The endless conversations about cataloguing and classifying, every little fragment of carved stone, sliver of painted frieze, flake of gold or gum assigned to its place and dynasty. Slow, long-distance arguments by letters and learned articles among people just like his father and Thomas here in Cairo, in London, New York, Paris, Berlin. Usually the very thought of it annoyed him but tonight he was filled with a happiness, a rightness with his place in the world that made him tolerant. He heard Thomas saying goodnight to his father, coming upstairs to bed in the room opposite his own. Then, soon afterwards, Thomas' snores. He listened for his father's footsteps but this must be one of the nights when he was working late on his own because he was still moving about downstairs. When Tutty struck a match to look at his pocket watch, it was nearly midnight.

He dozed for a while and woke to hear a knock at the side door to the yard. Normally one of the servants would have answered it, even at this hour, but his father must have been waiting because he was there almost at once, asking in Arabic where they'd got to, why were they late. Tutty could understand his father's Arabic, but not the low reply in the same language. The door closed, then there were at least three voices in the study below, the clink of coffee cups. Tutty thought wearily, Site foreman and friend, probably. On past experience, the haggling over coffee cups about workmen's pay and food rations on excavations could go on for hours. So it was a pleasant surprise when the visitors left after not much more than half an hour, his father's slow footsteps came upstairs at last and the house went quiet. Tutty waited another half hour to make sure then tiptoed down to the study in stockinged feet. He lit a candle and looked round the familiar chaos of his father's study. Every horizontal surface was either covered in papers or crowded with porcelain figures of gods and goddesses, scarabs, fragments of mummy cloth. The growing candle flame wavered over a shelf with a row of small bronze Bastets, their shadows swaying on the wall like a line of cat-headed chorus girls. The jackal jaw of Anubis reflected the flame from the top of a funerary jar. All of those were so familiar to Tutty that he hardly glanced at them. The scarabs, annoyingly, were kept in no sort of order and were hiding all over the place as if they'd uncurled their carved or moulded legs and scuttled there, on shelves, under papers, on top of books. He picked up and rejected some of the more valuable-seeming ones in ivory or semi-precious stones, not wanting to deprive his father more than necessary. One, being used casually as a paperweight, seemed promising. It was larger than the rest, deeply but crudely carved, made of black stone that absorbed the light rather than reflecting it. The feel of it in his hand was weighty and satisfying. Because he hadn't been able to block out entirely the life-long conditioning of his Egyptian upbringing he recognized it as a heart scarab – black basalt from the New Kingdom, fairly common, found in mummy wrappings and believed by some authorities to represent the heart of the dead person.

"You'll do, beetle," he mouthed at it, put it in his pocket and went back upstairs.

He waited until after the performance the following evening to take it to her, watching from a cafe table as the audience strolled out into the sunshine. With his new sense of mission, the men seemed to him to have a nasty glossiness to their faces as if they'd feasted on sticky cakes. A few minutes later the black-robed man and his assistant came out too and walked away up the street. Within seconds Tutty was across the road, through the curtain and into the back room. She was rolling up her bandages, just like the night before, and looked scared when she recognized him.

"There, I've got him."

He put the scarab down in a nest of jumbled bandages on the table. She gave a little scream.

"It's just like his." He blessed his luck, but then heart scarabs weren't especially rare. She put out her hand to touch it, then looked up at him. "What happens now?"

"Pick it up."

She picked it up, biting her lower lip with sharp little blue-white teeth. The look on her face, half-scared, half-trusting, went to his heart. He realized that simply bringing it to her wasn't enough. The other Englishman had used some mumbo-jumbo ceremony to put the curse on and he must do the same. While he was desperately trying to think of something she gave him his cue.

"Do I have to lie down?"

She didn't say it in a coquettish way but humbly, like patient to doctor. He nodded, struck dumb, and followed her to the room where the performances were given. She got up on the trestle table and lay back, arranging her swathes of dyed muslin neatly round her legs, then clasped the scarab to her breast with both hands. Tutty stood by the table, throat dry, struggling for words. He knew not a syllable of Egyptian but then the bogus priest almost certainly didn't either. Anything would do as long as it sounded foreign. A dim memory of prep school days came to his rescue. *"Gallia est omnis divisa in partes tres."* She gave a little shudder of satisfaction and closed her eyes.

Tutty wasn't missed because dinner tended to be an irregular meal at his father's house and that night didn't happen at all. The professor was out somewhere and Thomas dined off dates and lemonade in the study, while getting on with the task of cross-indexing recent finds – pitifully few of them and not especially interesting, but it had to be done. He'd worked through a couple of columns of them and had gone to the window for some air when he heard the rumbling of cart wheels in the street below and the foreman's voice, telling the driver to be careful. This surprised him because the professor had said nothing about new discoveries. He went outside and saw the cart drawn up by the house and the professor and foreman standing in the back of it, staring at something wrapped in reed matting. Heart bounding with hope, he called out to them.

"Ah, Thomas, come and look at this."

He clambered into the back of the cart. The thing under the matting was the right shape for a mummy case and the professor looked unusually pleased with himself. With his eyes on Thomas, he signed to the foreman to uncover it. Blue and gold glinted in the low sun. A royal, impassive mask stared up with a rearing cobra over its forehead. Thomas took a step forward, lifted the painted lid and registered the smell of the emptiness inside.

"Modern pine. It's a fake."

He stared at the professor, wondering for an instant if anger had sent the man insane, but found a grin on the piratical face.

"Of course it is. We've just bought it in the bazaar. Not a very expert fake, but it will serve its purpose."

Later, still labouring over the cross-indexing, Thomas heard the cart lumbering away.

Tutty chanted his way through all the tags he could remember from Caesar's Gallic Wars then, because the girl still hadn't moved, launched himself on *Arma virumque cano* and the next dozen or so lines of Aeneid I, filling in the gaps with irregular Latin verbs. When even those failed him he took a deep breath and intoned as sonerously as he could manage *Te absolvo. Nunc dimittis servum tuum in pace*, hoping that she didn't happen to be a Roman Catholic. She sensed at least the finality in his voice, opened her eyes and sat up.

"Is it done?"

He nodded, exhausted. She sat there for a while, still clasping the scarab to her breast, like a bird staring at the open cage door and not knowing what to do with freedom. Then a smile spread across her face. She raised her arms, slid off the table and did a wild little dance round the room chanting, "Free, free, free," muslin drapes flying back from her knees and calves. Tutty's feeling of happiness and rare achievement was stronger even than desire. He wouldn't have traded it for all the wisdom of all the kingdoms of Egypt. Her dance took her to the curtain between door and street. She twitched at it, looked out. Then, "Oh." She dropped the curtain, froze.

"Not another rabid dog, is it?" Tutty asked.

She shook her head. "It's him. The priest. The one who put the curse on me."

He went past her, looked out through the gap between curtain and doorframe.

"Him, you mean? The tall one in the panama?"

A tall, over-elegant man in a white linen suit and panama stood so close that if Tutty had shouted to him he'd have heard. He was in his late thirties or early forties with a pale, oval face with gold-framed glasses and a little pointed black beard. He wore an assortment of antique rings on his fingers and carried a black cane topped with the silver hawkshead of the god Horus. He was standing there reading a note, smiling to himself.

"He's come to get me." She was shrinking against the wall. "He knows what you've done and he's come to put the curse back on me."

"No, of course he's not." Anger at seeing all his good work ruined made Tutty resourceful. "We're stronger than he is. You can put a curse on him instead."

"I can? How?"

"Just put the beetle between your hands and say what you want to happen to him. Or you don't even have to say it, just think it. But quickly before he goes."

The man was folding up the note, tucking it away in his pocket with dandyish care so as not to spoil the line of the jacket. The girl stood motionless, eyes shut, and hands in prayer position at her chest with the black scarab between them. She was gripping it so hard that anything less tough than basalt might have cracked. The man flicked a piece of straw off his shoe with the end of his ebony cane, took a slim gold watch out of his waistcoat pocket and consulted it. Then he turned and walked away, in no hurry.

"He's going," Tutty told her. "Have you cursed him?"

She nodded, eyes huge and greedy, and came to stand beside him. They watched as the pale back receded down the street then blurred into the red-gold dusk. Then suddenly she put her arms round Tutty, pressed her mouth against his. He was so surprised that he didn't start to return the kiss until it was too late and she took her arms away.

"I'm ever so grateful. Really, I'm ever so grateful. Can I keep the beetle?"

"Of course." Then, seeing the excitement on her face, it occurred to him to ask her. "So what did you curse him with?"

She looked at him, as if he should have known the answer. "Death, of course. I cursed him with death."

She wouldn't go away with him at once. She said she had things she must do. If he wanted he could come back later, much later when it was dark. Feminine stuff to pack, he supposed. She must have clothes other than blue beads and gold muslin. Although it would have been a more satisfying end to his drama to whisk her away at once, at least the delay gave him time to think. He did his thinking walking round the city, first the crowded bazaar with the lamps lit outside the stalls and smells of spiced meat everywhere, then to the river bank and the slanting masts of the moored feluccas against a white sky. The night was hot and heavy, with distant lightning flickering towards the Nile delta, palm fronds hissing against each other like cockroaches in a faint breeze. The toughest question was how to explain her to his father. If he followed his original plan of escorting her home to England, even though the two of them would be travelling as chastely as sister and brother – or very nearly - the professor would have to know and couldn't be expected to like it.

After hours of walking, and many cups of coffee in small cafes, he decided that it was late enough to go and fetch her. The best thing would be to put her up at a hotel for the night then go home and face the music. With that settled, he walked quite jauntily back through the city towards the white cube of the house, thinking he'd like another chance to manage the kiss better, with some warning next time. He watched from across the road in case the brute had come back, but saw no sign of activity so crossed and pulled the curtain a little aside.

"Hello. I'm back."

It came to him that he didn't even know her name. There was a scuffling in the back room, a little light coming through. He got to the doorway in two strides.

"Hey, stop that."

His first thought was that the brute had come back after all and was trying to throttle her. It was only when his eyes adjusted to the lamplight that he saw what he'd interrupted. She was wearing normal clothes, a pink dress, a straw hat with a ribbon but the hat was disarranged because when he came in she'd had her arms round the flute player and the two of them were kissing with a confidence and enthusiasm that showed it wasn't the first time. At his shout they sprang apart, but not very far.

"What's going on?" He wished, even as he said it, that he didn't sound so much like a village constable, but what was a chap supposed to say?

"This is Lou. He's French."

She said it quite defiantly in her little voice, as if that explained everything. The lad – no more than 17 or 18 surely – stood there smiling at her. In normal clothes, he was even better-looking than in his flute-player's robes, hair dark and curling, eyes wide, lashes long and thick as a calf's. Lebanese-French, Tutty thought, or Syrian-French. Not that it mattered.

"Well, we're not taking him too."

"Lou and I are going away together," she said.

There was a new confidence about her. He noticed a bulge under the bodice of her dress. She saw his eyes going to it and pulled out a little linen bag, hastily cobbled together.

"We've wanted to for weeks, only I couldn't because of the curse. Now I've got the beetle, it's all right."

She popped it back inside her dress.

"Where are you going?"

Her forehead wrinkled. "Where the river comes out to the sea. Alex . . ."

"Alexandria," the boy said obligingly, probably catching onto one of the few words he understood. "I play, she dance."

His fingers mimed flute playing while his body imitated her sinuous dance movements.

"But you can't go back to that."

"Why not? Specially now we don't have to give all the takings to that bastard. There's more money in the Alex place, from the sailors."

"What about your parents?"

"What?" She stared. He might as well have been speaking Latin again.

"Won't they want you back?"

She laughed, a harsh little sound. "You're joking. They chucked me out when I was thirteen." Then, as if to get away from the memory, "Come on, Lou. Time we were going."

She moved towards the door. The flute player picked up a small bag and followed. Bemused, Tutty stood aside for her. She swept past then turned back suddenly, put her arms round his neck and kissed him again, taking him as much by surprise as before.

"Thank you. I'll never forget you. Thank you for the beetle."

Then the curtain flapped and they were gone.

It was past midnight and several drinks later when Tutty turned for home at last. He thought, on the whole, that he'd probably made a bit of an idiot of himself, but not too much of an idiot when all was said and done. And it had been a difficult situation. She wasn't the kind of girl his kind of chap married. Even if it hadn't been for all the other reasons against it, the memory of her small, hard voice, *I cursed him with death*, placed her in a different and harsher world than his own. At least now there wasn't a lot of explaining to be done to his father – unless he missed the scarab. On that score, there were no guarantees. In the usual confusion of his father's study it could be months or years before that happened. On the other hand, if he suddenly wanted it to illustrate some point or other, there'd be no peace for the household until it was found. If so, he'd just have to confess and give him some suitably edited version of the story. Still, he couldn't help being apprehensive as he approached the house. By then, his father and Thomas should be in bed. He decided to go in through the side door from the little yard to save waking up the servants. It was annoying, in his tired and nervy state, to find the yard blocked by his father's expedition cart, drawn up practically touching the house wall. To squeeze past it he had to put a foot on its back step, which brought his eyes level with the thing in the cart.

He screamed. He'd seen mummies before, all too many of them, all his life. But none like this. None with bandages so fresh and white, standing out from the shadows of the mummy case and practically glowing in the dark. None with an oval face as white as the bandages and fresh as if it had died that day. None with a bristling black beard. Never, in all kinds and conditions of mummies, one that wore gold framed glasses. A voice was screaming in his head and screaming out of his head, not caring who heard.

"We cursed him. We cursed him and he's come back to me."

His father was there almost at once, fully dressed and wide awake. He got Tutty inside and up to his study, fending off inquiries from the rest of the household, ordering them sharply to go back to bed and stay there. With the study lamp lit and the dancing Bastets wavering over the wall, Tutty poured out his whole story.

"I never believed any of the curse stories. I know you didn't either. But she cursed him – she meant it, with the black scarab – and now he's come to my doorstep. A mummy, you see. He made her into a mummy – so when she cursed him – I didn't believe it, you see, but I did it – so it made him into a mummy instead and . . . oh, God."

He sipped the brandy his father had poured for him and shivered. The professor waited. After a while Tutty said, "I suppose he really is dead.'

"Oh, yes, he's really dead."

Tutty hung his head. The professor didn't speak for a while, roving round his study. Then, at last: "What scarab did you say you took."

"The black one, the heart scarab."

The professor laughed. "After all these years, you still can't tell a fake."

"What?" Tutty's head swung up.

"A fake. The bazaars are full of them. I bought one so that I could show my students the differences between a bazaar souvenir and the real thing. Your death-cursing scarab was hacked out a few weeks ago by a ham-fisted faker with a cold chisel. It's no more a real scarab than you're a real Pharaoh."

"But the curse?"

"From Caesar's Gallic Wars? My dear boy, if that's the best you can do with an expensive education, I should have had you apprenticed to a plumber."

"But he's dead. He's out there wrapped up in a mummy case and he's dead."

"Yes, but it's nothing to do with you. This was meant to be kept secret so I want your promise not to tell anybody else, but at least it will set your mind at rest from this nonsense. Your promise?"

Tutty nodded.

"The man out there was a dealer in Egyptian artefacts. He had certain other businesses as well, hence that degrading peep-show you attended. He died today. Because of his interests, some of his associates thought it appropriate that he should be buried in the old Egyptian manner – or at least as close to it as modern sensibilities permit. For instance, no attempt was made to hook his brain out through his nostrils."

Tutty groaned and spluttered brandy.

"It was done with some secrecy, so as not to offend the bureaucratic meddlers," the professor said. "Later tonight, his body will be transported along the Nile towards its final resting place. I'm sure nobody could wish a more appropriate ending for him than that."

"He was a rotter," Tutty murmured.

"You may be right. If so, he won't be the first man to be more honoured in death than his life deserved. Now, my boy, drink up and go to bed. Tomorrow we'll talk. It may be time to think of sending you back to England."

"Oh, yes, please."

Almost a prayer. The professor helped Tutty to his feet, watched his unsteady progress across the study and the door closing behind him. Idly he picked up a few assorted scarabs from under his papers and arranged them in a row. He would miss the heart scarab, which had been a good example of its kind, and assuredly no fake. If a man were inclined to super-stition – which of course he wasn't – he might even think it had played some part in ending the career of a man who had defiled the old gods. But there were too many things to be done before morning. First, the little bags of gold coins to be sorted out for the foreman's friends, who had done their job efficiently, wrapped and delivered the goods precisely as ordered. Then, with their help, the mummy case must be lidded, straw-swathed and carted with its contents to the waiting felucca that would carry it as quickly as possible downriver to the docks. One other thing – the job the professor had been thinking about when his son screamed from the yard – was filling in the delivery label. The dead man had two particular customers, both rich and secretive collectors, both – in the professor's view – richly deserving what he had to send. New York or Hamburg? He smiled, enjoying the luxury of hesitation, his hand unconsciously rearranging the line of scarabs.

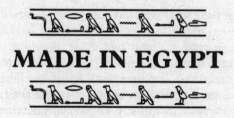

MADE IN EGYPT

Michael Pearce

We end our exploration of ancient Egypt with a new Mamur Zapt story by Michael Pearce. Captain Gareth Owen is the Mamur Zapt, or head of the secret police in Cairo, in the years leading up to the First World War. At that time the British retained a strong hold over Egyptian affairs, but there were continuing tensions with the Turks and other nations, such as the French, who believed that they had controlling rights in the region. Pearce writes with a sharp and caustic eye and his wry observations bring a suitable end to over four thousand years of Egyptian history and craftsmanship.

"It is not in the bazaars, Captain Owen," said Miss Sharpnell severely, "that one will find the true indigenous art of Egypt."

"No," said Owen, heart sinking. It had been a mistake coming. When Paul Trevelyan had invited him to the presentation, he had agreed in the interests of making up the numbers. He had not bargained on Paul inviting other people for the same reason; such as this formidable group of ladies newly out from England to study the Egyptian Arts and Crafts Movement. He had foolishly referred to the appliqué canvases of the Tentmakers Bazaar.

"Meretricious!" pronounced Miss Sharpnell with a sniff. "Surely Egypt has something better to offer? What is going on in the villages?"

"Well, they all work very hard –"

"Pots?"

"Pots?"

"They make them, I presume?"

"Well, yes, but –"

And used them. Sometimes, for example they embedded them in the dried mud of the village dovecote and pigeons rested in them. Did that count as indigenous art?

"One looks for the skill of the craftsman," said Miss Sharpnell in the same unforgiving tone.

"Quite so."

Over at the front of the terrace, where the flower-sellers pushed their roses and carnations through the railings at the tourists, and the pornographic postcard merchants hung their pictures – indigenous, possibly, but was it art? – an ushapti vendor was proffering a little wooden image to another of the formidable ladies.

"But is it authentic?" she demanded.

The ushapti vendor was shocked; or affected to be.

"Madame," he said, "go to the Museum. And if they do not say it is worth at least ten pounds, come back to me and I will give you ten pounds!"

And if he's still here when you get back, thought Owen, *I* will give you ten pounds. He saw an opportunity of escaping from Miss Sharpnell, however, and excused himself and went across.

"Actually," he said, "it would be worth your going to the Museum anyway. They always have surplus ushaptis for sale. Genuine ones."

"Well, I'm not really –" the lady was beginning, when Paul Trevelyan clapped his hands.

"I wonder if I could have your attention, ladies and gentlemen, for the actual presentation?"

The reception was being held on the terrace of the Hotel Contentale, and the presentation was to the Consul-General in recognition of his services to Egypt in the prevention of illegal exports of works of art.

Old Gasperi, the Director of the Museum, was making the

presentation. He went up to the table at the back of the terrace which held the gift that was being presented and drew off the cloth which covered it. A little mutter of appreciation ran round the spectators.

"And I can assure you," said the Consul-General, smiling, "that it will remain at the Consulate. I have no intention of taking it back to England, illegally or otherwise."

Old Gasperi took the mask in his hands.

"A fine piece!" he said lovingly. It, too, had come from the Cairo Museum. The Museum had so many objects in its care that it could afford to let some of them go. He fondled it for a moment and then suddenly removed his spectacles and peered closely at it.

"But, one moment!" he said. "This is not the original. It is a copy!"

"But, Owen, you were there!" said the Consul-General accusingly.

Owen was only too well aware of this. Various people, including Miss Sharpnell, had already pointed it out to him.

"What did you say you were? The Chief of Police?"

"The Mamur Zapt. Head of the Khedive's Secret Police," said Owen sulkily. "A quite different thing."

The difference, however, was lost on Miss Sharpnell. She pursed her lips.

"Under your very nose!" she said.

"Never mind the difference," said Paul Trevelyan, who had been organizing the reception and therefore felt responsible. "It'll be ages before the Parquet arrive." The Parquet, the Department of Prosecutions of the Ministry of Justice, and not the Police, much less the Secret Police, which concerned itself only with political activity, was the body which handled criminal investigation in Egypt at that time. "Get on with it without waiting for them!"

"But I brought it myself!" cried old Gasperi. "Only half an hour before!"

"But which did you bring? The original? Or a copy?"

"The original, of course!"

"Are you sure?"

"Of course I'm sure. I looked at it when I picked it up at the Museum. And Morpugo looked at it too."

"Morpugo?"

Morpugo was the Deputy Director of the Museum, a tall, thin, rather aesthetic-looking Levantine, with a large silk handkerchief, red to match the pot-like tarboosh, which, like all Egyptian civil servants, he wore on his head, overflowing from the breast pocket of his immaculate suit.

"Copy?"

Morpugo took umbrage.

"We don't deal in copies here, my man. If any copies turn up, we give them away. To people who can't tell the difference!"

"But might not the copy have been substituted? Without your knowing!"

"I took the mask out of the glass case myself. And I can assure you that it was not an imitation."

"I can confirm that," said Gasperi. "We looked at it together."

"And then what did you do with it?"

"Put it on my desk. Where it remained for the rest of the morning. Until Monsieur Gasperi collected it."

"And you yourself? Where you at your desk all the morning?"

"All the morning," said Morpugo triumphantly.

"All the morning," echoed the Coptic clerk who shared the office with him, glumly.

The guests had already been gathering on the terrace when M. Gasperi had arrived and placed the golden mask on the table that had been provided. It had at once been covered with a white cloth and had remained like that until the moment of unveiling and presentation. There had been people present the whole time.

But had anyone been actually keeping an eye on the mask?

"A general eye," said the maître d'hotel.

"But a more particular one?"

"Well, Mustapha –"

Mustapha, the waiter, had been charged with responsibility for the table; that is, with standing near it and seeing that nobody bumped into it and knocked it over. It was a particularly flimsy table with rickety folding legs and might well have been.

"Well, we didn't want a table which took up too much room," said the maître d'hotel defensively.

"And Mustapha had been standing by it the whole time?"

"Not for a moment did my eye waver, Effendi!" Mustapha declared.

"Except –" said Miss Sharpnell, who was standing nearby and listening to every word.

"Except when I went to fetch a glass of his special for Gasperi Effendi," said Mustapha, injured.

"Weren't there drinks on the terrace?"

"Yes, but he prefers seventeen years."

"Seventeen years?"

"Glenlivet," said the maître d'hotel. "It has to be the seventeen-year-old one. And while Mustapha was away," he added, giving Miss Sharpnell a baleful look, "I myself stood here engaging Gasperi Effendi in conversation."

"But while you were talking –?"

"I kept my hand on the mask."

"That is so, Effendi," said Mustapha. "And when I returned I saw the signor with his hand on the mask and thought: that is the way to do it. And after that I, too, put my hand on the mask."

"The whole time?"

"The whole time."

This time even Miss Sharpnell did not demur.

"It must have been before," said Owen.

"It could have been any time," said Mustapha.

"But how –?"

"Magic," said Mustapha. "There is some conjurer abroad."

As a matter of fact, there *was* a conjurer abroad; down in the street along with the other jugglers, acrobats, snake-charmers, musicians, dancers, flower-sellers, peanut boys and exhibitors of monkeys and stuffed crocodiles. Owen went down to him and found his hand taken confidingly by a tame, dog-faced baboon dressed in little red trousers.

"I wish I knew, Effendi," the conjurer confessed. "If you find out, Effendi, perhaps you could tell me. Then I could use the trick myself."

Owen had not really expected otherwise, but it had occurred to him that those below in the street would certainly have been keeping a hopeful eye turned up towards the terrace and might have seen something.

Alas, no. And the same went for the guests on terrace. No one had seen anything. Indeed, the consensus was that no one had gone near the table.

"Not after the first minute," said another of the formidable ladies, the one who had queried the ushapti's authenticity.

"But in the first minute . . .?"

"A little, bald-headed man went up to the table and nearly knocked it over."

"It was after that," said the maître d'hotel, "that I stationed Mustapha beside it."

"A little, slinky man," expanded the formidable lady breathlessly, "with crooked eyes."

Owen recognized at once from this description the identity of the possible malefactor.

"Well, the damned table was in the way," said the Consul-General. "It wasn't my fault!"

"Yes, it was," said his wife. "You know how clumsy you are."

And after that she had taken care to see he didn't do it again.

"I think everyone saw it," she said. "Because after that everyone gave the table a wide berth."

"It was a silly table to use," said Miss Sharpnell. "Anyone could see that it was unstable. They ought to have used one of those nice woven stands you see the peasant women in the market using to put their things on. A good example of indigenous —"

"Do you think," said the Consul-General, "that you could

get that woman away from me? Right out of Cairo, preferably. As far away as possible. One of those villages in the south –"

It would certainly be a week, thought Owen gloomily. However you travelled, it would take at least two days going there and two days coming back. Not to mention the bit in the middle. What *could* he do with her?

And what, meanwhile, about the mask?

"What about the mask?" he said.

"Damn the mask!" said the Consul-General.

"Dead!" said Miss Sharpnell decisively, and dismissively.

"Well, isn't that what you would expect?" said Owen. "After all, they lived three thousand years ago."

"Life goes on," said Miss Sharpnell, "and a people moves on. And we must move with them. It is at the living Egypt that we should be looking."

He had taken her to Karnak and to Luxor; to the Valley of Kings and the Valley of Queens; to the Ramesseum and the Medinet Habu; to Der el Bahari and to the Temple of Mut. And in the end, on a lovely evening when they were standing together on the river bank, and the setting sun was reddening the Nile, and Miss Sharpnell had taken off her eye-shade to study the effects, and Owen had suddenly noticed that she was younger than he had thought, and the fragrance of jasmine was in the air, she had allowed herself to be softened.

Possibly alarmed by this lapse, she had, however, on the following morning, pulled her eye-shade back firmly over her face and retreated again into her angular self.

It was then that she had pronounced her dismissal. "Dead," she said, "all dead.

"Cannot you take me," she went on, "to some village where I can see the ordinary life of Egypt, the craftsmen at their work? It is only out of that that a true, living indigenous art can arise."

Stung, he took her to the village at Der el Bahari. Spread out on the ground in front of the houses were mummy hawks, bits of mummy cases, little clay soul-houses, ushapti images of soldiers and workers in the field, mummy beads and scarabs.

Behind the houses, in caves in the rock, were the workshops where men were making the bits of mummy cases, the mummy hawks, the models, the ushapti images etc. Their heads were bent over their work and their faces frowned with concentration.

"A high standard of skill, I think you'll find," said Owen. "Of course, the elements of the craft are passed on from generation to generation."

Miss Sharpnell was silent.

They wandered into a workshop where men were busy making old bangles with fine, multi-coloured enamel bands running round them and little enamel discs dangling from golden chains, perfect replicas of Pharaonic jewellery.

"You wouldn't be able to tell them from the original," said Owen. "The gold is genuine."

He picked one up and showed it to Miss Sharpnell.

"This is work for the upper end of the market," he said. "They send these to the big jewellers' shops in Cairo."

"Where they are sold as replicas?"

"In the most reputable shops, yes. But the temptation to do otherwise is considerable. As replicas they would sell at about twenty pounds. As originals it would be more like a thousand."

"And which do they make them as?"

"I don't think they would understand your question. They make them, that's all."

Miss Sharpnell moved on to the next workman, who was making a Pharaonic mask. She touched it, almost lovingly.

"It is beautifully made," she whispered.

"How many of these would you do in a year?" Owen asked the workman.

The workman looked up briefly.

"One," he said.

"It's not just the work, it's the gold," explained the overseer.

"And who does it go to?"

The overseer named one of the big shops in Cairo.

"Usually," he said.

"Usually?"

"Not the last one. A man came down from the big Museum in Cairo and said the workmanship was so good that it ought to be shared. He bought it for the Museum."

"Did he so?"

"It was a Mask of Thutmose."

"Yes," said Owen, "so it was."

"I don't agree with this policy of selling off surplus exhibits," said Morpugo, "even if it does raise money for the Museum. No exhibit is surplus. All are part of Egypt's heritage and should be kept in Egypt. In public hands, too."

"You mean the Museum's hands?" said Owen.

"Certainly."

"Of course, the Mask of Thutmose wasn't actually being sold."

"It was being given away," said Morpugo, "which almost makes it worse."

"But to a worthy recipient?"

Morpugo sniffed.

"A man who could not tell the difference between an original and a replica," he sneered. "On whom the original would be wasted. So why give it him?"

"That's what you thought, is it?"

"Yes."

"And switched the replica for the original while it was on your desk?"

"Yes."

"What about the clerk?"

"I did it while he was opening the door for Gasperi."

"Tell me, when did the idea come to you? Before you went to Der el Bahari? Or when you went in to the workshop?"

"I had objected to the idea in the first place, when Gasperi had first proposed it. But he had overruled me. 'We have plenty of Masks of Thutmose,' he said. 'That is not the point,' I retorted. 'Every one is original and therefore should be kept.' But, as I say, he overruled me. I was still smarting when I went to Der el Bahari. I go down every six months to examine the latest finds. I knew about the workshops, of course, everyone does. The quality of the work in Der el Bahari is very fine. You can sometimes pick up some lovely things there. For oneself, you know. Well, I saw the mask, the work was breath-taking. And then the idea came to me: let Gasperi give this to the Consul-General, if that was what he was so keen on, and let us keep the original. If no one could tell the difference, what would it matter. I forgot about Gasperi himself, unfortunately."

"At least I can take it out of the country now," said the Consul-General.

The presentation had been reheld inside the hotel, as it was thought that, given the circumstances, more private proceedings this time might be preferable. Again, though, but this time deliberately, it was the replica and not the original that was presented.

"Actually, I'm happier with that," said the Consul-General, looking down at the mask in his hands.

"I think I'd better take that from you, dear," said his wife, hastily coming forward.

"I shall regard it as a tribute to Egyptian workmanship," he said, handing it over.

"But it's not authentic!" cried the formidable lady in anguish.

"But it is indigenous," said Owen. "An excellent example, don't you think," he said, looking at Miss Sharpnell, "of the work of the Egyptian Arts and Crafts Movement?"